White
Dreaming of a White...
Christmas
Flight of the White Wolf
While the Wolf's Away
Mated for Christmas
Wolf to the Rescue (novella)

Silver Town Wolf
Destiny of the Wolf
Wolf Fever
Dreaming of the Wolf
Silence of the Wolf
A Silver Wolf Christmas
Alpha Wolf Need Not Apply
Between a Wolf and a Hard Place
All's Fair in Love and Wolf
Silver Town Wolf: Home for the Holidays
Tangling with the Wolf (novella)

Wolff Brothers
You Had Me at Wolf
Jingle Bell Wolf

Run with the Wolf
Wolf on the Wild Side
A Good Wolf Is Hard to Find

Highland Wolf
Heart of the Highland Wolf
A Howl for a Highlander
A Highland Wolf for Christmas
The Wolf Wore Plaid
The Wolf of My Eye
Her Wolf for the Holidays

Billionaire Wolf
Billionaire in Wolf's Clothing
A Billionaire Wolf for Christmas
Night of the Billionaire Wolf
Wolf Takes the Lead

Red Wolf
Joy to the Wolves
The Best of Both Wolves
Christmas Wolf Surprise

SEAL Wolf
A SEAL in Wolf's Clothing
A SEAL Wolf Christmas
SEAL Wolf Hunting
SEAL Wolf in Too Deep
SEAL Wolf Undercover
SEAL Wolf Surrender
SEAL Wolf Pursuit (novella)

Heart of the Shifter
You Had Me at Jaguar

Heart of the Jaguar
Savage Hunter
Jaguar Fever
Jaguar Hunt

Jaguar Pride
A Very Jaguar Christmas

HEART OF THE WOLF
Heart of the Wolf
To Tempt the Wolf
Legend of the White Wolf
Seduced by the Wolf
Night of the Wolf (novella)
Day of the Wolf (novella)

WHAT A *Wolf* WANTS

TERRY SPEAR

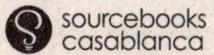

Copyright © 2025 by Terry Spear
Cover and internal design © 2025 by Sourcebooks
Cover design by Craig White/Lott Reps
Cover image © Anetta/Adobe Stock

Sourcebooks and the colophon are registered trademarks of Sourcebooks.

All rights reserved. No part of this book may be reproduced in any form or by any electronic or mechanical means including information storage and retrieval systems—except in the case of brief quotations embodied in critical articles or reviews—without permission in writing from its publisher, Sourcebooks.

No part of this book may be used or reproduced in any manner for the purpose of training artificial intelligence technologies or systems.

The characters and events portrayed in this book are fictitious or are used fictitiously. Any similarity to real persons, living or dead, is purely coincidental and not intended by the author.

All brand names and product names used in this book are trademarks, registered trademarks, or trade names of their respective holders. Sourcebooks is not associated with any product or vendor in this book.

Published by Sourcebooks Casablanca, an imprint of Sourcebooks
P.O. Box 4410, Naperville, Illinois 60567-4410
(630) 961-3900
sourcebooks.com

Printed and bound in the United States of America.
BVG 10 9 8 7 6 5 4 3 2 1

To Robbyn Mays, thanks so much for reading my books, starting with the jaguars and shifting to the SEAL wolves and many more! I'm glad reading gives you another place to go while you're dealing with the difficulties of MS. And thanks for sharing my stories with your family and friends. That proves you're a good shifter at heart!

CHAPTER 1

Charlene Cheswick was excited about moving to Oyster Bay, located on the Oregon coast. She couldn't wait to leave Portland, Oregon, and move to where it was quieter, had less crime, and she could listen to the soothing waves crashing on the beach. Her new home overlooked the bay and the Pacific Ocean. Yet it was forested too, wilder for a wolf to explore. After a year filled with so many losses, Charlene was ready for a fresh start.

With the sun peeking through fluffy white clouds on the warm summer day, she drove to the nearest mini-mart service station to fill her tank with gas and grab a slice of pizza so she didn't have to make a mess in the kitchen on the last night she would be there. As soon as she filled her tank, she headed inside to get her slice when she saw a man in a gray suit and another one in a black suit speaking with a third man backed up against a rack of chips. Immediately, she figured the suited men were police detectives and the man in the ragged jeans and rumpled shirt was someone in trouble. The jeans-clad man handed over a package to the gray-suited man and he pocketed whatever it was. Having been a former homicide detective herself, Charlene thought the whole scenario seemed wrong.

The guy wearing the jeans glanced at her, his eyes widening. Before she could make herself scarce, both suited men cast a look over their shoulders at her. She continued on her way to the fast-food restaurant to get her pizza and leave. If she'd had a badge, she would have faced the suited men down, but she didn't want to have any issues with them when she was just a civilian. The jeans guy hurried out of the store, but the suited men headed into the restaurant. She suspected they meant to try to intimidate her because of what she had seen, though she wasn't sure what that was. Taking a bribe? Taking some drugs? Something illegal, she was sure.

She ordered a slice of pepperoni pizza to go and paid for it. While she waited for the guy to cut her a slice and give it to her, the two suited men came up behind her. They stood way too close to her, antagonizing her.

"Do I know you?" the gray-suited man asked her, his voice dark with threat, his light-brown hair cut short, his eyes a glacial blue.

The other suited man was a little taller and blonder, his eyes green, his build a little heavy. She noticed things like that, having been in the business she'd been in.

"I'm a homicide detective out of Destin, Florida, here on vacation, so I doubt it. And you are?" She lied about still being a homicide detective because she assumed that would keep him from harassing her. She didn't give her name either. She didn't need to unless he asked for ID. Her driver's license still listed the Destin address because she had only been renting the home in Portland and Oregon wasn't a permanent residence for her—yet.

"I'm DEA Special Agent Pete Cohen. Sorry, you just looked like a girl I'd dated."

"Nope." She knew that was a total fabrication. She got her pizza and said, "Have a great night." Then she hurried out of there.

She didn't have to look back to know they were watching her. She went to her car and was sure that they would make a note of it having a Florida license plate. Maybe even run her plate to see just who she was. All she needed was to get caught up in some crooked cops' business when she was about to leave for her dream home. Not that she wouldn't love to take the bastards down.

She was only about ten minutes from there, on the way home, when a police car flashed its lights at her. Now what? She hadn't been speeding, she'd turned her signal on whenever she was making a turn, she had stopped at all the signals… Being stopped didn't make any sense.

Anxious and angry, she parked the car on the shoulder, waiting for the officer to speak to her. He took a damn long time before he walked from his car to hers. Ass.

She got a look at his dark-brown hair, dark-brown eyes, and crooked nose that looked like it had been broken at least once. She smelled his cologne, his arrogant scent, and saw his overconfident swagger.

"Let me see your ID," the officer said.

She handed it to him. "What did I do wrong?"

"You pulled out at a red light, making a right turn, but didn't fully stop."

"I did. I always do." She knew not to argue with a cop, but the DEA agents in the convenience store had set her on edge.

"Let me see your badge," he said to Charlene.

Badge? Her lips parted in surprise. How did he know she'd had a badge? Did Agent Cohen call the police to hassle her? "I'm on vacation here. I didn't bring it with me."

"Destin, Florida," the officer said.

"Where's your badge? Where's your ID? Do you have a business card? How do I know you're a real cop?" She figured it was time to rattle him a little, even though he had a patrol car so she knew he was a cop.

He handed her his card with his name—Lawrence Baker. He was a police officer with the Portland Police Bureau. "I'll just write you a warning this time but watch yourself the next time you pull up to a red signal or stop sign." He handed her a warning slip.

"Thanks." She was furious. The officer had no business stopping her, and she highly suspected, since he knew she'd had a badge, that Agent Pete Cohen had been the one to sic the officer on her. She was so glad she was leaving Portland soon.

When she arrived at the house, she was still irritated, but she enjoyed her pizza and a glass of red wine before she got ready for bed. She was excited about settling into her house in Oyster Bay tomorrow and eager to manage the two homes she had turned into rentals on the coast.

She—and her renters—could enjoy the beaches, hiking trails, and forested parks. Deep down, she had always felt connected to her grandfather, who had shared his love of nature with her while on walks on the Oregon beaches, or through the woods, when she was a young girl. She had loved his tales of times past when her family had lived in these parts—of her mom getting lost as a wolf pup in the woods, of her grandmother chasing off a black bear, of collecting all kinds of different berries and making jellies with them. Returning to her family's roots, a place she'd left as a child but had never truly left behind, had always been a dream of hers.

Besides, living in a home on the West Coast meant she could run out her wolf door, disappear into the woods, and explore to her heart's content. Hmm, maybe some of the red wolves who were bachelors would want to rent her places for a stay there. Maybe she would even fall for one of them. That could be a real boon.

She couldn't wait.

Red wolf DEA Special Agent Ethan Masterson spoke with Ferret, his local drug informant. He was usually reliable, and Ethan liked him. Ethan figured Ferret could do some good things with his life if he just had the right encouragement and stayed off the drugs. Ethan had even aided Ferret's mother and sister when they'd had health issues while Ethan had been trying to help Ferret get his act together. Ferret had lived in the Portland area all his life and had been in and out of treatment centers for drug abuse, locked up in jail several times, but he knew most everyone involved in the drug trade. Ethan had managed to accomplish several drug busts with the information Ferret had fed him. So he'd truly been invaluable to Ethan's missions and Ethan would help him get his life straight however he could.

After tonight though, Ethan was retiring, at least on the books. He'd already put in his thirty years, and he was ready to retire, yet his boss, Barney Grainger, had a solo deep undercover mission for Ethan to take and he was already set up to move into the new home the agency was providing for him in Oyster Bay. He just had this one last job in Portland tonight, and he was looking forward to making a big bust and taking down two of the men who had been involved in killing his parents a year ago.

Everyone on the team was eager to move into the drug house and take the perps down. At Ethan's command, they busted through the front door and headed through the two-story house. Ethan at once smelled the scent of a red wolf—female type—and he was immediately alarmed. If she was involved in all this, he couldn't arrest her because she was a wolf. His own wolf pack would have to deal with her. He smelled other scents: male, female, all human. What he didn't smell? Any sign of drugs. Or scents of Kroner, Oakley, Thor, or Benny or any of the other guys that Ethan was after. His team always kidded him that they didn't need to take drug-sniffing dogs on these cases because he could find the drugs no matter where they were hidden.

With a sinking suspicion they had the wrong house, he moved up the stairs without backup to confront the she-wolf before his men got involved. He immediately heard water running in a bathroom. New age music was playing loudly over the sound of the shower, which could be a ruse. He wasn't sure what he was going to do with the she-wolf, but he had to come up with a plan of action quickly.

"Clear!" "Clear!" his team members were calling out as they searched the rooms downstairs.

Ethan moved quickly but quietly toward the room where he heard the water running. The door was open to the master bedroom, and he went inside and headed for the bathroom. Again, he smelled the female red wolf's scent in the bedroom, and he wondered if his informant had steered him wrong. Man, would Ethan be pissed. This was his last night on the job in the city of Portland, and it would be a bust, instead of him busting someone for dealing in drugs. But more than that, he'd have to leave without taking down the men responsible for murdering his parents.

He cautiously stepped into the large master bathroom and saw the she-wolf in the shower stall in all her naked glory, wet red hair curling over her shoulders, her eyes wide as she gawked at him through the shower glass. He couldn't see the color of her eyes because of the steam and the fog on the shower glass. But he could see her shapely figure and rosy-peaked nipples. She threw the shower door open, and though wolves were used to seeing each other naked when they shifted, he expected her to scream, grab a towel, cover herself up, and yell at him to get the hell out of her bathroom..

But she did the unexpected—shifted into her red wolf as soon as she smelled he was one—and bit him on the arm!

He cried out in shock and surprise. Hell, he wished he'd controlled his reaction a bit more. He certainly hadn't wanted to alert his men he was in trouble.

Then she shifted back, grabbed a towel, and wrapped it around herself just as two of the men on his team raced into the bedroom to come to his aid.

"What the hell are you doing in my house?" she asked, furious, her green eyes flaming with fire. *Now* he could see their entrancing color.

"I'm DEA Special Agent Ethan Masterson," he finally said as the two men came up behind him with their weapons aimed at her. "We had word that this was a drug house."

She tilted her head to the side as if she was mocking his ineptness. He was a wolf. He could smell there were no drugs there.

"Did you find anything?" Ethan asked his men, casting the words over his shoulder while not taking his eyes off her for a second, afraid she might shift and bite him...*again*. He was certain his men hadn't found any drugs, but he had to ask.

DEA Special Agent Renault Green hurried into the bathroom then, his eyes widening—almost in recognition—when he saw the woman clad only in a towel, her skin and hair dripping wet. "No, sir. We had an agent question your contact again, and Ferret said that he told us the address is 101 White Birch Road, not 101 White Pine Road. But we know Ferret mixed it up either accidentally or on purpose and now he's trying to cover his ass."

"I recorded his words. I know he told us this address. All right. I'll be right down to give the next orders," Ethan said to Renault.

Agent Manx Ryerson, one of the other men on his team

that was right there, snickered, and Ethan cast him a cutting look. Agent Pete Cohen slapped Manx on the back, like he felt the same way as his pal.

"Yes, sir," Renault said, and he and the other agents headed out of the bedroom, into the hall, and descended the stairs. "Wrong house," he told the other men downstairs.

"I'm sorry for the mix-up." Ethan's arm where she'd bitten him was throbbing like crazy now and he noticed some blood staining his shirtsleeve. He knew she'd broken the skin, but a wolf could have done a lot more damage—like crushed the bones in his arm or ripped away at the muscle. She had only reacted out of anger and frustration, and he didn't really blame her.

"I hope you're going to take care of any of the damages." She didn't say it in a way that said she was hopeful, but more that she expected it.

"Uh, yeah, I'll have some red wolves take care of it within the hour." Ethan would make it up to her as quickly as he could, though he also had to go after the men who had killed his parents. But he couldn't leave her in a lurch like this either.

She quirked a brow.

"We have a wolf pack out of Portland that I belong to, and they help with any issues we have with our wolves."

"Good. Then they can deal with you too."

He fought smiling at her comeback. She was feisty and he liked that about her.

He was damned glad this was his last job in Portland. Yeah, he really had wanted it to go well, but man was it ending on a sour note, even if he took down the bad guys after this fiasco.

"I'll, uh, let you get dressed and you can tell me what needs to be repaired."

"Thanks for letting me do that." She didn't sound thankful but annoyed to high heaven. Then she reached into the shower stall to turn off the water.

He inclined his head, feeling like he was standing two feet tall. It didn't seem like anything he said to her was going to make it right with the wolf. She wasn't in their wolf pack, or he would have known her. He was surprised he hadn't known anything about her. Maybe she had just moved here, and no one had met her yet. The news would have been all over the pack already otherwise.

He hurried off and when he was downstairs, he talked to his team members. "All right, we're going to the correct house this time, but I need to inspect the damages here and make sure I can get someone out here to replace the owner's door and the frame."

The men looked disgruntled about that when they were eager to do this drug bust.

Manx Ryerson said, "Hey, we never have to explain ourselves if we hit the wrong house. It's just an honest mistake."

Ethan glowered at him. "We do this the way I say." As far as he was concerned, hitting the wrong house during a drug bust was never right. It meant they hadn't done their job!

He knew they weren't used to him stopping a mission like that to help out the homeowner whose home they had wrongly trashed. But he couldn't leave her alone at her place with a broken door. It would be unsafe for her to stay here tonight. And her belongings wouldn't be safe if she went somewhere else for the night.

"Wait for me outside," he told his men, who were milling around in the foyer, waiting for him to say when he was ready to go.

They all moved outside while he walked through the house and saw the wreck his men had made during their search. It was fine when they hit the right house. But certainly not when they hit the wrong one.

He called Leidolf, his red-wolf pack leader, and said, "Hey, I have a problem." He almost said *we*, because it was up to the pack to make things right, but he had caused the problem. Technically, his informant had, but *he* hadn't broken into the she-wolf's place.

"What do you need?" Leidolf asked, knowing if Ethan was calling him at this late hour, he was in some kind of wolf trouble.

"A cleanup team and a new door and doorframe for a home in Portland." Ethan gave him the address.

"What happened? Did your team hit the wrong house?" Leidolf was a canny wolf, and he often knew what was what before anyone had to tell him.

"Yeah. Unfortunately. My informant gave me the wrong address. The woman is a red she-wolf, but I don't know her."

"Hell. What's her name?"

"We didn't get that far."

Leidolf said, "All right. Cassie and I will be up there shortly and try to make it up to her."

"All right. I'll let her know that you'll be arriving soon." Actually, *Ethan* needed to make it up to her, but he didn't think she was interested in speaking with him any further. He didn't blame her either.

They ended the call, and he walked through the rest of the house, just shaking his head at seeing the overturned floor lamps, couch cushions tossed all over, and in the kitchen, the drawers that had been yanked out and all their contents dumped on the floor. He would get some of this straightened up until someone else came to take over. Then he could get on with the mission, hoping that the guys they were after wouldn't have been tipped off by now that he was coming for them.

He was lifting one of the drawers off the kitchen floor when the she-wolf walked into the kitchen.

"Wow. Are you always this destructive on a raid?" she asked.

"These guys hide things everywhere. We don't have time to be careful. They're deadly."

"This is beyond conducting a search speedily." She stood there, her arms folded across her chest. Her hair still wet, she was wearing jeans, tennis shoes, and a silky shirt, no bra.

That had him taking a second look. He hadn't meant to. He'd already seen her naked, for heaven's sake, and they were used to seeing others naked to shift into their wolves... but of course that was with wolves he knew. There was just something provocative about the way her nipples were poking against the fabric of her shirt that was wet where her hair had dripped water. He should have kept his mind on straightening up her apartment. But hell, she was the kind of woman he would have liked to date, bite and all. She raised her brows at him.

He cleared his throat and began putting all the kitchen drawers back, damn glad that none of them were broken. "I'm Ethan Matheson," he repeated, hoping she would give up her name, but she didn't. He was so in the doghouse with her. "And you are?"

"You would think before you raided a house, you would have learned that."

Trying to appease her, he said, "I've called our pack leaders—"

"*Your* pack leaders, not *ours*," she said.

"Uh, yeah, and they're bringing a team to help clean up the house. I'm really sorry about this." He truly was but she didn't appear to be satisfied with his apology. Hopefully, putting the place back in order would make a difference. Though she might have nightmares about this. He knew she could have suffered some trauma from the experience, and this wouldn't make up for that.

"So you can get on your way and raid the right place this time, if it *is* the right place?" she asked.

"Yeah. We do good work. Most of the time. We just got the wrong information from the informant."

"Does it happen very often? Be honest with me. Or did I just luck out?" She arched a brow.

"It happens once in a blue moon." Thankfully. He finished picking up the drawers and putting them back in place while she just watched him, her glower stern.

When he began rescuing her silverware from the floor, she said curtly, "Put them in the dishwasher."

He almost smiled. It had been a long time since he'd pissed off a she-wolf this bad.

Then his good friends Tori Rose and Sierra and Adam Holmes—all three red wolves who worked at the Portland Police Bureau—arrived, for which he was truly grateful. When Tori had been hired last year, she had caught the guys' attention because of her dark, shiny hair cut in a long bob, her seductive red lipstick, and her long legs that looked longer because of the high heels she wore. But she was one hell of a good investigator, keeping them all on their toes. Sierra, the sketch artist for the bureau, was a vivacious redhead with the prettiest blue eyes. Adam had fallen for her in an instant. If any other bachelor wolves in their pack had been interested in her—which, truth be told, they had been—they had been out of luck. Despite the job he had to do as a homicide detective, Adam was always upbeat, and all the women loved his dimples when he smiled.

They lived in one of the bedroom communities of Portland, so they were close by. It would take Leidolf and Cassie longer to get there since they lived out in the country where they owned a ranch and tons of acreage where members of the wolf pack could run.

"Hey, thanks for coming to help us out on such short notice," Ethan said to his friends.

They smiled at Ethan, but then Tori and Sierra glanced at Ethan's arm, and he suspected they smelled his blood. Thankfully, they didn't ask him about it.

Adam said, "Leidolf said you hit the wrong house."

"Yeah." Ethan was glad that Leidolf had called on them to help him right away.

"Go," Tori said. "All your men are waiting anxiously for you to go after the right perps, and we know you want to finish this job before the criminals get away. We've got this."

"Thanks, guys. Sorry," he said to the she-wolf again, and then headed out to get his team together and hit the correct house before the guys he was after vanished like the last four times he had intel on them and just missed apprehending them.

Normally, Charlene thought of herself as good-natured and great about getting over her grievances quickly, but this was truly too much. What a mess! Not once in her ten years as a homicide detective in Florida had she arrested the wrong person. Maybe she had just been lucky, but she was still angry about Special Agent Ethan Masterson pointing a gun at her while she was taking a shower! If they hadn't torn up her place, she wouldn't have felt quite so irate.

But God, Ethan was gorgeous, if she could look beyond the reason he had been there. He was tall, probably at least six feet like her father had been. His square jaw exuded masculinity and portrayed a sense of power and confidence. High cheekbones made him stand out among men. Auburn hair, trim mustache, and a beard gave him added character. But it was his hazel green eyes that had captured her attention—from surprised, to shocked, to interested, then regretful—probably because of barging into her home when she wasn't their intended target.

What gave her real chills was seeing Special Agent Pete Cohen and the other agent who had been with him when Cohen had hassled her at the convenience store. She couldn't imagine all the agents at her house were crooked, but she didn't feel confident in telling the only wolf there what she suspected of two of his fellow agents. And Renault? He was her ex-boyfriend, Noah Westmoreland's best friend. What was he doing living here in Portland? Like them, he had been born and raised in Florida.

"I'm sorry. We haven't been properly introduced. I'm Sierra and this is my mate, Adam Holmes. This is Tori Rose. We all work for the Portland Police Bureau, though I serve as their sketch artist. Tori and Adam are homicide detectives with the bureau."

Charlene let out her breath. "I'm glad for the assistance." She appreciated that they were fellow wolves.

"We truly understand your frustration," Sierra said. "I would have felt the same way."

"Thanks."

Once the dishwasher was full, Charlene started the cleaning cycle and then went into the living room to right the standing lamps and put the cushions back on the sofas and chairs. The place had been rented fully furnished, so it wasn't even her stuff that had been tossed about like that. She could just see having to pay damages to the owner.

Then a couple of men, also both red wolves, arrived and

said they were measuring the frame for the door and would take care of it in the next couple of hours. One of the men said, "We've got access to resources, and we'll get this done as soon as we can."

"Thank you." She got on her phone and called the man who was the manager for the house rental. "Hi, Fred? This is Charlene Cheswick. I'm sorry to call you so late at night, but the DEA busted through the rental house's door, and a crew is here to replace it. If anything looks different from when I rented it, like the new door they have to put in? It wasn't my doing."

"DEA?" He sounded surprised.

"Yeah." She was so exasperated. Couldn't they have waited at least until she'd left tomorrow morning? Then they could have gone to an empty house and not terrified anyone. Like her. "They got the wrong house."

"I'm on my way to the house to look over things. You're moving out tomorrow, right?"

"Yeah, so this was a shock."

"All right. Well, I'll be over in just a little bit."

"Thanks."

In most cases where the police stormed into the wrong house, nothing came of it for months, if ever. And the people whose house was damaged were stuck taking care of the catastrophic mess on their own and dealing with the trauma of the whole experience. At least she was leaving here and not returning, so she wouldn't have to relive the nightmare of a red wolf DEA special agent roaring into her bathroom to try to arrest her. She could just imagine reliving the experience every time she took a shower. She guessed she hadn't heard them bust through the door because her music had been turned on a little loud.

She did hope she hadn't hurt him too badly. She usually didn't let her emotions get away from her, but when she smelled he was a red wolf, she had just reacted. And tasted his blood. At least she didn't go so far as to break any bones. He'd been wearing body armor and gloves, but that hadn't protected his arms that were only covered in a long-sleeved shirt. She could tell he was well built, in good shape, probably from working out and running as a wolf when he could.

She hadn't felt the need to apologize to him since he had been standing in her bathroom with a gun pointed at her and she had been naked and unarmed. Until she shifted and took a bite out of him. It had at least made her feel a little better. Luckily, Ethan hadn't taken her aggressive nature as a sign of being guilty. She knew she had been innocent, so she hadn't thought he might believe she was truly guilty when he realized she was a wolf too. Then again, not all *lupus garous* were the good guys.

"I guess they went upstairs too," Tori said, sounding apologetic.

"Yeah. But they didn't touch my bedroom. I don't know about the guest bedroom." Charlene led them up the stairs.

"At least Ethan could smell that there were no drugs in the place," Sierra said.

"Unfortunately, the others weren't wolves so they couldn't." Charlene walked into the bedroom where only one drawer had been pulled out of a chest of drawers. "I guess they didn't have time to do anything in here before they checked on Ethan." She wasn't going to tell them she bit him. They might think she was a little unstable for biting a fellow wolf. Or not. Maybe they would have reacted the same way, given the circumstances.

Charlene put the drawer into the bureau while Adam checked the guest bathroom.

"Everything's good here," Adam said. "We'll stay here until they replace the door."

"Thanks. It'll be nice having some police detectives here to make sure I don't have a break-in from another source." Then she heard her manager call out from downstairs. Charlene hoped he wouldn't be too upset about what he saw. Most of all, that the owners wouldn't be.

CHAPTER 2

ETHAN CONFIRMED AGAIN THAT THIS WAS THE CORRECT house where the murdering drug lord Kroner was holed up and realized that it had a black roof, not a gray one like the house they had entered by mistake. The siding was gray, not white like the she-wolf's home. He'd seen the pictures. He should have realized it was the wrong place, but he had relied too much on the address Ferret had given them.

Ethan still felt bad about breaking into the she-wolf's house and was exasperated with himself for thinking about it because he needed to get his head in the game so no one on his team was hurt. These guys they were looking to take down were ruthless and had been involved in several home break-ins and five murders—that they knew of.

With a prick of heightened awareness, Ethan gave the signal to break down the door, some of his team going around the back of the house to break in through the back door at the same time. He was truly thankful they hadn't busted down two of she-wolf's doors.

The coordinated effort of them busting through the doors made a lot of noise, stirring the dead if anyone was asleep in the house. There were no lights on inside, so it was possible that everyone was asleep. Hopefully, the guys they were after weren't off committing other crimes while the city slept or had gotten word that Ethan and his men were coming for them.

As soon as Ethan headed inside, he motioned for his team to secure various rooms and he started up the stairs with three of his men, the darn carpeted floors creaking with his weight. The whole place reeked of drugs—methamphetamines, coke, and marijuana. Drug paraphernalia covered the beat-up coffee table, beer cans sitting next to it. A couple of half-empty whiskey bottles sat on another table in the living room, cigarette butts filling ashtrays on several of the tables. The place smelled of dust, cigarette smoke, drugs, booze, and filth. These men made so much from drug money, but this was how they lived. Now this was completely different from the she-wolf's pristine home.

He went into a bathroom on the way to the bedrooms and gave the all clear sign. Then he forged on to the first of the rooms and slowly turned the knob on the closed door. Not locked. Ethan assumed no one was in there unless it was a case of subterfuge and they were ready for a firefight. He knew Kroner, the leader of the gang, wouldn't go down easily. He'd been to prison several times and he vowed he would never go back.

Ethan pushed open the door, and it creaked as it slammed against the wall. Nothing happened. Damn, he hoped they weren't all still out on the town. It was a little after midnight and anything was possible since his men hadn't been watching the right house. But they couldn't have waited to do this another day, afraid the word would get out to Kroner and his gang that the DEA had raided the wrong house and suspect they were the actual targets.

One of his team members went into the bedroom and

one stayed with him to assist while Ethan and two others went to check out the next bedroom. Then more of the team headed up the stairs, having cleared the rooms on the first floor.

Ethan led the men toward the next room. It was a three-bedroom, two-bath house, so they still had two more bedrooms and the attic to search. He reached the next door and twisted the doorknob, but it was locked.

One of the men hit the door with a tactical door ram, splintering the hollow-core door into pieces. Gunfire from the perp burst through the opening, and Ethan put on a gas mask and threw a smoke grenade into the room. He was already past the door, so he hurried to check out the last room while his men put on gas masks. They all heard someone choking and coughing in the room.

The room smelled mostly of one of the men he was after, Benny Coates, one of the newer guys in the gang.

Ethan couldn't make any headway without the floor squeaking under the carpet all the way down the hall to the last bedroom, the master bedroom. When he reached the door, he tried the doorknob, and it was also locked. Two of the team members had gone into the other room and no more gunfire had been exchanged so hopefully they had Benny, or whoever had been shooting, in custody. The officer with the door ram came to slam it into the last door and as with the other locked room, shots rang out from this one.

Ethan tossed a smoke grenade into the room. Two more of his team members joined him, masked. He headed into the room, having a difficult time seeing through the smoke, but then the gunfire started again. One of his men fired in the shooter's direction and made a hasty exit out the bedroom door. The other dove behind the bed, unable to get off a shot. Ethan had managed to take cover next to a tall chest of drawers. Coughing, the man was still shooting when his gun jammed. His heart beating wildly, Ethan rushed him, wanting to take him into custody at all costs.

Ethan was nearly to the man when he recognized him. The shooter was Kroner, and he had just unjammed his gun. *Shit!* Ethan lunged at him, wishing he could leap as a wolf, getting so much more distance than when he was in his human form. But Kroner got off a shot before Ethan slammed into him and knocked him onto his back and into the bathroom on the title floor. Ethan's men were trying to get into the bathroom to help him. Kroner struck Ethan in the jaw while Ethan wrestled with him to get him flipped over. The guy was 220 pounds and six three, so he was like an immovable giant.

Ethan and two of his team members finally managed to turn him over and secured his hands behind his back with zip ties. They had an even harder time getting him to his feet. He was coughing from the smoke, his eyes half-shut, blinking back tears.

"You're dead, Matheson," Kroner promised, his brown eyes tearing up from the smoke and appearing blacker with rage.

Ethan ignored the threat. He and another of his team members hauled Kroner toward the stairs, then down them to a waiting police van. Ethan and his men took off their gas masks and began securing all the evidence.

"We got Benny too," Renault said.

"Good." Ethan was damned glad they got Kroner and Benny at least, though he was disappointed they hadn't gotten Oakley, Thor, or more of the gang.

"Hey, you're bleeding," Renault said to Ethan.

Ethan glanced at his arm. He wasn't feeling any pain yet from the bullet that had hit his left arm, just above where the she-wolf had bitten him.

"An ambulance is parked out front," Renault said, looking concerned that Ethan might have lost a lot of blood and wasn't thinking too clearly.

Ethan had to have his bullet wound checked out by their wolf doctor, but he knew he couldn't just leave without getting it bandaged up here to stop the bleeding. Thankfully, he still wasn't feeling any pain. He watched as they loaded Kroner into the police van. That meant at least two more bad guys were off the streets for a while. Since Kroner had shot Ethan, he hoped the drug lord would be charged with attempted murder this time, until the authorities could ensure they had enough evidence proving he was responsible for Ethan's parents' murder.

"Hey, Renault," Ethan said, hoping the agent knew the she-wolf and it wasn't just his imagination that Renault recognized her.

"Yeah?"

"You looked like you recognized the woman whose house we raided."

Renault ran his hands through his hair and looked a little sheepish. "Uh, she was dating a friend of mine."

"Her name?" Now Ethan would finally know who she was.

Renault smiled, appearing amused that the she-wolf hadn't given her name to Ethan. "Charlene Cheswick."

Ethan wanted to know if her boyfriend was a wolf. Though sometimes wolves dated humans if there were no other wolves around to date. "What was your friend's name?"

"Noah Westmoreland."

"I don't know him." Ethan was thinking out loud that he didn't know a wolf in the area by that name, though he hadn't known Charlene either.

"He isn't from around here."

"Destin, Florida." Ethan snapped his fingers. "That's where you transferred in from."

"Right. I was surprised to see her here. It's sure a small world."

"Yeah." But if Noah wasn't here, because Ethan sure hadn't smelled a male wolf's scent at the house, then maybe she had left him behind. Ethan walked over to the waiting ambulance.

One of the EMTs cut Ethan's long-sleeved shirt to bandage his arm. "You'll need to have this taken care of at the hospital."

"I'll drive myself, thanks."

"Did they have a dog in the house?" the EMT asked, looking over the bite wound.

Ethan glanced at the bloodied wolf teeth marks on his arm. "That happened another time."

The EMT bandaged that wound up too. "You need to

make sure the dog had all his shots, and you'll need to get some too."

"Right. That's just what I'll do."

The department was throwing Ethan a retirement party tomorrow afternoon. Though he hadn't told any of his fellow agents about his next mission, his red-wolf pack leaders and his closest law-enforcement wolf friends knew what he was doing next. For now, he was done with work, so he would just run in tomorrow and enjoy the celebration.

He had to get his arm looked at tonight, though. He didn't want to tell the doctor, or anyone else, that a she-wolf had bitten him because he'd raided her house by accident.

His boss, Barney Grainger, called Ethan as he was driving down to Leidolf's ranch to have his arm looked at.

"Are you going to be able to do the mission from Oyster Bay?" Grainger asked.

"Yes, sir." Ethan still wondered why his boss wanted him to do this solo, instead of having someone else handling it who was still on the force and not retiring. Sure, he could use that as his cover, but he suspected there was more to it than that. Like someone in their department was on the take. Maybe that was even the reason why they hit the wrong house tonight.

"I figure you'll be out a week or longer after having been shot, depending on how bad it is. Renault informed me you didn't go to the hospital."

"No, sir. I'm seeing my family doctor and she'll fill out the necessary paperwork on me."

"All right. Well, you take it easy, and when she approves you returning to work, let me know."

"I will."

"Great job on catching two of the men."

"Yeah. I can't wait to take down the rest."

"We'll do that. You just get the intel."

"Yes, sir." Ethan and his boss ended the call. He wanted to get the bastards himself, but he knew he would need the team to do it. These guys were just too dangerous for one agent to tackle alone.

"Damn, they did a job on your door," Charlene's manager said to her as he walked into her rental house, making his way through the debris.

"Yeah, but I have some, um, friends coming to take care of it," Charlene said.

"All right. And the rest of the house?"

"You can check it over, but thankfully, there was no other damage," Charlene said.

"Okay, I'll make a quick walk through the house, if you don't mind."

"Go ahead."

The manager walked into the kitchen and was checking it out when Tori said to Charlene, "So this isn't your house."

"No, I'm just renting it."

Then a couple walked in through the door, both green-eyed redheads, the guy tall and commanding, his eyes immediately taking in his surroundings, and the woman petite and friendly, offering her a warm smile. The man said, "Hi, I'm

Leidolf Wildhaven. This is my—" He paused as he saw the manager walk out of the kitchen.

"He's the manager of the house rental," Charlene told Leidolf.

Then the manager went upstairs, and Leidolf continued, "This is my wife, Cassie, and we truly regret what happened to you."

The manager came back downstairs. "When are they taking care of the door?" he asked Charlene.

"In a couple of hours."

"Okay. I'll check it out in the morning, send a picture of it to the owners, and make sure it passes inspection with them."

"Thanks so much." Charlene hoped the owners would be happy with it.

Then the manager left.

"We'll stay here until the door's replaced if you have anything else you want to do," Leidolf said. "The rest of you don't have to stay here either."

"Do you need us to do anything else for you?" Adam asked Charlene.

"No, thanks. I appreciate that you came to help me with everything," Charlene said.

"It is our pleasure. It's always good to meet other red wolves," Tori said.

"I agree," Sierra said. "We'll have to have lunch sometime."

Tori seconded that suggestion.

Adam smiled. "I think that's an invitation for the ladies only."

"Yeah, I'm all for doing it," Cassie said. "We didn't catch your name."

Because Charlene hadn't given it. She really wasn't going to be around to have lunch with the ladies or anything else. Portland was a three-hour drive from where she was going to be living. "I'm Charlene Cheswick and I thank you for the lovely offer, but I'm moving to Oyster Bay tomorrow."

"Oyster Bay," Cassie said, sounding surprised.

The others smiled.

"You'll love it there," Toni said. "It's really beautiful there."

"Yeah, I've been there too with Adam," Sierra said.

"I'm renting out two homes for visitors to the area to stay at," Charlene said, thinking maybe she would end up with some friendships with the red wolves out of Portland after all.

"Oh, great. Do you have any business cards?" Cassie asked. "We'll share them with the whole pack."

"Yeah, sure. I'll just go get them." Charlene finally felt things were looking up after this disaster and headed up the stairs to her bedroom. She grabbed some business cards, then took them downstairs to give to everyone.

"We'll pass them around to the other pack members," Leidolf said. "We always encourage our pack members to buy goods or services from other wolves and we would be happy to have you join us, even though you'll be living some distance from our pack. But you're a red wolf and if you're ever out this way, you're welcome to come to our parties and other functions anytime. There are no wolf packs out in that vicinity, though there may be a lone wolf or two living out that way. We never met any while we were out there, but just like you being here, we didn't know it.

"We have plenty of acreage at the ranch, and we have pack members who also own a reindeer ranch that has lots of acreage. If you're ever out that way, you can run as a wolf there where you'll be safe too." Leidolf gave her one of his ranch cards. "You can also stay with us when you visit."

"Thanks."

"Are you going to be around in the morning? We could have breakfast together instead of lunch," Toni said.

"Yeah, sure. Breakfast would be fine. Do you have any suggestions?"

"The Egg Stop. They have the best breakfasts, cute decor, and a really nice staff," Tori said, the others all agreeing.

Charlene hadn't heard of it, but she thought that would be fun. Tori gave her the address to the place, they agreed on a time, and then she, Adam, and Sierra said good night and left.

Charlene motioned to the living room. "We might as well get comfortable."

About that time, four guys arrived with the door and frame, and they all started working their magic. Leidolf actually went to help the men install the framing and the door, which impressed her. Since he was the pack leader, she figured he would just sit back and watch.

Cassie asked Charlene, "What made you move out here from Florida?"

"My grandfather was from Tillamook, and I loved coming out to visit him. He taught me how to gather berries and make fruit pies and jam, how to fish in the rivers, and how to navigate the woods safely as a wolf. I always wanted to move out here to be on the Oregon coast, but my parents didn't want to leave Destin. When they passed on, I sold everything to fulfil my dream of living out here." She'd had such happy times here. After she lost her family in Florida, everywhere she went that she had spent time with them reminded her of what she'd lost and made her sad. She'd wanted to start anew in a place where she felt at home.

"That sounds like a lovely dream."

"I just hope it works out and I can stay in the area." Charlene never knew how things would go in the rental business.

Leidolf got a call then and answered it. "Thanks, Doc." He said to Cassie, "Well, Ethan not only was shot in the line of duty when he took down one of the perps he was gunning for, but he was bitten by a wolf."

Charlene felt bad then. She was the wolf who had bitten him when he had a dangerous job to do. Though she hadn't thought of that at the time.

"Oh, no," Cassie said. "Is he going to be okay?"

"Yeah, he was shot in the arm, but Dr. Redmann will be taking the bullet out and he'll be good as new before long, thanks to our faster-healing genetics," Leidolf said.

"And the bite mark?" Cassie asked.

"Uh, the she-wolf drew blood, but didn't do any real damage," Leidolf said, then winked at Charlene as if he knew just who had bitten Ethan.

Cassie glanced at her and smiled. At least they didn't

seem perturbed with her for biting a fellow wolf in their pack when she hadn't been doing it to protect herself, but in anger.

"Is he being hospitalized?" Charlene asked. "I mean, for the bullet wound?"

"We have a clinic at the ranch now. Any shifter who is injured will be treated there. Dr. Rita Redmann is our new doctor, and she treats all kinds of injuries. Ranch-related, police-related, and she delivers babies too. But only of the shifter variety. Of course, if someone was trespassing on our property and was injured, she would take care of them until they could be transported out of there."

"That's good to know." Charlene hadn't needed a doctor for anything while she was here, but she never thought of seeing a shifter who could take care of health-related emergencies for a wolf pack.

The men finished putting in the door and then she thanked them and the pack leaders as they said their good nights. Once they left, Charlene headed to bed.

As soon as she slipped under the bedcovers, she closed her eyes and envisioned Ethan's hazel green eyes gazing into hers, regretful, surprised, and maybe even a little interested. He had the prettiest natural auburn hair she'd ever seen on a guy. Too bad he had led the raid into her home. Maybe if he hadn't and she had met him earlier under different circumstances, she might have even dated him. If he was single, of course. What did she know? Though she knew it couldn't have lasted if she had because she was leaving town.

Still, it was a shame she couldn't have gotten to know him before this. Then he would have realized her house wasn't a drug house, and they wouldn't have had that unfortunate first meeting.

CHAPTER 3

AT THE RANCH, LEIDOLF GAVE ETHAN HELL IN THE RECOVery room once he learned Ethan had driven there himself.

"Why in the hell did you drive down here to see the doctor? Cassie and I would have brought you here after we left Charlene's house. Or the doctor would have met up with you in Portland. Or we would have sent an ambulance to get you." Leidolf looked so sternly at Ethan that he wanted to smile.

Ethan only nodded, woozy. He didn't like imposing on anyone, and he really hadn't felt that bad at the time—probably because of the adrenaline pumping through his blood.

Doc wanted him to stay the rest of the morning at the clinic, but Ethan said, "I'll be fine once I have more sleep."

Leidolf wasn't about to allow Ethan to drive himself home. He put out the call for help.

Brad Reddington and Josh Wilding arrived at the clinic then. Brad was a good friend and also a subleader and had quickly volunteered to drive Ethan's car back to Portland. Josh, one of Ethan's best friends, was part owner of the nearby reindeer ranch and a retired homicide detective who had worked with Ethan on several cases. Josh took Ethan home in his car. When they arrived at his home, Ethan was exhausted, feeling the pain from the bullet wound and the wolf's bite.

"Hell, man, I didn't figure you would be shot on your last Portland assignment," Josh said, getting Ethan settled in his bed like he was his big brother.

"Yeah, I rushed him, but Kroner unjammed his gun at the last moment." Ethan didn't regret his decision. He felt he saved other members from his team getting shot, and as a wolf, Ethan would heal up much faster.

"At least you got one of the people who was responsible for your parents' murders," Brad said, bringing him a glass of water and setting it on the bedside table.

"Yeah. It would have been nice to get the whole gang, but I'm still going after them."

"Well, if you need any of our help, just let us know," Josh said. Then he chuckled. "We take it that the she-wolf whose house you raided bit you."

Brad smiled. "I figured it must have been a love bite."

Ethan shook his head. "I don't think making friends with me was on her mind at the time."

"You're not going to let that stop you, are you?" Josh asked.

Nope. "I have every intention of making it up to her one way or another."

They both laughed.

"I look forward to seeing you do it," Brad said.

"Yeah, the same with me," Josh said.

Ethan hoped he could pull it off. Both Josh and Brad were happily mated. Most of his friends were, and Ethan had done his fair share of giving them a hard time when they were courting their mates. Not that he was courting Charlene, but any interest he might show in a female wolf was a chance for them to give him a hard time back.

"Do you need anything else besides sleep?" Brad asked.

"No, guys, thanks so much for bringing me home."

Brad shook his head. "Leidolf was sure pissed that you had driven to the ranch to see the doctor on your own like that."

Josh agreed. "Yeah, we all agree. It would have been nothing for any of us to come get you to see the doctor."

"Next time, I'll keep it in mind."

"You'd better," Brad said. "We're all here for each other. Get some rest, Ethan."

"Sleep well," Josh said. "We'll check on you later."

"Thanks, guys. See you later."

Then they left him to sleep for the rest of the morning. Sleep wouldn't come though as Ethan kept thinking about the night's events—catching Charlene in the shower and taking Kroner and Benny down. Then Ethan got a call. At this hour? It was Tori. "Yeah, Tori? You know that I have finally gone to bed after seeing Doc, don't you?"

"Yes, but I wanted to check on you. How are you doing?" Tori asked.

Ethan did love that about his fellow red-wolf pack members. They were sincerely concerned about each other's well-being. "I've been better. But I'll heal up soon enough. At least I don't have to work when I wake up."

"Yeah, but even if you hadn't retired, you would have been off from work, recuperating from your injuries." Tori was one of his close friends, being a fellow law-enforcement officer, but she, like many of his red wolf friends, also knew about his new undercover mission.

Ethan knew Tori was concerned about him because of his injury, but he suspected she had an ulterior motive for calling him this early when she could have checked on him later in the morning. He realized she had mentioned his *injuries*. Aww, hell, she must know about Charlene biting him.

"Okay, so I wanted to give you a bit of news. When you move to Oyster Bay, you'll know someone there already," she said.

"Who?" Ethan was going to miss his friends in the Portland area, but hopefully this additional assignment wouldn't take too long.

"Charlene Cheswick will be in Oyster Bay," Tori said.

"Who?" He couldn't believe he had heard Tori right. The she-wolf whose house he had just raided?

"She didn't tell you her name? The she-wolf who bit you tonight after you invaded her home."

He groaned.

Tori laughed. "She's moving there tomorrow. Maybe when you get moved in, you can apologize to her for breaking into her place and tearing it up, or maybe she'll even apologize to you for biting you."

He doubted that would ever happen! Though he was all for apologizing to her again. Worse, he wasn't moving to Oyster Bay to retire, but moving there as part of a deep undercover operation. If he did meet up with her, he would be lying to her about his reason for being there. Not a great start to trying to make amends to her, but he had a job to do.

"Well, I'll let you ponder that. Get better quick, and I'll see you at your retirement ceremony in the afternoon, Ethan."

"See you there, Tori." He couldn't believe it when he learned that Charlene was going to be living in Oyster Bay too. He hoped they could bury their differences because they were both red wolves and would be living in a small community...together. He hoped his undercover job didn't impact her in any way, shape, or form.

Then he got a call from Adam. "Hell, doesn't anyone sleep at this hour?" Ethan asked Adam. It was only four thirty in the morning!

Adam laughed. "I had to check in with you. I wasn't going to because I knew you needed to recuperate from your injuries, but Sierra wouldn't let *me* go back to sleep this morning until after I had called you."

"I'll be fine. You know how we are. I'll be perfectly fit soon."

"Good, we're both glad to hear it. Um, so the she-wolf bit you, eh?" Adam laughed again.

"Hell, that's why you really called me." Ethan couldn't help but be amused.

"Yeah, Sierra had to know what had happened."

When Ethan explained about the shower and how Charlene had already been naked so she could easily shift, Adam chuckled. "No wonder she bit you."

"Yeah, I had it coming. She could smell I was a red wolf by then so she knew she couldn't turn me. And she didn't do as much damage as she could have if she'd been defending herself against me."

"Well, now we can go back to sleep knowing the whole story and that you're going to be all right. We'll see you at your retirement party. Oh, just a heads-up. Charlene is moving to Oyster Bay, if you didn't know it already."

"Tori told me."

Adam laughed again. "I knew she would beat us to tell you the news. Get some rest. We'll see you in the afternoon."

Ethan smiled, feeling a little better that his friends knew what had happened between him and Charlene and could have a good laugh. He couldn't quit thinking of the beautiful redhead and her heated green eyes though. *Charlene*. A pretty name for a pretty she-wolf. He hoped if she gave him a chance to get to know her, he could put a smile on her face the next time he saw her because he had every intention of purposefully running into her when he moved to Oyster Bay.

Though he had no intention of breaking into her home like he did in Portland.

In the morning, Charlene was anxiously waiting for the manager to show up at the rental home to check out the new door. She had breakfast scheduled with the she-wolves of the wolf pack and she hated being late for anything.

"It looks good, Charlene," the manager told her as soon as he arrived and inspected the door.

She was glad he liked the door, but the owners had the final say. She glanced at the clock on the living room wall.

She was ten minutes late to the restaurant, and it would take her ten minutes to get there.

Then the rental manager sent pictures of the new door to the owners and got a text back. "I told them it looked great to me. They said it looked fine and they were sorry you had to go through all that."

"Boy, me too." Charlene thanked the manager. She'd already packed her bags, and they were in her car. She gave him the keys to the new door. "I had a pleasant stay here. Tell the owners that I thought their place was lovely. Thanks."

"I will. You were a great tenant."

They said their goodbyes and she got in her car to drive over to the restaurant to meet up with the ladies. She was looking forward to this as her last hurrah in Portland. She just wished she had known there were other she-wolves in the area that she could have socialized with while she had been there for the month.

She parked at the restaurant and went inside. The three ladies were waiting for her and smiled brightly to see her. "Sorry if I'm a little late to the party. The manager had to inspect the replacement door and he got it okayed with the owners, so it's all good."

"Oh, wonderful," Cassie said. "Breakfast is my treat. You can order from the menu or serve up your own meal from the buffet. They have everything you could want, even special omelets made to order."

They all took their seats at one of the tables and the server brought them menus. "What would you all like to drink?"

"Hmm, this maple espresso black tea sounds good," Charlene said.

"Lavender Earl Grey tea for me." Cassie started looking over the menu.

Tori said, "Apple blossom tea for me."

"I'll have the lavender tea also," Sierra said.

Then they all had a chance to look at their menus.

"I'm getting the breakfast bar," Charlene said. "It looks scrumptious."

The others all wanted to get the same thing. They headed to the breakfast bar and began serving up their food—fruit, hash browns, ham or sausage, and everyone ordered omelets, grabbed glasses of apple juice or orange juice, and then headed back to their table.

"Okay, so now that we're sitting down, I have to ask if the DEA special agent is all right after he was shot," Charlene said, concerned for Ethan, then took a sip of her espresso.

"Yeah, Ethan is doing great. We stopped by his place to check on him before we came to the restaurant," Cassie said.

"I guess he has some time off from work now." Charlene forked up some of her cheesy omelet. Hmm, sharp cheese just like she liked it.

"He has retired. He's going to be relocating to Oyster Bay, so at least you'll know one red wolf out there," Tori said, with a twinkle in her green eyes. She was wearing a light-gray suit, like she would be heading into work right after their lady wolves' breakfast.

Charlene couldn't have been more shocked to hear the news. She thought Tori was amused that she and Ethan might have a chance to get to know each other better after their initial fiasco of a meeting. "What? Why in the world would he do that? I mean, when all his friends live here and he's a member of the wolf pack." Charlene couldn't understand why a wolf would move so far away from a working pack that he belonged to.

"He said he has had to deal with so much crime that he just wanted to get away from it all. Most of our wolves work out in the country or live out there. A few are in the city," Cassie said. "But as they retire, I think more of our wolves will move out of the city. It's easier if we want to run as wolves."

Okay, so Charlene could understand that, but why would Ethan move specifically to Oyster Bay? Where *she* was moving to?

The lights sparkled overhead and pictures of different kinds of fancy chickens—from silkies to frizzles—decorated the walls, while the tables were covered with red-and-white-checkered cloths. So cute.

The ladies had sure picked out a great restaurant. The food was delicious. "So I guess as a pack leader, you're busy with that all the time," Charlene said to Cassie.

"I'm actually also a wolf biologist and teach groups about the importance and habits of wolves," Cassie said.

Charlene smiled. "When you got your degree, that must have been easy."

Cassie laughed. "Yeah, I could tell the professors a lot that they didn't know about with regard to wild wolves."

"I bet." Why hadn't Charlene thought of an occupation like that when she was trying to figure out what to do with her life? Because a police officer had rescued her family from their crashed car when she was five, and she'd wanted to be a police officer. She enjoyed taking care of the rental properties in Florida, though, after she changed careers.

"We're sorry we didn't know about you beforehand," Sierra said. "In addition to being a police sketch artist, I also teach art classes to the kids in the pack and adult classes for pack members."

"That sounds like fun."

"It is. We have a great time." Sierra glanced over at the entryway to the restaurant and smiled.

The other ladies looked that way and saw Ethan, Adam, and Leidolf show up, surprising Charlene when she thought this was just going to be an all-girl's breakfast. She was sure it wasn't a chance meeting.

They pulled up another table to join with theirs.

"Sorry," Leidolf said, his green eyes alight with devilment. "We had to get breakfast too, and what better time to do it than when a group of lovely she-wolves are having theirs at our favorite spot to eat."

"Join us, mate of mine," Cassie said.

"Yes, don't be shy," Tori said.

Sierra looked glad to see her mate and she moved over to sit beside Adam, leaving her chair available to Leidolf so he could sit beside his mate. Charlene guessed Tori wasn't mated since no one had said anything about it. But darned if Tori didn't move into the seat next to Adam so she would leave a free seat next to Charlene. Now Ethan would have to sit down next to Charlene.

"Girl, boy, girl, boy, and so forth," Tori said.

Charlene had to chuckle. She couldn't help herself. Smiling, Ethan took that as a sign that she wasn't going to bite him if he sat down beside her. He was dressed in jeans and a long-sleeved dress shirt and looked like he was on a date, not ready to work as a DEA special agent.

Sierra was wearing a skirt, heels, and a pretty blouse, appearing to be ready to go to work at her job as a police sketch artist after breakfast. Likewise, her mate, Adam, was dressed in a suit, suitable for a homicide detective. Leidolf and Cassie were dressed in jeans and short-sleeved shirts, looking like they were on vacation.

The server came and asked the guys what they wanted to drink. The guys told her that they would get the breakfast buffet. After she took their drink orders, she left, and Adam and Leidolf went to get their meals.

Tori hopped off her chair and said, "I'm going to get seconds."

"Me too," Cassie said, smiling at Tori, and left the table.

Smiling, Sierra wordlessly left the table to get a new plate of food.

Ethan said, "I'm really sorry about your place. Leidolf said everything was fixed though."

"Yes, and the homeowners approved the changes this morning. So I have to thank you for calling on everyone to do that. I wouldn't have been able to otherwise. I heard you were shot while you were apprehending the bad guys at the correct house." Charlene sipped some more of her tea.

"Yeah, and bitten before that."

Charlene smiled.

Ethan chuckled. "I expected you to do quite a few things, but that was totally unexpected."

She *wasn't* going to apologize for that. "You took it well. Afterward, I considered that it had been a mistake on my part if you had believed I truly was involved in the whole business. Bad wolves are out there after all."

"I didn't smell any drugs in the house, and that made me suspect that we had it wrong."

"But not before you made a wreck of my place."

"Yeah, I'm sorry."

"I bet you made sure the next place was the right one."

He smiled. "Hell, yeah."

She shook her head. "You might as well get your food so the rest of our party can return to the table. I suspect they all left so we could clear the air."

Ethan sighed. "They did. They're a great group of friends."

"I promise I won't shift and bite you again, just in case you're worried about that."

"That's good to know. I'm already hurting enough, though if you have a good reason for it again, I wouldn't hold it against you. Do you want anything more?"

"No, I'm still eating what I have here."

"Okay. I'll be right back." Then Ethan got up and went to the buffet table.

She was surprised he was so nice to her after she had bitten him. She probably wouldn't have been if the roles had been reversed, and that had her thinking about *him* coming out of the shower naked and her having a gun aimed at him.

The unbidden thought of him dripping wet made her body heat and she felt like she was having a sudden hot flash.

Then everyone returned to the table with plates of food and took their seats. They all began to have conversations around the tables and Charlene said to Ethan, "I hear you're moving to Oyster Bay."

"Yeah, I hear you're going that way too."

"Yeah, we might even be neighbors. But you'll no longer be on the force so you won't be breaking into any more houses. Though if you were, I would let you know my address so you wouldn't give me any more trouble." She took a bite of a juicy, green grape.

He laughed. "No more warrants, no more break-ins. But I'll gladly take your address and your phone number."

She smiled, fished out one of her business cards, and handed it to him.

He looked at the card. "So you rent out properties."

"I do. Do you want to rent one until you find a place of your own?"

He chuckled. "I've got a place."

She sighed dramatically. "I'll have to scratch you off my list of prospective renters then."

He laughed and gave her his phone number and the address to his new place.

Tori finished the food on her plate and said, "Hey, I've got to head in to work, but this was grand. We'll have to do it again when you come back to the city, Charlene."

"Yeah, Sierra and I have to go in to work too," Adam said, standing and helping Sierra from her chair.

Leidolf said, "I've got some things to take care of at the ranch."

"And I need to get some materials ready for a speech I'm making to a group at a college," Cassie said.

That she probably knew by heart, Charlene was thinking.

"We paid for your bill too, Ethan," Leidolf said. "We'll all see you at your retirement ceremony this afternoon."

"Thanks!" Ethan said. "I appreciate it. I'll see you there."

Then everyone except the two of them left the restaurant while Charlene asked for a refill on her maple espresso black tea. She hadn't expected everyone to leave so all at once, but she suspected it was in part for her to visit privately with Ethan a little longer.

"I'm going back for seconds. Do you want anything?" Ethan asked.

"Sure, I'll get some more fruit." She rose from her chair and joined him. "So I take it that you took the bad guys down and just didn't get shot and lose them."

"They're in jail, but trying to get bonded out, of course."

"Great. Hopefully they won't be." She'd considered telling Ethan she had been a homicide detective, but she'd given up her job and didn't really want to have to explain why. For now, she was the owner and manager of rental properties. It was amazing how someone's view of her could change when they learned what she used to do. Sometimes not in a good way. She always suspected that the ones who were shocked and didn't have anything more to do with her had dirty little secrets they didn't want her to know.

"After they shot at us, I believe they'll remain incarcerated. But you never know."

She got a new plate and added some cantaloupe, honeydew melon, and more grapes. They were so sweet. "So what are you going to do for a job when you move to Oyster Bay?"

"I have a retirement check so I'm going to chill for a little while and figure things out."

"Oh, sure. And recuperate from your injuries." She noticed he was favoring his injured arm and had winced a few times. "I still can't figure out why you would leave your friends behind."

"I'm not. I'll be seeing them. But I might have a new friend there to enjoy some wolf runs with."

"Me?"

"Yeah, I still have to make it up to you. Would you like to have dinner out when I arrive there this evening?"

She smiled. "Okay, I'll bite."

He laughed. "You sure did."

She laughed and then she saw Renault on the other side of the breakfast bar getting food. "Fancy seeing you here."

"My favorite spot to eat." Renault smiled at her and then glanced speculatively at Ethan. "I didn't expect you to be out and about after getting shot last night."

"It's barely a scratch. See you at the retirement ceremony."

"Yeah, sure," Renault said and then he continued to fill his plate with food.

Charlene and Ethan headed to the table with their plates of food. He had taken seconds of practically everything.

"So when are you actually moving to Oyster Bay?"

Renault sat at a table close to them. Charlene smiled at him and then Ethan said, "Right after the retirement party. If you would like to come to it, we would love to have you there. I mean, especially me. But some of my, um, friends will be there—Leidolf and Cassie, Sierra and Adam, Tori, and Josh Wilding and his mate, Brooke. Josh is retired from the Portland Police Bureau, but we worked a lot of cases together. So it won't be just a lot of people you don't know, but some of the people you've met. And then we could caravan out to Oyster Bay together. After that, we could have dinner tonight there."

"Then I could see the guys at the retirement party that you were working with who raided my house too?" No way.

"Yeah, I guess that's a no-go."

"I'll take you up on dinner. Just let me know when you get in. Not too late though. Around six would be a good time for me." She mentioned that only in case he got hung up with his friends for hours and didn't arrive until eight or nine. She wasn't waiting that late for dinner because he was enjoying being with his friends longer and couldn't part company. Which she totally understood. But they could have dinner another night.

"Of course. I totally understand."

They finished their breakfast, and he walked her out to her car. "Until tonight then," he said.

"Tonight." She slipped into her car and waved goodbye and left for her next new adventure. Maybe she would even have a wolf to date on occasion, but she would see how that all panned out. The last DEA special agent wolf she had dated hadn't worked out well at all.

CHAPTER 4

ETHAN COULDN'T HAVE BEEN MORE THRILLED THAT Charlene seemed to have forgiven him for wrecking her house and was willing to have dinner with him tonight. As soon as he arrived at the office for his faux retirement ceremony, everyone cheered him on, and he was especially glad to see his red wolf friends there. Of course he was glad to celebrate with the men he worked with all the time too. Once he was gone, he would still be seeing his wolf friends. And they had helped him out with situations more times than he could count.

He wished Charlene could have been here too, but he totally understood why she hadn't wanted to be.

"So"—Tori clinked her glass of apple cider against Ethan's—"it appeared things were working out okay between you and Charlene. I had thought of inviting her to your retirement ceremony but—"

"She had to get on her way. She wasn't too fond of the other men on the team who did all the damage to her place."

"Sure."

"I had invited her because I knew you were going to ask that question next. You make a great detective, you know," Ethan said.

Tori smiled. "Yep, that was my next question. I overheard the two of you exchanging phone numbers and addresses.

That's a good start. And you stayed and visited with each other for a while longer. That's a good sign. You're leaving for Oyster Bay after the party, right?"

"Yes, and as long as I don't celebrate here for too long, I can have dinner with her tonight."

The place was so noisy he was glad that with the wolves' enhanced hearing, he could make out what Tori was saying without humans overhearing their conversation.

"Wow, that's great. I was going to suggest that you get on the ball with that. You never know when some wolf might run into her on a visit to the area and you would lose out." Tori smiled and sipped her apple cider.

"A date with Charlene?" Adam asked, emphasizing that it was a singular event. "Good show."

"One date," Ethan said. "We'll see how it goes. We might not be compatible in the least."

"After she bit you and you're both still speaking to each other," Cassie said, joining them, "I would say you're doing all right."

Leidolf agreed. "It was just a wolf's way to get to know you."

Ethan laughed. "A lick or a nuzzle would have been lots more welcome." His arm where she had bitten him was healing, but the bite mark would still be visible for a couple more days. Which was why he was wearing a long-sleeved shirt around his fellow law-enforcement friends.

"A date? For when? Tonight?" Sierra asked. "And you're still here?"

Yeah, Ethan was ready to chase Charlene down, caravan

with her, and then get settled into his place before he picked her up at her house to take her somewhere nice for dinner. Actually, flowers were in order, and he would make a reservation at the nicest place they could go to. He would tip the hostess to make sure they had a window seat so they could see the sunset while they had dinner. Not having had serious relationships with any she-wolves before, he had never worked so hard to win a she-wolf over, but he figured she deserved it.

"After we hit the wrong house, we didn't think Ethan was ever going to come out of the woman's house," one of his DEA team members said, laughing.

"Well, he had to make right by the lady. Don't tell me you wouldn't have been trying to help her out after the mistake we made," another of his men said.

"I bet he'll ask her out on a date."

"Are you kidding? The way she was glowering at him and then at us? No way."

"Yeah, he'll ask her."

"Did you ask her on a date?"

Ethan laughed.

"Hell, he did!"

"No way. Really?"

Ethan smiled. They knew him too well. "Dinner tonight."

"You lucky dog. Why isn't she here tonight?" Pete Cohen asked. He was one of the men who had torn up Charlene's kitchen to such an extent during the raid, according to another of Ethan's team members. And then ended up rushing into the bathroom to come to Ethan's aid when he heard him call out in pain. Known to have a sweet tooth, whenever Cohen was on surveillance with anyone, he would have a package of candy bars to eat while gathering intel. Even now, he had a candy bar in hand.

"After seeing you guys and what you did to her place?" Ethan asked.

Cohen shrugged. "Yeah, I guess so."

The other men who had been at the raid shook their heads.

"If anyone can turn ordinary metal into gold, it's Ethan," Manx Ryerson said. "Hell, I would have stayed and helped her clean up her place."

"As if," Renault said. "You've probably never cleaned up after yourself ever, from seeing the sight of your desk. The notion of you cleaning someone else's place up? No way."

The other guys laughed, but Ethan agreed with them. Manx was a slob. He had at least three half-empty coffee mugs on his desk at all times and food wrappers from fast-food restaurants stacked on top of his desk or stuffed in his desk drawers. Ethan wondered if he was that bad when he went home to his wife. His good friend Pete Cohen was the opposite, almost obsessively neat. Even when he ate his candy bars on a stakeout, he had a trash bag with him that he would put all his wrappers in. Ethan couldn't see the two of them working together, let alone being such close friends.

Ryerson said to Ethan, "We'll miss you."

Cohen scoffed. "You're glad Ethan's leaving so he doesn't hassle you about your messy desk any longer."

Ryerson shook his head. "No. Renault will take his place and he'll hassle me instead."

"You're damn right I will. As soon as Ethan said he was retiring, I knew one of us would have to pick up the slack," Renault said.

Though Ethan was having a good time at his retirement party, he knew several of the people had to get back to work—even his wolf friends—while he didn't want to miss his window of opportunity to have dinner with Charlene.

"Off I go," Ethan finally said. He gave his wolf friends hugs and received lots of slaps on the back from his DEA team members. He spoke with his boss, who took him aside to ask about his wound.

"I need a doctor's report," Grainger said.

"Yes, sir. Thanks for working with me all these years. I'll have my doctor send you the report." Frankly, Ethan had forgotten all about it.

"I hate to see you go."

Then Ethan told his boss goodbye and he'd keep in touch. He headed out to his car and drove off. After working at the agency for so long, it seemed unreal that he no longer had a desk he would work at there.

He was barely out of the suburbs of Portland when he got a flat tire, then a second and a third one. What the hell? That's when he saw a bunch of cars pulling over with flat tires both behind and in front of him. Then he saw the culprit. A big construction truck in front of the cars had accidentally dropped a bunch of nails on the highway. Ethan counted about thirty cars with flats on the shoulder by the time the truck ran out of nails.

He immediately called Leidolf. That was the thing about a pack. They could provide better services than anyone, but boy, if Ethan missed his date with the she-wolf tonight because of this mishap? He was going to be royally pissed.

The problem was that though one of the men in his pack was getting the replacement tires for his car, the city had to send out a highway maintenance vehicle to clean up the road or they would all just be driving over the same area where the nails were located.

He decided he'd better call Charlene to tell her he was on his way but experiencing some trouble, just in case this took longer than he planned. He pulled out his phone and called her number. "Hey, Charlene, this is Ethan. I'm on my way, but I barely made it out of the suburbs when a construction vehicle dropped a payload of nails all over the road."

"Oh no."

"Yeah, they still need to clean up the road before someone can come with three more tires that I need to change out."

"Oh, wow. And you called me because?" Charlene sounded amused as he heard running water in the background, and he immediately thought of her being in the shower.

But he knew she couldn't be in the shower while she was on the phone. "I just wanted to let you know I'm picking you up for dinner, but I'm having a roadblock that might take a while to clear out."

"Okay. Well, we still have time. You have a three-hour drive to get to Oyster Bay, and if you are delayed as much as by an hour and a half, you'll still be here on time for a date."

He smiled. She didn't tell him that if he ended up reaching her place later than the allotted time, she would give him some leeway. "All right. Well, I'll be there when I get there."

"I'll see you in a little while." Then they ended the call. He waited and waited and waited for the county maintenance truck to come to clear the road. He felt like he was on a stakeout. Police cars had arrived to block off the road until it was cleared of nails.

A half hour passed, which seemed like hours, and then a maintenance truck swept the area with a magnetic metal collector. Ethan was grateful it had arrived. Then the truck finally drove off and Ethan was hopeful that his new tires wouldn't get any new nails.

Ethan called George. "Hey, if you can get here now with the tires—"

"I'm just on the other side of the police barricade that they're now taking down, sitting with all the other vehicles bringing tires to their customers."

"Thanks, George."

"Sure thing." George finally parked behind Ethan, then helped Ethan change out his tires. "I'll let Leidolf know you're taken care of."

"Thanks." Ethan was so glad to get on the road again. He wanted to call Charlene and tell her he was on his way, but he figured she would think he sounded way too needy.

Charlene had gotten a kick out of Ethan calling her to make sure she knew he was held up not because he was still having a good time at his retirement party but because he had some real trouble. She appreciated it, but she also was certain he could get there on time, despite the problems he was dealing with for now.

She finished making a tuna salad and sat down on the patio to eat it at the table where she had a view of the bay. The deck was a little bigger than at her grandfather's cottage, but it had the same pretty views of the water, the seagulls, the waves striking the rocky shoreline. Steps led down to a private beach like at his place, which made it just as special. Trees along the cliff provided a woodland setting.

It was a hotter June day than usual at seventy-eight degrees, but a breeze swept off the water and made it feel cooler. Normally it would have been only a high of seventy and a low of fifty, perfect for running as wolves tonight. She loved this place. She hoped Ethan would want to go for a run later with her tonight. The sun would set around nine so she figured they would have dinner, and he could return home and then meet up with her later. She assumed he would want to get settled into his own place.

She finished her lunch and put her empty dish in the dishwasher. After that, she checked the tidal schedule to ensure that she didn't get caught when the tide came in and made sure she had a good two hours to explore.

She wore jeans and a pair of waterproof hiking boots suitable for rock climbing and her windbreaker, tucking a bottle of water and a first aid kit in a backpack and her cell phone into her windbreaker pocket. Then she locked up her place and left her deck to take a walk down to the beach. At first, the beach was sandy, but she wanted to make her way to a hidden cove—a small, sheltered bay that tourists couldn't see from the cliffs and most locals didn't know about. It was tucked away between rocky structures that formed a jagged semicircle. That was part of the reason she had bought the house.

Little tidal pools were filled with sea life, looking like tiny sea aquariums. She knew never to turn her back on the ocean because sneaky waves and the undertow could be a real danger. Then she got a call on her phone and fumbled to pull it out of her windbreaker pocket, nearly dropping it in the tidal pool, She saw it was Ethan on the caller ID and chuckled. She guessed he really needed a friend in Oyster Bay.

"Hey, I wanted to call you to tell you that I'm on my way again."

"Good. I hate it when I get a nail in my tire, but three tires at once? That's awful."

"The wolf pack members are great. They helped me take care of it."

"That's great."

"Is that the ocean I hear in the background?"

She took a deep breath of the sea air. "Yes, I'm just taking a walk to check out some of the tidal pools."

"I can't wait to do that too. Just watch out for rogue waves."

"Right. We could do this sometime, and I thought we could take a run as wolves later tonight after dinner, if you would like." She thought it would be even more fun to do with another wolf.

"Yeah, that would be great. I would love to do that. I'll let you go. You need to be careful on those rocks. The seaweed and plant life can be slippery, and you could fall and break a leg."

"Thanks, I'll see you later." She was being careful to step on only bare rocks and not on top of any of the plant life that was exposed when the tide went out. Other areas were covered in mussels and barnacles that were now closed up. In the water she saw fish, a crab, a green anemone, and even colorful sea slugs. She was taking pictures of all of them, planning to eventually frame them and put them on her home's walls and in her rental units.

She had been out there for quite a while and was cautiously making her way across the craggy rocks to another tide pool. She saw some pretty coral there and snapped some more shots. She was searching for more tidal pools when she saw a wave coming in and braced herself. It splashed across her boots, and she realized the tide was coming in. It was time to get herself back to the beach and up to her place.

Except for the waves and the intermittent cry of a seagull, it was really quiet out here, no people anywhere. It was just lovely.

Time just flew while she was out there, and it wouldn't be long before Ethan arrived for dinner. She was really looking forward to it, more so than she thought she would. Despite the reason they had met, knowing a fellow red wolf was welcome.

She headed up to her home and unlocked the door and got another call from Ethan. "Hey, did you get more nails in your tires?"

He chuckled.

She liked a guy who could see humor in a sore subject.

"I'll be there on time. I'm nearly there."

"Oh, you're early."

"I promise I didn't speed too much."

She laughed. "Where are we going to eat?"

"The Seabreeze Restaurant," he said.

She found it on her computer. That was a really nice restaurant. She would wear a skirt. "Okay, I'll be ready. That sounds great." As soon as they finished talking on the phone, she hurried to go through her clothes and finally picked out a breezy boho skirt and a long-sleeved peasant blouse. She quickly pulled off her hiking boots and stripped down to her bra and panties, then dressed in the skirt, blouse, and a pair of high-heeled sandals. Oh, and she needed to brush her hair and redo her makeup.

She was all ready when her doorbell rang. She hurried to get it, but when she opened the door, she didn't see Ethan as she had expected, but a man delivering a vase of a dozen red roses. From Ethan? What a sweet gesture.

She thanked the deliveryman and signed for the flowers, then took them into her house and set them on her dining room table. She read the card and it said, "From a secret admirer."

She frowned. She would have thought Ethan would just sign his name to it. A few minutes later, her doorbell rang again, and this time, she was delighted to see it was Ethan. And he was carrying a vase of two dozen red roses.

"Wow," he said. Just the way he looked at her and what he said made her feel like a million bucks, and she loved it.

She hadn't dated since she moved to Portland after the tumultuous relationship she'd left behind in Destin. Noah had never looked at her like Ethan did, not in the eight months she had dated him. Never had he brought her flowers. So this was welcome.

Ethan was dressed in a long-sleeved, button-down collared shirt, nice trousers, and dress shoes and looked divine. He handed her the vase of roses and smiled.

She smiled back. "Thank you so much." Then she carried the vase into the house and set the flowers on the table next to the others. They were beautiful.

He glanced at the other flowers and frowned. "It looks like someone else beat me to it."

"Yeah, my secret admirer. I had hoped that they were from you."

He looked over the card from her secret admirer like a police officer would who was on the job.

"I have no idea who it could be from. I don't know anyone in the area." She was glad she had dressed up for dinner since Ethan had.

He led her out to his car and got the door for her.

"You know," she said, "I wouldn't have eaten without you if you had been delayed later than the specified time."

His expression lit up. "Seriously?"

"Yeah, but only because I felt sorry for you for the nails in your tires and that you were so worried you wouldn't make it in time for dinner."

He chuckled. "I had no idea. I really figured you would stick to your guns."

She sighed. "Well, you're trying so hard to make it up to me for raiding my rental house. I give you an A for the effort."

"Thanks." He got into the driver's seat and headed for the restaurant. "Do you want me to look into who your secret admirer is?"

She smiled. "Sure. If a guy wants to pursue me, I want to know who it is. Otherwise, it's creepy."

"Yeah, that was my thought too, especially since you're not from here and don't know anyone yet."

"But now that you are retired, can you investigate something like that?"

"I still have friends on the force, so yeah. Adam or Tori would check into it for me in a heartbeat."

"Oh, great. So I haven't looked to see where your home is located."

"About a mile from yours. I could actually take a run to get here."

She smiled. "You didn't raid the rental home I was staying at in a unique way to meet me, did you?"

He laughed. "Yeah, that was it. I wish I'd been that clever."

She smiled. She was glad he was going to look into the person who had delivered the flowers anonymously. She didn't need a stalker bothering her when she was starting over here, and she was relieved she had a wolf who could help her if she had any real trouble with someone. It was disconcerting that she had this new, weird mystery. She had just wanted to enjoy her time with Ethan.

When they arrived at the seafood restaurant, it had other dishes too—steaks, burgers, and even pizza. They walked in, and she was so surprised that Ethan had been thoughtful enough to make a reservation for them, which she so appreciated. Noah was a wing-it guy and never made reservations. If a place was too crowded, they just left and ate somewhere else. He would never wait in a long line for anything, and he would never plan a date in a way that really showed he cared.

The place was packed, so it was good that Ethan had made a reservation, or they could have been stuck waiting for dinner like a whole line of people were doing, sitting on benches outside. At least the weather was nice, the breeze from the Pacific Ocean cooling things down further.

The restaurant had miniature trees covered in fairy lights in various locations to give it a festive outdoors appearance. The walls were covered in whitewashed wooden panels, above blond wooden floors. All the booths and chairs were covered in aqua-blue vinyl and sea-glass walls between booths gave patrons more privacy. Large pictures of sea creatures from octopuses to sharks and sea turtles hung on the walls. She loved the color scheme and the decorations.

They ended up with a front-row seat overlooking the ocean, which would be divine for a view of the sunset on the water while they ate their dinner. This couldn't have been more romantic.

The server brought them a bottle of champagne and a couple of glasses, and Charlene's jaw dropped. For a moment, she was afraid it was from her secret admirer, but Ethan nodded to the wine steward, and he poured their champagne for them.

When the steward left their table, Ethan reached his golden bubbling glass of champagne out to Charlene's, and they clinked them in a toast. "To new and much better beginnings," he said.

"I second that." She drank some of her champagne.

Wow, when he wasn't trying to take down bad guys, Ethan was truly chivalrous. She was glad she could see him in a whole different light, and she was truly glad he was no longer working as a DEA special agent.

CHAPTER 5

ETHAN ORDERED COCONUT SHRIMP TO GO ALONG WITH his and Charlene's champagne for starters. They couldn't have had a more perfect table for watching the sun set over the ocean. Charlene was sipping her champagne and seemed to be enjoying herself, smiling, happy, not like she'd been when he'd first met her. He was glad he had chosen this place to have their dinner, and he had plans for taking her all over Oyster Bay and the surrounding coastal communities to sightsee, if she wanted to.

"So do you have any siblings?" Charlene asked.

"I had a brother who died in Hawaii due to a surfing accident. I always figured I would be the one to bite the dust first in the line of work I do."

"I'm so sorry."

"Thanks. It was a tragedy. What about you? Do you have any siblings? Parents? Other relatives?" he asked.

She took a deep breath and let it out. "No. I had a twin sister and parents, but they were caught in a hurricane in the Florida Keys and didn't make it." Her eyes filled with tears and she swallowed hard.

He immediately reached out and took her hand and caressed it, trying to do what he could to show he was there for her.

"I–I haven't spoken with anyone about it since it

happened, except for Noah, and that didn't go well. You're different. I just feel…well, that you would be more sympathetic. I had stayed home to manage the rental properties while my family went to the Florida Keys, my choice. I was devastated. It happened three months ago, and I still feel bad about it."

"I'm so sorry. I totally understand." He assumed she had survivor's guilt and he wanted to help her navigate through those feelings any way that he could. He was glad she felt secure in speaking to him about it. He wanted to be there for her. "My dad and mother were both DEA special agents and died in a shootout with a drug gang—the same group I was trying to take down. First, my mom, and then my dad went after them with a vengeance. He hadn't been working the case. He wasn't allowed to because he had a personal stake in it. I was still working on becoming an agent with the DEA at the time. I knew how he felt, but I couldn't stop him even though I tried."

"Oh, how awful. But you went after the drug gang once you became a special agent, even though it would have been personal for you too," Charlene said.

"Yeah. My boss, Grainger, had a similar circumstance with his father being a police officer and dying on the job. When he became a police officer, he found the man responsible and put him away. So he knew just what I was going through and backed me all the way. He also knew I wouldn't just go in shooting and ask questions later. You know the house we hit—the correct house—was where we captured two of the men who were part of the gang who killed my parents. But there are still two others that we know of who are living the free life."

"I'm glad you got two of them anyway."

"Yeah. I wish I could have gotten all of them." If he had, he wouldn't be doing this undercover work next. But he wanted to locate the rest of the men and coordinate with his boss to send his former team to apprehend them. He wasn't supposed to try to take them down by himself at any cost. He was fine with that. Ethan didn't care who did it as long as it got done.

He didn't like that he couldn't tell Charlene what he was doing either—that he was still after the men who had ambushed first his mom and then his dad, but he didn't want to blow his cover. Yet she was a red wolf, and he felt it was kind of a betrayal if he didn't tell her.

"Oh, wow, look at the sunset over the water." She lit up with happiness.

He loved seeing her like that. The sky was filled with clouds and the sky, beach, and water were all colored different shades of lavenders, oranges, and yellows. Just beautiful.

Then the server brought Charlene's wild Northwest salmon, garlic mashed potatoes, and brussels sprouts and Ethan's plate of flame-broiled halibut, baked potato, and green beans to the table.

"Enjoy," the server said with a smile. She bounced off to see to another table.

"Oh, this is so good," Charlene said after eating a bite of the salmon. "Have you ever been here before?"

"No. I haven't. I have to tell you I'm so glad I can enjoy

this with you and explore the beaches with you too, if you would like to."

"Yeah, sure. I would love that. It's more fun doing it with someone else."

Which made him wonder again why she had left Destin and come to a place where she knew nobody. Which he blamed on always overthinking situations as a detective. She probably was thinking the same thing about him being here.

After dinner, they ordered dessert. He had planned to go the full course with her, perfect for a first date if she was hungry enough. She was and they both got a slice of white chocolate cheesecake since neither of them had eaten it before.

Once they'd finished their dessert, he wanted to go to her place to shift before they ran as wolves because she had a wolf door to go in and out of.

"Do you want to shift at your place?" he asked.

"Uh, yeah, sure."

"I don't have a wolf door," he said.

She smiled. "You'll have to be risqué then when you want to shift at your place."

He laughed. "Yeah."

"Well, everything, including the cheesecake, was delicious. Thanks."

"You're most welcome." He paid for the bill, and then they headed out to his car. "You don't have any clue who might have sent you the vase of flowers?"

"No."

"The manager of your rental unit wouldn't have, would he?" Ethan asked as he drove to her place.

"No. I mean, if she had, she would have signed it. Wait. That guy who was working with you—the DEA agent named Renault?"

"Yeah, I was just going to ask you about him. He said he knew you from when you were dating his friend in Destin, Florida. Was this friend a wolf?"

Charlene rolled her eyes at Ethan. "Yes, he was a wolf—with a bad temper, I might add."

"And he's the ex-boyfriend?"

"Noah Westmoreland? He and I broke up about a month before I moved out here." Then she changed the subject. "Do you think you'll miss your job? The excitement? Taking down the bad guys? Making it safer for the innocents?"

"Maybe to some extent. But it's time for me to start a new phase of my life. I needed to retire before I started just shooting these guys and asking questions later. They're bad news and rarely give up without them shooting at us. We located three hundred weapons in one guy's house."

"Who would need that many weapons for any reason?"

"Exactly."

"What did you like about your old job?"

"I liked helping victims, getting the bad guys behind bars, and providing some closure to families. Though in my own experience, you never really find closure."

"I imagine so."

Then he finally pulled into her driveway, and they got

out of the car and went inside the house. "Back to Renault... Would he have sent you the flowers?"

"Maybe. He was always nice to me when he came to see Noah so they could get together to shoot pool or something. Noah didn't seem to notice or care."

"Noah would have noticed," Ethan assured her. As wolves, they smelled the interest people had in each other and if Renault was showing Charlene that he liked her, he was smelling like it too.

"You're probably right." She locked her door and unlocked the wolf door. "Feel free to take any of the rooms to shift in."

He began stripping right then and there. He was a wolf after all, and he was interested in Charlene. He wasn't shy about stripping and shifting in front of any wolves and he wanted her to know that.

She gave him a crooked little smile and then stripped off her clothes nearby, laying them on a chair, then shifting into her beautiful red-wolf form. Since she had done that earlier and bitten him, he already knew what she looked like as a wolf. For shifters, it was just as important to like the appearance of their wild animal form as it was to like their human physique.

Then he shifted into his wolf, and she smiled. It appeared he'd passed the test. She poked her head out the door to the back patio, making sure the coast was clear, and then pushed the rest of the way through. She waited for him to follow her out of the house, and then she preceded him into the woods.

Douglas fir and hemlock trees filled the forest, making a canopy that was catching a light rain. Charlene had smelled rain in the air, and now a misty fog covered the ground. Sword ferns, vine maple, and wild rhododendrons covered the forest floor. It was perfect for wolves to disappear into the vegetation if anyone was on a nearby hiking trail. But this late at night, no one was out there anyway. They listened for sounds of anyone, just in case. Frogs were croaking, bugs singing to each other, the waves coming in, splashing against the rocks down below, an owl hooting in a tree off in the distance and another returning the conversation, but the place was devoid of any human dialogue.

She was glad that they could run as wolves like this without fear of being shot at. Dinner had been grand, and she was so glad that Ethan and she had connected in this way. She knew if he was still working for the DEA in Portland, they would have had the obstacle of living too far away from each other. But here? Who knew?

Her undercoat of fur was keeping her dry, in addition to the canopy overhead, but she was surprised to see it raining. She hadn't thought they would get any for another couple of days. The fog rising from the ground really made it seem like a mystical, fairy woodland, something from out of the medieval past. Running as wolves made her feel more connected to the land and that past.

Ethan was following her from a short distance behind, marking this as *his* territory all over the place. She wanted to laugh if she could have. She knew it was an instinctual part of their wolf behavior, but she wouldn't give into it while she was running with another wolf. When she was out here alone, sure, to let other animals know that a wolf was on the prowl.

She smelled the ocean, the rain, the scent of Douglas firs, and a bunny rabbit that had scurried off through the brush in a hurry. She spied a red deer farther away in the woods, and when it saw her coming, it bounded away. Glancing back to see if Ethan had seen it, she realized he was no longer behind her. Then she heard movement coming through the underbrush to her left, and for a moment she was afraid it was a wild boar. She turned to see Ethan and she smiled and shook her head. He nuzzled her face in greeting, a few tendrils of black coastal huckleberry and red huckleberry threaded through his fur. She thought it was too funny.

When he shifted, they wouldn't need to pull the thorny plants off him. They would just drop all over her floor. That gave her an idea. Maybe she and he could pick berries sometime and make jam together. That would be awesome, if he was willing to do that. Tart Oregon grapes were out here too but they wouldn't be ripe until the fall, and they could make that into jam later on. The more she did with him, the more she saw other possibilities.

They heard a coyote howl and others followed suit. She hadn't planned to howl, but she figured now was the time to show she had a wolf pack out here. Two wolves made up a pack, though she'd never thought she would be thinking she would be part of a wolf pack that would include the wolf she had bitten!

She howled then and Ethan quickly joined her in her

wolf's serenade. She thought they sounded beautiful together. She licked his face, and he nuzzled her neck, then licked her face too. Then together as one, they howled, sending their wolves' verse dancing through the forest, the coyotes now silent. *Good.* Hopefully they had chased them away.

Then she and Ethan turned around and headed back to the house. What a delightful night to run as wolves...and with a companion? Even better. Especially when she heard the coyotes howling. She suspected it might be a good idea if the two of them ran together anytime they wanted to take a run on the wild side and not on their own.

They made a dash for the patio that was covered, protecting them from the downpour, now that the trees didn't provide them with cover. Then she went through the wolf door first and Ethan followed her.

She shifted and got them some bath towels because although their bodies were dry, their legs and faces weren't. "Did you have fun running through the berry bushes?"

He chuckled as he dried off and then began pulling on his boxer briefs. "I thought I smelled a coyote or heard one so I headed in his direction to chase him off. The next thing I knew, I was in a thicket of thorny huckleberry shrubs." He picked up the thorns, stems, and berries he had dropped on the floor when he shifted, since the plants didn't have his fur to hold onto any longer. He found her trash can in the kitchen and threw everything out but the berries. He set those on the counter.

"If you would like, we could pick berries sometime and make jam out of them."

"I was hoping you would say that."

She laughed. "Right."

"Yeah, right. I used to go picking wild blackberries and currant berries with my parents and we would make jam afterward. It's so much wilder flavored and beats anything you would find in the store."

"Oh, I agree. Okay, that's a date. When we both have time…"

"Tomorrow afternoon?" he asked.

She smiled. "Sure."

Once they were both dressed, he gave her a kiss, not waiting to see if she would reject him. She didn't. She'd had an absolutely wonderful time with him. It might not always work out that way as they started to really get to know each other. But for now, yeah, this was just what she needed.

She had enjoyed being in a relationship with a wolf and had dated wolves several times over the years. One would never have left Florida, not even to visit Oregon with her. One had a mother who didn't like that Charlene had been a homicide detective, and she was always finding ways to stop them from having a date.

Another just hadn't been romantic in the least. He had wanted to settle down, but she couldn't have imagined anything duller. Date night was a TV show and popcorn—at home. No eating out, movie theaters, or dancing at clubs. But being with Ethan? This was lots more like what a good relationship should be. Considerate of what she might like to do, no one interfering in their date plans, eager to get together with her. She loved that about him.

She opened her mouth slightly to his mouth in an invitation to take this a little further if he was game. And he was. He deftly kissed her deeply, like a man who knew how to do it in a sensuous way that made her want more of the kiss, and more of him.

But then she figured she had better cool it and call it a night before she ended up inviting him to stay over for the evening, when she was always a lot more cautious about new relationships than that.

He pressed his forehead to hers in a parting way, holding onto her shoulders, appearing to have a hard time letting go and leaving. She smiled. "Tomorrow, be ready to pick berries. I'll make us lunch before we go hiking."

He smiled. "That sounds good. What time?"

"Eleven? I like to do things early."

"I'll be here at eleven." Then he pushed his luck and kissed her lips again, not softly or gently, but telling her just how much he liked kissing her, and she kissed him back in the same way, letting him know he was making all the right moves.

He smiled and left her house, and she locked the door after him. She leaned her back against it, hoping she wasn't making a mistake or going too far too fast. She hadn't dated anyone new since she'd called it quits with Noah so she was a little rusty at getting into a new relationship. She waved at Ethan out the window.

He was smiling, waving back. She was sure she made his night as much as he had made hers. She just hoped they would continue to enjoy the time together. It would be awful if they ended up not liking each other at all and had to live close to each other in such a small community.

CHAPTER 6

ETHAN WAS AFRAID HE WAS MOVING TOO FAST WITH Charlene, though when a wolf really, really liked a wolf, they didn't delay getting to know each other. But with this job hanging over his head and his boss expecting results, he would have to concentrate on that soon. He'd absolutely had no plans to live in Oyster Bay after he finished this mission when all his friends were in Portland or the surrounding communities.

Yet, if he and Charlene continued on this path and ended up mating, he was ready to settle down and start their own pack on the coast. He smiled at the idea. Then he frowned as he tossed his clothes in the washing machine and took a shower. He wasn't sure how she was going to take the news that he was still working this dangerous job.

He got out of the shower, dried off, and pulled on a fresh pair of boxer shorts, then called Tori. "Hey—"

"How did it go with Charlene? You took her out to dinner, right?"

"Marvelously. But I want you to check into something for me."

"About your case already? You were supposed to be resting up for the week after being wounded twice on the mission."

As if the wolf bite counted for anything. And *that* didn't go in the report.

"Not to mention," Tori continued, "it wouldn't hurt for you to get to know Charlene a bit better while you have the time off."

"No, it's not about the case. Charlene received flowers from some unknown person. A secret admirer."

"Uh-oh, so you have some competition that you are needing to eliminate."

Ethan laughed. "She doesn't know who sent the flowers, and she wanted me to learn who might have. The delivery was from Coastal Florists." He gave Tori Charlene's address and when the flowers were delivered.

"I'll check on it first thing in the morning unless it's a case of life or death."

He smiled. "Thanks."

"She has no idea who might have sent them?"

"She has an ex in Destin, Florida, by the name of Noah Westmoreland, and Renault saw her during the raid on her home. He knows her, was a friend of Noah's, and you know he was working in Destin before he transferred to Portland. Anyway, since she left Noah, Renault might have learned where she was moving to and sent her the flowers."

"He has no chance with her. He isn't a wolf," Tori said.

"Yeah, but Renault doesn't know that. I'm sure it would give her some peace of mind to know who sent them."

"True. If I learn he did it, what do you want me to do about it?" Tori asked.

"Just let me know. Hopefully, he won't try to pursue her out here. We both thought it was bizarre that whoever sent the flowers did so anonymously. If he was really interested in her, he should have said so."

"Right. It would creep me out if anyone did that to me."

"Exactly."

"Before I let you go, tell me that you also got Charlene flowers," Tori said.

"Yeah, you bet. I was damn glad I had, though I still missed giving them to her first."

"At least you also thought of doing it. I hope they were nicer than what he, whoever he is, gave to her."

"Doubly so."

"At least so you say."

Ethan laughed. "Thanks for looking into this for me."

"You know you can always count on me. I'm glad the night went well with Charlene. I'll talk to Adam about it and he'll help me look into it. Good night."

"Good night, Tori." Ethan knew they wouldn't share what they were looking into with anyone except the pack leaders and Adam's mate, Sierra, because she worked at the police bureau too.

Ethan got into bed, lay on his back, and started thinking about Renault. Ethan could understand if Renault realized Charlene had left her boyfriend behind and he thought he had a chance to date her now. But that would be a long-distance relationship and Ethan couldn't see that working out or why Renault would even consider it. Which meant someone else probably sent the flowers.

He rolled onto his side and closed his eyes, but he couldn't quit thinking about the mystery. He opened his eyes, grabbed his phone, and turned it on. He thought about calling Charlene, but she could already be asleep. Yet, he wanted to ask her more about who might have sent her the flowers.

He sighed. Would she be angry with him? Tired of his asking her? Amused?

He called her and her phone rang and rang and rang. Hell, she was asleep. But then she answered the phone and he thought she would sound half-asleep. She didn't.

"Hello, you. Do you have a change of plans for tomorrow?" she asked. "I was charging my phone in the living room so it took me a few minutes to get to it."

"No. I just wanted to let you know I talked to Tori and she and Adam are going to look into who ordered the flowers."

"I'm glad they're looking into it and that you'll be around if someone starts to actually stalk me."

"I am too. He won't get far with it."

"No. All you and I have to do is turn wolf and that would be the end of it."

He chuckled. "I'll let you get some sleep then."

"You too." Then they called it a night.

He was glad he had moved here and could watch over her personally. He took a deep breath and released it. He would get to the bottom of the mystery one way or another.

Charlene couldn't get to sleep. She kept racking her brain for a reason why anyone would send her the flowers and who it might be.

She finally fell asleep and woke to her phone ringing early the next morning. She glanced at the caller ID. *Tori*.

"Hello?" Charlene said.

"Hey, I hope I didn't wake you too early, but I wanted to tell you that Ethan has Adam, Sierra, and me on the job of trying to track down your mystery flower sender."

"Thanks, Tori. Last night, Ethan told me that you would look into it."

"Yeah, I was just calling to see if you have any other ideas about who it might be once you had more time to ponder it last night."

"Other than Renault, or even my ex-boyfriend trying to get in touch with me, I can't think of anyone else."

"Did you tell your ex-boyfriend where you were moving to?"

"Actually no, but he did work with Renault in Florida."

"Your ex-boyfriend is another DEA agent?" Tori asked.

"Yeah, and he could still be in touch with Renault since they're friends. Actually, Renault might have even told him that he ran into me at the raid on the house I was renting. Renault could have easily learned where I was going to live next and told my ex. Though truly, I don't know why Noah would care. He and I ended things on a sour note, and we haven't spoken to each other since."

"The flowers wouldn't be from one of the people you purchased any of the homes from, right?"

"I don't think so. The houses that I'm renting out were owned by two older couples who wanted to move closer to their kids in other parts of the state. The person who owned the home I'm living in had a new job and was moving with his family closer to Portland where he would work."

"Okay, so that sounds like nothing that would hold any real leads. Did you eat in town when you were looking for places to buy? Maybe stay at a hotel overnight?"

"Oh yeah, sure. I ate breakfast, lunch, and dinner at different restaurants while I was here overnight. And I did stay at a hotel to really get a look at several different places."

"Did anyone stand out to you at any of the places?" Tori asked.

Charlene could tell that Tori was good at her job. She was thorough in helping Charlene to recollect what she couldn't on her own about people she might have met.

"Well, I found the places about two days after I moved to Portland, so it has been nearly a month since then. It has taken that long to buy the properties and renovate them. Which means I did talk to a couple of people about doing the work on all three of the houses to update them and an interior decorator to furnish the rentals. I'll think on it and get back to you in case anyone comes to mind."

"Maybe something will jog your memory. Even returning to the places you ate might help. Go with Ethan though, in case the person works at one of the restaurants. Same with the hotel. Take him along so everyone will know you have someone in your life. I know, it's just for pretend, but it could help stop real trouble before it starts, hopefully."

"Okay, I'll do that. Thanks, Tori. I'd considered doing these things, but I just wasn't sure it was really necessary."

Once they ended the call, Charlene called Ethan.

"Hey, good morning!" Ethan sounded like he was a real morning person. She usually was too, but not this morning.

"Good morning, Ethan. Tori called. She was trying to jog my memory about who I might have run into here who would have sent the roses, and I mentioned eating at three different restaurants while I was here looking at places. She suggested I return to them to see if I can recall anything. So if you're at all interested, do you want to eat with me this morning while we check out the restaurant where I had breakfast?"

"Hell, yeah, I'll be right over to pick you up."

She chuckled.

"Where are we going?" he asked on Bluetooth.

"The Beach Breeze Café."

"Oh, great, I had wanted to try that place out while I was here."

"Well, this will be fun while we're on a fact-finding mission." She was used to trying to solve mysteries as a homicide detective. As long as this didn't turn into a dangerous situation.

It didn't take long for Ethan to get there.

She opened the door and locked it behind her and climbed into his car before he could get out. "Onward and upward. This is my treat, um, for helping me out so much."

"You deserve it," he said.

She sighed and shut her door. "Thanks." Okay, so she really needed to tell him she was sorry about biting him. If she hadn't ever seen him again, she could have lived with not apologizing. But because they were doing so much together, she had to. "So about biting you—"

"It's nearly healed up."

Shoot, she should have asked him about his gunshot wound first thing this morning. "I apologize for biting you."

He glanced at her and smiled. "I deserved it, truly. As soon as I didn't smell any drugs in the house, I should have known we weren't in the right place. And smelling your she-wolf scent added to the awareness that your house wasn't where we should be."

"But you were so sure that it had to be the right place. Your informant gave you the wrong address. Did you talk to him about it afterward? What if he was giving the bad guys time to escape?"

"Yeah, I talked to him. I wasn't supposed to be working the next day, but I had to go and see where his head was at."

"And?"

"He swears he gave us the correct address, but I had recorded the conversation, and he hadn't. I could smell deception on him, and I told him I didn't believe him. He got really nervous, wouldn't look me in the eye, and was tapping his foot on the floor incessantly."

"So he purposefully steered you to my house."

"Yeah. I questioned him about why he had lied to us and sent us to someone else's home."

"I bet he had a story on hand for that."

Ethan pulled into the parking lot at the Beach Breeze Café, and they both got out of the car. "Yep. He changed his story and said he always gets the two tree names mixed up. I asked him how much Kroner paid him to change the address. He swore Kroner hadn't or we wouldn't have caught the dude. I had to admit that was true. If Kroner had paid Ferret off, that meant Kroner would have known that my team and I would go to the wrong place and then head to their place, and Kroner would have packed up and moved already."

Ethan opened the door to the restaurant for Charlene, and they walked inside. A hostess seated them and left menus with them.

The last time Charlene had gone there, she had loved it. Paintings of sailing boats and fishing nets, fake crabs clinging onto them, seahorses, and seashells everywhere were hanging on the walls, and a treasure chest was filled with candy at the cashier's desk. A fishing boat was situated in the middle of the restaurant, filled with buffet food for breakfast. Fruit, hash brown potatoes, biscuits, cinnamon rolls, and doughnuts were set out, and scrambled eggs, sausages, and ham filled the warming trays and covered platters.

"So then why did Ferret lie to you, Ethan?" Charlene opened her menu.

"I asked if he thought we would tip Kroner off by hitting the wrong house, and then Kroner would hear about it and take off. Ferret was sweating like he'd been on a desert island, sitting in the sun on a blistering hot day. I suspected that he was afraid to tip Kroner off himself—the old adage that they kill the messenger coming to mind. While with our clumsy raid of your house, if any news source had learned of it, 911 reports from nearby neighbors, or just anything that clued them in, Kroner could hear about it and then alerting him of the raid would have come from us, not Ferret."

"Aww, okay, that makes total sense."

A server arrived at their table and they both asked for coffee. Then he left to give them a little longer to look at their menus.

"Though you caught Kroner and the other guy."

"Right, so no new source or 911 calls had been made."

Charlene glanced around the restaurant. "I didn't have any interaction with anyone in here other than the server, as I recall. I don't remember any customers who were in here at the time. I mean, some families were here, but I wasn't paying any attention to them. I was on my phone looking at house listings though, so I might have missed if someone was watching me."

"Well, I'm glad we could have breakfast together anyway. This is nice."

"It is. I love the decor and the food is great."

"So what do you want to do for breakfast? Buffet or order from the menu?"

"I want to try the Spanish omelet with crispy potatoes and toast," Charlene said. "And sausages. Fruit comes with it."

"Okay, I'm going to get the buffet. They have everything I want and more. It looks like they have a good lunch and dinner menu too."

"Yeah, we'll have to try it some other time. Would you like to take a walk along the beach and see the tidal pools with me after breakfast?" Charlene asked.

"Yeah, I would love to do that."

"I should have asked you about your arm."

"The teeth marks are nearly gone."

She laughed. "I meant your bullet wound."

He smiled. "Oh, that. It's still there, but it's healing. Thanks for asking."

CHAPTER 7

After breakfast, Ethan drove Charlene back to her house. Luckily, Ethan was wearing shoes that were perfect for hiking over the rocks in case she wanted to do that.

"You are dressed right to go adventuring," she said, glancing at his weatherproof hiking boots and jeans.

"Yeah, just in case you wanted to hike or beachcomb after breakfast."

"Well, good call." She changed her shoes to hiking boots and brought a hiking pack with a first aid kit and a couple of bottles of water.

Ethan took the pack from her so that he could carry it. He had thought of wearing the right clothes but hadn't thought of taking a backpack. It had been a while since he'd enjoyed a hike like this in his human form.

She led the way to the spot she had been checking out when he had called last night while on the drive there. He loved hearing the sound of the breaking waves on the rocky beach and seeing the tiny creatures in the tidal pools. He hadn't done anything like this since he was a little kid. She started taking pictures of the sea creatures and he watched her for a moment while she crouched down, getting up close and personal.

"I'm going to print the ones I really like and hang them up in the house and at the rental homes. I wanted something that was my own creation and taken of the local area."

"I like the idea. How are your rentals doing?" Ethan hoped they would be successful.

"I already have both of them rented out for the next six months. I'm thrilled. I suspect I'll have lulls at times in renting them, especially if storms threaten the area. Um, no hurricanes though. The water is fifty to sixty-five degrees, too cold for hurricanes to really form. The cabins are newly refurbished and have always been single-family dwellings, though property was zoned for rentals. So it gives visitors to the area some new places to stay. They're in great locations too, within walking distance of the beach, with forests to hike in, and close to places to eat. I was looking for the best locations for rentals, not realizing that I might have wolves renting them who would love the freedom to roam in the woods, or even on the beach at night as long as the tides aren't in."

He wondered if that was another reason for Charlene taking refuge on the West Coast: no hurricanes. Because of her family's deaths, he completely understood her concern. "Yeah, you better believe Cassie and Leidolf will be watching your reservation days, and if they aren't booked? They'll encourage some members of the pack to come out there for a visit."

"That's amazing."

"Yeah, they're great. I don't know how other wolf packs are run, but ours has really good leadership. They want to do everything they can for wolves in the pack and those who are in the area, even though you live so far away."

"You too now," she said, taking pictures of a starfish.

Hell, he had to remember Charlene thought he was living here permanently. "Yeah, right."

"Well, I'm glad to be part of the pack."

"Good, because you'll have to come to the holiday celebrations. They're lots of fun."

"If we're still speaking to each other by then, we can go together."

He chuckled. "Sure. That would be perfect." He had hoped he would be done with his mission well before the holidays, but he never knew how things would go. He'd had a lot of success with another mission like this five years ago. Within three days, he had found the culprits and had them put away.

His wolf doctor said he couldn't work for at least a week, or he might raise suspicions about his bullet wound. It was still aching, and he knew the injury still had a few weeks to go before it was totally healed, though as a shifter he healed in half the time that humans did. He was lucky the bullet hadn't hit a bone, or an artery. He had the doctor send the report to his boss, who was surprised it wasn't that bad, considering how much Ethan's wound had bled—according to witnesses he had spoken to.

Ethan got a call on his phone, and he pulled the phone out of his pocket. When he looked at the caller ID, he saw it was his boss. He glanced at Charlene. She was still taking pictures and moving to another tide pool.

He answered the call, "Yeah?" He was trying not to sound like the caller was his boss in front of Charlene when he was supposed to be retired.

"How are you doing?" Grainger asked.

"I'm doing well, considering." Ethan hadn't expected his boss to inquire about his health. Not that it wasn't appreciated, but he'd had the doctor send the report to him.

"Kroner was released from jail based on a clerical error."

Ethan's heart practically gave out. "Shit." He glanced at Charlene.

She looked back at him. She'd heard his comment and knew there was some kind of problem. But luckily, with the sound of the waves and the wind blowing in his direction, carrying his boss's side of the conversation away from her, she couldn't hear what was being said over the phone. If Ethan and Charlene had been together in her home and she was sitting nearby and listening, she could have heard the rest of the conversation because of their outstanding wolf's hearing.

"Also, I just learned that Kroner's cohort Oakley Osburn has a great-aunt living in Oyster Bay," Grainger said.

That was the thing Ethan really liked about his boss. He would do whatever it took to help his agents get to the bottom of a case, loving to get his hands into the nitty gritty of it himself in a covert way.

"You might want to watch that situation. The word is Osburn's close to his great-aunt and when he can, he visits her every few weeks. And Kroner has gone with him on several different occasions." Grainger sent Ethan a picture of Mrs. Osburn's home and of her. She had short, white curly hair, and was wearing a pink three-quarter-sleeved shirt and white jeans and sturdy shoes. She was a pretty, grandmotherly type and he hoped she wasn't involved in all this drug business.

"Do you know when Osburn visits there usually?" Ethan asked his boss.

"Sundays, if he goes at all. He takes his great-aunt to church and then out to lunch. But there's some consensus he has been there late at night on other days. That's why I wanted to get with you on it. Watch for him and see if he also leads us to Kroner."

"All right, sir. I'll sure do that." Ethan realized Charlene was fully watching him now. He was sure she would begin to suspect something was up, and he wasn't going to continue keeping the secret from her. He finished the call with his boss and sighed. He'd been frowning about the whole situation, and when he realized it, he smiled at Charlene.

"Do you have some kind of a problem?" she asked.

"That was my boss. Kroner, the guy I arrested and who shot me, was released from jail because of some clerical error."

"Oh no."

Ethan would have left it at that, but he didn't want to any longer. He was dating Charlene now and she had a right to know. "Yeah. I want to arrest whoever the clerk was who did that because now the bastard is back out again and on the run. My boss wanted to warn me. Everyone who had a part in arresting Kroner needs to watch out for him, if he doesn't just try to leave the area permanently."

"Do you think he would come after you here?" Charlene asked, looking worried.

"Let's return to the house and talk."

She was frowning, not looking happy with Ethan in the least.

He told himself that she could be a target now that Kroner was on the loose, should he learn Ethan was seeing her, which was the main reason he had to tell her what was going on. When Kroner was in jail, Ethan had felt Charlene was safe and Kroner wouldn't even know Ethan was seeing her or where he had ended up.

"This sounds ominous," she said, walking with Ethan back across the slippery rocks as he caught her arm once to keep her from falling. They reached the sandy beach and finally made their way to the stairs to her deck.

"It is. Kroner and his buddies all had a hand in killing my parents, both DEA agents, for going after them. Now I've done the same thing as they had done by arresting him—which would have been fine if Kroner had just stayed in jail."

They finally reached her house and went inside. He set the backpack on the dining room table, and she got them some glasses of ice water. "Okay, tell me what is going on."

"I'm not retired."

"What?" Charlene set the glasses of water on the dining room table, then sat down. "Explain."

Then he explained about how he was on one last undercover mission, but he wasn't going to be really working on it until next week because of his injury. Until the news about Kroner being out of jail upset the whole apple cart.

"If your boss staged this whole business with the retirement ceremony, does he believe someone in your department is consorting with the enemy? I mean, why else pretend that you're retiring in front of your whole department?"

"Yeah. I think that's why he has me doing this solo." He didn't know how Charlene was taking the news just yet.

Charlene let out her breath in a heavy sigh. "Is it because your informant gave the wrong address to my house?"

"No. There have been some earlier situations where we went to raid a place where Kroner was known to be and then voilà, he vanishes without a trace—four times in fact. My informant had nothing to do with those cases. My boss knew I was after these men for killing my parents, so he was sure I wasn't the one who was sabotaging the mission."

"You're still a DEA special agent." She seemed to be mulling that over, trying to figure out the implication. "Who else knows?"

"Leidolf and Cassie, and the red wolves who work with the Portland Police Bureau: Tori, Adam, and Sierra. Others in the red wolf pack too. They'll help me if I need a quick backup."

"They are three hours away."

"Yes, but they would drop everything and be here to help me out."

She shook her head. "They're still three hours away. So the house you bought—"

"It's the DEA's. My boss had it rented for me, but no one in the department knows about it."

"Oh, you aren't really living here. Why did you set up here, in this specific location?"

"He wanted me to check out Shelby Bay."

"Just down the coast from us."

"Yes. Oakley has been known to be there and there's a house that he might be working out of, but my boss didn't want me to be living that close to where the perps could be."

"So you haven't moved to Oyster Bay permanently." Charlene sounded like she was still trying to come to grips with the fact that Ethan wasn't really retired. "That makes sense because you truly wouldn't leave your friends and the wolf pack behind." She appeared disappointed as she pushed her windswept hair out of her face.

"Yeah, but that was before I met you."

She frowned at him. "I'm sorry, but this is a lot to take in. I'm a red wolf too. You could have confided in me from the beginning."

"I wasn't supposed to, and I thought you would be safer if you didn't know."

"I was a homicide detective out of the sheriff's department where I lived before."

His jaw dropped. "Seriously?" Now it was his turn to be shocked at the news.

"Yeah, for ten years. After my family died, I had to take care of my parents' rental properties and the funerals and all, and I just couldn't focus on going back to my job. I left the force to take care of everything. Then my boyfriend and I broke up, and I was ready for a big change in my life, which is a lot of the reason why I came out here. It was always a happy place for me when I visited my grandfather. My twin sister actually preferred the crystal-clear aqua waters of Destin to the wildness of the Oregon coast. The last few times, I was the only one to visit my grandfather. I always felt…revitalized, joyful, when I came here. The Destin beaches are crowded with tourists in the summer. Here…it's so peaceful."

Ethan understood how she felt, but he also looked at her with a new sense of awe. She wasn't just a civilian any longer. Well, she was now, but she had been trained in police techniques so she would be better equipped to deal with someone who might be a danger to her. Not that he wanted her to have to protect herself from these men. "I'm glad you're here. But why didn't you tell me you had been with the sheriff's department when you were in Florida?"

"Would it have made any difference?"

"Yeah. As a former police officer, you would know better how to manage someone who was trouble."

"So that means you don't have to protect me any longer?"

He smiled. "Of course I want to protect you. But…well, I would have felt like I could share what my mission is, that as a former homicide detective, you would understand. Believe me, I've dated women who hated that I worked as a DEA special agent. They just felt it was too stressful, not knowing if I would return from a raid in one piece. Once I was shot in the leg and ended up in surgery and off the job for a month. Instead of being there for me, the woman I was dating ended up dumping me. She said she couldn't deal with it. She left Portland for good, so she is no longer with the pack."

"Oh, that's awful. I guess not everyone can handle it." Charlene cleared her throat. "When I was shot—"

Hell. "I hope the guy who shot you is dead."

She smiled.

"What happened?" He felt awful that he knew so little about Charlene and thought he had been the only one who had suffered an attack from a perp while on the job.

"The shooter was a woman, actually. Noah was dating her, but she wasn't a wolf. Then he met me, and he was at once interested in me because I was a wolf. He's a gray wolf, not a red wolf, by the way. When he broke up with his short-term girlfriend, she went ballistic. They'd only been together for a couple of weeks, but she had decided he was hers forever and ever. He later explained to me she'd told all her friends that she and Noah would be married before long. She found out that he was seeing me, and she started stalking me. This crazed blond came out of the dark when I was returning home from a trip to the funeral home and started screaming obscenities about me stealing Noah from her. I tried to reason with her with my police training, to talk her down. But it was of no use.

"I couldn't avoid being shot but I yelled out, trying to get anyone's attention so they could call the police. But it was a dark night, full moon, with just some light from a streetlamp. I could see, but others probably couldn't tell what was happening if they'd heard me. She shot me in the shoulder, and I was afraid she would keep shooting until I was dead, as angry as she was. I ran at her and shoved her down. She whacked her head hard on the pavement and that knocked her out temporarily, long enough for me to grab her gun and call the police.

"They were there within minutes and took her into custody. At the same time, an ambulance transported me to the hospital. We didn't have a wolf doctor to take care of our injuries like you have here. I ended up in the hospital for a week and finally got out. But the doctor put me on two months' leave to recover, physical therapy, the whole thing. Noah had been laughing his ass off because I should have been back to work after a month."

"What an ass."

"Yeah, I know. I was still having to deal with my family's death, so it was a lot to manage. As a DEA special agent, Noah was busy working his cases and I swear he was staying away more because of all I had to deal with."

"I wouldn't have." Ethan rose from his chair and went to Charlene's. He pulled her from it, then hugged her. "I would have been there for you."

"Yeah, I think you would have been."

They moved to the living room, more relaxed now, and he felt a real shift in their relationship, not so superficial, better, deeper. "What happened to Noah's ex-girlfriend?"

"She was sent to prison for attempted premeditated murder. She had done it before when she was sixteen and her boyfriend started seeing another girl behind her back in high school, but the court records had been sealed. So Noah hadn't known about it. Anyway, she ended up with thirty years in prison."

"Good for that."

"So you said you were shot another time?" she asked.

"Uh, yeah. I just didn't dodge fast enough."

"You sound like me."

"Yeah, it was another drug bust. I was hit in the same arm too."

"Did the guy go down for it?"

"Absolutely. I'd had other problems with him before that. He'd attempted to cut me with a knife and went to prison for a few years for attempted murder that time too. While he was in the joint for shooting me, another prisoner killed him over drugs. So that was the last time I had to worry about him."

She sighed and kissed Ethan on the mouth. "Now I'm sorry I didn't bite your other arm instead."

He laughed, thinking that's how they would always remember their first encounter. He kissed her back, pressing for entrance. She softened her mouth to his, parting her lips and encouraging him to dip his tongue inside and kiss her deeply. He cupped her head, her silky hair falling over his hands. He kissed her again, loving the feel of her full lips against his mouth, the way she licked his lips and kissed him more firmly. Her hands were on his shoulders, caressing, holding him steady, her eyes closed. He closed his eyes as he enjoyed the impromptu kiss with Charlene. He was completely tuned in to her, her skin soft, her scent sweet, mixed with the fresh, salty sea air.

She finally pulled her mouth aways from his, licked her lips, and smiled. He smiled and kissed her mouth one last time.

"What can I do to help you catch these bad guys?" she asked, sounding serious as could be.

"Nothing, really. I'm just glad if any of this comes your way, you might be able to handle yourself better. But I don't want you in harm's way." He hadn't expected her to offer, but he didn't want her to get involved in this. She might be trained in dealing with the bad guys, but she wasn't part of the force now and she didn't have a paycheck or even health insurance from the DEA's office to cover this if she got injured. She would have to use her own, which wasn't really fair to her. Not to mention his boss would be ticked off if he learned of it.

"You're here alone, and if you're undercover, I make the perfect girlfriend for you, as long as you don't have an ex-girlfriend coming after me."

He laughed. "No."

"Good. Then it's settled. Just tell me what you want to do first to take these guys down. Oh, I have a question. I thought you were retired and couldn't do anything about it, but if there's someone in your department who's crooked, then you need to know who it is."

"Right."

"I saw something odd when I went to the service station closest to me the night of the raid."

"Oh?"

"Yeah, a guy named DEA Special Agent Pete Cohen looked like he was taking a bribe or drugs from some grungy-looking guy. And Pete was with someone else, the other man who rushed into my bathroom to save you."

"Manx Ryerson."

"Right, him too. Cohen looked like he was bullying the grungy guy, but when they saw me watching the situation—the hazard of being a former police officer and an alert and wary wolf—the grungy guy took off and Cohen and Ryerson followed me into the restaurant."

"To intimidate you." Ethan was so angry, he wanted to arrest the both of them for bullying Charlene.

"Right. But I told Cohen I was a homicide detective on vacation there from Florida, so he didn't ask for my name, though my driver's license still showed my address back in Florida. Still, I think he decided I might be more trouble than I was worth. But my wolf senses said the two men were dirty, shaking down a druggy or small-time drug dealer. I might be wrong, and they were just talking to one of their informants, but since they followed me to turn up the heat, I don't think so. Then the most bizarre thing happened. Some patrol officer named Lawrence Baker, stopped me for a traffic violation that he damn well knew I hadn't done. But the really weird part was that he asked to see my police badge. I had only told Agent Cohen that I was a homicide detective. No one else in Portland knew it."

"Well, hell. So Agent Cohen sent the police officer to harass you. Then Agents Cohen and Ryerson saw you at the rental house and knew just where you lived."

"Yeah, at least for the one night."

"Without evidence, we can't prove anything, but I'll let my boss know." Ethan hoped they might be able to get somewhere with the information, but no matter what, he wished he'd known before his retirement party. Though he figured at the time, Charlene hadn't been sure if Ethan had even been one of the good guys.

CHAPTER 8

CHARLENE HADN'T TOLD ANYONE THAT SHE WAS A former homicide detective because it changed the way people viewed her and she had moved on. If she could help Ethan with his mission, she was doing it. She was glad that she'd mentioned what Agents Cohen and Ryerson had done at the convenience store.

"Okay, so what do you plan to do?" she asked Ethan.

"This business with Kroner being out of jail is problematic. I'm just a little worried that you could be in as much danger as me if he learns that I'm seeing you."

"We're dating, you're staying in Oyster Bay when you ultimately retire, and I'm helping you with this so you can get this done sooner than later." Some men didn't like it when women told them what was what, but Ethan just smiled wickedly at her. "I mean, if you really don't want to stay in Oyster Bay after you're done with the mission...I'll understand. But if you are interested in the least..."

He smiled again. "Hell, yeah. I'm all the way interested in seriously dating you. I don't want us to take any unnecessary chances where you're concerned though."

"I have never been shot on the job," she said. "I'm good at risk assessment—unless it has to do with a former girlfriend of a guy I'm dating. So what do you want to do next?"

"We'll have lunch at the restaurant where you went to, so

that you can try to remember anything from when you were there the last time," Ethan said.

"So you're still interested in who sent the flowers to me? It seems to me that's the least of our worries."

"I am. We'll also watch for any sign that Kroner is in this area, but I suspect he'll be heading south. Our men are after him. If Kroner comes here, we'll let my boss know at once. But until then, I'm on the Secret Admirer ID Taskforce."

She laughed. "Okay, so we still have time before we go to the restaurant. Is there anything else you would like to do?"

"We have intel that one of the men, Oakley Osburn, sees his great-aunt on occasion in Oyster Bay. She's seventy-nine years old, and he takes her to church on Sundays sometimes and to lunch after that. But there's a possibility he's there some other nights too. He's Kroner's second-in-command who runs everything when Kroner is unavailable. We could check out the area where she lives just as a drive-by." He pulled out his phone and showed Charlene a picture of the woman.

"She looks like a sweet grandmotherly type," Charlene said. "Okay, let's do this, partner."

"All right." He sounded more resigned than glad about allowing Charlene to help him with his work.

But she didn't care. If she could assist him and give him a better chance at accomplishing this mission sooner than later, she was doing it. They headed out to his car and then he drove her to the housing development where Oakley's great-aunt lived.

"Do you ever miss being on the force?" Ethan asked Charlene.

"No. I loved my job while I was working there. I wouldn't have left the job if it hadn't been for my family's deaths. But at that point, I couldn't handle anything more." Then she sighed. "Besides, Noah and I had irreconcilable differences. It was just time to move on and start over again."

"If you're willing to talk about it, what happened between the two of you?" Ethan asked.

"Oh, a bunch of things. He had no empathy for me about my family's deaths. He hadn't really liked that we had been so close to each other. His family had been gone for a decade so I never knew them or how he had interacted with them. He never really talked about his parents, which made me think he wasn't that close to them. Whenever I would ask him about his family, he would say it was the past and it wasn't important. But I knew that wasn't true. Our past shapes us and it would have helped me to understand him better."

"That's so true."

"He was fine with me being on the police force with a regular paycheck, but he really didn't like it when I quit my job. He felt I wouldn't earn enough off the rentals."

"So he wanted a mate who was bringing in a good income."

"We never got to the mate question. It never would have happened, believe me. But yeah, I didn't really think that he cared about the financial aspect until I told him I was quitting my job and that's when it came to a real head. He was mad when I didn't do what he wanted me to—stay with the job. He had asked me about the inheritance I had received, but he hadn't gotten much from his parents when they passed, so I believed he thought the same was true with mine. I wouldn't tell him because I knew we were going nowhere with our relationship. Because I wouldn't enlighten him, he said that's just what he thought—my parents had been barely scraping by and hadn't left me with anything. He assumed the properties were all mortgaged, but they were all free and clear."

"Well, that *wouldn't* have been me, for sure. If you had your heart set on quitting the force, I would have been behind you all the way. We have to do what makes us happy, and you certainly needed to make the change for your own well-being. As to family, I'm an open book. I was close to my parents and my brother, and I would be happy to talk to you about my family and learn more about yours."

She smiled. Ethan was a lot more like the kind of wolf she should have been dating all along. "That's why I'm helping you with your case."

"I appreciate it, but only if you don't get hurt."

When they reached Oakley's great-aunt's address, Ethan drove by it slowly like he was visiting someone in the area, searching for the right address to go to. The gray Cape Cod-style house had a deck out front, a bright-red door, and pots filled with geraniums hanging from the porch overhang. A little gray stepping-stone walkway invited visitors to approach.

"I hope she's not involved in any of this," Charlene said. "You never know though. The sweet little great-aunt with the apple-pie smile could be just as wicked and as dangerous as her grandnephew."

"That's so true. I met up with a grandmother whose grandson was selling drugs and asked her about him. She was out in front of her house tending to her roses. Her long, white hair was done up in a bun, her expression sweet until I asked her about him. She hit me with a hand trowel. I deflected the blow, but I sure hadn't seen that coming."

Charlene laughed. "I can see that happening. What did you do with her?"

"I calmed her down. I didn't arrest her. She was just protecting her grandson after she'd raised him from a baby. Her daughter was in prison for selling drugs, stealing property, and deadly assault. The boy's father never even knew he had a son or cared. The grandmother was the only one who had been there for him. So she was really protective. She felt awful about hitting me afterward. I assured her I was fine. Renault was with me. I don't think I've ever seen him laugh so hard."

The more Charlene got to know Ethan, the more she thought how caring he was about people even when they hit him with a trowel or bit him on the arm as a wolf. And Renault? She could see him being amused about it.

They saw Oakley's great-aunt leave her house and walk to the mailbox while Ethan continued to drive on past the house.

"She looks so sweet," Charlene said, watching out the side view mirror as the woman retrieved her mail and headed back up the walk. "It's still too early for lunch. Let's go to Shelby Bay. We can take a look around town, like a girlfriend and boyfriend who are just visiting there. Do...do the men you're after know what you look like?"

"They do. They don't know my vehicle. It's a rental and doesn't look anything like my own vehicle."

"Aww, okay, good. We don't have to get out, but just drive around the area where these guys have been staying before."

"Yeah, that's what I'm supposed to do." He sounded glad and not as concerned now that she was going with him.

They drove around the area to the house where Grainger thought Oakley might be doing business. There was no sign of any of the men at the house, but there was a car parked out front. Charlene quickly took a picture of the license plate before Ethan drove past it. She called up Tori. "Hi, Tori? Can you run a license plate for us?"

"Does this have something to do with the flower delivery at your house? Or"—Tori paused—"this doesn't have anything to do with Ethan, does it?"

"Yes. The black Mercedes is parked at one of the perps' houses in Shelby Bay," Charlene said.

"He told you." Tori sounded shocked.

"I'm his partner in this so he can retire for good."

"Oh wow," Tori said, her tone of voice one of concern.

"I'm a former homicide detective out of Destin. So I'm fine with this kind of work."

"Oh my, you didn't tell any of us that. A fellow homicide detective, woo-hoo! If I need any help with a case, I'm running what Adam and I are working on by you."

Smiling, Charlene figured Tori would tell the rest of the wolf pack, which was fine with her.

"Okay. Well, that makes a difference, and I'm so glad that you're there to help watch Ethan's back in this. You don't know how worried all of us have been that he was doing this on his own and we're so far from there to reach him. I'll look into this, and I'll get back to you," Tori said.

"Thanks, Tori!" Then they ended the call.

Ethan was smiling at Charlene. "I won't hear the end of this from Tori and Adam now."

"What?"

"That you're working with me on this."

"I have to figure out a way to keep you here. It's the best way I can think of."

He laughed. "Thanks. I figured it was kind of a working vacation, until I realized you would be here and then things quickly changed for me."

"Good. That works for me. So what do we want to do now?"

"By the time we get back to Oyster Bay, we can have an early lunch. And if you would like, we can go whale watching after that," he said.

"Oh, absolutely. That's something I really wanted to do when I got settled in Oyster Bay."

"Okay, then. We'll go this afternoon after lunch." When they arrived at the Starfish Deli, he called the whale-watching tour that had the best ratings. "Okay, we're on for one o'clock. No storms this afternoon, so that's good. Do you get seasick?" Ethan asked Charlene.

"No, never. What about you?"

"No, hopefully I'll be good."

"That's great."

Then Charlene got a call from Tori and put it on speaker. "Hey, the license plate belongs to a Clara Snyder. She's sixty-two and lives in Portland. I did a check into her background, and she had bought the car and another at the same time. It doesn't make any sense. She's a retired high school teacher and she doesn't have that much income from her retirement."

"But she paid for the cars in full?" Charlene asked.

"Yeah. So that's kind of suspect, especially since the car was at Oakley's house. But otherwise, I don't see anything that shows she has a connection to him or anyone else that you're looking for."

"Why have two cars when there's just one of her? And where did she get the money from to pay for the two cars?" Charlene asked.

"What if one of the guys you're after paid for the cars. He doesn't have any real connection to her, as in he's family, but he has somehow hooked up with her to purchase the cars in her name," Tori said. "Then there's no tie to him that we would easily see. If he's one of your guys, he might even have gone through another party to make the arrangement to approach Clara."

"Does she have any family? Wouldn't they be worried if someone Clara didn't know just gave her money to buy a couple of cars?" Charlene asked.

"Yeah, that was something else I checked into. She was an only child, never married, no kids, her parents are gone. She doesn't have any living relatives. So we figured she was the perfect choice to approach with the offer of purchasing a couple of cars through her."

"You are doing a great job of checking into this," Ethan said.

"Well, when I learned who owned the car, it made me curious, and I couldn't quit looking into it. Adam has been giving me a hard time about it—in his humorous way. I want to go ask her about the cars, but I'm afraid that will spook her, and she'll tell whoever it was who gave her the money that a police officer is asking questions."

"Okay, well, be careful, Tori. Not only do we not want to spook Kroner and his cohorts, we don't want you to get hurt in the process," Ethan said.

"I'll be careful."

"Let us know what you discover," Ethan said.

After that, they ended the call and he and Charlene walked inside the deli. Black chairs and white tables and booths on a black-and-white-checkered floor set the scene. Black-and-white pictures of sea creatures hung on the walls. She pointed them out to Ethan. "That's what gave me the idea of taking photos of marine life, but in color, to add to the walls in my home and the rental homes."

"That would be so nice. I like the idea of having photographs in color too."

They took a seat in one of the booths and ordered a grilled chicken, bacon, and cheese sandwich for her and a hot pastrami and Swiss on rye sandwich for him.

When the server left to put in their orders, Ethan asked Charlene, "Okay, does anyone working here seem familiar, or do you recall if any customer seemed unduly interested in you?"

"No, nothing. I really wasn't paying any attention to anyone. Even though as wolves we often are wary of our surroundings, I was just focused on eating. The food was great."

"Totally understandable." He was certain she would have seen someone if they were obviously watching her since she was a wolf, and though she'd been enjoying her meal, wolves did notice things that might make them wary. He was glad to have some enjoyable time to spend with her like this.

Their sandwiches were soon delivered to their table, and they began to eat.

"I can see why you enjoyed this place. The food is great," Ethan said.

"Yeah, even if my secret admirer isn't from here, I'm glad we came here for lunch." She took another bite of her sandwich.

"Me too. Have you ever been on a whale trip?"

"No, not me. I'm really looking forward to it. What about you?"

"No, never."

"Don't tell me. You work too much."

He laughed. "If some of my friends had wanted to do it, I would have gone along. But going by myself? Nah."

"Oh, sure. The same with me. This is going to be fun. We need to drop by my place so I can change into tennis shoes for the boat trip and grab a jacket. It'll be cold on the water."

"Absolutely. I'm wearing rubber-soled shoes and I have a jacket in the car so I'm all set."

After lunch, they drove over to Charlene's place, and she changed shoes and grabbed her jacket. Then they headed over to the boat docks where they would take off on a smaller Zodiac boat. Unlike some of the large boats that carried thirty to forty people to watch whales, the Zodiac would take a max of five customers. For this trip, it was just the two of them, so this was nice and personalized.

They met Captain Rusty, who greeted them and then gave them safety tips and made sure they had life vests on before he headed out. "Okay, are you ready to go see some whales?"

"We sure are," Charlene said.

The captain motored out through the narrow harbor, and they saw sunbathing seals.

"Oh, wonderful." Charlene began taking pictures. "They're beautiful."

The sun was shining off the choppy water as the captain steered into the bay. He moved into calmer water as soon as he could. They began trolling for whales, and it wasn't long before they saw a pod of dolphins.

"Those are Pacific white-sided dolphins," the captain said.

The dolphins approached the boat and rode the bow waves and looked eager to make their acquaintance.

The captain waved at the dolphins near the boat. "This is a large group—about ninety of them but they can reach up to 300 in a pod."

"Wow." Charlene was taking pictures like crazy.

But so was Ethan, thinking she might even want to use one of his pictures in her rental units if he could take any good ones.

"The dolphins come up north from California and visit Oregon and Washington over the summer," Rusty said.

"That is too cool for us," Charlene said.

When the dolphins moved off, they didn't see anything for a while, but then they saw Flipper and his relatives! Bottlenose dolphins! They were about ten in number, Ethan thought.

"The bottlenose dolphins can be loners or even swim up to a thousand in a pod. Though most pods consist of about ten to thirty dolphins hunting fish together," Rusty said.

Once the dolphins left, they had to wait patiently to watch for whales, but Ethan was thrilled they had gotten to see the two kinds of dolphins. If they didn't see a whale, he would take Charlene out again on another whale-watching trip. He could see where this could be addictive. He was just glad they were loving the boat ride on the ocean and feeling the sea breeze whipping across their bow and that neither of them had gotten seasick.

Just when it seemed like they wouldn't catch sight of any whales, they saw two gray whales feeding on the kelp beds. Captain Rusty moved the boat closer and then just stopped. Before they were ready for it, they were surrounded by four whales, curious about the boat.

"Oh," Charlene squealed, pointing at the tail of a whale.

Ethan smiled at her and was enjoying seeing the whales as much as he was enjoying seeing Charlene having fun doing this.

After watching them for about a half hour, the whales finally left, and after the beautiful experience, Capt. Rusty motored them back to the dock.

They thanked the captain for a delightful trip and then headed off to Charlene's home.

"That was incredible," Charlene said.

"I agree."

"I think you took as many pictures of all the marine life as I did."

He laughed. "I'm sure of it. You can use any of the ones I got if you think they're good."

"Oh, thanks. I sure will."

For dinner, they headed over to the Pelican Brief Pub where Charlene had eaten the first time she was here in Oyster Bay. Once they sat down and had their menus in hand, Ethan asked her, "Do you recall seeing anyone who might have anything to do with sending flowers to you?"

Charlene looked over her menu. "Nah. I really didn't think this would work, but I'm glad we had the meals together and checked the restaurants out just in case."

"Yeah, it was worth trying and I've enjoyed the whole day."

"Me too."

"So what's the best case you ever worked on as a homicide detective?" Ethan closed up his menu.

"Whenever I could catch a murderer and had enough evidence to put him or her or both away, those were the best cases. The family would suffer forever from the loss of their loved one or ones, but at least the guilty party would be sitting in prison so he or she couldn't do it again. But I was also involved in helping to locate missing kids when there was an urgent need and I wasn't in the middle of a murder investigation. Even during murder investigations, I would spend practically every waking hour of my own time searching for kids who went missing in the area. My boss joked that he needed to create a one-person missing persons bureau that I worked at full-time because my success rate was so high, whether I was recovering missing children who just got separated from their parents on one of the boardwalks or runaway teens."

The server came to take their orders and after Charlene ordered a lobster meal and Ethan ordered a rib eye steak dinner, the server brought them a small loaf of sourdough bread and butter and glasses of white wine and water, then left to take orders from another table.

Ethan sliced off a piece of bread for Charlene, who thanked him and began buttering the bread. He cut off another slice for himself and buttered it. Before long, the server brought their lobster and steak dinners. They thanked the server and then began eating.

"So what was the best case that you ever worked on?" Charlene asked Ethan.

"It's pending. Taking down Kroner and his cohorts was supposed to be my best case, since they were the ones responsible for my parents' murders. But with Kroner out and on the run, and no trial yet for Benny, and the others still free, it will be a while before I learn if it's the best case or not. One of my earlier cases involved a boy, though, who had stolen a thirty-dollar fountain pen from an office supply store. He didn't want the pen so much as he wanted to prove to his friends that he could steal like they could. He figured it would be easy to grab because it was so small, but it had a security sticker on it."

"How old was he?"

"Fourteen. He was just too young to start out on the wrong foot. I told him it wasn't worth it to be involved in a life of crime, even if his friends had talked him into stealing. He was new to the area, so I figured it was a case of new-kid syndrome where he was trying to make friends and fit in, but he was doing it with the wrong crowd. I told him he would have to return the pen and clean my car once a day, three times a week for the month. I even showed him how to do it right the first time."

"Oh, good for you. What about his parents? What did they think of that? Some would have been grateful that you had helped the kid out, but others would have tried to protect their kid and lawyered up. I had to deal with both." Charlene pulled out some of the lobster meat from a claw and practically purred.

Ethan smiled at her. "I told him the situation was that I could either talk to his parents about this and we would work out this deal, or I wouldn't tell them and he could just pretend it never happened."

"Hmm," she said.

Ethan cut up some of his steak. "He opted not to tell them. But I said if he got caught doing it again, breaking any law, not just stealing, I would tell them everything. The first day he was supposed to arrive to clean the car, he was late, and I told him if he was late one more time, he would have to wash the car four times every week during the month. I had a job to do, and I couldn't put up with his tardiness. I don't think anyone had really set down rules for him. He was surprised to see me ready to wash the car with him. I think it set him at ease. In any event, I mentored him, we visited and talked about school issues, family issues, and I ended up taking him on police rides. I had him filing papers in the office and he became a regular figure at the police bureau. He was a good kid. He just needed a little guidance."

"What about his friends?"

"They ended up in juvie. Peter graduated high school with honors and became a policeman. I was so proud of him."

"That's wonderful. What about his parents? Did they ever learn about his earlier theft?"

"They were thrilled he decided to do something with his life. They had found out I had him washing my car after the first week when he went home all wet. He finally told them what had happened, and they came by and thanked me."

"Aww, so that had a great outcome."

They ate in silence for a while and Charlene finally said, "I admire you for helping that kid out."

"The funny thing was he ended up bringing his new friends over to help wash the car once a week after his month was up, and they all went on police ride-alongs several times. I began getting a steady stream of more teens from the high school who wanted to do it too. The guys all gave me a hard time about it at work."

She laughed. "I bet." She thought Ethan was so cute. She thought he would make a good wolf daddy someday. "Everyone who worked with me gave me a hard time for being such a bloodhound, whether it was finding missing people or finding the murderer in a homicide case."

"We're well suited to police work," he agreed.

"But we also are well suited to most anything that we can use our wolf instincts for."

"Most assuredly."

"We didn't get to do our berry picking today, so I thought we could do that in the morning, if you would like to." She drank some of her wine.

"Yeah, sure. With us wanting to check out the restaurants and the whaling trip, I'd forgotten all about it."

"When you mentioned the whaling trip? That's what I wanted to do instead. It was just so much fun."

"It was great."

They finished dinner and he paid for it, and then they left the restaurant. As soon as they got into his car, Charlene got a call and she frowned. She couldn't believe the name on her phone screen.

"Any trouble?" Ethan asked, observant as always.

"Noah is calling."

CHAPTER 9

To Ethan's surprise, not only had Charlene's ex-boyfriend called her, but she put the call on speakerphone, which was thoughtful of her so he wouldn't be left in the dark about what was being said. He was curious how this would play out between Charlene and her ex.

"Hey, Noah, what's up?" She was very businesslike in her approach to him.

"You didn't tell me you were moving to Oregon. I had to hear it from Renault. You know how that makes me feel?"

She smiled and reached over and squeezed Ethan's hand. "You and I broke up two months ago, Noah. We hadn't spoken to each other in all that time."

"I just figured you needed some time alone for a while."

"For two whole months?" Charlene sounded incredulous.

Ethan felt the same way and couldn't imagine parting company with Charlene for all that time without keeping in touch with her if he really cared about her.

"I had no idea you would move across the country." Noah sounded furious that she had the nerve to do that and had not even given him the courtesy of telling him.

Ethan was glad that she had gotten away from the disagreeable wolf. She deserved a whole lot more.

She shook her head. "We were not good together. I know that now. And you said that yourself several times." Then she paused and frowned. "You didn't, per chance, send me a bouquet of roses, did you?"

"That son of a bitch." Noah sounded growly, ready to turn wolf and tear into the offender.

Ethan took his irate response as a no, and he suspected right away that Noah thought his friend Renault had sent them to Charlene.

"Pardon?" Charlene asked.

"Renault Green. He said that he was with a DEA team that raided your home accidentally. That's how he knew you had moved to Portland."

So Noah didn't know that Charlene was living in Oyster Bay now then?

"Then he asked me if I'd moved to Portland too, wanting to know if we were together or not. I told him we were taking a break, but yeah, we were getting back together. The bastard."

"He's supposed to be your friend, *and* you and I broke up permanently, not temporarily. If it had been just a temporary situation, I wouldn't have moved to Oregon. He's living in Portland now and if he thinks he can see me—"

"He's not a wolf, damn it!"

Charlene took a deep breath and let it out. "Okay, listen, not that it's any of your business, but I'm seeing a wolf. I'm not dating Renault, so you can quit being perturbed with him. Unless you two have had a fight about something else, he's still your friend."

Silence.

"I've got to go now. I hope you find what you're looking

for in a relationship with a she-wolf, Noah. Truly, I do, but we just don't have what it takes. Bye." She didn't wait for him to say anything further and hung up on him.

Ethan smiled at her, glad she'd told it like it was. "So do you think that Renault sent you the flowers or not?"

"Well, we know for sure now that Noah hadn't. But I would say it's inconclusive as to whether Renault had. Did you notice that Noah thinks I still live in Portland? If Renault knew I had moved to Oyster Bay, he didn't tell Noah any differently."

"Hmm, then it's still possible Renault doesn't know that you moved either, and he might not have sent you the roses. The guys knew I was having dinner with you after the retirement party, but they could have assumed that we were doing that in Portland. I was moving to Oyster Bay after that."

"You told them that you were having dinner with the woman whose home you tore up?" she asked, sounding a little bothered by the idea.

He was afraid he was in the doghouse with Charlene because of it. "It just came up. Adam, Sierra, and Tori said something about the date to me and then one of my team members heard the news and it spread like wildfire."

"Like it would within a wolf pack."

"Exactly." Then Ethan smiled at her. "Thanks for letting me listen in on the conversation."

"It was necessary in case Noah wasn't getting the message or he thought I wasn't really dating a wolf. I'm dating you and working with you on your case. So I wanted everything to be out in the open with you. And I wanted him to know for certain that it's over between us. I can't believe he thought we just needed some time away from each other."

"Yeah, for two whole months." Still her comment about being open with Ethan made him feel guilty that he hadn't been that way with her to begin with. "I appreciate it and I'm sure glad we're dating."

"I know that it doesn't mean you'll be staying in the area, but for now, I'm enjoying spending the time with you," she said.

"The same thing here."

"Thankfully, the rentals are easy to maintain while I can get other things done. I have a maintenance guy lined up if there's any trouble with either rental home and a cleaning crew who will take care of cleaning when the occupants vacate the premises. Everything for booking is automated and then I just keep up with reservations and answering emails from registered guests or those interested in renting one of the places."

"That sounds like a great deal."

"Yeah, it frees me up to be able to go on a mission to help you catch bad guys, though I guess the drawback would be you finishing your mission and leaving Oyster Bay since the house you're staying at isn't really yours."

"Well, if we're still dating, I'll have to find a solution to that situation then. But I will be glad to get these guys all behind bars. And this time Kroner for good. Then we'll be free to just do whatever we would like to do," he said.

"Okay, that sounds like a deal."

"We haven't been to the hotel yet where you stayed

overnight. Maybe we should run by there and see if anything jogs your memory about someone who was overtly friendly and might have sent you the roses?" Ethan asked. "Since your ex-boyfriend didn't send them, and Renault might not have either."

"Sure thing. Let's go."

When they arrived at the hotel, Charlene glanced around at the lobby, but then she took Ethan's hand and led him into the Ocean Breeze Pub. The decor was ocean-themed with beach scenes of up and down the coast of Oregon, making the pub perfect for having a cocktail and watching the sun set.

They sat at a booth that looked out on the ocean and ordered their drinks. The server soon brought them their cocktails.

"Did you come to this pub when you were here before?" Ethan sipped some of his piña colada.

She lifted her margarita and licked the sugar off the edge of the glass.

He immediately thought of kissing her.

"For a drink, sure," she said. "It was the night that I arrived. I spent time driving around the area looking at homes I might have been interested in seeing and then let my real estate lady know which places I wanted to see in the morning. I had dinner at the restaurant we went to tonight, then came here to stay the night and had a drink before I went to bed." Then she saw a man watching her from the lobby.

Ethan glanced at what she was looking at. "Do you recognize him?"

"No, but he appeared to be taking a long look at me, which seemed odd."

"I wonder if he works here."

"Or just comes here to drink at the pub."

"Looking for women."

She smiled. "Well, if that's the case, we need to do this." She leaned over, cupped Ethan's face, and kissed him with passion.

Oh yeah, he was all for this. He kissed her back, not caring if anyone thought that they shouldn't. If that was the guy who was interested in Charlene, Ethan wanted him to know that he was in her life now, and she didn't have time for another man in her life.

They broke free of the kiss, smiled at each other, and did a brief sweet kiss. "Hmm, once I finish my mission here, I might have to rent one of your places until I find one of my own so we can continue to…do this," he said.

Charlene laughed and sipped some more of her drink. "I love their drinks here."

"Yeah, this one's great too. Not watered down like at some places."

"I agree. And I love that they'll fix it with sugar on the rim of the margarita instead of salt." She licked her lips.

He smiled. "Yeah, I liked tasting your triple sec, tequila, and lime juice, mixed with the sugar on your lips, just the perfect sweetness."

"Hmm, your piña colada with its rum, coconut cream, and pineapple juice is so sweet and delicious on your lips too." She got a notification on her phone and said, "Do you mind me taking this? It's about the rentals."

"No, go ahead." He glanced at the lobby but the man they'd seen was gone.

"Oh wow," she said. "Both my places are now rented through twelve months." She showed him the listings.

"Aww, hell," he said, frowning, amused, but at the same time, *not*.

"What's wrong?" She sounded worried.

"They're all bachelor wolves."

She laughed out loud. "I was worried they were some of the guys you've been after or have taken down in the past."

He smiled. "No, it just means I'll have to really step up my game."

"So far, you're doing great."

"It's my new mission."

She laughed. Then she got a call from Tori and thought she might have some news about the mystery man. "Hello, Tori. Ethan and I are having a drink at the hotel where I'd stayed. I'll put this on speakerphone."

"Oh, that's great! Hey, I got the information on who sent the roses. It was Renault."

"No. Why would he do that? I mean, he's living too far away for me to date him seriously, and he's not one of…uh, one of us, but also, why send the roses anonymously?"

"I know, right?" Tori sounded just as surprised about it.

"I can't believe it," Ethan said. "I know he hasn't had a girlfriend in a while, but I can't imagine he would think a long-distance relationship would work."

"Well, he knows me from Destin, and he always acted like he was interested in getting to know me better. Maybe Renault is too worried about rejection to meet a woman and start up a relationship," Charlene said.

"Yeah, he hasn't had much luck with women. But why send the roses anonymously? That doesn't make any sense. And he hasn't gotten back into touch with you either, which is really strange," Tori said.

"Okay, well, since he's a DEA special agent, I'm not worried about his interest in me. And if you want to mention that I'm dating Ethan in front of him at some point, go ahead and do it," Charlene said. "Once Renault learns of it, that should be the end of his interest in me."

"Adam, Sierra, and I will make it our mission. We'll set things up so we can be sure to talk about your newfound friendship that is going famously well where he can overhear us. And we'll mention that we're hoping to hear wedding bells in the future," Tori said.

Charlene smiled at Ethan. "Yeah, that works for me."

"The same thing for me," Ethan said. "Let's go for it."

"Yay! We'll definitely do it and let you know how it goes," Tori said.

Charlene took a sip of her drink. "Good. I'm just so glad it's someone I know and he's not bad news."

"Yeah, I agree," Ethan said. "I know him pretty well, so I'm not worried about him."

"Okay, good. I'm going to get with Adam and Sierra and hatch our plan," Tori said.

"Thanks, Tori," Charlene said.

"Thanks," Ethan said. "We look forward to hearing how it went."

They ended the call and Charlene ordered another drink from the server for the both of them. "That guy who was eyeing me?" Charlene said.

"Yeah, he left."

"He's over there talking to a lady in the pub now."

"Maybe he was just waiting for her, and you distracted him," Ethan said. They got their second set of drinks and clinked their glasses together. "This has been a great day."

"Oh, I so agree. I never expected to have such fun companionship when I moved here. I wish you didn't have a mission here but I'm really glad you're here."

"Me too. I never expected to be dating a wolf while I live here. I'm having a blast with you." He leaned over and kissed her sweet mouth and she quickly fed into his need to kiss her. Yeah, she was just the person he needed in his life.

CHAPTER 10

ETHAN AND CHARLENE FINISHED THEIR DRINKS AND then he drove her home. He couldn't believe that everything had changed for him when he had met Charlene and she ended up in Oyster Bay too. He was totally thinking of making this his permanent home. He loved it here and he loved being with Charlene. When he parked at her place, he walked her to her front door.

"I had a lovely day with you," he repeated, and she agreed, right before he kissed her.

She kissed his mouth with delicious intent, really getting into the kiss. She was so amazing—confident, caring, fun to be with, had a great sense of humor, and eager to go on all kinds of adventures—and he knew she was enjoying the intimacy between them as much as he was. Things were so looking up.

Then she pulled her mouth away from his and sighed. "Why don't you come over for breakfast in the morning and then we'll go hiking for berries."

"Yeah, I'm all for it."

"Don't hesitate to tell me if you have to do something work-related or if you're feeling like you need to rest a bit because of your injury. Other than seeing you wince some, I keep forgetting about your bullet wound," she said.

"So far, so good. I'll let you know though if anything's going on that you need to know."

"Okay."

They kissed briefly and said goodnight. He was already wanting to stay the night with her, and he hadn't felt that way for another she-wolf ever. He'd been happy to date them and kiss them good night and that was it. He had been feeling some pain from his wound, but he'd been sucking it up so he could enjoy the time he was spending with Charlene. He didn't want *anything* to interfere with their plans.

At home, he took a shower, then headed for bed, glad that the mystery of who had sent the flowers to Charlene had been resolved. He wondered how Tori, Adam, and Sierra were going to subtly mention that Ethan was seeing Charlene in front of Renault and how he would react.

Ethan closed his eyes and swore he could still feel Charlene's sensuous mouth pressed against his, the way she licked the seam of his mouth and gained entrance, the way her pheromones always sent out devilishly sexy hints that she was as into him as much as he was into her.

For the first time since he'd met a she-wolf that he'd dated, he had wanted so badly to show her that he was the right wolf for her.

Ethan woke early the next morning, ready to have some more fun with Charlene and was thinking that if she was interested, he would grill some steaks for them tonight for supper.

He dressed in cargo pants, a long-sleeved shirt, and

hiking boots. This time he took a hiking bag with bottled waters, energy bars, and a first aid kit. He called Charlene before he headed over, just to make sure she still wanted to do this. "Hey, it's me. I'm about to come over, if you're ready for me. I was thinking about grilling steaks for us tonight too, if you would like to do that."

"Oh, absolutely. I'll see you in a minute."

"I'm on my way over." He drove over to Charlene's house, and she had left the door open for him. Grabbing his backpack from the car, he walked inside her home, calling out, "It's just me."

"I'm in the kitchen. I love how close we live to each other. How would you like your eggs?"

"Over easy would be great."

"Sausage or ham or both?" she asked.

"Sausage appeals this morning." He put his backpack next to the door and joined her in the kitchen. "Do you want me to make the coffee?"

"Yes, thanks."

But first, he wrapped his arms around her waist and kissed her cheek as she slipped some sausage links into a frying pan. "Good morning."

She turned her head to smile at him and kiss him back. "Hmm, good morning."

Then he let go of her and made them some coffee. "Have you scoped out the area where the berry patches are?"

"I saw a few when I went through the forest on my first trip here. We went a different path when we were running as wolves that one night and I saw a few that way too. Oh, if we're going to have dinner here, we might as well run as wolves afterward too."

"Yeah, that sounds like a winning plan." But he realized that's probably why his arm had been bothering him when they ran the first night as wolves. It didn't matter. He was healing up day by day, and he wasn't giving up the opportunity to run with her if that's what she wanted to do. Then he got a call on his phone and pulled his cell out of his pocket. "It's...Renault."

Charlene nearly dropped her spatula into the frying pan that she was cooking home-fried potatoes in. "No."

"Yep." Ethan answered the call, pretending he had no clue why Renault would be calling him, and said, "Hey, how's the job going without me?" He put the call on speakerphone in case Tori and his friends had already let the cat out of the bag about Ethan dating Charlene and that was what Renault was calling him about.

"I hear you're dating Charlene." Renault sounded perturbed.

No good morning, hello, no talking about work, just the topic of Charlene—which indicated to Ethan that Renault had really wanted to make something more of getting together with Charlene.

"Uh, yeah, news travels far and wide and...fast. She told me that you and she had known each other through your friendship with her ex-boyfriend. But she had been ready to move on. Did you know that she and Noah had broken up two months ago and he hadn't even realized she was living in Oregon for a month? She said Noah still wouldn't have known except that you saw her at her place and told Noah about it." Ethan was trying to catch Renault in a lie while he made some toast for them, then found the butter and strawberry jelly in the fridge and set them on the table.

"Right. I wanted to make sure they weren't together any longer—which was the only reason I called him about her. I really thought he would say they'd broken up for good. Instead, he was furious that she was living in Portland and never told him she was leaving." There was a significant pause before Renault said anything further. "You're really dating her?"

"Yep. I've found a kindred spirit in Charlene." Wolf-wise for sure, and he loved being with her. He set the table. "We have a lot in common. We just suit each other. I hope everything's going well for you at work."

But Renault wasn't done talking about Charlene. "Noah applied to take your vacant position and the boss just hired him, so I would watch your back if I were you. He's not happy with Charlene either."

Charlene quickly dished up their eggs, sausage, and potatoes before she burned them. She appeared a little off-kilter when she heard that Noah would be in Portland. Ethan poured cups of coffee for them, then rubbed her back to reassure her that everything would be fine. He couldn't believe it. Would Charlene even want to return to Portland and be with her ex-boyfriend now? He didn't think so, but now he was going to have to deal with the wolf. Which he had no problems with, but he didn't want it to become a wedge between him and Charlene if she still had some feelings for Noah.

"Okay, that's good to know."

"The boss probably already told you that Kroner was mistakenly released from jail and now he's in the wind. You know he wants your hide."

"Yeah, but I'm retired now, and I won't be as important to him as others who are still working for the DEA and pursuing him so they can return him to jail." Ethan swore that Renault wanted to give him all the bad news just because he was now dating Charlene. Ethan didn't want to rub it in that he was having breakfast with her, which could sound like he'd stayed overnight with her, so he didn't mention it.

But then Charlene did. She grabbed the slices of toast and added them to their plates. "Hey, Renault, you didn't send me some roses, did you?"

Silence ensued. She had really surprised Renault that she and Ethan were together this morning and that she had been listening in on the conversation the whole time.

"Uh, no. Why?"

"Oh, I just thought they were lovely, but the gift tag had gotten wet and so I couldn't read the ink-stained words. I just thought maybe, since you realized I was in the area, you had sent me a housewarming bouquet of flowers," she said, sitting down with Ethan to eat. "I was afraid to ask you though in case you hadn't sent them."

Ethan just smiled at her and shook his head.

"No, I didn't send you any flowers. I didn't realize I was interrupting anything. I've got to get to work. Glad you're both enjoying each other's company. Talk later." Then Renault hung up on them.

Charlene speared a sausage link with her fork and pointed it at Ethan. "I wanted him to know that we are really together. Just in case he had hopes that we weren't. Though with Noah being in the area, Renault would give up pursuing me in a heartbeat, knowing him."

"Renault will be sure to tell Noah. I can't believe my boss hired him. Though my position is technically vacant, and if Noah met all the qualifications, I could understand why he got the job. But hell, now he'll be in the area and how much do you want to bet that he'll be pestering you again?" Ethan scarfed up some of his eggs. "These are great tasting, by the way. I love the lemon and pepper seasoning you added to them."

"Thanks. I should have asked if you would like that first." She took a sip of her coffee. "Noah will be three hours away and I have a wolf at my back now." She smiled at Ethan, then bit into her sausage. "Why did Renault think Kroner would be after you instead of the DEA agents who are still on the payroll and have to be tracking him down?"

"Renault knows Kroner threatened to kill me when I took him down this last time. But I'm sure Kroner will want to stay as far away from me as he can."

"You're retired and if he reads the news at all, he could know that you are. You wouldn't have a badge, a gun, or the backing of the department. At least as far as he knows," Charlene said. "So he might... Wait, your boss didn't set you up to be the prey, did he?"

"No. Kroner's escaping jail time wasn't planned." Though Ethan thought about it for a moment, then discounted the idea. His boss, Grainger, would have had Ethan agree to the plan if he had thought that was the best way to catch these guys.

Charlene sighed and sipped some of her coffee. "I absolutely can't believe that Noah is coming to Oregon. He was Florida-born and he swore he would never leave there. He liked to surf on his off time. He's going to be so pissed off when he learns I'm not even in Portland any longer and seriously dating you here in Oyster Bay. I'm sure Renault will tell him just where we are so maybe he can get back in Noah's good graces."

Ethan leaned back in his chair. "The water-stained note was genius."

She laughed. "Yeah, I just wanted to see what he would say. I swear if we could have seen his face, he would have been blushing when I asked him if he sent the flowers to me."

"I'm sure you embarrassed him. He shouldn't have sent them anonymously. That would make him a beta wolf, if he had been a wolf."

"Right. That's exactly what he is. And the fact he wants to clean his hands of trying to date me and he'll want to sic Noah on you? Totally beta behavior."

Then Ethan got another call and pulled out his phone, thinking Noah might already have gotten the word and Ethan was going to get hell for it from him, but it was Adam. Ethan put the call on speakerphone.

"Hey, we played out our little drama in front of Renault so he overheard us talking about you dating Charlene. He was all ears," Adam said.

"I just got a call from him." Ethan ate another bite of his sausage before his breakfast got cold.

"No way." Adam sounded incredulous.

"Yeah."

"Did he tell you the other news?" Adam asked.

"About Noah taking my old job?"

"Yep. That's what Renault said, pretending to innocently overhear us talking about you dating Charlene. He told us right away that you might be bound for trouble because Noah still thinks he and Charlene are together. That's when I asked him if Noah knew you both were living in Oyster Bay," Adam said. "He said he didn't tell him, but the word would probably get out that both of you were living there now. Of course we know Renault is going to tell Noah right away."

"Thanks for warning us," Ethan said. "Charlene and I are having breakfast together, by the way."

Adam laughed. "Good. I hope that Renault knew it too."

"He did."

Adam laughed again, but then he got serious. "You know we've already talked to Leidolf and Cassie. The wolf will be in our territory when he arrives in Portland and so he has to play by our rules. If he wants to make trouble for a couple of wolves in our pack—the two of you—then he'll have the whole wolf pack on his back."

"Wow," Charlene said. "I never knew the pack would come in handy for making my ex-boyfriend back off. Thanks to all of you for helping out."

"Yeah, thanks." Though Ethan was ready to fight the wolf on his own terms.

"Okay, well, I have to go. Tori and I need to investigate a homicide. We suspect Kroner had something to do with it."

"Hell," Ethan said. "I'm still pissed off that the clerical error set him free."

"Yeah, the bureau is looking into it, making sure that no one coerced or bribed the person who is responsible for making the error."

"I sure hope not," Ethan said. Then he would really be angry. Not so much if the person was coerced, but if they received money for it? Yeah. "So who was murdered?"

"A known drug dealer who was in competition with Kroner. I've got to run. I'll talk to you both later. Have a fun day," Adam said.

"Thanks, we are off to pick wild blackberries and make jelly," Charlene said.

"That's the life. You both deserve it."

They told Adam to be safe on the job and he said the same to them and then they ended the call.

"Well, I hadn't thought someone might have actually released Kroner on purpose," Charlene said, then finished her eggs.

"I know. It would be a criminal act for sure. Especially if Kroner's release had resulted in someone else's death." Ethan carried their plates into the kitchen, and she grabbed the butter and jelly and put them in the fridge.

"Are you ready to go berry picking? It's time for us to just enjoy ourselves."

Ethan put the frying pans they had cooked breakfast in into the sink and added soap and water to let them soak. "Yeah, I'm ready to go. When we return, I'll clean these up."

"Okay." She grabbed a backpack and added a couple of bottles of cold water.

"I've got some energy bars for us if we need them too."

"Oh good. I've got a couple of buckets to use to collect the berries."

"Perfect. I didn't have anything that would come in handy."

She showed him her bear noisemaker too, then tucked it into her bag.

"Oh, great idea."

"Yeah. They have around 25,000 to 30,000 black bears in Oregon. When I visited my grandfather, we were always aware that running around in the woods we could encounter a bear."

"For sure. I've run with some wolves before and ran smack-dab into a black bear on about five different occasions over the years."

"Were you ever in real danger?"

"We were in a pack of three to five wolves, so we managed to scare them off each time."

"That's good. And it's scary."

"I agree. We worked well together as a deterrent to bears for sure. Coyotes and mountain lions too."

Charlene and Ethan headed out of the house and began walking along a path in the woods, talking to each other and making noise so that if they came upon any black bears, they would scare them off. "Did you see the weather report? We're supposed to have fog tonight," she said.

"Yeah, I figure it will be perfect for running as wolves."

"Oh sure, that would be great," she said.

Right now, the sky was clear and sunny, and the temperature was sixty-five degrees. Perfect for hiking and berry picking. In the fall and through the winter and spring, it could be really rainy, so summer was ideal for doing this.

They found some purple Oregon grapes, but they weren't ripe yet. "These are really tart, but add some sugar, and it makes it perfect for jelly. I used to pick them with my grandfather. We can do that when they ripen in the fall."

"Yeah. I would like to do that. Why was your grandfather living out here when your parents were in Florida?" Ethan asked.

"Mom and her family were from the Oregon coast. She was on spring break in Florida when she met my dad. He had taken over his parents' rental properties and she wanted to stay with him there. My grandfather didn't want to leave his native Oregon. So my sister and I visited him every summer and he came out to Florida for Christmases. We had a feast with him in Oregon during the weeks of Thanksgiving and Easter. We loved going to both areas, though I wished that Granddad could have been with us all the time while my sister and I were growing up. My grandmother died when we were six months old so we never knew her. What about you? Were your parents from Oregon?"

"Yes, from the Portland area. They both wanted to be in law enforcement from the time they were young and actually met at the police academy. And that was all she wrote. They fell in love, the only wolves in law enforcement at the time.

Like us, they were good at what they did. They both eventually became DEA special agents. My grandparents were from there too. I've traveled all over, but I always came home."

"Is that going to be a problem for you in the future? I mean, being away from Portland? Your friends?" she asked.

They found some blackberries and began picking them before they moved on. "No. Not when I have someone in my life who makes my days and nights so special," he said.

"Hmm, I feel the same way about you."

"I...hope you're not having nightmares about me raiding your house." He'd thought about it earlier and meant to ask her if she'd had any issues from his terrorizing her.

"Ooh, more blackberries," she said and hurried over to get some. "Yes, on the nightmares. I was listening to the music too loudly with the shower water running on high and I thought I heard a bang, but I figured it was a car that had gone by the house and had backfired or something. And then everything was quiet after that so I didn't think anything further about it. You guys didn't holler out that you were DEA or anything."

"No, as dangerous as these guys often are, we go in without announcing ourselves. You would have heard us for sure and figured out that we were in your home if we had been yelling."

"I would have. Boy, I would have been mad."

He laughed. "I figured when you bit me, you had been angry."

"Yeah, well, if I'd been really mad, I would have bitten you a lot harder. That was more like a love bite."

He smiled while they continued to pick blackberries.

"Anyway, so yeah, I've been having nightmares about you pointing a rifle at me. What about you having nightmares about me?"

He chuckled. "I did actually have one about being attacked by a wild red wolf—female type."

She chuckled. Then she glanced in the direction where she heard a noise. "Oh, oh, a bear is coming." Charlene yelled, "Go, ha!" and fumbled to pull her bear noisemaker out of her backpack. She backed away and was too close to the edge of the cliff. It crumbled and she screamed out as she fell.

CHAPTER 11

ETHAN'S HEART PRACTICALLY LEAPT OUT OF HIS THROAT as he dove to catch Charlene, but she'd already fallen and caught herself on some rocks below the edge of the cliff before slipping all the way to the beach's rocky bottom sixty feet below. Around two-hundred-and-fifty pounds of muscle, and six feet in length, the male black bear was still coming, and Ethan didn't have a choice. He scrambled over the cliff, though he was more prepared for it than Charlene had been. At least there were lots of foot and fingerholds on the rocks. The bear could climb the cliff and trees too, but he just peered over the edge and watched them down below. Then he ambled off.

"Are you okay, Charlene?" Ethan asked, hoping to hell she hadn't been hurt when she slipped off the cliff.

"Yeah. What about you?"

"I'm good. I made more of a calculated climb. Are you able to climb back up here?"

"I can. Is the bear still up there?"

"Yeah, I hear him sniffing around."

"Well, he better not be eating all our blackberries."

Ethan smiled, thinking the berries weren't half as important as climbing back up into the woods away from the cliff and the bear. The tide was coming in, the waves crashing against the rocks below them. The rocks they were clinging to were slippery and about fifty feet above the water. They couldn't hold on forever where they were either.

He was listening to the bear snuffing around, waiting for it to go away. But Ethan's injured arm was really aching. He hadn't planned to climb cliffs anytime soon! He would have left that activity for a later time when he was completely healed.

"How are you doing?" Charlene called out to Ethan.

"Good. How are you doing?"

"I need to make it up the cliff soon or I'm not going to have the strength."

"I'm listening to the bear." Ethan didn't want to tell her he was eating their berries, which was the reason the bear was sticking around.

"He is eating our berries, isn't he!"

"I'm afraid he is." Then he glanced down at her, and damn, she was climbing up to reach him. "Be careful, honey." He hadn't called her a term of endearment yet, but it sounded so natural to call her that.

She smiled. "I am, thanks. How is your injured arm doing?"

He had to be honest with her. "It's killing me."

"Ohmigod, Ethan. We've got to get you out of here."

"And you. I think the bear might have moved on." Then Ethan's phone started to ring in his backpack. "They'll have to leave a voicemail."

"If it is one of your friends, they wouldn't be able to come rescue us anyway. It would take too long."

"No. We'll be out of here before you know it." He began to

move up the cliff, and when he reached the edge, he looked to see if the bear was there to make sure it was safe for Charlene to join him. The bear had knocked over their buckets and the berries all were gone. Ethan could smell the bear's scent where it had headed off into the woods and disappeared. "It's all clear."

"Good. I need to get on solid ground and give my arms a rest."

"Yeah, I hear you."

"I'm sorry. You have to be way worse off than me," she said.

"Nah. I have more muscle mass than you and it had to be tough to hold on as long as you have." He climbed onto the ridge and reached down to help her up if she needed it.

She was nearly there, and he grabbed her arm and hauled her all the rest of the way up and into his arms.

"God, you scared the life out of me when you slipped off the cliff," he said.

"Yeah, me too." She hugged him tight. "Thanks for coming to my rescue."

He chuckled. "I wanted to come for you, but I was trying to get out of the way of the bear too."

She smiled and kissed him, then glanced at the berry buckets. "He ate *every* one of our blackberries."

"Yeah, I know. So are we done for now or—"

"Let's get some more. I want to do this."

He gave her another kiss and hug. He was so proud of her for not giving up. Though if the bear came back, they would probably call it a day. But he was ready to collect the blackberries and make jelly with her after that.

They had to go in another direction where they hadn't already cleaned out the wild fruit though. They finally found some more patches of blackberries and picked them all, filling their buckets.

"Woo-hoo! We got them before the bear did. But we better head back to the house before he decides to see if we picked some more blackberries for him. All the blackberries we collected should be enough to make a good batch of jelly out of them." She took Ethan's hand and headed for home. "Oh, who called you on your phone?"

"Let me check." Ethan let go of her hand and pulled his phone out of his backpack. When he saw the caller ID, he shook his head. "Oh, you won't believe this. Noah was the one who had called."

"Ohmigod, no way!"

"Yeah, I take it he's an alpha wolf."

"He is. So are you going to call him back?" She sounded amused.

"No. We're busy on our berry-picking date. When we get back to your house, we'll be in the business of making jelly." He got a call before he put his phone back in his backpack and he glanced at the caller ID. "He's persistent."

She laughed. "Yeah, I could have told you that. He doesn't know that you're an alpha like he is. He probably thinks he can intimidate you and you'll leave me alone."

"It's not happening."

"That's what I like about you. Someone who will stand up to him. Even if Renault was a wolf, he wouldn't have stood up to Noah."

"You're worth it." Ethan tucked his phone into his backpack.

"Thanks. Besides, Noah would never have gone out to pick blackberries with me and then make them into jam or jelly. This was really fun."

"That's part of life, experiencing stuff like that. And the blackberries are so much wilder and tastier than the store-bought brands," he said.

"Exactly. Plus, having the encounter with the bear made it all the more…exciting."

He laughed.

They finally reached her home, dropped off their backpacks near the door, and he began cleaning the frying pans from breakfast. Charlene brought out lemon juice, pectin, and sugar, and then washed the berries. Then she soaked the berries in salt water. She dried them after that.

"These are perfect. Some are perfectly ripe, others a little underripe, which makes a great combination. Overripe blackberries lose their pectin and sharpness. So we did great," she said.

"That's good to know. Do you want me to mash the blackberries in the pan?" he asked.

"Sure." She added some lemon juice to it.

He simmered them over the stovetop for a few minutes to break the berries down, and then she strained them through a jelly bag. She added some of the seeds back in so it was more of a jam than just all jelly.

He began mashing the berries with a potato masher. "Boy, they smell good."

"They do. It makes me think of still being out there picking them."

Then they cooked the mixture with sugar and pectin, and he began stirring it constantly to dissolve the sugar. They boiled it for five minutes and then after they finished cooking it, they sterilized the jars for the jelly.

"Should we have lunch now?" she asked.

"Yeah, that was fun." He was cleaning everything up so they could make lunch. "Unless you want to order pizza instead of making lunch."

"That sounds fabulous." She sighed. "Oh, you shouldn't have been doing all that work with your arm. I keep forgetting that you're injured because you keep acting like there's nothing wrong with it. But after cliff hanging, it has to be sore."

"I was mixing and mashing with my good arm. My injured arm only hurt when I was hanging onto the cliff."

She shook her head. "And when you were running as a wolf? Why don't we just grill steaks tonight and enjoy the sunset instead of running as wolves? Especially after the trauma I'm sure your injured arm has experienced today."

"Sure, that would be fine." Ethan wouldn't have let on it was bothering him, but it was probably a good idea to give his arm a rest.

They ordered a supreme pizza with all the toppings that would be there in half an hour. Then they settled on the back deck with glasses of water.

"Now this is the life," she said, watching the seagulls flying over the ocean.

"Yeah. I couldn't have found a better place to retire, even if I hadn't thought that's what I would be doing here." Then he got a call on his phone and looked at the caller ID. "It's Noah again."

"You might as well get it over with."

"That's just what I was thinking." Ethan answered his phone. "Hello?" He put it on speakerphone so Charlene could listen in or jump into the conversation if she wanted to.

"This is Noah Westmoreland and I'm—"

"Charlene's ex-boyfriend from Destin, Florida." Ethan wanted Noah to understand that he knew the situation between Charlene and Noah perfectly well.

"*Current* boyfriend. There has been a slight misunderstanding between us."

Ethan wondered why Noah didn't talk to Charlene about it and called him instead. "Well, from what she tells me, the misunderstanding is on your part. We're dating, if you didn't know that for certain. I understand that you took over my old job. Congratulations are in order. Grainger is one of the best bosses you could ask to work for. I want to wish you luck with that. And I need to tell you to watch your back. If Grainger didn't warn you, someone in the department might be dirty. Just be careful who you confide in."

Noah didn't say anything for a moment and Ethan thought he might realize that Ethan was trying to help him out, but not where Charlene and his relationship were concerned.

"Charlene and I aren't through with each other, and you had better watch your back where I'm concerned."

"That's good to know. Good talking to you. But our pizza just arrived"—not that it had, but it was a good excuse to show they were dating whether the wolf liked it or not—"so I have to let you go. Enjoy Portland. It has a lot of nice things to offer."

"Listen, here, you—"

Ethan ended the call.

"You know he's not going to give up that easily." Charlene sipped some more of her water.

"Yeah, but I don't have any trouble seeing him wolf to wolf."

"You have been injured! And he's a gray wolf. He's bigger than you. Though if it comes to that, I'll be there to fight him too."

"I don't want you in a fight with him. I mean, if he decides to come here to see me eye to eye, I'll deal with him."

"Does anyone know where you're actually living?" Charlene asked.

"No. Except for you. I gave you my address. Well, and our pack leaders, and Adam, Sierra, and Tori. But no one in the department except for my boss knows."

"Okay, so if Noah comes here, he isn't going to find you."

"Correct. So he'll come and see you most likely instead." Which Ethan didn't want.

"Which means you'll need to stay here with me. You know, to protect me from the big bad wolf."

Ethan smiled.

"I'm serious."

"It will be my honor and my pleasure." Ethan hadn't

expected that to happen! Noah had really screwed that up with Charlene.

Then their pizza arrived, and they ate it on the deck. This was great. At his home in Portland, he had a deck that overlooked a backyard. It was pretty, but with an ocean view like this? Perfect. No traffic noises, dogs barking, just the sound of the ocean waves pummeling the rocky beach below.

Once they finished their lunch, he said, "I've got to go out and buy some steaks and pack an overnight bag for tonight. Do you need anything at the grocery store?"

"What else do you want with the steaks?"

"Corn on the cob? I can grill them and maybe we could have baked potatoes or french fries."

"I have the potatoes."

"Okay, I'll get some corn on the cob. What about fixings for breakfast?"

"I can make us pancakes or waffles if you would like. I have everything we need for that."

"Milk? Bread?"

"Rolls to go with our steaks?"

"I'll get some of those too. I'll be back in a little bit."

"Have a safe trip."

"Thanks. If Noah calls you, just let me know."

"I sure will. He'll probably move to Portland and will take a little time to get settled in before he begins working at the job, which means he might end up taking a drive out here to see me."

"I hope to be here when it happens."

"Yeah, me too." Then she gave Ethan a hug and kiss before he left.

Now she was his kind of she-wolf girlfriend. He gave her a generous kiss and hug back, and then he left to grocery shop and pack his bag. He was thrilled it had come to this so quickly in their relationship. Noah really hadn't played the game right, especially if he thought Ethan would ever let him ruin what he had with Charlene.

CHAPTER 12

Despite how Charlene and Ethan had met, she knew he was the kind of wolf she would get along well with. Mainly because he was so apologetic about raiding her house by accident. Noah was the kind of agent who would mark it off as the hazard of being in that business if he had raided her home accidentally and hadn't already known her.

She really was glad that Ethan was here and dating her. She couldn't imagine Noah would feel he could keep up any kind of a relationship with her when she lived so far away. Maybe not quite so far away as Florida, but she was not moving back to Portland to see him, and he better not think of quitting his job so that he could join her in Oyster Bay and renew their friendship.

She changed the sheets on the bed because she wanted them to be fresh for when Ethan stayed with her the night, and hopefully he would stay longer than that. She was thrilled and eager to take their relationship further.

Before she could do a load of wash, Noah called. Why did that not surprise her?

"Hello, Noah. I heard you moved to Portland and took Ethan's position at the DEA." She started the wash cycle on the washing machine.

"Do you belong to the red wolf pack out of Portland?"

She hesitated to answer Noah, not expecting that line of

questioning. She thought he would give her hell for seeing another wolf or beg her to reconsider seeing him. But belonging to the local wolf pack? Had Leidolf and Cassie talked to him?

"Yep. I guess since you'll be in the area, you'll be joining them too. They're great wolves. They can really help us out in a crisis." And keep Noah from causing trouble for Ethan and her.

"Hell, I was already read the riot act by the pack leaders. Did you sic them on me?"

She wanted to laugh. "No. And neither did Ethan. Why? What did they say?"

"That we are in their pack territory, they know about our situation, and I had better not cause any rift in the pack. Even though I'm not a member of the pack, I have to live by their rules because I'm in their territory. Though they offered for me to join them. I wouldn't have thought their territory would encompass your area since you're so far away."

"Ethan has always been a member of the wolf pack. They took me into the pack before I came out here, and there aren't any other wolves or wolf packs out here. You're going to join our pack, aren't you?" She hoped Noah would because he might pay more attention to the leadership and not get himself into hot water that way. Not only that, but they really could be a help to him.

"How do you feel about it?" Noah asked.

She was surprised that he would ask her opinion on it. He usually was hardheaded about doing things his way and he didn't care what others thought about it. "I love them. And yeah, I would recommend you do it."

"All right. I've never been with a pack and neither have you, so I was wondering how it would work out. But if you think it will be a boon, then I can sure try it out."

"They have great leadership. They help their pack members out pronto if they get into a bind. So go for it. Truthfully, I didn't know about them all the month I was living in Portland until right before I left."

"When Ethan and his team barged into your house thinking it was a drug house."

"Right. And the pack leaders and others helped get the house back in order. So are you working now or are you still just getting settled in?"

"I'm starting work soon, but I want to see you. Tomorrow maybe? If you're free?"

"I'm dating Ethan. That's not going to change. You know how it is for us as wolves. He and I have a physical and emotional connection but also a chemical attraction to each other. There's no denying what I feel for him already."

"I still want to see you."

"All right. But Ethan will be here when you get here." She didn't know why Noah thought she would change her mind about them after all this time apart when they hadn't even spoken so much as a word.

Noah let out his breath. "All right."

"And no fighting between the two of you."

"Tomorrow morning at eight then?"

Noah wasn't promising he would be civil, she noted.

"Sure, you can have breakfast with us. I'm making pancakes. Do you have my address?"

"Yeah, Renault gave it to me. I can't believe he thought he could date you."

"Neither can you."

Silence.

"I'll see you tomorrow then." She said goodbye and hoped this wasn't a mistake. She knew Noah wasn't going to let this go though. But she was glad that Leidolf and Cassie had spoken to him. Whereas they had been thrilled to meet her and welcome her to the pack, they were hard on him because he was an alpha male. She understood that they needed to set down the rules right away so they wouldn't have trouble in the pack from an outside alpha wolf causing issues.

By the time she had finished washing and drying her sheets and remaking the bed, Ethan returned to her house. She loved his company.

"Okay, I have some...well, weird news," Ethan said, putting the steaks in the fridge until he was ready to grill them.

She frowned at him. "Oh, me too." She just hoped that the two men didn't have a fight. But she wondered if Noah had called Ethan back about seeing her tomorrow.

"Do you want to share yours first or—" he asked.

"You go ahead." She rubbed his good arm. "Does this call for a cocktail?"

"Uh, yeah, or a glass of wine. I brought a bottle of merlot."

"Okay, that sounds good."

He poured them each a glass of wine and then they went out on the back deck and sat down together on one of the rattan couches to drink it. It was so comfy out here with him.

"Okay, so my boss called me," he said.

"Does he want you to start doing some surveillance early? I'm ready." The sooner they caught the bad guys, the better.

"He wants to send an agent to work with me."

"Oh." She knew if that happened, she wasn't going to be able to help Ethan with the mission. Except maybe behind the scenes, if Ethan needed her to. But another agent who would be armed with a gun and a badge would help to protect him better than she could.

"The weird news is that the agent will be Noah."

"No way. My ex-boyfriend? There's not another guy working in your department whose name is Noah, right?" She could have fallen off the couch she was so surprised.

"No, it's your ex-boyfriend. Apparently, Renault had talked to Grainger about hiring Noah as soon as he knew I was going to retire months ago since they were best friends. So he'd already applied for the job."

"Okay, so what was the deal with me then? I mean, Noah was planning to move to Portland and wasn't going to tell me? Which was fine, but what I don't understand is why he made a big deal of me leaving Destin without telling him!"

"Yeah, that's exactly what I was thinking. But maybe Noah was waiting to learn if he liked the job first before he talked to you about it and asked you to join him."

"Possibly, but he could have handled that a lot differently when he knew he had the job and got mad at me for having already moved to Portland. He should have been thrilled to know I was going to be in the same place he would be, though of course I wouldn't have been once I moved to Oyster Bay. I really never thought he would leave Destin, but I had told him how much I loved Oregon and wanted to return there and that might have influenced him. But then the other question is, once Renault learned I was here, why did he send me flowers and try to stir things up?"

"I suspect Renault thought the two of you had broken up for good because you had already moved here and hadn't told Noah." Ethan took a drink of his merlot. "So my boss thought since the place I'm staying at is a three-bedroom home, Noah could stay in one of the guest bedrooms."

"Ohmigod, no."

"Yeah. The more Grainger thought about it, the more he decided that he didn't want me to work alone. He figured that the new guy, who had worked as a DEA special agent in Florida for years, would be perfect to fill my vacant position. Grainger knew there's no way that Noah would have anything to do with the mole in the organization so he could back me up without any problem."

"So that's why Noah called me and said he wanted to see me in the morning."

"Because he knew you lived out here too and he could possibly date you while he's staying in Oyster Bay." Ethan shook his head.

"Which isn't happening," Charlene said.

"So was that your news then? That Noah is coming to have breakfast with us in the morning?" Ethan asked.

"Yeah. I had no idea he was going to be living with you." Charlene couldn't believe how quickly their plans could be torn asunder.

"All right. That'll work out. He'll see that we're together.

The thing is I can't really tell my boss no, I can't work with him," Ethan said.

"No, and you shouldn't. This way you'll have some legitimate backup. If nothing else, Noah is good at his job. He has earned all kinds of accolades through his work. He's just not a good choice as a boyfriend for me." She took a sip of her wine and then she smiled, thinking she had the perfect plan. "Okay, so how about this. You stay with me, and Noah can stay at the DEA's rented house. That way the idea that he isn't dating me will really sink in."

"That works for me. Hopefully, he won't tell my boss that I'm staying with my girlfriend."

"He better not. So the other news is that Leidolf and Cassie talked to Noah about becoming a member of the pack and essentially a team player."

Ethan laughed. "Knowing Leidolf, he gave Noah a dressing-down in case he thought to create problems in the pack—particularly with regard to you and me."

"Yep." She chuckled. "Noah needed that."

"I'm glad to hear it. I packed a few things with me to stay for a couple of nights at your place. I only brought my clothes with me to Oyster Bay for while I am on the mission because the rental house was completely furnished. I put most of my stuff in storage until I figured out where I was going to permanently retire."

"When is Noah moving into your place?" she asked.

"Tomorrow morning. After we have breakfast, I'll go to the rental house with him and pack my stuff up to bring it over here."

"I sure hope this works out." She was still worried Noah might give Ethan a hard time. She didn't think Noah would leave Ethan in the lurch if Kroner or his other cohorts were gunning for him though. Noah still had his reputation to maintain as a great DEA agent, and he was new at the job so he had to prove to the boss that he made the right hiring decision. Not to mention that if Ethan was injured or killed during the operation, Leidolf would look into it himself to make sure that Noah hadn't had anything to do with it.

"If you feel like you need your own personal space or it's not working out between us, I can always move back to the DEA rental house," Ethan said.

She smiled and leaned over and kissed his cheek. "No. *You* are going to work out beautifully. When I said I hope this works out, I was referring to you and Noah working together on the mission."

"We have a job to do, and if he's as dedicated to his work as you say he is, we won't have any trouble."

"I sure hope not."

"Truthfully, I doubt he'll want to have me, Leidolf, and the rest of the pack on his case."

"Okay, I'm feeling better about all this. I was worried you would be staying at the other house, and he would slip away to try to start up a romance with me again."

"That's not happening."

"No, it isn't. But he might not believe that until he sees it for himself. I was worried I wouldn't be as much of a help to you in taking these guys down since I don't have a badge. I guess this leaves me out of working with you on the case."

"Yeah. It's better this way. I don't want you getting hurt and I'm glad I'll have Noah as backup. Are you ready for me to grill the steaks?"

"I sure am."

Once the food was done, they opted to go outside on the back deck to eat. She hadn't thought she would have companionship like this, so she was glad that she had furnished the deck for company with two couches and two chairs, a coffee table and a table with four chairs. The patio was covered, so when it rained, they still could sit outside. It was just perfect for watching the sunset and eating meals out here, especially when the weather was really beautiful. They sat at the table and started to eat their steaks, corn on the cob, and baked potatoes.

"This is delicious," Charlene said. "I'm so glad that you offered to cook the steaks."

"Me too. I love grilling steaks, but I can make us grilled chicken, brisket, you name it."

"It all sounds great to me. After dinner, let's just find something to watch on TV." She didn't have a fancy grill, but she figured if things worked out between them, that would make for a nice investment.

"Yeah, what appeals to you?"

"Oh, some kind of a survival show? I always think of how it would be if one of our kind went on a trip like that and turned wolf to catch our food, were protected from the biting bugs because of our double wolf coats, could drink the water without boiling it or purifying it, take care of poisonous snakes with a chomp, chase off wild boar and crocs, or take them down to cook up and eat."

He laughed. "That sounds good."

They finished eating and cleaned up. Then they settled on the couch and started watching a show where a man and woman who didn't know each other but had some survival skills worked together to survive for twenty-one days to see if they could do it—naked.

Poisonous snakes, fire ants, biting insects, ticks, mosquitoes, bad water, hot sun, and cold nights, constant rain, and crocodiles or alligators—depending on the area—plagued them. As wolves, they could deal with any of those situations without any problem.

"We ought to sign up for a challenge like that," Ethan said with his arm around Charlene as they cuddled on the sofa.

She laughed. "Yeah, but they only do it with people who don't know each other. You have to also film what you're doing while you're out there."

"Right, but we would do that when we were in our human form and then we would turn off the cameras for the night and sleep as wolves."

"Yeah, we would make it without any issues then. And they would be amazed at our toughness. But these are just reality shows so they have a production crew close by to check on them. I'm afraid we would be outed."

"We'll skip that challenge then." He kissed her and once they finished the episode, the couple making it through the Amazon jungle on their own for the allotted time, bug-bitten, their bodies starved and dehydrated, Ethan turned off the TV. "Are you ready for bed?"

"I sure am." She rose from the couch and helped him up.

He grabbed his bags, and she led him to her bedroom. She couldn't believe she was doing this with Ethan already, and yet it just felt right.

Ethan was letting Charlene take the lead here because he wasn't sure how far she wanted to go. Just to curl up and sleep together? Have unconsummated sex? He would be happy to do either with her, but he wanted her to make the choice. He set his bags on the floor out of the way, wondering if she was going to dress in nightclothes and if he should just wear a pair of boxer shorts. She didn't give him much time to think about it as she began to tug off his T-shirt and then tossed it on the floor.

He smiled. Okay, so they were going to get naked, and he figured they were going to be intimate with each other. Though not all the way because for wolves that would amount to a mating for life. He slipped her shirt over her head and smiled at her leopard bra.

"Wild, huh? That's me."

He laughed. "Yeah, I knew that the moment you bit me when I was armed to the teeth, ready to arrest you—though the fact you were a wolf meant I had to do something else, truly." He ran his hand over her bra, squeezing her breasts gently, enjoying their softness in his grasp. Then he leaned over and kissed her mouth.

She quickly wrapped her arms around his neck and gave him a searing kiss on the lips, then delved deeper, her tongue ravishing his as if she had held back long enough. He could enjoy kissing her all day. He slid his hands around her back and fumbled to unfasten her bra. He felt it release, and he pulled the straps down her shoulders, off her arms, and then was able to caress her naked breasts. Full, luscious, making his arousal twitch with growing need.

She quickly toed off her shoes and he slid his off so he could unfasten her pants, then pull them down. He smiled to see her panties matched her leopard bra. She eagerly unfastened his belt and unzipped his pants, then tugged his pants down his legs until he stepped out of them. He yanked off his socks before she could free him from his boxer briefs. They'd already seen each other naked before they shifted to run as wolves, and of course when he'd seen her leaving the shower when he'd raided her home, but this experience was more intimate while they were undressing each other.

Once she pulled down his boxer briefs and he kicked them aside, he began kissing her again, wanting her to know it wasn't just all about the sex, but about showing the feelings he had for her, the admiration, caring, protectiveness... which made this all the more powerful to his way of thinking. He slid her panties down her legs, and she maneuvered out of them. As if she was afraid that he was waiting for her to take him to bed, to assure him that this was what she wanted too, she broke free from the kiss, pulled the covers aside, climbed onto the bed, and patted the mattress next to her.

"Come on. Let's do this," she said.

He smiled. Hell, yeah. He climbed onto the mattress, hoping he didn't look like too much of a hungry wolf and would cause Charlene to change her mind, but truth be told, she looked just as ravenous.

As soon as he was next to her, she rested her leg over his hip, exposing herself to him, telling him wordlessly what she wanted—at least he hoped—and he began to stroke her inviting clit while kissing her mouth with exuberance.

Their hearts beating wildly, she was kissing him back. She pressed her leg hard against his hip, her body tensing as he stroked her. Her hand was free to tweak his nipples and she moved her mouth to them, kissing and licking one and then the other. He felt an incredible rush of heat and passion that he'd never experienced before. Then she moved her mouth to his again, her tongue licking his lips and then tonguing him, her fingers combing through his hair, making him feel divine.

But then she was stopping, tensing, holding her breath, ready to shatter, he suspected. She closed her eyes and breathed out. "Oh, oh, yes, don't stop, keep going, yes, there, aww, Ethan."

He continued to stroke her for a few seconds, inserting a finger and feeling the tremors from her climax reverberating still deep inside her, and she smiled at him. "Wow. My turn."

"I'm ready."

She began to stroke him, kissing his mouth, their pheromones shouting to each other that they were so right for each other. Their hearts were still pumped up, the adrenaline shooting through their bloodstream, and he hadn't felt this good, free, and spontaneous, in a long time.

She continued to stroke him with finesse. She was just irresistible to him.

He was trying his darnedest to hold back, to enjoy her touch longer. Her strokes were doing him in, but before he could stop, he was coming. He exploded with climax, feeling on top of the world.

She smiled at him and kissed his mouth. "I could just send you to the shower to wash off, or I can come with you and clean you up," she said.

He laughed. "How can I resist an offer like that?"

They headed to the bathroom and started the shower, stepped in, and began soaping each other up. Now this was perfect. He'd never washed with a she-wolf in the shower. Never in the bathtub either, and she had one of those oversized ones that would be perfect for two.

For now, this was wonderful. Soaping each other up, kissing, laughing as she slapped suds on his chest, and they bubbled up and she poked them to pop the bubbles. He did the same to her, concentrating on the ones collecting on her nipples, which had her laughing hilariously. This was more than just sexy. It was fun too.

Then they got down to the business of washing up each other's private parts, and rinsing off, then toweling each other dry.

"I'll be in bed in a minute. I need to dry my hair, or I might get you all wet," she said.

"Truthfully, I don't mind at all. All I care about is that you and I are together like this. What a beautiful night."

"Oh, I agree."

"I'll take care of drying your hair for you." This was the first time he'd ever dried a woman's hair for her. He loved doing it for Charlene. Everything he did with her came so naturally. He already felt such a strong bond with her. He combed his fingers through her hair as he dried it, thinking how glorious it had felt when she had combed her fingers through his hair while he was stroking her to orgasm.

"Hmm, that feels really great. I'm going to have to have you do that every night, a great head massage."

He laughed. "I loved it when you did it to me."

"I'm so glad. You looked like you were loving it." Then she and he went to bed, and they immediately cuddled with each other. "This is so nice."

"Yeah, I agree. I'm so glad that you asked me to stay the night."

"Me too."

Then they got quiet, and he thought this was truly the best night he'd ever had.

Ohmigod, making love to Ethan had been monumental and sleeping with him was so nice. They woke a couple of times, kissed each other, and fell back to sleep, cuddling.

She hadn't even thought once about Noah coming here to have breakfast with them in the morning. She was glad for that. If Ethan hadn't been here with her, she might have.

She kissed Ethan and hugged him as he kissed her back and he said, "Hmm, so special."

"This is the nicest night ever."

"Yeah, I agree. Tomorrow we can watch the sunrise, then we'll have breakfast?"

"I would like that. I hope that Noah won't be a problem when he comes for breakfast," she said.

"He won't be."

She sure hoped Ethan was right about that.

CHAPTER 13

EARLY THAT MORNING, NOAH ARRIVED AT CHARLENE'S house to have breakfast with her and Ethan. He knew Charlene was nervous that Noah might start a fight, but Ethan had a lot of training in dealing with volatile situations like this and believed he could talk Noah down if he needed to. Still, they were two alpha wolves interested in the same she-wolf, so Ethan figured it could go either way. Noah could man up and accept he had lost out or not. Ethan was hoping that Leidolf and Cassie had put the fear of the wolf pack in him, and Noah would mind his manners. Ethan didn't want Charlene upset by any of this.

Ethan went to greet Noah, and the two wolves measured each other up right away. Noah was six two, so taller than Ethan by a couple of inches. Ethan's auburn hair was redder than Noah's. Noah's eyes were blue instead of hazel green like Ethan's. He stood tall, a little confrontational, then shook Ethan's hand. It was a powerful handshake, but not one that said he was trying to outdo Ethan, just attempting to match his strength, which Ethan appreciated.

Ethan had planned to treat Noah like a guest arriving at the house, while Ethan was the man of the household. It was the only way to establish territory and convey that to another male wolf. Of course, Ethan liked the idea that he would play that role with Charlene permanently, but he was doing this for her benefit in the meantime, so Noah would leave her alone.

Charlene had made herself scarce, getting the batter ready to make pancakes, while Ethan and Noah worked out this situation between themselves. Ethan finally stepped back to allow Noah entrance into the house.

To Ethan's amusement, Noah actually gave him a half-hearted smirk, as if acknowledging that Ethan had played the game just right—for a wolf.

"Hey, Noah," Charlene called out from the kitchen, "why don't you sit down at the table, and I'll serve up the breakfast in a minute."

Which meant she was telling him to keep his distance from her. Ethan waited for Noah to comply. He suspected Noah wanted to go into the kitchen and give her a hug or kiss or something, but then he glanced at Ethan, who was just standing there waiting for him to sit down at the table.

Noah finally sat on one of the chairs, and Ethan got everyone cups of coffee and then set the table. "I take it you brought some of your clothes with you to stay at the DEA rental house," Ethan said.

"Yeah. They're in the car."

"Okay, good." Ethan helped Charlene bring in the plates of pancakes and slices of ham and set them on the table.

Then Charlene sat down next to Ethan at the table across from Noah, showing him whose side she was on.

"This looks great, Charlene. Thanks for inviting me to have breakfast with you." Then Noah turned his attention to

Ethan. "I take it that Charlene knows you're not really retired from the department."

Ethan swore he brought the matter up to see if Charlene didn't know about it and then Ethan would be put on the spot with her in front of Noah. Before Ethan could say that she did know all about the situation, she spoke up.

"Yep, and I was going to help Ethan with his mission. He shouldn't be doing this on his own, so I'm glad you're going to be working with him on this." Charlene took a sip of her coffee.

"You're no longer a homicide detective," Noah reminded her.

"Right. No badge any longer, but I could still have helped Ethan with surveillance." She ate some more of her pancakes.

"The way we're going to work the living arrangements is that I'll be here with Charlene, and you'll stay at the rental," Ethan said.

Noah was about to take a bite of his ham, but his jaw dropped. Then he shook his head. "All right."

Ethan was glad the wolf was finally getting the point that Ethan was with Charlene and Noah had lost his chance with her back in Florida.

Ethan gave Noah some of the backstory on three of the men who were still at large. "Thor is a big dude. That's the name everyone calls him. He's Timothy Morton, but the guy is six five and more like a bear—black-bearded, black hair, eyes as black as coals, and he's the real muscle of the group. His father was abusive, a drunk, worked construction, and his mother died of cancer when Thor was ten. Thor had five siblings, all boys, all of them in trouble from time to time. With his big size, he intimidated everyone, even when he wasn't trying to, except for Kroner.

"Then we have Kroner—Jet Kroner—the leader of the drug gang. He's almost as big at six three. He calls all the shots. He had his own gang when he was in middle school, and he continued having the same gang through his school years and beyond. He has a good family—well-to-do. His father was a retired judge, his mother a retired dentist. He was a spoiled only child, got everything he ever wanted, but he wanted to make a name for himself on the dark side.

"Oakley is smart, cagey, a follower, but when Kroner isn't around, he takes charge. He has one sister who is a schoolteacher, his father is a minister, and his mother is busy with the church. But he feels closest to his great-aunt who adores him. He has a dark side to him as well.

"Benny Coates was just arrested. They had three other gang members, but they died during turf wars. Benny is relatively new to the gang by a few months. I believe he was hung out to dry, wanted to be like Kroner who took him in on a whim. But the guy was smart, streetwise, and a thug in his own right. I had hopes we could flip him to turn on Kroner and the others. There are others who work for Kroner, but they're small fries and we don't know their names."

Noah said, "Then there's the mole in the organization."

"Yeah, at least one. Kroner's the one who had my parents murdered," Ethan said. "And he's the one who shot me on this last mission."

"You're working on this case when it's personal for you?" Noah asked.

"Yeah. Grainger had a similar situation with his dad being gunned down when he was serving as a police officer. Grainger's boss let him track down the men who killed his father, so he's fine with me working this case. I have too much to lose by getting myself killed, so I'm not going to go all Rambo and try and take these men out without playing by the rules."

"Good to know. That's the same with me. Grainger said you're still recovering from the gunshot wound. How's that going?" Noah asked.

"It's healing." Though it would be doing better if Ethan hadn't gone cliff hanging when the bear charged them.

"But it's still bothering you."

"Yeah, but it won't get in the way of me doing the job."

Noah smiled a little at that and Ethan thought that's what Noah wanted to hear—that Ethan was a worthy partner, even if he was still suffering from a gunshot wound.

"So all four men are wanted for a number of murders, racketeering, drug running, you name it. The three we need to catch won't hesitate to shoot us." Ethan told Noah all about the great-aunt who lived in Oyster Bay and that they needed to go there before church services to see if they could capture Oakley.

"Grainger said you weren't supposed to try and take any of these men down on your own," Noah said, then ate the rest of his pancakes. "That you're supposed to call it in."

"Right. That was before you arrived to help me out. The

rest of the team is three hours away. They might not get here in time to take the gang members down if we find them, and then they could get spooked and disappear again. And there's still a mole in the organization, I believe. So if he got word that we were gunning for Oakley, he could just give him a call and warn him."

Ethan told Noah about the botched cases where the four men always seemed to get word that the DEA was on their way to grab them. He also told him about the clerical error that caused Kroner to be released back out into the public and the case Adam and Tori were working on that might be a homicide that Kroner had something to do with.

"What do you think about all this?" Noah asked Charlene.

"I'm ready to help you both out if you need my assistance." She finished her coffee. "And I hope you learn who the mole is and take him or her down."

"Yeah, I want to deal with that too," Noah said. "Someone like that can get a lot of the good guys hurt."

"I agree." Then Ethan got a call from his boss. "Yes, sir."

Grainger asked, "Are you meeting with Noah?"

Ethan glanced at Noah. "Uh, yeah. Noah's here and we're discussing how we're going to handle this. I'll let him know. Thanks. Out here." Ethan put his phone back on the dining room table. "That was Grainger. He said that the clerk was paid to make the clerical error in Kroner's favor so he would be released. She has been arrested for her part in the crime."

"Hell," Noah said.

"I know. I hope she realizes what she has done if Kroner is responsible for yet another murder," Ethan said.

"What about this mole in the department?" Noah asked.

Charlene got everyone refills on their coffee. She seemed relaxed with them speaking about the case and not talking about her dating Ethan any longer, and he was glad.

"I'm not sure who it could be. There are six to ten of us who go on these various missions, augmented by local law enforcement. It's even possible it could be someone in the Portland Police Bureau who's involved in leaking the planned raids to the men we are after."

"But the last time you went after these guys, you went to the wrong house, and then you managed to go to the right house and catch two of the men. Was anyone on vacation when it happened, or out sick who didn't know about the actual timing of the raid and that's how you managed to capture the two men?" Noah asked.

"Grainger is looking into it. On the police end, Adam and Tori, who are both red wolves—"

"I met them. They came by to see me because they're part of the wolf pack and knew I was taking over your job. They said they were thrilled another wolf was going to be working with them." Noah sounded pleased that he'd made some friends already.

Ethan was glad that he had. A new wolf was welcome if he or she contributed to the pack. "That's great. They're good folks."

"Adam and his mate, Sierra, and Tori had me over for dinner last night," Noah continued.

"That's great. So the two of them are looking into who might be a mole in their bureau. They are homicide detectives, so they don't go on the drug raids with me normally. Though when we have an issue having to do with wolves, we all stick together. And if I'm working on a case that has to do with a murder, we all work on it together. Adam and Tori have access to information about who's working what jobs and who's off on vacation, that sort of thing, at the bureau. So they'll be looking into it. Covington, their boss, is great to work for. He's aware of the fact one or both of the departments might have a mole, but we're keeping it just between us for now until we can find the culprit."

"Okay, good. I'm at a bit of a disadvantage coming into the job from out of state and not knowing anyone," Noah said.

"Yeah, but that's what makes it perfect. You haven't been involved in any of the shenanigans in the department, not to mention you're a wolf and we trust you for that reason alone," Ethan said. "I'm sure that also helped you to secure your job."

"Renault put in a good word for me too. I'm glad I can be here to help you out."

Ethan thought Noah was having a real change of heart about him and Charlene. He was glad about it. He could use a good partner on this last mission. He noticed that Noah was glancing surreptitiously at Charlene, but she was ignoring him completely, appearing not to want to give him the idea that she felt anything for him any longer.

"Grainger said that you'll take the lead on this mission because you're from here and know the players. He also told me not to tell anyone in the department that I'm out here with you working on the case since you're supposed to be retired," Noah said.

"Not even Renault," Ethan said, knowing the two of them were good buddies. "Not that Renault is anything but one of the good guys, but if he accidentally let it slip up that we're doing this together, whoever the mole is might get the word."

"Yeah, not even Renault," Noah said. "Everyone believes I'm not starting the job for a few weeks to get moved and settled in. I had lunch with Renault yesterday afternoon. I told him I had found a house and purchased it in Portland, but that I had to return to Destin to sell my house and get my household goods ready to move. Which is why it worked out well that I'm living in Oyster Bay with you so that I don't run into anyone that I'll be working with in Portland. I didn't even tell Adam and Tori what I was doing, not realizing that they knew just what you were doing out here."

"Okay, good. Adam, Sierra, Tori, our pack leaders and a few other wolves know, just in case we need some additional support," Ethan said.

"Oh, that's good to know."

They finished eating breakfast and Charlene and Ethan cleared the dishes from the table. He started soaking the pan that Charlene had used to make the pancakes. "I'll take care of that after it soaks."

Ethan noticed Noah watching their interactions, the way Charlene was smiling at him, helping him put things away, touching him in little intimate caresses. Nothing passionate, but just enough to show she really cared about him and that

Noah didn't stand a chance to date her. Maybe they could be friends, but not in an intimate way.

Ethan wondered if Noah had ever helped her with cleaning up after meals, or if he left it to her to manage if she made meals for them. He shouldn't have cared about their past relationship, but he wasn't used to dating a woman whose boyfriend still wanted to be with her, and he certainly wasn't used to befriending a girlfriend's ex and working with him. Not only that, but Ethan really wanted to measure up in Charlene's eyes and prove to her, and to Noah, that he had what it took to make her happy.

"Did you ever date Tori?" Noah suddenly asked Ethan.

If he was trying to create dissension between Ethan and Charlene, it wasn't going to happen. "Yes. When she first arrived, she dated quite a few bachelor males, including me. We've worked together, socialized at the wolf pack gatherings, and she's a great woman, but we just don't have that spark that wolves have when they know they're with the one they really want to be with for a lifetime."

Noah nodded. "She seems really nice. Maybe I'll ask her out on a date when I get back to the Portland area after this mission."

"It wouldn't hurt to try," Ethan said. Though if Noah did start dating Tori, he hoped he wouldn't treat her the same way as he'd treated Charlene. Then again, Ethan could not imagine Tori putting up with it either. But maybe Noah would change and realize that, when he had some competition, he might just have to work harder at keeping the she-wolf.

"So Sunday is our first real attempt at taking these guys down," Noah said, sounding eager to get it done.

"Yeah. Charlene and I checked out his great-aunt's place." Ethan showed him pictures of the house and surrounding area, and of the church where Oakley took her on occasion. "Now, we don't know for sure if he'll be taking her to church that day. I'm sure it will be hit or miss, but hopefully we'll get a break and it'll go smoothly."

"What about Shelby Bay?"

"We drove by the home Oakley's been seen at, but we didn't see any sign of him. There was a car parked there that belonged to a Clara Snyder though." Ethan explained what they had learned about her.

"Okay, that sounds like we're getting somewhere with this. What about putting some surveillance on the house in Shelby Bay?" Noah asked.

"We could do that. What about tonight? About two in the morning? What about using your vehicle this time? I have one that's a loaner that no one knows. My own car is at Adam and Sierra's home."

"Yeah, no one knows mine either. I bought it when I got here so I didn't have to drive my rust bucket all the way across country."

"Okay, good. If you're ready now, we can go to the house. I'll pack my clothes and you can get settled in," Ethan said.

"That sounds good to me." Noah said to Charlene, "Good to see you again, and glad you found what you're looking for, but I still want us to be friends."

"Of course," Charlene said and smiled at him, the first time she had done so since he had arrived.

Then he left the house and Ethan gave her a hug and a kiss. "I'll be back in a little while."

"I'll make some room for your clothes. I never envisioned having to share space with a wolf so I'm hogging everything."

He smiled. "Well, I can use one of the guest bedroom closets, if you have room for clothes in there. Anything will work for me as long as I get to stay with you." He hoped he didn't sound too desperate to stay with her or she might think he wasn't alpha enough.

She smiled at him. "We'll work it out. It will be no problem at all." Then she kissed him back and whispered, probably worried Noah might be just outside and could hear them, "It looks like Noah has come around."

Ethan kept his voice low too. "Yeah, I think so. I'll see you in about an hour or sooner." He sure hoped she didn't change her mind about him staying with her. Both of them had lived alone, so living with each other might take some getting used to.

"Okay. That sounds good."

Then Ethan left to get this done, thrilled with the way things were working out between Noah and him and with Charlene even more so. He had thought they might invite Noah over for some meals as a means of wolf camaraderie, but Ethan really needed this time to get to know Charlene better too.

CHAPTER 14

Charlene was so thrilled to get everything moved around so Ethan would feel welcome in her home. She headed for her bedroom first to move her clothes and give Ethan equal space in her closet and dressers. She had a great big master bedroom closet so she'd just spread out all her clothes in there. She would have to squeeze things up a bit, but it was easy to do and still left them plenty of room to both share the closet.

She was sure glad Noah had behaved himself at breakfast and kept the conversation on the mission. He seemed happy that the pack was taking him in and that he'd made friends with some of the pack members already. She was thrilled Ethan had come into her life.

After she finished sorting through her drawers and cleaning out some of them, she heard a car pull up in her driveway. Ethan was back already. She figured he might talk to Noah for a while, but she guessed he just wanted to be with her instead, which pleased her to no end.

She opened the front door and headed outside to help him carry in his bags of clothes. "You returned quickly."

"Yeah, I just packed everything up while Noah was unpacking his stuff. He hadn't brought a whole lot of clothes. He said that he would stay in one of the guest bedrooms in case you needed to have your space and sent me packing. Then I would stay in the master bedroom again."

"He didn't say that."

"Yep." Ethan had a twinkle in his eye.

She laughed. "I guess he's hoping it will be so." She carried some of the bags of clothes in and set them on the carpeted floor in her master bedroom suite.

"Are you sure you want me to bring all my..." He peeked into the closet. "Oh, it looks like there will be plenty of room for the two of us."

"There is." She began hanging up his suits that were already on hangers in the closet. "You can organize your clothes any way that you want, but I'll just hang them up for now so they don't get wrinkled." Then she showed him the drawers he could use for the clothes he wanted to fold away. "I'm going to move some of my toiletries out of the drawers in the bathroom to free up some space in there too."

"Okay." He continued to put his clothes away until the bedroom was clean again.

"While Noah is working here with you, I was thinking we might have him over for a meal occasionally," Charlene said from the adjacent bathroom. "Since he's on his own and doesn't have anyone to talk to, I thought it would be kind of nice. Maybe he could even go for a wolf run with us, once you're healed up."

"I thought of that too, but for now, I want to spend the time with you."

She smiled. "You're still worried about him trying to get on my good side and win me over. You don't have to worry about it."

He called out, "Hey, are these pictures of you and your family?"

She returned to the bedroom and picked up one of her favorites off her dresser top. "We were at the beach in Destin."

"Beautiful. Your family, the beach, the water. I can see why your family loved it there."

"But crowded. Do you see how many people are on the beach? As soon as it warmed up, tons of tourists invaded it."

He laughed. "Can I help you hang it up?"

She hesitated. "Uh, sure." She went and got a hammer and a picture hanger, and then he held the picture up on different walls until she picked the place she wanted to hang it. A special place over an antique chest in the living room—her mother's favorite piece of furniture.

"Thanks." She appreciated him for helping her to decide where the picture would go and that he understood how important her family was to her. "After lunch, do you want to take a walk on the beach?"

"Yeah, I'm all for it."

They checked the tide schedule, then dressed for the walk. Ethan carried the backpack, and they headed down the stairs to the beach. What was fun about her beach was that it was practically private, rocks jutting out into the ocean keeping other beach walkers from reaching the area below her home except maybe during low tide.

"Ohmigod, look at these huge mussel shells filled with brightly colored, juvenile, ochre starfish and baby gooseneck barnacles that look almost pearl-like. They're beautiful." Charlene began taking pictures of them. "Isn't that the most stunning thing you have ever seen?"

"Besides you and seeing your enthusiasm at seeing such a sight? Yeah, it is truly magnificent."

"Coming down here with you and seeing this has made my day."

"I can see living here will be a really great experience," Ethan said.

"For sure." After taking a ton of pictures, she and Ethan began checking more tidal pools, but they didn't see anything as spectacular as the mussels filled with small starfish.

They spent a good two hours on the beach, just enjoying the water, listening to the sound of the breakers, and feeling the sun shining through the clouds. Then they headed back to the house.

"Do you want to go to the Fort Stevens State Park and see the shipwreck of the *Peter Iredale*? It's only an hour away from here," Charlene asked.

"Yeah, I would love to. I figure when we can't do our surveillance, we can enjoy some trips close by."

"Okay, let's go."

He loved that about Charlene. She was eager and ready to do things at a moment's notice, just like he would be. Flexible. Fun-loving. "Do you have an ice chest? We can take some cold bottles of water and snacks in case—"

"We get lost in the woods?"

He laughed. "In case we get hungry or thirsty."

"I have an ice chest and we can take backpacks in case we get lost in the woods—but together."

He smiled. "It's a deal."

They were already dressed for hiking, so they gathered some

snacks, bottled waters, and the ice chest filled with ice, then drove to the park. He enjoyed every moment he was spending with Charlene. It was like taking a mini-vacation with her every day.

When they finally reached the park, they didn't have too far walk to see the shipwreck. It was just beyond the parking lot and the tide was still low so they could walk out to it. They looked up the description and discovered it had been a four-masted steel sailing vessel from England.

Charlene gave Ethan an abbreviated account of it. "A sudden squall forced the *Peter Iredale* onto the beach on a foggy morning. The ship has been rusting on the shore for almost 120 years." She looked at the rusty frame of the hull. "After all that time and with the salty water washing over it, it's amazing that any of it is still here."

"I know. It's iconic. I'm glad they didn't remove it."

"Yeah, me too. Though there were several parties who wanted it for salvage. Coming here makes for the perfect date," Charlene said.

Ethan had her stand in front of the vessel and took a picture of her and it, but then he took one of them together. After taking several more pictures of the vessel, they walked to a Civil War military installation that had been guarding the mouth of the Columbia River up through World War II. Then they hiked two miles around Coffenbury Lake and saw the South Jetty observation tower where visitors used to see views of the Columbia River.

"This is just so neat," she said, holding Ethan's hand.

"Yeah, this is great." With Charlene especially.

They walked another trail through the park and then

finally got into his car and headed back to the house. He was glad he hadn't been shot in the leg! He wished he could go running with her as a wolf again. Maybe tonight.

"Ribs for dinner?" Ethan carried the ice chest into the house and then emptied it.

"Yeah, that would be good."

"I was thinking we could run as wolves after dinner."

She set their backpacks on the table and gave him a serious look. "Your arm needs to heal up more. Besides, we got lots of exercise today. I was thinking of watching a movie. Since you have to leave at two in the morning for your stakeout, we'll go to bed early."

He pulled her into his arms and kissed her soundly. "You just want to go to bed early because—"

"Hmm, yeah. You caught me."

He chuckled and they kissed each other again.

Then they made dinner and sat outside to eat. "I love your view," he said.

"It's like having the most special seat at a restaurant, though when it's chillier out, we can enjoy indoor seating and we'll have the same great view."

"And we won't have to tip the hostess to get the best seats in the house."

She laughed. "You're right."

They ate their meal, then went inside to have hot cocoa and enjoy the movie, settling down in the living room together on one of the couches, snuggling, watching a science-fiction thriller where a teen could make others see things that weren't there.

"Now that would be a cool power to have," Charlene said. "Especially for criminal pursuits."

"Yeah, you could take down criminals. What if you could make them think that you were one of the bad guys so they would spill the beans to you, and then you could just arrest them without anyone shooting you."

He smiled. "That would come in handy."

"You could make the bad guys think they were armed with bananas instead of guns."

Ethan laughed. "You would be a handful if you had a power like that."

"You had better believe it." She kissed him and sighed. "I love that we can pick this up whenever we want to."

"Hmm?"

She began kissing his mouth. "Let's finish the movie sometime later. I'm thoroughly enjoying it, but I just keep thinking of something I would rather do with you right now. You have to get up early and we need to make our own kind of magic together."

"I'm always up for that."

"I noticed."

He turned off the TV, she raced off down the hallway, and he chased her into the bedroom to make love.

Ethan had set his phone alarm to go off twenty minutes before Noah was to arrive at two in the morning. When the time came, he kissed a sleepy Charlene. She kissed him back and wrapped her arms around him. "Good luck on your surveillance and don't let Noah give you any guff."

Ethan chuckled. "I won't. Get some sleep. I'll join you later." Then he left the bed, dressed, and made some coffee to fill his thermos.

He heard Noah's car drive up and quickly went to the door to wave at Noah to let him know he was about ready. He didn't want Noah to ring the doorbell or knock on the door and wake Charlene if she had managed to fall back asleep. He grabbed his backpack, his thermos, and his gun, then headed out to Noah's car.

Noah was also armed with a thermos of coffee. "Morning."

"Morning. Surveillance is one of the jobs I dislike the most." Ethan shut the car door and buckled in.

"Yeah, me too. Lots of sitting and waiting and not much in the line of results. But sometimes we hit the jackpot."

"I agree."

"Aren't you going to miss this kind of work once you're done with this mission?" Noah asked as he drove them to Shelby Bay.

"I had thought I might. Solving crimes. Bringing in the bad guys. Testifying against them. Now that I have Charlene in my life, no. I'm so glad to be here." That was the truth and Noah might not want to hear it, but Ethan had to be honest about it, though he didn't want to rub it in that he was with Charlene and Noah wasn't.

"Now that I'm in the new job, I'll probably work there for about a decade."

"Yeah, as long as we live, it helps to move to a new job on

occasion so no one notices that we aren't aging like regular humans," Ethan said.

"True." Noah finally reached Shelby Bay and drove by Oakley's house. He found a good place to park so they could watch the house surreptitiously.

Then they sat in silence and immediately saw a car drive by. At this time of morning, it was quiet, except for the lone car. It drove to Oakley's house and Ethan and Noah perked up.

"It's not the car we saw before," Ethan said.

"Buying drugs or delivering them maybe. Watch for a license plate number."

"Got it. Red Chevrolet Camaro." Ethan called it in to Tori because he didn't want to alert anyone in the department that he and Noah were working on the case.

"Oh man, it's two thirty in the morning. I was sound asleep," Tori said.

"Yeah, I know, but you love it." Ethan gave Tori the make and model and license plate number on the vehicle. "Thanks, I appreciate it." He knew she loved helping him. She was a good trooper. "Hey, hold on. Here's another." A blue Kia Rio drove up. The Camaro had already driven off. He gave her the number to the other one.

"I take it you're doing surveillance," Tori said.

"Yeah, with Noah. We're at Oakley's house."

"Okay, well, I'm looking into this. Just call me if you have any other license plate numbers."

"Will do." Then they ended their call.

"You have a good working relationship with Tori," Noah said.

"Yeah, we need Tori and Adam, and Sierra too, as part of our law enforcement team. Of course Grainger doesn't know I'm using them as a resource because of the mole we think is in the organization."

"That's really helpful. I've never worked with wolves before on the job."

"If you like socializing with other wolves at all, you'll love going to the pack activities at the ranch. You'll meet other single she-wolves too."

They watched as more cars stopped by the house. They would go inside for a few minutes and leave again. Tori sounded really tired the last time Ethan had to call her, but she was getting the information back to him about each of the car owners.

"Oh no," Tori said. "That last car? It belongs to Renault."

"No way," Ethan said.

Noah frowned at Ethan. "He couldn't be the mole. Maybe he's investigating the situation on his own."

"I can't believe it either. But hell, he's known about all the missions I've been on."

"He was with you on the mission when you raided Charlene's house. You caught two of the guys. If Renault had been a mole, he would have made sure that both Kroner and Benny weren't caught," Noah said.

"I know. That's puzzling. Then again, Benny was new to the gang and Kroner still was released." Ethan couldn't believe Renault would be down here on his own, trying to catch these guys. Grainger wouldn't have sent him without telling Ethan. Ethan planned to just watch the perp's house and then share the information with his boss. He sure wouldn't be knocking at a dangerous perp's door on his own without a whole backup team. "Why did Renault move from Florida to Oregon?"

"He said he wanted a change of pace. Like me, he was from Florida. His family had broken up when he was a kid and he'd been on his own since he was sixteen. So he worked really hard to finally make his way up the ranks and become a DEA special agent. I just can't imagine him working with them." Noah sounded shook up that his friend could be involved with these guys.

"We'll have to approach this situation with caution. He may not be in league with them." Even so, Ethan would be wary of Renault until they knew for sure what was going on with him.

"I agree. I would hate to lose a good friendship by accusing him wrongly of being a mole in the department. On the other hand, I'm damn glad I didn't tell Renault what I was doing and where I would be," Noah said.

"Yeah, I'm doubly glad for that."

When there was no further action after two hours of surveillance, they finally went home. "Hey, don't worry about your buddy. We'll figure out what's going on." Ethan was really concerned about Noah and how he felt about his friend. He didn't want him worrying about it until they could investigate the matter further and learn the truth.

"Thanks." Noah sounded appreciative that Ethan genuinely cared how he felt. "In the morning, we'll be camping near the great-aunt's house an hour before church, right?"

"Yeah, why don't you come by and eat breakfast with us in a couple of hours? And then you and I will head out."

"Are you sure?"

"Yeah, just get some sleep for the next couple of hours and we'll do this."

"All right. Thanks."

"See you in a little bit." Ethan grabbed his thermos and backpack.

"See you." Then Noah drove off and Ethan headed into the house.

He left his thermos in the kitchen, his backpack on the table, and headed for the bedroom, eager to rejoin Charlene. He put his gun in the bedside table drawer on his side of the bed, then slipped into bed with her, hoping he wouldn't wake her, but she quickly pulled him into her arms.

"I treasure being with you. You make every moment special," he said, kissing her, not having wanted her to stay awake for him, but he would have done the same for her, had their roles been reversed.

"I feel the same way about the time I've spent with you. I've never trusted or cared for anyone like I care about you." She caressed his face, her touch loving and gentle, welcome.

"The feeling is mutual. I feel safe with you."

She chuckled and kissed him. "When I'm not biting you."

He smiled. "You know I'm falling in love with you."

"Oh, yeah, you're definitely making me feel the same way about you."

He hugged her and nuzzled his face against hers. "We're having breakfast with Noah in the morning before we go to the great-aunt's house to see if we can take Oakley down. We'll have breakfast at six."

"Hmm, okay."

And that was the end of talking for the rest of the morning, knowing they needed to get some sleep so they could function for the next part of their mission. He would tell her about Renault when they woke.

CHAPTER 15

Charlene was so relieved when Ethan returned to sleep with her. She'd had a devil of a time getting back to sleep after he had left because she missed his comforting cuddles. She was dying to know what he and Noah had seen while they were on surveillance, but she knew they had to sleep too so she had kept the talking to a minimum once Ethan returned to bed.

She woke to find Ethan had already left the bed and was in the kitchen making coffee. She hurried to dress and joined him, hugging and kissing him. "Good morning, you," she said to him.

"Good morning, honey. So would eggs and ham be all right to fix? I probably need to go to the grocery store and pick up some more groceries. I left the food I had bought at the house for Noah so he would be all set up."

"That was sweet of you. Eggs and ham for breakfast will be great to have."

"Last night, one of the cars that arrived at Oakley's house was Renault's."

"No way. Are you sure it was him? Maybe someone else was driving his car." Charlene just couldn't imagine that Noah's friend was the mole in the organization. He always seemed really nice. But for the right price or even blackmail, an agent could be turned. "Oh, poor Noah. He must be angry or upset about it."

"He was kind of quiet once he learned of it. I hope he doesn't confront Renault about it, trying to discover if Renault is involved with these guys. I just don't want either of us to jump to the wrong conclusions."

"I agree." She poured cups of coffee for them.

"I hear Noah's car pulling up now. Hey, after we do this, no matter the outcome, I'm ready to return home and take a nap with you."

She laughed. "Yeah, wolfish naps are the best. Especially if you have a cuddly wolf to snuggle with. I couldn't wait for you to return home to me so we could spoon each other again after your surveillance mission."

He smiled. "The feeling was mutual. Being at home with you in bed was preferable to drinking coffee in Noah's car with him and collecting license plate numbers of all the vehicles that dropped by Oakley's house. Poor Tori. I kept her awake for most of the time we were doing surveillance, feeding her all the plate numbers so she could track down who owned them."

"But nobody you were looking for dropped by?" Charlene set the table for breakfast for the three of them while Ethan went to get the door for Noah.

"Unfortunately not or we would have taken them in right then and there." Ethan opened the front door before Noah could knock. "Good morning. I told Charlene what we learned last night. I hope you got some sleep."

"I did, though I was still perturbed about the situation with Renault. But you were right. We have to just put that on the back burner and deal with these other guys, then sort out what's going on with him," Noah said, walking into the dining room with Ethan. "Morning, Charlene."

"Morning, Noah. I hope you're not as tired as I am," she said, "and I didn't even stay up as long as you guys did."

"I know you were worried about us," Noah said, though he gave her a wink like he didn't really mean she was worried about him, just about Ethan.

"Of course I was. I know you dodge bullets well, but Ethan?" She smiled at Ethan.

Ethan chuckled. "Okay, ham and eggs. Or omelets with grated cheese?" He took over the kitchen to prepare breakfast.

"Ham and eggs," both Noah and Charlene said.

She was impressed. She figured she was going to be making breakfast for the guys again, which was fine with her. They had a job to do. She could relax for the rest of the day. Well, sort of. She would be worried about Ethan and Noah while they carried out their mission today.

Once they finished breakfast, she said, "I'll clean up. You guys be safe."

"We will be," Ethan said. Then he kissed her. "I'm not going to be quiet about it any longer. I have to tell you that I love you, honey."

She smiled brightly at him and hugged him tight. "I love you too and I didn't want to wait any longer to say it either." It was so easy to say that to Ethan. Though she had planned to reveal it to him when he returned to her to take a nap.

She realized that she and Noah had never said they loved each other, but with Ethan, it came so naturally, and she really meant it. She thought Noah had already left, but he was standing near the front door watching them.

He smiled a little but didn't seem to be offended or upset about it. She was glad because she wanted to be friends with him. As *lupus garous* belonging to such an exclusive and small group of people, it was important.

She and Ethan kissed each other again and the guys left, and she cleaned up the kitchen. Later, she heard someone pull up in the drive. It wasn't Noah's car, so she wasn't sure who it could be. She peered out the window and saw it was Renault. *Ohmigod, what was he doing here?*

She took a deep settling breath and called Ethan, hoping he wasn't in the middle of a bad situation. "Hey, Ethan, I hope I'm not interrupting anything."

"No. We've been watching to see if Oakley arrives at his great-aunt's house, but he hasn't yet. We'll keep observing to see if he arrives or if his great-aunt goes to church on her own. What's going on there?" Ethan sounded like he was concerned something might be wrong.

She was glad he was intuitive like that. "Renault just drove up to my house."

"Shit."

"He's not going to hurt me. He doesn't know that I know about him parking his car at Oakley's house. I just wanted to make you aware that he's here. He's still sitting in his car."

"You be careful with him," Ethan said, sounding worried about her.

"I've got this." She wouldn't have worried Ethan, but

she didn't want him being upset with her if she hadn't told him that Renault had come by and something had gone wrong.

"Okay, well, you call if you have any trouble at all."

"I will. Love you."

"Love you too, honey," Ethan said.

Then she answered the knock at the door and smiled brightly at Renault. "Well, this is a pleasant surprise. To what do I owe the pleasure?"

"I was in the area, and I wanted to come by and see you."

"Come in. Do you want some coffee?"

"Yeah, sure. That will be great. You have a nice place here." He walked over to the windows that looked out on the deck and the Pacific Ocean. "Beautiful."

"Yeah, I love it here. It's been so nice, and it'll be fun to see it during the different seasons."

"For sure."

"Let's sit out on the deck and have our coffee," she said.

"Perfect."

They settled on a couple of chairs on the back deck and drank their coffee.

"So the reason why I'm here is that I wanted to apologize to you for not telling you the truth."

About the roses he'd sent her, she thought. "Oh?"

"Yeah, I um, sent the roses to you."

She smiled. "Well, that was sweet of you."

He sighed. "I never thought Ethan would win you over."

She laughed. "We just hit it off from the very beginning."

"When we raided your place, that was the first time you

had met him?" Renault sounded like he couldn't believe they would be that enamored with each other that quickly.

"Yeah." She sipped her coffee. "Well, thanks for the roses. They were lovely."

"I bet Ethan didn't bring you any."

"He did." She laughed. "Twice as many. But yours were beautiful too. Why did you send them to me anonymously? That's what I couldn't understand." Except that she knew he was a beta male.

"I knew Noah had gotten Ethan's job. Then here you were at the house we raided, and he hadn't said anything at all about you already being in Portland. So I assumed he and you had split up. I called him and asked, and he said no. I knew you would have moved there together if you had still been a couple."

"Okay, but the other thing that puzzles me is why did you send the flowers to me when we live so far away from each other? I mean, it would be impossible to date much," she said.

"Yeah, but I knew you and I've always liked you and I wanted to see if we could make it work. Noah didn't appreciate you like I did. Maybe you would have even wanted to return to Portland to be with me if things had worked out between us."

She smiled. "Do you want another cup of coffee?"

"Yeah, sure. I would love some. I...kind of thought Ethan might be here."

She sensed something was going on with Renault, but he was having a hard time coming out with it. "He went to get some groceries. I called him to tell him you were here. He said he would try to see you before you leave. But he's also running some other errands, setting up his bank account, and other stuff."

"Oh, seeing Ethan would be great." Renault smelled a little nervous about the prospect of meeting up with Ethan at her house.

Maybe he was afraid Ethan wouldn't like it if he knew Renault was visiting her alone when he had sent her the flowers. She was thinking that this might be a great way for Ethan to talk to him and maybe get at the root of what was going on with Renault without tipping his hand. Noah would have to go to the DEA house and stay there without Renault seeing him though.

"Let me text Ethan to see if he wants to have lunch with you. I know he would love to connect with you since you worked so close together."

"Okay, yeah, that would be great," Renault said.

She thought Renault might say he had to run, so she was surprised when he agreed to it.

"Great." She texted Ethan then. Having lunch with you and Renault at the house. He's eager to see you. You're out running errands, grocery shopping, setting up a bank account.

Ethan texted back: Okay, my car is in your garage, but Noah can take me grocery shopping and I can bring some home. What do we need?

She gave him a list. Get one of those roasted whole chickens. We can make mashed potatoes and green beans to go with it for lunch.

Ethan texted: Got it. No luck here. Great-aunt went to church with a couple of women. No sign of Oakley.

Charlene texted: Okay, see you when we see you. Stay safe.

You too.

"Okay, Ethan is picking up a roasted chicken so you can have lunch with us."

"It's not really too much trouble, is it? I don't want to put the two of you out in any way." Renault sounded like he didn't want to get on Ethan's bad side.

"Nope, not at all. He's eager to see you. So how about if we go for a walk on the beach. I'll just let Ethan know where we've gone to if he gets home before we do." She wanted to let Ethan know that she and Renault wouldn't be home so Ethan could "sneak" into her house while she and Renault were gone. Otherwise, Renault might wonder how come he didn't hear Ethan's car return to the house. Not that Renault was a wolf and could hear things like they could as wolves. But the rumbling sound of a garage door opening, or lack thereof, was another story.

Charlene texted Ethan: We're walking on the beach so you can drop by the house anytime you want. I'll let you know when we return.

Ethan texted back: Good plan. We'll try to hurry. We're almost to the grocery store and then Noah can drop me off at the house.

She texted: Perfect.

She grabbed her backpack and added a couple of bottles of water. "Are you ready, Renault?"

"Yeah. I haven't been to the Oregon coast to walk on the beach before, so I look forward to it."

"Then you're in for a treat." She took him down to the tide pools where she'd taken Ethan before. Sure, it was special to do this with Ethan, but she was on a mission to make sure that Ethan could get home with the groceries without Renault catching him arriving home with Noah. That would take a lot of explaining.

CHAPTER 16

"Why the hell is Renault seeing Charlene at her house?" Noah asked Ethan as if he was still dating her as soon as Ethan told him what was happening.

Ethan said, "I don't know. I'll see if I can learn what he was doing in Shelby Bay."

"Just be careful. We don't want to tip him off that we know he has had contact at that home."

"Yeah, I will be. I was disappointed that we weren't able to catch any sign of Oakley at his great-aunt's house, but I knew his turning up there could be a long shot."

"I agree. It can take weeks to take these guys down, so I'm not giving up hope," Noah said.

Ethan was glad that they were working together when he hadn't been totally sure in the beginning.

They arrived at the grocery store and hurried through it to pick up all the groceries they both needed. "How about if I grill steaks at the DEA house tomorrow night for the three of us?" Noah asked.

"That sounds like a great idea." Ethan liked that Noah was trying to really develop some wolf camaraderie with them.

They paid for their groceries and then Noah drove Ethan back home. "Okay, good luck with your quest concerning Renault."

"Thanks, I'm hopeful we'll learn what he was doing, and

we can clear him of being a suspect." Ethan carried the groceries into the house while Noah drove off.

Ethan texted Charlene: I'm home with the groceries. I'm just putting them away so no rush on coming home. Just do it when it feels natural.

It took Charlene a while to text him back and she finally said: Okay. The tide's coming in so it's perfect timing for us to return. We'll probably arrive in about twenty minutes.

He texted: Perfect.

He finished putting away the groceries. Then he started peeling the potatoes, slicing them up, and boiling them. Afterward, he began frying the green beans.

Before long, he heard Charlene talking to Renault as she was coming up the steps to the back deck.

Ethan went to the back door to greet them. "Hey, Renault, good to see you." He shook his hand. "Have you been missing me?"

"Yeah. Frankly, I have been. You were great at the job. Have you been missing the job?" Renault asked.

Ethan laughed and pulled Charlene into a hug. "No. Not at all."

Renault smiled. "I can see where she would make you feel differently about working at the office any longer. All I've got to say is Noah really missed out."

Charlene smiled. "He'll do great finding someone he's a whole lot more into than he was with me. It's all good. Hmm, lunch smells delicious."

"So what brings you around here?" Ethan asked Renault.

"Well, if Charlene hadn't told you yet, I came to apologize

to her for not telling her I had sent the roses anonymously. She said you beat me by bringing two dozen."

Ethan laughed. "Yeah, but your delivery beat my arrival at her house."

Renault smiled, looking more lighthearted now that he'd come clean about the flowers with both Charlene and Ethan. Renault even helped Charlene set the table and brought everyone glasses of ice water.

"That wasn't the only reason I came here—I mean, to apologize to Charlene. I kind of have a situation at work. Since you're no longer there, but I know you well enough to realize you weren't sabotaging our missions, I was trying to catch who might be the one responsible," Renault said, sounding as serious as could be.

"That's a dangerous thing to do on your own," Ethan said. At least Ethan had Tori and Adam's backup if he had really needed them to intervene while he was in Portland.

"It's just as dangerous for all of us on the force if we have someone in the department who is on the take," Renault said.

"True." Ethan brought in the roasted chicken while Charlene got the bowl of mashed potatoes and Renault dished up the green beans. "So what do you have in mind doing? Is Grainger sanctioning this?"

"I asked Grainger if I could surreptitiously learn who might be involved. The boss said not just no, but hell no. He said I was too valuable to lose." Renault sat down at the table and forked up some of the chicken Ethan had carved up.

"He's probably right about that. Do you have any suspects? Anyone who seems suspicious?"

"Agents Pete Cohen and Manx Ryerson."

Ethan glanced at Charlene. She raised her brows.

"They were with us on the raid at Charlene's house, but I checked the roster and both of them were on five of the raids where we took heavy fire. We had kept the mission plan secret except for just a few key players. So neither of the agents had a lot of time to get the word out if they were involved in this. They only had enough time really to warn them we were at the door, ready to knock it down." Renault dished up some green beans and mashed potatoes.

Ethan thought about those missions as he ate one of the drumsticks. "Okay, so two of our agents were wounded on three of those raids."

"Right. So I would discount the men who were injured because they were right in the line of fire, pushing forward, trying to take down the perps. Even I got winged on that first job."

"Yeah, I remember that."

"Hell," Renault said, "if you hadn't been there for me, I would have died."

"We got lucky."

"Did any of your men die?" Charlene added butter to her potatoes.

"No, but we had enough injuries that might not have occurred if someone hadn't warned the drug dealers before we bashed in their doors," Renault said.

"True. I figured a good way to narrow down the search was to discount anyone who had been out sick, injured, or on vacation because they wouldn't have been aware of our missions," Ethan said.

"Exactly. Not once did Cohen or Ryerson take any bullets. In fact, I couldn't account for their whereabouts during this last raid. Which could have been another reason why we would get hit so hard. Two of our men weren't there helping us to take down the perps," Renault said.

"They must not have warned Kroner that they had hit the wrong house and were coming to his house next," Charlene said.

"No one but I knew who we were actually targeting," Ethan said, "because of previous botched cases. About the other cases, Renault, you could be right. I was so busy making sure our injured men were getting seen to, and that the drug dealers we caught were being hauled away, that I don't remember what either of those men had been doing."

"They looked like they hadn't been in a fight at all. The rest of us were sweating, had gas-mask marks on our faces when we removed the gas masks, and I didn't see that they'd even worn gas masks."

"Hell." Ethan wished he had been more observant of the two men.

"Don't feel bad about it. I didn't catch on until the raid on Kroner's house. I found your informant and took tougher measures to learn how come we hit the wrong house. He said that an agent, he didn't know which one, told him he would make it worthwhile to him if he changed the name of the street that we were supposed to hit. Nothing too noticeable, something that could be a reasonable mistake. But he also asked who the drug dealer was, and Ferret told him he didn't know and he wouldn't give the agent the actual address either."

"Aww, hell. I *thought* Ferret had lied to me. He was sweating and nervous, tapping his foot, avoiding eye contact, even looking up at the ceiling as if he was trying to come up with a story. But I couldn't learn from him why he had given me the wrong street name." Now Ethan was truly irritated about it. He sure wished the hell he knew who the agent was. "Ferret did know who the drug dealer was. I just kept who we were going after under wraps from our team until we arrived at the house."

"I just kept thinking something wasn't right because we had all these near-misses on capturing the perps," Renault said.

Charlene mentioned what she had seen at the convenience store. "I mean, it might not have been anything, but Ryerson and Cohen acted suspicious to me."

Renault shook his head. "Especially after Ryerson and Cohen followed you into the restaurant to intimidate you."

"What are you thinking of doing to prove who the mole or moles are?" Ethan asked, hoping he wasn't being taken for a fool because the mole was really Renault who was trying to learn if Ethan thought it was him.

"I got word that Oakley had a home in Shelby Bay, but it's in another person's name and so it took a lot of digging to unearth it. Oakley doesn't know what I look like so I actually followed another guy who often buys drugs from Oakley. That's how we learned Oakley was involved as a dealer initially. I figured this dude would be going to his source. I followed him from Portland, long drive, I know, but I didn't realize he would lead me all the way out to Shelby Bay and to this home that is associated with Oakley."

"That was risky." Especially since Ethan and Noah had caught Renault at it and worried about him working with the criminals.

"Yeah, I know. But the thing of it was, I went to buy the drugs for evidence, had a microphone on, and the whole thing. But no one sold me anything. They denied having drugs there."

"But there was nobody to back you up. What if someone was conducting surveillance and saw you going there and thought you were involved in all this?" Ethan asked.

"To tell you the truth, I would have asked you to go with me because I trust you, but you went and retired on me. I figured I could rely on Noah, but he has gone back to Florida and who knows when he's returning to take over your old job. Plus, being new on the team, he might not want to go rogue to help me solve this."

"I imagine he wouldn't. Just like it's too dangerous for you to do so. What did you find out when you went to the house?" Ethan asked. Maybe Renault saw something that would help them.

"I didn't see Oakley. I didn't see anyone I recognized. Just some small fish. I figured Oakley and the others might be lying low after the raid on Kroner's place and us netting one of the guys."

Ethan sure wished he could confide in Renault. He didn't want Renault to go off half-cocked and get himself killed because he was determined to do this on his own, yet Ethan understood how he felt. Ethan certainly felt the same way about catching these bastards.

On the other hand, Ethan didn't want to expose Noah and his mission to Renault who still could be the mole. They needed to look into his financial background and see if he was getting money that couldn't be accounted for. Or buying expensive items he couldn't afford.

"I shouldn't involve you in all this since you're no longer with the force, but you always gave me good advice, saved my butt a few times when I arrived in Portland, and I just thought if anyone had any sound words of wisdom it would be you."

"Thanks. The department will get whoever the mole or moles are. I don't like that you're doing this on your own and putting yourself at unnecessary risk without Grainger's approval."

"I second that," Charlene said, then began eating the rest of her chicken thigh.

"You know it could be someone in the police bureau, not even in our department," Renault said, serving up some more green beans on his plate. "The meal is delicious, by the way."

Charlene said, "I agree. Thanks for lunch, Ethan."

"My pleasure. On the business of someone in the police bureau being involved, Grainger has talked to the bureau chief who is having someone look into that."

"Oh, good. I was going to see if your good friends Adam or Tori might be able to check into it quietly. I was going to drop by your house to talk to you about all this, but I don't have your address."

That was going to be tough to explain since Ethan couldn't give out that address to anyone in the department.

"Ethan is staying with me." Charlene smiled brilliantly at Renault. "So if you're looking for him, he'll be here if he's not running errands."

Renault's jaw dropped. Then he smiled. "Well, hell, who would have thought it would progress that quickly?"

Renault had no idea. "Yeah, I was going to rent a furnished place to make sure I liked it out here before I actually bought a home, but then Charlene told me to come stay with her and save on the rent. So my own household goods are still in storage in Portland. Staying with Charlene has worked like a charm." He only mentioned the storage situation in case Renault had been checking *him* out!

"Yeah, we've been having a great time," Charlene said. "Ethan has been the best company."

"I'm glad. You deserve someone who is good for you," Renault said.

"Thanks. Noah and I will remain friends," Charlene said. "He just needs to find the right woman for him."

"That's good to hear. You won't be living that close to each other, but when you come into Portland, I hope we can all get together sometimes," Renault said.

"Sure, that would be great. But you know, I agree with Ethan about you trying to do this undercover work alone without your boss even backing you. You could be murdered by these guys, and no one would ever know what had happened to you," Charlene said. "I have experience with this stuff as a homicide detective, so I know what I'm talking about."

"Yeah, I know you do." Renault sighed. "I really felt Ethan

and I were a team, watching each other's backs, until he retired."

Ethan was surprised Renault had felt that way. Renault really hadn't been a very open person with him or anyone else on the team since he had joined them, but Ethan had figured it had to do with his background or maybe his personality. He'd been a good agent, serious, contemplative, thorough on his investigations, an expert sharpshooter who had even saved Ethan's life once. Ethan had liked his work ethic and was grateful to him for taking down a perp who could have killed him. Ethan truly hoped he hadn't gone to the dark side.

Renault ran his hands through his dark hair. "Okay, listen, the truth is someone has been tailing me. That's… that's another reason I had to speak with you, Ethan. I–I really don't know who else to turn to. I've gotten to the point that I don't trust anyone in the department and not in the police bureau either. But you and Noah, of course. I don't know who is following me, but as wary as we are and as long as we've been in this business, you know when you've got a tail."

Ethan believed him.

"It's a black Mercedes."

Instantly, Ethan thought it might be the same car belonging to Clara Snyder that they had seen at Oakley's house. "Did you get the license plate number?" He hoped they could confirm it was the same one.

"No. So I don't know who it belongs to or what they're up to. Maybe Grainger is having me followed to see if I'm the mole and will lead him to these guys. Maybe it's one of them or their henchmen. I just don't know where to turn. I mean, I thought of asking Grainger, but if he believes I'm the mole, he wouldn't tell me the truth anyway."

"Maybe you should take a vacation and get out of Oregon for a while," Ethan said, wanting Renault out of harm's way. He thought that might be the best way to get him out of this situation if he wasn't the mole.

Renault shook his head. "I've got to do this. I've got to find these guys and take them down, if not for my own sanity, to do what's right by your parents and for you."

Ethan knew how he felt. He wanted resolution in this case in the worst way.

Then Tori called Ethan and he said to Renault and Charlene, "I'm going to take this outside. I'll be right back."

"Sure," Charlene said and then she engaged Renault further. "When you went to Oakley's house, did you see any sign of drugs?"

"Hey," Ethan said to Tori, closing the back door and heading down the stairs to the beach so that he could make sure his call was private. "We have unexpected company. Renault arrived to talk to us." He explained to Tori what that was all about.

"Talk about putting you on the spot. From what we could gather about the murdered victim, he was trying to take over Kroner's territory as soon as he saw he was arrested. He didn't care that Kroner was released. We guess he figured if the DEA could take Kroner down once, they would have him back in cuffs again before long. Fatal mistake on his part. The victim has been wanted in several felony crimes also but get this. We ran the license plates on one of the cars in Kroner's garage and it also belongs to Clara Snyder."

"Hell, is she just that culpable or is she at the heart of all this?" Ethan asked.

"We have a financial team looking into her finances. If nothing else, the IRS will get her on tax evasion because she's been collecting all this money to buy cars and not reporting it as income."

Ethan wondered if there wasn't more to Clara than met the eye. "What if Clara isn't who she says she is? Being a retired high school teacher could be just a cover."

"We're looking into it. So far, it appears she is who she says she is. Maybe she has just been bamboozled into doing this. You know how it is. People from all walks of life can easily be scammed," Tori said. "How are things going with you and Noah?"

"Surprisingly well. I think he might be setting his sights on another she-wolf and he has given up on Charlene."

"Oh? That's a quick change of heart. Who is the new she-wolf?"

"You."

Tori laughed. "Noah would definitely get more than he bargained for with me."

Ethan smiled. "That's what I figured. Let us know if you get anything more on Clara and hear anything about where Kroner might have gotten off to."

"I will. I'll talk to you later."

"Thanks for the update." Ethan climbed back up the steps and found Renault getting ready to leave.

"Hey, thanks for having me over for lunch," Renault said.

"I'm serious about you taking a vacation. Psychologically, it's not good to feel everyone could be a threat, and if Kroner or one of his cohorts is following you, that's not good," Ethan said. "Especially since you don't feel you can trust anyone to be there for you if they come for you."

"Thanks."

Then Ethan frowned. "Did the Mercedes that's been tailing you follow you here?" All they needed was for Kroner or his criminal friends to learn Ethan was staying here and then Charlene could be more at risk.

"I don't believe so. It followed me to Shelby Bay and then I lost it when I left there."

"So the Mercedes followed you all the way from Portland to Shelby Bay?"

"Yeah. There aren't a lot of ways to reach Shelby Bay, and though I tried to ditch him, he kept finding me. That's why I knew I had a tail. I'm sorry. I didn't think of what that might mean for Charlene, but I don't believe anyone followed me here. I was really taking all kinds of detours and backtracking to get here," Renault said, sounding sincere.

"Still, that worries me."

"I can handle myself," Charlene said, sounding annoyed that they would treat her like some defenseless heroine.

"I have an idea though." Ethan thought if he could catch the bastard who had been following Renault, it would be worth it. Especially if it meant stopping him from going after Charlene, if he knew Renault had been to her house. "Oceanside Grocery is five miles from here.

Go there and I'll meet you. I'm driving a dark-green sedan, Honda Accord. I'll go in, grab a couple of things from the store, get some gas in case it takes a while to ensure you're not being followed, and then leave. You'll do something similar and then drive back to Portland. I'll follow you halfway there and see if anyone's trailing you. If you pick up a tail, I'll nail his ass. If nothing happens in the one and a half hours I'm following you, I'll return to Oyster Bay."

Renault looked relieved. Ethan was glad he had come up with the plan to protect his back. But he didn't want to leave Charlene alone. Calling on Noah to come there and watch over her probably wouldn't go over that big with Charlene. Still, he had to talk to her about it. He was sure Noah would be all for it.

"Okay, I'll meet you at the store then," Ethan said.

"Thanks, Ethan. I really, really owe you for this," Renault said.

"No trouble at all. Maybe we can catch this guy and end his stalking." And put an end to the stalker coming after Charlene if that was next on his agenda.

"But you're no longer with the force," Renault suddenly said, as if remembering that fact.

"We'll figure it out one way or another, but I'll watch your back."

"Okay, I'm off." Renault left the house then.

Ethan gave Charlene a hug. "Are you all right with all of this?"

"Yeah. You be safe though."

"What if Noah stays with you while I'm gone?"

Charlene smiled. "No. I'm fine. If I feel like I'm in trouble, I'll call Noah and he can be here in a couple of minutes, as close as the DEA house is to ours."

"All right." Ethan kissed Charlene, hoping she'd be fine on her own. He wanted to make Noah aware of what was going on, but he didn't want to upset Charlene. He called Noah on Bluetooth as he headed for the grocery store. "Hey, we have a development."

"Is Renault the mole?"

"He said he was looking into this himself without Grainger's approval."

"Hell, he's going to get himself killed."

"Yeah, but also from what he says, the car that we spotted at Oakley's house has been following him. The black Mercedes. I'm meeting up with Renault at the grocery store and then following him halfway to Portland. If I see the Mercedes, I'm going to try to catch the driver and see what's going on," Ethan said.

"So someone's been following Renault and he went straight to Charlene's house."

"Yeah, but Charlene said she'll be fine."

"I'll make sure of it."

"Keep out of sight. I'm glad you're going to be there for her if she needs you, but I don't want Charlene pissed off at me if she thinks I sent you to protect her."

"All right, but if someone is out to get her, I'll be there and all over him. If I can, I'll do it without her ever knowing about it. I'm taking a backpack, my gun and badge, and

I'll run over there. I don't want to drive over to her place, or she'll hear my vehicle," Noah said to Ethan.

"Okay, sounds good. I'll call you later to let you know what's going on."

"I'll put my phone on vibrate. Out, here."

Ethan smiled. He really liked having Noah as a partner. It made him feel like he could really accomplish the mission with him by his side. Ethan soon arrived at the grocery store and saw Renault's car there. There was no sign of the black Mercedes. He hoped that Renault wasn't imagining all of this, but on the other hand, if it really was the same vehicle he and Noah had seen at Oakley's house, he believed Renault was right in being worried about the driver's intentions.

CHAPTER 17

With no intention of sitting around while Ethan was off on a grand adventure, protecting Renault if he needed protecting, Charlene was checking on properties for sale on the coast to see about buying a third one. She'd had three rental homes in Florida, and she'd planned to look for a third property when she finally got settled here.

She called Jennie Dosier, the real estate agent she had worked with for the other coastal homes. "Hey, Jennie, I'm ready to start looking for another rental place. I've seen a couple that look like they would be good prospects. Maybe you can find a couple of other places I could also check out."

"Yeah, sure, would seeing them today work for you? I've got three new listings I'm sure you would be interested in, based on the others you've already purchased."

"Oh, great. Yeah, I'm free now if you want to..." Charlene frowned as she saw Noah sneaking into the dense forest next to her home where she and Ethan went for their hikes. What the hell? *Ethan!* He had to have called Noah and made sure that he came to protect her.

Even though she had said no on calling Noah, she couldn't be upset with either of them. They were only looking out for her safety. She was amused that Noah thought she wouldn't see him. Though, to give him credit, she had just gotten lucky by being at the living room window when he moved into the forest. If she'd been anywhere else in the house, she would never have known he was out there.

"Are you okay?" Jennie asked.

"Uh..." Charlene continued speaking with her agent. "Yeah. If you can meet me here in a half hour, that would be great."

"I'll call the homeowners to let them know we'll be dropping by."

"Okay, perfect. I'll see you soon." Then she called Noah to let him know where she was going. "Hey, Noah."

"Hey, what's up?" Noah sounded both surprised that she would call him and a little anxious.

She wanted to laugh because he was trying to act like he wasn't hiding in the woods next to her house. "Ethan must have told you that Renault had a tail and whoever it was might have seen him come to my place."

Noah was silent. She figured that Ethan had told him *not* to let her know he was doing this, or she would be mad at Ethan.

"Okay, well, you can keep hiding in the forest watching for bad guys if you want or stay at the house while I'm gone. I'm going to look at some houses to see about buying another rental property. The real estate agent will be here soon, and I just wanted to let you know where I'm going."

Noah sighed heavily. "Hell, Ethan told me not to let you know what I'm doing. I'll stay at the house. If someone comes there looking for you, I'll handle it. Just so you know, Ethan didn't tell me to watch over you. He just told me he was trying to watch Renault's back and that there could be an issue with the guy tailing him knowing Renault had been at your place."

"I'm glad that you are here."

"I'm on my way to the house."

She chuckled. Then she opened the back door to let him in.

"Sorry about that. I really hadn't thought you would catch me at this."

"Truly, I got lucky. Have you heard anything from Ethan?"

"Not yet. But nothing may come of it."

"True. Here, have some water." She fixed Noah a glass of ice water. "Make yourself at home and protect the place."

"I was supposed to be protecting you."

"I'll be fine. If anyone comes, they wouldn't be following me to go house hunting," she said. "You can tell Ethan that I caught you and you're in the house, and you can tell him what I'm doing if he calls."

Noah laughed. "He's not going to be happy that you caught me at it. He's going to believe I did it on purpose."

"I'll let him know the truth when I speak with him."

"He'll wonder if I'll make a good partner in this business."

She smiled. "I'm sure he knows you're good at your job."

Her real estate agent finally arrived, and Charlene joined Jennie in her car. She was excited about the possibility of adding another rental home to her properties. Of course, none of them might be right for her, but if one was, she would be thrilled.

She was also glad Noah was at the house observing things while she shopped for another house to buy. But she had to admit she was watching to make sure no one was tailing *her*.

Ethan went inside the grocery store to grab a couple of items according to plan. He saw Renault getting a candy bar and a bag of chips. Ethan picked up a box of popcorn and a bottle of wine to have later with Charlene for a movie night experience. Despite carrying out this mission and everything else that was going on, he wanted to show Charlene that he was always thinking of them as a couple and wanted to do fun things with her.

Ethan glanced through some other aisles, then saw Renault paying for his goods in the self-checkout line. As soon as Renault left the store, Ethan checked out, then went to put some gas in his car. Renault was doing the same thing. Ethan went to the pumps on the other side of the cashier's station and behind Renault so he could see him when he left.

Once Renault was on his way, Ethan finished pumping gas and saw a black Mercedes start to pull out of the car wash. No way could it be the same car that had been following Renault and they had seen at Oakley's house. But Ethan saw the license plate and it was the same car that Clara owned. Ethan jumped into his car and blocked the Mercedes from fully exiting the car wash.

Ethan was out of his car in a flash with his gun and his badge out, shouting for the occupant to get out of the vehicle.

For a moment, the person sat hidden behind the darkly

tinted windows—illegally tinted and they could get him for that if nothing else. Renault must have been watching his rearview mirror and turned his car around to return to assist Ethan. Ethan called for police backup.

The driver wasn't shutting down his car, and when he saw Renault's car pull up, he tried to make a dash for it over the cement curb that was supposed to direct the car-wash patrons around and into the travel lane near the gas pumps so they didn't hit another vehicle. The driver couldn't back up through the car wash because two other cars were sitting there in line to wash their cars.

If the guy didn't bust his tires or scrape the underside of the car, he could get away. Ethan couldn't allow it. Especially when he might know that Renault had been to Charlene's house. Ethan shot out two of the Mercedes's tires. Renault was out of his car, racing around to the other side to shoot out the Mercedes's other tires.

Now the car was riding lower over the curb, but the guy gunned the car again and was driving on flat tires.

Ethan jumped into his car and followed the black Mercedes onto the road. He didn't want to mess up the DEA's loaner car—Grainger would have something to say about that—but Ethan just couldn't let the guy go. He got to the side of the Mercedes on the two-lane road and bumped it, knocking it onto the shoulder. The driver kept control of his car and returned to the road but before Ethan could bump him again, he had to pass him because of an oncoming car.

Renault was behind the Mercedes and Ethan slammed on

his brakes. The Mercedes tried to circle around him, but the driver didn't have enough room to maneuver and ended up clipping Ethan's car. Renault immediately slammed into the Mercedes's tail, crunching it between his car and Ethan's.

Ethan jumped out of his car, heard the sirens of police cars en route, and headed to the driver's side, shouting, "Turn off your engine, show your hands, and open the door."

Renault had maneuvered around the black Mercedes and was slightly behind the back passenger door on the right-hand side in case anyone tried to exit the vehicle from that direction.

The driver's side door opened just a little and Ethan thought the driver was going to leave the car—until he saw the gun. He kicked the door into the driver, realizing it was Thor, Timothy Morton, the guy who was the size of a giant. Ethan continued kicking the door repeatedly, denting it, but also keeping Thor from shooting him. Ethan was still recovering from his earlier bullet wound and he sure as hell didn't want to get killed when he knew he had finally found the she-wolf he wanted to mate for life.

The police arrived and surrounded the car. Ethan showed off his badge to the officers. "He's armed and was trying to shoot me through the door. It's Timothy Morton, a.k.a. Thor, and he's wanted on multiple warrants that are out for his arrest."

It was a standoff for the moment. Thor finally backed off and the bashed door closed as much as it could. At least, he couldn't shut the door all the way and lock it.

Ethan signaled to Renault to grab the back door of the

car. Ethan figured it would be locked, but he thought it might distract Thor.

As soon as Renault yanked at the rear car door, Ethan pulled open the driver's door, reached in, and grabbed Thor's meaty, muscular gun arm. He yanked it out through the open door and kicked the door at the same time as hard as he could. Ethan heard the bone crack in Thor's arm. Total win. No one got shot. He'd known Thor wouldn't give up without a fight, no matter what.

Thor dropped his gun on the pavement and the police moved in to help to confine him until the EMTs could arrive to take care of his arm. They found several more guns, an assault rifle, and tons of ammunition.

Out of earshot of the officers, Ethan said to Renault, "You take care of this. You collared him."

"But you—"

"I'm undercover. I can't be in the news. Take care of it. I'll let Grainger know what's going on. You need to tell him you've caught Thor. But as far as everyone else in the agency is concerned, I'm retired. If anyone sees anything about it in the news, I was just making a citizen's arrest because I was a former special agent. I'm out of here."

"Okay, sure. We'll talk later." Renault appeared shocked to learn Ethan was still on the force.

Then Renault called Grainger and told him he got Thor and was going with him and a couple of local police officers to the hospital to have Thor's arm x-rayed.

Ethan took off to Charlene's house, calling her first before touching base with Noah because he wanted to make sure she was okay. He was damned glad they had caught another of the men who had been involved in murders, drug charges, and other criminal pursuits.

"Is everyone all right?" Charlene asked, sounding worried.

"Yeah."

Before Ethan could tell her what had happened, she cleared her throat. "Hey, I can't talk right now. I'm looking at some other homes that I could turn into another rental house."

That surprised the hell out of Ethan. She hadn't mentioned to him beforehand that she was going out to look for another rental house. Not that she had to tell him everything she was doing, but he was worried that one of the men he was after might be following her now. And Noah hadn't texted or called him either to tell Ethan that she had left the house.

Here Ethan figured she was safe at home with Noah discreetly watching over her.

"Just meet me at home when you're through with your business," Charlene said. "You can tell Noah what's going on."

"At your house? You know Noah was there?"

"Yeah. It's not his fault. Talk to you later."

"All right. Love you." He headed for the house, not calling Noah because he figured he would just talk to him when he arrived. He sure hoped Thor ended up in jail and didn't get out. But what was Noah doing at Charlene's house when he was supposed to be watching her place in secret?

CHAPTER 18

Charlene was dying to know what had happened with Ethan and the guy who was tailing Renault, but she couldn't talk with him about what was going on while she was with the real estate agent. Ethan had sounded annoyed with her that she wasn't sitting at home staying safe while Noah was secretly watching out for her. She was glad he was concerned about her, but she had been thinking about looking for the additional property to rent, and while he was doing his business, she wanted to do hers.

If Charlene and Ethan were right for each other, they could talk things through like this, and everything would be fine. In a way, it was good to have these little bumps in their relationship because if they could successfully deal with them, she knew they were right for each other. If they couldn't, things wouldn't work out. She understood how he was feeling, but she hoped he also understood how she felt.

Jennie said, "Hey, two more listings just came up that are similar to what you have already purchased, though one is larger—a four-bedroom and three-bathroom. Do you want to check them out? They look good."

"Yeah, let's check them out." One of the other listings Charlene had seen looked like it might be perfect for what she wanted, but she had to look at the others too. The other two homes she had seen online needed a lot of work. She could do it, but if she could find a reasonably priced home to rent out that was more ready, she would prefer that.

Still, she felt a little like she should go home and learn what had happened with Ethan and Renault. She sighed. That was Ethan's business, and he would tell her later. This was her business and she wanted to do this now. Homes could be snapped up just like that, and she didn't want to lose out on a good bargain if she found one.

"Okay, this one might be right up your alley," Jennie said. "The couple are divorcing. They both want as much money as they can get out of the place, but they want it done quickly, so I'm sure we can get them to come down significantly on the price."

When they arrived at the house, they walked inside and checked the place over. The first thing Charlene wanted to see was the back deck and the view of the ocean from it. That was one of the things that really enticed people to rent her places. But she loved the detailed molding around the floors and the tile floors throughout the living room, kitchen, and dining room. The house was about two miles down the road from her own home, so it was a nice location.

"What do you think?"

"So far, I like it." Then Charlene looked through the bedrooms and bathrooms and it truly was a much bigger house than she normally rented out. But for bigger groups, she thought it might work.

Normally, she would have just decided on a place and purchased it, not having to ask anyone else's opinion, but she realized she wanted Ethan's input. She had never thought she would feel that she would have to ask anyone else to help her make a choice. But she really wanted to include him in the decision-making, and that was a big change for her when she was in a relationship.

More than that, she realized just why she wanted his input. She wanted him to live with her—permanently. She just hoped when she told him, he was of a like mind. With Noah, she had told him what she was going to do; she didn't ask him what he thought of it. "Let me call my boyfriend and have him meet us over here to look at the house."

"Oh, sure. Go ahead," Jennie said.

Charlene called Ethan and said, "Hey, have you gotten home yet?"

"No, not yet. I'm about ten minutes from there. Is anything the matter?" Ethan sounded worried that she was in trouble.

"No, but I would like you to help me decide on buying one of the houses for the third rental. I'm only two miles from my house, so we'll just wait for you here." She gave Ethan the address.

"All right. I'll be there pronto."

"Don't break any laws getting here."

He laughed.

She loved his laughter and she felt he was over being perturbed with her about not telling him what she had been up to while he was watching Renault's back.

When he arrived at the house, he hugged Charlene and kissed her. "I'm so glad you're fine."

"I'm so glad that you are."

"I'll let the two of you look at the house alone together." Jennie went outside to give them some privacy.

Once Jennie had closed the front door, Ethan pulled Charlene in for another warm embrace. "I had to protect Renault if anyone bad was following him, but my main concern truly was you. I didn't tell Noah to go watch over you. I just told him what I was concerned with and what I was doing. He wasn't supposed to let you know he was observing your place."

She laughed. "He was hiding in the woods, but I just happened to look out the window and saw him move into them. It was pure dumb luck."

"Oh, good. I was going to give him hell for not doing it undercover."

She smiled. "You don't need to now. I want to learn what had happened to you and Renault, but I also want your opinion on buying this house as a rental."

"Really? Yeah, sure. I would be honored. So Renault and I took down Thor and he is off to jail."

"Ohmigod, really?"

"Yeah."

"That's so great." She hugged him back and kissed him.

"I know, right? I'm glad we got him. So, what do you think about the house?"

"I love it, but I want you to look at all the bedrooms, the bathrooms, kitchen, deck, view, et cetera."

"Wow, this is a really big place." He discussed the open-layout plan with a kitchen that opened up into the dining room and living room.

"Yeah, I know. I was thinking"—she sighed—"that maybe I could move here if you would like to move in with me permanently." That was the real reason she had wanted him here, but she hadn't wanted to say that over the phone.

He smiled. "Are you asking me what I think you're asking?"

"A mating? Yes." She smiled. "If you agree and we want to have kids, this place is bigger. The beach access is great, and they have the same situation with walking right into the woods from the house."

"Yes, on both counts. You have made me the happiest wolf alive." He wrapped his arms around her and lifted her off the floor and kissed her.

She smiled. "You make me feel the same way."

"I want to take you right back to the house and mate you," he said.

"Yeah, I'm pretty impatient about it too." But then she took his hand and started walking him through the house. First things first.

"Well, the other home is lovely, but then you've decorated it beautifully," he said.

"And it's smaller. So having a family there would probably mean we would need to have the bigger place and yet the other house is big enough for renters."

"True." He eyed the master bathroom—the shower and the large whirlpool tub with jets. "Yeah, this works."

She laughed.

The bathroom had individual sinks and lots of cabinetry for supplies. The toilet had its own separate little room.

"I love this closet in the master bedroom. It has even more room than the other house. The living room is bigger, and even the kitchen is," Charlene said, walking back into the kitchen and checking out the pantry. "The kitchen is more open to the dining room and living room. This is really nice. It would be better for having friends from the Portland area visit, and we could entertain guests while we're cooking."

"We'll have to get a wolf door for the house."

"Yeah. I had one installed in the other house, but not in the rentals. With all the wolves renting them in future months, I'll need to have those all fitted with wolf doors."

"We will."

She smiled. She really liked that she had a partner in managing the rental houses. "I guess when you truly retire, you'll also be a rental manager."

He smiled. "I can be on top of any maintenance needs too. You can take care of other customer complaints."

She laughed. "That works for me." But she suspected he would help her with customer complaints too. "So about this place, what do you think?"

They went out on the back deck and looked at the view of the ocean. The deck was even bigger than the other home's.

"Yeah, I think you're absolutely right about this being perfect for us and for a family. How about we make an offer on the house, and then if we buy it, we'll fix it up the way we want before we move in?"

"And furnish it just like we want so it's a combination of our tastes?" she asked.

"That will be perfect." he said.

She smiled and told him the listing price. "The couple who own the home are divorced and they are looking to get the most money they can, of course, so they can split the proceeds between them. But Jennie said that she felt she could get them to come down on the price. It has just been listed, so it's possible someone else might snatch it up. They haven't even had an open house yet."

"Let's make an offer."

"All right. Let's do it." She was so glad he was ready for being with her.

They walked out to the driveway where Jennie was in her car speaking on the phone. She quickly ended the call and left the car. "I've got a couple of people who want to see the house already and so does another Realtor. What do you think about it?"

"What's the lowest offer the owners will take?" Ethan asked.

"Five thousand less, that's if no one else wants the house."

"I'll pay cash, no loan, no getting it approved. It will be a done deal," Ethan said.

Charlene thought the same, but she was surprised Ethan stepped in to say it first. Was he planning on spending his own money on the house?

"Okay." Jennie had them sign the contract with the offer and Ethan gave her the earnest money. "Let me call them and see what they say." Jennie called the owners in a conference call. "You have an offer on the house." She gave them the dollar amount. "The offer is cash, so no loan approvals, which can be a real incentive to sell quickly. Sometimes the loans fall through, so you have to start the process all over again with someone else, and getting a loan approval can take a lot longer. We haven't shown it to anyone else, but they need to do some work on the place—painting, replacing the carpeting, and refinishing the deck."

Jennie waited for a minute and then smiled. "All right. I'll draw up the contract and get the ball rolling on this. Thanks so much." Then she smiled at Charlene and Ethan. "You've got another house."

"Yes!" Charlene said.

Smiling, Ethan squeezed Charlene's hand.

"I'll email the contract to you within an hour if that works for you."

"Yes, perfect. We want to look through the house again one last time before we leave," Charlene said.

"Yes, by all means do."

Charlene and Ethan walked back into the house, and she threw up her arms and said quietly, "Yes! I would have paid the full price. I think if the couple didn't jump at the chance to sell the house to us, they might have had some other offers. Maybe even a bidding war since it had just been listed."

"They were too eager to just sell the house and split the proceeds," Ethan said, gathering Charlene in his arms and kissing her soundly. "Which worked out great for us. I'm so glad we got it. I should have talked to you first about me paying cash for the house, but as a couple, my money is yours."

"We'll have plenty of funds to do any renovations we want and fully furnish this house too then." She kissed him back, loving how kissable he always was. "Let's take this other business to our other home and get on with it."

"All right. Now you're talking."

They left the house and thanked Jennie and headed home. When they arrived there, Noah let them into the house. "No one came by. What happened?"

Ethan told him what had occurred. "Grainger was glad we caught Thor, even though Renault now knows I'm not retired. He told Renault he can't tell anyone else at work."

"Oh, that's not good. But at least following Renault resulted in capturing another of the men we needed to take down." Noah sounded pleased. "How did the house hunting go?" Noah asked Charlene.

"We found the perfect place to buy and made an offer and it was accepted, so we're just waiting to sign the contract and get it done," Charlene said.

Noah looked a little surprised that she said *we*. Then he nodded. "Great. Did Ethan tell you I'll grill steaks for us when you want to have dinner at my place one of these nights? Maybe tonight and we can celebrate both successful endeavors today." Noah looked hopeful that they could. Charlene felt sorry for him. Not only had he lost out on Charlene as his girlfriend, but he hadn't even been able to help take down Thor.

"Yeah. Tonight will be great. Will six be good for you?" Charlene asked.

"Yep, and I'll get us some champagne," Noah said.

"That sounds great," Ethan said.

Then Charlene got the contract from her real estate agent in an email.

Charlene and Ethan said goodbye to Noah, and Charlene was glad Ethan hadn't told him they were mating. They could tell him tonight, which would be another big reason for celebration, but they needed to do this first.

"We were thinking alike about not telling him what we were doing," Charlene said. "I got the contract. Let's get this done first."

They read it over, signed the contract, and sent it back to Jennie.

Then Charlene put her phone on the table and Ethan swept her up in his arms. "Time to make all my dreams come true."

"Mine too."

He carried her into the bedroom and set her down on the bed, then slipped off her sandals. "I never dreamed I would be pairing up with a red wolf who was a former homicide detective."

"I never thought I would end up with a DEA special agent who was still actively with the force. We make a great pair."

"I totally agree. Everything about you makes me know this is the perfect match. I thought so before, but when you asked me to help you decide on the other house, even before you said you wanted to mate me, that clinched the deal that you were the right wolf for me."

"I love how protective you are, and yet even when you're perturbed with me about things, you just get it over it in a heartbeat."

He smiled. "Yeah, with you it's easy." Then he removed his boots and socks and she rose from the bed to pull off his black growling wolf T-shirt.

"I love this T-shirt, perfect for undercover."

He laughed. "Black is for the intimidation effect."

She smiled and ran her hand over his chest. "The wicked teeth of the snarling wolf add to the effect."

He pulled off her camisole blouse and then reached lower to slide her breezy skirt down her hips and pulled it off. "You're beautiful." He kissed her jaw and neck and moved his mouth to her throat, his hands on her breasts, massaging her through her bra.

He always made her feel so sexy and impassioned. Then he rubbed his package against her mound, and she smiled and kissed his mouth with pent-up need. "You are beautiful." She unfastened his belt and unzipped his cargo pants, then pulled them off his hips and he kicked them aside.

Then she saw his injured arm. She couldn't believe he could take down Thor when he was still injured. She gently kissed Ethan's arm.

"It's getting better with your tender loving care."

Right, like him lifting her and carrying her to the bedroom?

He removed her bra and panties, and she removed his boxer briefs and smiled to see his full arousal. "Always ready for you," he said.

She quickly moved onto the bed so he wouldn't try to lift her and set her on the mattress. He was soon nestled between her legs, kissing her again. He rubbed his stiff erection against her, connecting with her mound, stirring their pheromones to the nth degree.

God, how she loved making love to him. But this time it

would be all the way. A consummation—a wolf's mating, no longer two wolves on their own, but a couple, the start of a pack of their own.

He was kissing her slowly, surely, deliberately taking his time to warm her up, but she was already hot and eager to consummate their relationship. Their pheromones were heating up and teasing each other, testing their resolve, enticing each of them to make this the ultimate and permanent connection. Her need grew sharper, more profound, and she was filled with deep happiness. She had finally found her mate. He made her feel empowered, uplifted, like she was the only one who mattered. Just like he was the only one who mattered to her.

She kissed his mouth and he surrendered to her completely. She stroked his tongue with hers, telling him in no uncertain terms that she was already completely warmed up. He responded with the same enthusiasm, kissing her, running his hands over her shoulders, ramping up the need between them. This was what she truly needed in a partner—the passion and the love he shared with her.

His kisses were magical, intensely pleasureful as she licked his lips and kissed him again.

She was wet for his penetration, enjoying the foreplay but wanting the consummation that would make them mated wolves forever. He moved his mouth down her neck, making her skin tingle. He kissed her breasts with lingering gentleness, his hand sweeping down her bare tummy to her short, curly hairs.

Then he began his exploration, finding that spot that

screamed with pleasure as he began to stroke it. He made her feel glorious, and she loved him for it.

"Such a lover," she whispered against his ear.

"So easy to love," he whispered back, his heated breath warming her to her toes.

A wind was blowing off the ocean, the waves crashing against the shore, the air cool in the house, but she was on fire. She nearly lost it when he poked a finger into her feminine channel, and she climaxed before he could stroke her further. She cried out with shocked pleasure.

He was about ready to enter her but quickly said, "I love you."

"Oh, I love you too. Do it."

He smiled and pressed his engorged erection all the way in and began to thrust.

Yes! They were a wolf couple forever! And she kissed him with no holds barred.

Ethan couldn't have felt any more right about this—taking such an exquisite lover and friend as his mate. He felt empowered to save the world with Charlene right beside him.

He didn't expect her to push at him to roll off her, but he wasn't parting from her until they were done, unless of course she really wanted him to. The next thing he knew, she was riding on top of him, rocking to his thrusts, looking thrilled, enthusiastic, sexy, on fire. Their hearts were beating wildly, and they were united in the moment, coming together until he felt he was coming apart and orgasmed deep inside her. He rolled over so he was on top again, continuing to thrust until he was completely spent. Their bodies were sweaty, her smile contagious. He kissed her soft, sweet mouth again, glad she was the only one for him.

Then they embraced, enjoying the moment of mated bliss. Emotionally and physically sated, they were happily mated.

"A wolf run?" she asked, kissing his ear. "Oh, wait, what about your arm?"

"I'll be okay." He smiled at her, loving her, and yes, he wanted to go with her for a wolf run too—their first mated wolf run, but he was so enjoying being with her like this, just holding onto her.

"In a little bit," she whispered. "This is just too nice."

"I agree." He didn't want to release her for anything.

CHAPTER 19

CHARLENE AND ETHAN HAD TO GO TO NOAH'S HOUSE FOR dinner in a couple of hours, but they still wanted to run as wolves. They finally got out of bed and kissed each other. Since they were already naked after making love to each other, they just shifted into their wolves and ran through the house. They soon pushed through the wolf door, her first and then him. Once they were in the forest, they played with each other, licking and nuzzling each other's muzzles.

Then they began racing each other through the woods, off the human trail, though they didn't hear anyone on the human trails winding through the forest. They were having a ball running through the woods as mated wolves. He realized it felt differently while running with her now that they were mated, no longer courting, but one. Though he still couldn't anticipate her moves. That would come later when he'd been with her for longer. And that made it all the more fun to get to know all her quirky wolf moves and her human ones too.

They were side by side or chasing each other, barking, woofing, and then they paused to howl their joy of being mated, proud, thrilled, sharing the news with all the critters of the woods.

After their fun romp in the forest, they finally returned to the house, shifted, showered, and dressed. "Hey, let's make dessert to take to dinner. Do you like brownies?" she asked.

"I love them."

"Great. So does Noah and I do too."

She and Ethan made brownies together, filled with chocolate chips and pecans, and spread chocolate frosting on top.

When they were done, they drove to Noah's house for dinner. They were a little worried Noah might be upset that they had ended up mating since she had been his girlfriend before this.

"I think he'll be all right with it," Charlene said, sounding like she was trying to reassure Ethan.

Ethan smiled. "I sure hope so. I still have to work with him."

Charlene smiled. "He probably knew where this was going anyway. I kind of let the cat out of the bag when I mentioned *we* had bought the other house."

"True. I'm sure he would have caught on before long anyway."

They soon arrived at the DEA rented house and left the car.

"Hey, come in," Noah said, welcoming them inside. "Grainger called and said that I was to remain undercover. Renault wouldn't know about it, just in case he is the mole, and we have this all figured wrong. Oh, the brownies look good."

"Thanks. I know you like them, just like we do," Charlene said. "The steaks smell great."

"Yeah, I just started them. They're about done. Do you like medium rare too, Ethan?" Noah asked.

"Yeah, you know us wolves."

"Yep. You can open the bottle of champagne. So two down, two more to go. We're getting them behind bars for sure," Noah said, going back out on the patio to flip the steaks.

They joined him while Charlene carried the champagne glasses and Ethan popped the cork, then poured some champagne for them.

"We would only have one more big boss to capture if it hadn't been for the clerk releasing him. Believe me, they have her up on charges," Ethan said.

Noah dished out the grilled corn and steaks. "I wish we could take down the mole or moles too. That could make all our lives easier."

"That's for certain," Ethan agreed.

They all went inside to eat because they didn't want the cold night air to chill their food before they could enjoy their meal. With the big ocean-view window, they could see the full moon and stars glittering across the black night, suspended over the whitecapped waves on the ocean.

"The steaks are delicious and cooked to perfection, by the way," Charlene said.

"They are," Ethan agreed.

"Thanks. I'm glad we could do this. Congratulations are in order for you buying another rental house," Noah said.

"About that." Charlene took a sip of her champagne before she spoke further. "Ethan and I decided to buy that house for ourselves to live there, and the home we're now living in will be a rental. The new home is bigger, perfect for a family."

"You're going to mate each other." Noah sounded surprised that they were doing it so quickly.

"We mated each other," Charlene said. "I didn't want to spoil our dinner in case you were upset by it, but you know when you meet a wolf that's the right one for you, there's no sense in delaying a union."

"Yeah. I agree. And I'm glad for both of you. Congratulations." Noah smiled, but he still appeared as though he couldn't believe it.

Charlene believed Noah was okay with learning that she and Ethan had mated, and she was glad about it. "Okay, so what is your next mission?" Charlene might not be involved exactly as a paid DEA agent, but she could be involved if the men came to her place.

"I want to watch both Oakley's home and his great-aunt's place," Ethan said. "We need to stick together in case we have to take these men down though."

"Can I help?" Charlene asked.

"No thanks. We've got this," Ethan said, serious as could be.

"Okay, then I'll go forward with getting the rental houses fitted with wolf doors as soon as the units are vacated. I have one that will be empty tomorrow, and then it's booked for two weeks after that. I'll contact someone to install a wolf door. Or, as far as the contractor is concerned, a large dog door."

"Are you going to rent to people with pets?" Ethan asked.

"Yes, but they can't just let their pets out through the wolf doors because there are no fences around the properties. They could lose their pets."

"True. Humans will wonder why you have them then," Noah said.

"Nah. They were formerly owned by other people who actually lived there. I'll give that excuse if anyone asks," Charlene said. "But I doubt anyone will inquire about it."

Ethan got a call from Tori then. "Yeah, Tori? I'm having dinner with Noah and Charlene. Charlene and I mated each other."

"Woo-hoo!" Tori said. "Who all knows? No one said a thing about it to me."

"You and Noah and that's it," Ethan said.

"Well, I'm honored. I called about the two men I thought might have to do with being the mole."

"In the DEA?"

"In the bureau."

"Hell," Ethan said. "I'm putting this on speaker so Charlene and Noah can hear the news."

"Sure. The police officers are Lawrence Baker and Elias Davis," Tori said. "They've been under investigation for a couple of shady situations. A woman and her teenaged son had witnessed the officers shaking down a drug dealer and pocketing his drugs. The officers had been too busy chasing off the drug dealer to notice the witnesses. They never turned in the drugs, never wrote a report about the confrontation, and for several hours, the woman and her son were afraid to tell the police. Which makes sense because they wouldn't have known who else might be crooked on the force. Then they finally did, and the two officers have been under investigation ever since. Our boss has kept it a closely guarded secret until Adam and I talked to him about a possible mole with regard to your cases. He was so angry. Not with us, but to think these men had betrayed DEA missions and could have gotten some of your agents or our officers killed."

"How much more corruption have they been involved in?" Noah asked.

"Lawrence Baker's fingerprints were found on the scene of the recently murdered man that we're investigating—a drug dealer who was in competition with Kroner. Baker wasn't at the scene of the crime when the victim was found by a man walking his dog in a park," Tori said. "So why were his fingerprints on the man? That's really suspicious."

"So, he could have been hired by Kroner to kill the other drug dealer?" Ethan asked.

"That's what we think. We're keeping the evidence of Baker's fingerprints on the victim secret because we need further evidence to prove that he actually had something to do with the murder. Plus, of course, Adam and I smelled Baker's scent there. Kroner's too. But we can't use that as evidence in a court of law. Baker could say he'd talked to the drug dealer before and must have touched him, not even remembering that he had. He wouldn't have any corroboration with having made a police report of talking to the victim at some point though. Still, it would make it unlikely that we could prove he had murdered the victim without eyewitnesses or his own confession."

"I can get it out of him," Noah said.

Ethan smiled at him. "What about Elias Davis? Was there any evidence that could point to his being involved in the homicide?"

"No," Tori said. "But we're still looking into it. We didn't smell his scent there at all. The victim had been encroaching on Kroner's drug territory, and witnesses revealed to us that the two men had words several times where Kroner had threatened to kill him. So Kroner had motivation for sure. Kroner had killed his drug competition before—when he was a teen. His record was sealed in Medford, Oregon, but we were able to learn of it while we were investigating him further," Tori said.

"With regard to the current murder case, Kroner was released from the jail and, an hour later, the dog walker found our victim. So timeline wise, Kroner could have been involved. Also, Baker had taken off to run some errands. He could have been at the crime scene and killed the drug dealer before the dog walker found the body."

"What about a financial trail for Baker? What would he get out of the deal if he did indeed kill the drug dealer competition?" Ethan asked.

"Yeah, that's just what I was going to ask," Noah said. "Financial trails can really help to pinpoint a crime."

"We just got some financial data back on both Davis and Baker. They both have been receiving some large amounts of money—payoffs? They're not working anywhere else other than their regular police jobs," Tori said. "So they're not getting any extra income from moonlighting."

"So Davis is involved also," Ethan said.

"Yeah, in some criminal ventures, but not sure if he was involved in the murder of this latest guy. My boss held a news conference to see if we could get any new leads. We've had a ton of calls in on the murder, but nothing has panned out yet," Tori said.

"Sometimes media coverage can really help," Charlene said.

"Yeah, everyone's shaken by the death. It was in a park that families frequent. I've got to go. But when I learn anything more, I'll call you."

"Thanks, Tori," Ethan said.

"Yeah, thanks," Noah said.

"If you want, you, Adam, and Sierra could come to the coast for a visit and we could talk about all this," Charlene said.

Ethan smiled at her.

"I've got plenty of room at the DEA rental house. You all could stay with me," Noah said.

"Okay, let me talk to the others and we'll let you know. If we learn that Davis, Baker, or Kroner are in your area, our boss will most likely approve it," Tori said.

"Or in Shelby Bay since it's just down the road. We can set up a sting operation," Ethan said.

"But they're out of your jurisdiction, Tori," Noah said.

"We'll call the local police if we find any of the men involved in a crime in either Shelby Bay or Oyster Bay," Ethan said.

Charlene mentioned having to deal with Agent Cohen

at the convenience store and how she was pulled over by Officer Baker for a traffic violation that she hadn't committed right after that.

"Ohmigod, so Baker could be in cahoots with Agent Cohen too," Tori said.

"It certainly looks like that could be the case," Ethan agreed.

They finally ended the call so they could finish their meal, then ate the rest of their dinner, enjoyed the brownies, and thanked Noah for dinner while he thanked them for the dessert.

"Surveillance at two in the morning?" Ethan asked Noah.

"Yeah. I'll pick you up," Noah said.

Then Ethan and Charlene returned home, and he said, "I need to call Adam and Sierra and our pack leaders to tell them we're mated."

Charlene smiled. "I never thought when I found a mate, I would be sharing the news with a whole pack of wolves, and I love it."

Ethan laughed. "Yeah, you're now part of a much bigger family." They walked into the house, and he called Cassie and Leidolf first. He figured Tori would tell Adam and Sierra that they were mated right away. "Hey, Cassie, Charlene and I have some news."

"Let me get Leidolf on the phone. Is this about your case?"

Ethan smiled. "Something more of a personal nature."

"Ooh," Cassie said.

Charlene laughed.

"Leidolf! Ethan and Charlene are calling."

"Coming!" Leidolf joined her and asked, "Yeah, what's up?"

"We're mated," Ethan said, so happy to be telling them the news.

Charlene smiled at him. "Yeah, I had to think of some way to keep him in Oyster Bay after he finishes his mission here."

"Congratulations!" Leidolf said. "It looks like we're going to have a whole pack in Oyster Bay eventually. Our territory is expanding."

They laughed.

"As soon as you can get away for it, we'll have a pack celebration to honor your union," Cassie said.

"Oh, that would be lovely," Charlene said.

"Yeah, as soon as this case permits, we'll plan to do that. We'll let you know," Ethan said. Then they finally ended the call.

Ethan gathered Charlene in his arms. "Man, here I thought I wasn't going to find anyone following Renault, that he was just spooked. Then I was worried that I had sounded annoyed with you that you were out looking for a house and Noah wasn't watching out for you."

"And that I knew what he was doing."

"Yeah, that too. But I was only concerned about you."

"Which I totally understood. And you know what? I loved you for it."

"It's a damn good thing."

She laughed. She cuddled against his solid warmth, so

glad she had moved to Oregon to live her dream and ended up with her dream hero and, one day, a chance to start a family with him.

CHAPTER 20

AT TWO IN THE MORNING, NOAH SHOWED UP AT THE house to pick up Ethan again so they could do their surveillance of Oakley's house. Ethan kissed Charlene and she stirred and sighed, then pulled him into her arms and said, "Be safe, love of my life."

He smiled and kissed her again, hugging her. "Absolutely. Love you right back."

When Ethan and Noah arrived in Shelby Bay and parked near Oakley's home, it was dark. There were no lights on anywhere. Ethan let out his breath. "It looks like no one's home. Or if they are, everyone has gone to bed and there's not going to be any action. We can't get inside the house unless we see evidence that Oakley, or Kroner, is staying there."

"Yeah, it looks that way. What if Oakley got word of Thor's arrest and he has moved to a new location?" Noah asked.

"There's a good chance of that. What about his great-aunt's house?" Ethan asked.

Noah's lips parted. "Yeah. Do you want to check it out? I mean, I hate leaving here if Oakley or others end up here because they're just out partying or taking care of business. On the other hand, what if you're right?"

"Though Oakley might not go to her place, afraid we might know about his great-aunt and his going to church with her some Sundays, but at the same time, there was an indication that he went there some nights, so it's worth taking a chance to check it out."

"On it." Noah drove them back to Oyster Bay and they found a nice inconspicuous spot to park and observe her place.

Everything was quiet there too. Ethan preferred it when there was lots of activity and not all this quiet. The house was dark, and they couldn't really do anything. Then Ethan got a call from Charlene and immediately he worried something was the matter. She should have been sleeping, unless she was just worried about him and couldn't sleep.

"Hey, is anything wrong?" he asked.

"I heard someone outside the house. I could see the shadow of someone at one of the windows, tall, a man, I figured, looking for a way to peek in but all the lights are off in the house and the curtains and blinds are closed. I'm going to turn on the outdoor lights and shift, turn wolf, exit the house, and see what I can see. I'll take refuge in the woods."

"*Hell.* We're just down the road from you at Oakley's great-aunt's house. We're headed back there now. Just keep out of sight."

"I will. Thanks."

Then she ended the call and he figured she was shifting into her wolf and leaving the house. He hated that he couldn't keep in contact with her, but she needed to do whatever it took to keep herself safe.

Ethan explained to Noah about what was going on.

"If Thor relayed to Kroner or Oakley that Renault had

been to Charlene's house before you caught him near the grocery store, one of the men involved with Thor might be there," Noah said.

"Yeah, that's what I'm worried about. Are you speeding?" Ethan asked.

"Yeah. Have your badge out in case we get pulled…" Noah started to say.

A police car flashed its lights behind them and followed them until they pulled over on the shoulder of the road.

"Hell," Ethan said. Of all times to get pulled over…when he was in a rush to save the love of his life.

The patrol car parked behind them, and they waited in the car until the officer approached Noah's vehicle. Ethan was on the phone to the local police department right away to tell them a patrolman had just stopped them, and they were DEA special agents on an undercover mission.

The patrolman called out to them to turn off the engine and roll down the window.

Noah did and showed him his badge. Ethan showed him his.

"I'm on the phone with your supervisor. The homeowner called me that she has a prowler on the premises and could be in danger. We're en route there now." Ethan handed his phone to the patrolman and his supervisor talked to him for a minute.

"I'll give you an escort. Jenkins is the name," the patrolman said, handing Ethan's phone back to him.

"All right but hang back and no lights or sirens. If it's who we suspect it is, he or they won't hesitate to shoot it out with law enforcement. But it might be nothing. We have to be sure though."

The patrolman nodded and ran back to his car and Noah took off, speeding again.

The officer in charge that Ethan had been talking to, Detective Ty Richardson said, "We're sending more reinforcements to that location. It's better to be prepared than to be caught shorthanded."

"Right. We'll meet you there." Then Ethan ended the call.

"I wish we could let Charlene know that a bunch of non-shifter law-enforcement personnel are converging on her place," Noah said.

"Yeah. I know. At least we were already in Oyster Bay when we got the call from Charlene, instead of Shelby Bay." They were almost at the house because of it.

"I agree." Noah slowed and parked down the road from the house next to the woods. The patrol car likewise parked some distance behind them on the shoulder.

Then, armed with their guns, they headed through the woods toward the house.

Ethan saw Charlene in her wolf coat behind a cluster of pines, and she looked surprised to see the patrolman with them, but she kept hidden from him. Noah noticed her too, but the patrolman couldn't see her because of the dark.

The home's front and back porch lights gave the patrolman enough light to head toward, though Ethan heard the officer trip a few times in the woods over fallen tree branches and roots sticking up out of the ground and swear just as many times.

They didn't find anyone, but Ethan smelled Kroner's scent on the deck and around some of the windows. Damn it to hell. Ethan wanted more than anything to return to Charlene and make sure she remained safe.

Patrol cars gathered at the house and Jenkins asked, "Where's the homeowner who reported the intruder?"

"She hid in the woods. I'm going to get her." To Noah, Ethan said, "It's Kroner's cologne on the deck and around the windows." Ethan had to alert Noah so that he would be able to catalog Kroner's scent before the police all converged on the house and the scents would be all mixed up. "Let's check out the place and then I'll go get Charlene." Ethan had to grab her clothes so she could shift and dress before she returned to the house. He was sure Kroner hadn't gotten in, but they had to make absolutely certain.

Noah could fill the police in on who Kroner was and why he might be sniffing around Charlene's place.

Ethan went into the bedroom and checked it out, but he hadn't smelled any sign of Kroner in the house. He got some running clothes for Charlene and a pair of sneakers. He slipped them in a backpack and said to Noah, "I'll be right back." He headed out of the house.

He walked into the woods while the officers were examining the grounds around the house and deck. A couple of the officers had even descended the stairs from the deck to the beach to see if anyone had gone down there.

"Hey, it's just me," Ethan called out to Charlene.

She was soon coming out of hiding to greet him, nuzzling his legs, sniffing his crotch in a fun-loving mated way. He crouched down and hugged her. "God, I'm glad you're okay. It was Kroner but he had to have left." Ethan set the backpack down and unzipped it for her. She glanced around and seeing no one, she shifted and began pulling on her clothes.

Then he held her close, hating that he'd put her in this danger. Well, Renault had, but it would have only been a matter of time before Kroner learned that Ethan could have been staying there with Charlene.

"Hey, it's not your fault," she said. "I know you believe you're the one responsible for Kroner coming to the house. I'm sure that Renault was. It looked like you called in reinforcements."

"We had to. We were speeding to reach you and got pulled over."

"Oh, great." Charlene took hold of his hand, and they headed back to the house.

Once they arrived there, Charlene smelled the scents but there were so many around her place because of all the policemen there that she wouldn't be able to isolate Kroner's scent if he should return and she had a chance to smell it. At least he was glad Noah knew it now, having caught the scent before the policeman muddied the waters, so to speak. Noah looked relieved to see she was fine too.

The police took her statement, and she described a man of Kroner's height and build and then they left.

"What do you want to do about the sleeping arrangements?" Noah asked.

Charlene and Ethan looked at him.

"Okay, you know you can't stay at your house. It's been

compromised. Kroner or one of his buddies is bound to return at some time or another. Do you want to stay with me at the DEA house? Or maybe Charlene should stay with the pack at Leidolf and Cassie's ranch until we take this guy down," Noah said.

"I'm not going to leave Oyster Bay," Charlene said, sounding annoyed that Noah was acting like she didn't have any choice in the matter.

"Noah's right," Ethan said.

"I could stay at the house if you want me to keep an eye on things," Noah said.

"Then if Kroner returned, you would be the one who collared him?" Ethan asked.

"Yeah, it would look good for me."

Ethan laughed.

Charlene didn't look happy about it. "Okay, how about—if you are both worried about me—I stay at the DEA house and the two of you stay here and you can *both* take Kroner down if he makes a move on the house again."

Ethan didn't like that idea at all. He wanted to be with Charlene to ensure her safety.

"Or, we can all stay at our house and you both can take him down while I sleep." Charlene smiled at them.

Ethan loved her and smiled. "Okay, rather than us leave here and possibly compromise the DEA house, you and I can take a room at the hotel that you stayed at before, Charlene. So can Noah. We'll stay away from the DEA house for a while, but we can put surveillance on your house or even be there later. Let's pack some bags."

"Okay. I've got spare toiletries you can have," Charlene said to Noah. "You'll have to get some spare clothes until this is resolved if you don't return to the DEA house, but you can have one of my bags to use."

"Thanks," Noah said.

"I'll tell Grainger what's up," Ethan said.

"All right. I'm off to pack," Charlene said.

"I'll make reservations for us at the hotel," Noah said. "The agency will reimburse us for it."

"Seabreeze Hotel," Charlene called out.

Ethan got ahold of Grainger and told him what had happened. "Noah had been staying at the DEA house, but I was staying with Charlene, a former homicide detective."

"Wait, the one whose home we raided by mistake in Portland?"

Ethan smiled. His boss would want to know the details. "Yeah, we're dating now. Thor must have followed Renault to Charlene's house in Oyster Bay. I ended up there and we all had lunch together. When Renault left the house, we had plans for me to meet him at the grocery store and I would see if he was being followed. You know the rest."

"Right. Hell. Okay."

"Noah's making the reservations for two rooms at the Seabreeze Hotel in Oyster Bay."

"Okay, we've got you covered. Just don't let Kroner follow you there."

"No. We'll be careful." If Kroner managed to follow them to the hotel, Ethan was taking Charlene to the pack leaders' ranch where they had a bunch of ranch hands and others to keep her safe. "We didn't have any luck on surveillance either at Oakley's house or his great-aunt's place."

"Keep me informed."

"We sure will, sir."

Then they ended the call, and Ethan went into the bedroom to pack.

Charlene put some extra toiletries together for Noah and then kissed Ethan. "I'll be okay, Ethan."

"I just worry about you, you know."

"I'm fine. I can handle myself."

He knew she kept saying that but if Kroner had a gun, which he would have, she might not be fine. He grabbed her bag and his own. She put the toiletries in a small bag for Noah.

"What we need to do is make certain that if either Kroner or Oakley is watching the house, they have no idea where we're ending up," Ethan said.

Charlene gave Noah the bag of toiletries.

"Thanks, Charlene. I'm heading out first, like I'm leaving your house for the night. I'll drive around to make sure I'm not being followed until I finally head over to the hotel," Noah said.

"We'll do the same thing," Ethan said. "If you learn someone is following you, let me know and I'll come for you."

"Okay, the same with you. If anyone seems to be trailing you, let me know. I'll come to your aid. We'll take whoever it is down together."

Ethan didn't like the idea that Charlene could be in the middle of it, but if they could take these guys down, they had to do it.

CHAPTER 21

"I WISH WE KNEW WHAT KRONER'S VEHICLE LOOKED LIKE," Charlene said to Ethan as they took off in her car in a different direction from Noah so that if Kroner or one of his cohorts was following them, he couldn't track them both.

"I agree. But I kind of suspect he wouldn't have hung around after the police were all over the area. Still, we have to be cautious no matter what."

She was so tired that she just wanted to go to sleep. But she knew Ethan had to be too. Well, both he and Noah. She hoped Noah was all right.

They kept turning down into residential areas and back out again, and finally Ethan drove them to the hotel, sitting above a beach, all lit up, looking warm and welcoming. They parked and went inside. Flames flickered in a fireplace in the lobby, and complimentary wine was being served. Even house-baked goods and cordials were complimentary.

Wow, this was really nice.

Noah was already there checking into the hotel. They smiled at him and joined him at the registration desk. Then they got their key cards and went up to their rooms, not speaking to each other, just in case someone had seen them enter and thought they were with each other. So far, they didn't believe anyone knew Noah was an undercover agent working with Ethan. They didn't want anyone to realize that he was.

"Well," Charlene said, "this is like a honeymoon before the honeymoon."

Ethan laughed. "I'm glad you can see the positive side of this."

"Always. It helps me get through the bumps in life."

He unlocked their door and walked inside with her. The expansive room featured a king-size bed, ocean paintings on the walls, a gas fireplace ready to warm a cold night, and a soaking tub and shower for some sumptuous cuddling and more. The curtains were open, revealing a patio showcasing a view of the ocean, the whitecapped waves rolling onto the sandy beach. Binoculars rested on a table to use for bird-watching, along with lanterns to use while taking sunset walks on the beach. Luxury at its best. Now this was super nice.

They quickly dumped their bags on the carpeted floor, stripped off their clothes, and slipped under the silky beige comforter, sinking into the supersoft mattress. It was so late that they needed to sleep more than anything else. But of course, they couldn't shut down their inquisitive minds right away.

"What happened during your stakeout?" Charlene asked.

"No one was at Oakley's house and his great-aunt's home was quiet too," Ethan said.

"I guess that's why you could come to my aid so quickly."

"Even if they had been at one of the houses, we would have been on our way to rescue you."

Charlene ran her fingers over Ethan's chest in a light caress. "Okay, so I've been thinking. What if Renault is truly the mole? Even though he thought you were retired, Kroner still wants you out of the picture. Renault said he sent me the roses because he thought we could start seeing each other and I might move back to Portland. That seems pretty far-fetched to me. Renault didn't know where you were living because you were staying in a DEA safe house. He learned where I lived, knew we were seeing each other, and came to my house.

"I think he was trying to see me in the event he could connect with you, then tell you all about his stalker. Being the good agent you are, you would have to protect his back. If Renault was working for Kroner, the plan was probably that Thor would kill you, but instead you captured Thor. What if Renault, not Thor, had told Kroner that you had been staying with me? Kroner planned to eliminate you, and me too. That didn't work out for him either. I might have the scenario all wrong, but what if I'm right?"

"Then I need you to stay with Leidolf and Cassie until I take care of the threat," Ethan said.

She shook her head. "I know these men mean business. I've dealt with their kind before. Sociopaths who kill for killing. I've got my rentals to manage, and I live here. It could be months before we take these guys down. I'm not going to hide away at the pack leaders' ranch for months until that happens."

He hated to admit that it could even be years. "All right." This still changed Ethan's focus. Instead of searching for these guys and trying to bring them in, he was going to have to stay close to home to make sure they didn't take Charlene hostage or kill her to get back at him.

"We need to let Noah know what your thoughts are on the matter." Ethan grabbed his phone off the bedside table and called Noah and put it on speakerphone.

Then Charlene explained what she thought might be the case again.

"If that's the case, I'll kill Renault myself," Noah said.

"Yeah, that's the way I was feeling," Ethan said.

"I would rather he spend a long time in jail, and he would have to face the people he had helped put behind bars," Charlene said.

"True," Ethan agreed. "So we need to know what Renault's motive would be if he is involved in this business. Money issues? Drug habit? Blackmail of some sort? There has got to be a reason he would make a deal with these thugs, if he has."

Ethan was damn glad that Charlene had been okay when he and Noah came to her rescue, but if Renault was the mole, Ethan had to do a lot of rethinking the situation. "But Renault gave me Agents Manx and Ryerson's names as possible moles in the DEA."

"Yeah. I was wondering about that too," Noah said.

"Right. I had a case like that. A neighbor told us he was passing by a house where the murdered woman lived while he was walking his dog. He gave a description of the vehicle parked nearby that didn't belong there and then subsequently left. It wasn't until later in the investigation that I realized *he* was the one who had committed the murder," Charlene said.

"But he had sent you on a wild-goose chase looking for a mystery car," Ethan guessed.

"Exactly. What if Renault knew Cohen and Ryerson were taking drug deals but they didn't know that Renault was involved with Kroner too? The other thing I keep thinking about was Renault knew Noah was coming to Portland, and he would realize Noah wouldn't like it if he sent flowers to me."

"You're damn right," Noah said. "Only another wolf beat me to it."

Ethan smiled. He was damn glad he had. "But Renault's a beta and he also understood Kroner wanted to find me and he had to get that information no matter what."

"Right. That would mean Renault was more afraid of Kroner than he was of Noah. Which would make sense. Noah might have ended his friendship but—" Charlene said.

"Kroner would have ended Renault's life if he didn't do what he had tasked him to do," Ethan said.

"Right," Charlene said.

"Hey, Noah, I need to get hold of Tori and see if she can look into Renault's financial situation. We'll talk to you when we get up in the morning," Ethan said.

"All right. Talk to you later."

Then they ended the conversation.

Ethan called Tori, who promised to have her resource guy look into Renault's financial records. Then he answered a call from Leidolf, who promised to send some wolves to watch over Charlene's house. Both Tori and Leidolf wanted Charlene at the pack's ranch, but Ethan assured them Charlene wanted to stay in Oyster Bay for now.

Charlene snuggled with Ethan. "Why do you always call Tori so late? Why not Adam?"

Ethan smiled and kissed Charlene on the forehead. "She's much easier to talk to about a case when it's late now that Adam and Sierra are mated. I've been known to interrupt them at inappropriate times."

They finally fell asleep, but at seven, Ethan got a text and he groaned. Then he checked the text. "It's the guys. They're in the lobby."

Charlene laughed. "I guess we need to get up and dress so we can meet with them."

"Or you could wait for me in bed."

"No way. I want to go with the guys to the house and then we can leave them there."

"They need to go there on their own so they can set up surveillance. If we go with them—"

"Right. If Kroner or his men are watching the place, he will see us return and he could follow us back to the hotel." She let out her breath. "All right. But I'm hungry and want breakfast. So let's eat."

He smiled. "Okay, that works for me."

They both dressed and Ethan called Noah. "We've got reinforcements from the pack. We're meeting them in the lobby. If you want to join us, we can have breakfast together. They're going to house-sit for the time being."

"Oh, great. Be right down."

They met up with their reinforcements, Ethan introducing them to Charlene and Noah since neither of them knew any of the guys. "Brad Redding, a former Navy SEAL, is a subleader and works at the ranch, mostly in security, but as a subleader, he does a variety of other missions also. Josh Wilding, a retired homicide detective, has worked with me on missions before while he was at the bureau. Maverick Wilding, Josh's twin brother, owns and operates the reindeer ranch. And twin brothers Quincy and Pierce Nelson are both in security details at the pack leaders' ranch."

"Hey, good being here," Brad said, giving Ethan a hug and then Charlene. He shook Noah's hand.

"Welcome to the pack," Josh said to Noah and Charlene.

"I'm so glad to be with the pack," Charlene said.

"And congratulations are in order," Maverick said.

The dark-haired twins, Quincy and Pierce, total charmers with any new she-wolves they met, stepped up to welcome them to the pack and congratulate the new couple. "Notice how Ethan never once brought Charlene to the ranch so she could see any of the other bachelor wolves out there?" Quincy said. "All just as fit, strapping, heroic, and eager to make your acquaintance."

Pierce smiled. "Yeah. If she had known about us, things might have been different."

Ethan laughed. "In your dreams."

Charlene smiled. "Thanks to all of you. While you're at Ethan and my house, feel free to eat or drink anything we have there and make yourself at home."

"Thanks. We'll take shifts watching the place and let you know if we have any contact with anyone," Brad said.

"Great." Ethan was thankful Leidolf had sent so many men to help them. He suspected Leidolf was only going to send Quincy or Pierce, because he said he was sending four men not five, but Ethan swore the Nelson brothers came as a set. Then again, maybe it was Maverick who insisted on coming with his twin brother, Josh.

"Leidolf told us the whole situation. If anyone is armed and enters the house, we'll try to use nonlethal force," Josh said.

"But if we have to, we won't hesitate to use lethal force," Brad said.

They needed to take these guys down one way or another. Hopefully nonlethally, but no matter what, they had to stop these guys.

"Could you join us for breakfast?" Charlene asked.

"No, we really need to get to your place. We can park in the garage, right? We don't want Kroner or his associates to know you've got more company," Brad said.

"Yeah. My car is here at the hotel. Ethan's Bronco is in the garage, but you'll have room to park your vehicle."

"Okay, then we're off," Brad said, and the men left.

Then Noah, Charlene, and Ethan went into the restaurant to have breakfast. "What are we going to do now that the guys are house-sitting?" Noah asked.

"We're going to stay here for the day. And then tonight, we can do surveillance," Ethan said.

"When you do surveillance, I'm going to the house," Charlene said. "I'll join the guys there. If Kroner or his cronies come to the house after me, they'll never know what hit them."

Noah and Ethan exchanged glances.

Ethan took a settling breath. "All right. Sounds like a good plan." It was better, he figured, than leaving Charlene on her own at the hotel when he and Noah left to do surveillance.

He leaned over and kissed her and then they ordered their breakfasts. The server soon brought them coffee and tea.

Noah drank some of his black coffee. "Now I can really see what this is all about as far as belonging to a good wolf pack."

"Absolutely. When we were doing just our mission, it was up to us to do it." Ethan added cream and sugar to his coffee. "But when Charlene became a civilian target for these ruthless criminals, all bets were off as far as the pack is concerned."

"See, I told you they were a great group to join," Charlene said.

"I agree. Though how will we explain this to Grainger if they capture one of the guys?" Noah asked.

"They are friends of mine who are law-enforcement trained and who can protect Charlene while you and I are on stakeouts. Grainger will understand. It will be like hiring bodyguards for her. Woe to anyone who might break into the house and try to harm her." Ethan drank some of his coffee.

"Yeah, I like these odds better," Charlene said. "Then the two of you won't have to worry about me."

"We'll worry about you, but we'll feel better about you having protection," Ethan said.

They finished their breakfast and then they had to figure out the car situation.

"If I drive home, I'll have to park in the driveway," she said.

"And if one of the men is watching your place, they'll know your vehicle," Ethan warned.

"So I'll get a taxi to drop me off."

"All right. We'll follow the taxi to make sure you get home all right," Ethan said.

"That sounds good."

"But for now?" Ethan asked.

"Let's take a walk on the beach. Do you want to come with us, Noah?" Charlene asked.

"I hate to bow out but since Ethan and I are going to do surveillance tonight, I need to get some more sleep."

They would need to also, but walking with his mate on the beach first? That totally appealed to Ethan.

They headed to the beach while Noah returned to his room to sleep. Ethan strolled with Charlene along the beach on the chilly, foggy morning. It was beautiful as the sun was coming up and pinks, purples, and yellows were bathing the rocks and water in a wash of brilliant light.

"I love you," Ethan said, leaning down to kiss Charlene, so glad that he was the one saying that to her and not Noah.

As if she knew that's what he was thinking, she said, "If I had been with Noah, you know what he would have done?"

"Walked with you on the beach."

"Nope. Gone to bed so he would be ready for his mission tonight."

Ethan laughed. "He definitely *wasn't* the right wolf for you."

"I agree. But after our beach walk, I wouldn't mind going to bed."

"Not just to sleep though, right?"

She smiled and kissed him. "That too, but more also."

CHAPTER 22

AFTER A LOVELY BEACH WALK, ETHAN AND CHARLENE returned to the hotel room, showered, and went back to bed. They took a much-needed nap, made love, showered, and went to lunch. No one had called them from her house, so Ethan figured it was all quiet over there. Not that they thought anyone would try to break in while it was broad daylight out, but it was important to be prepared, just in case.

"Do you want to have lunch with Noah?" Ethan asked Charlene.

"Yeah, sure," Charlene said.

Ethan called Noah to see if he wanted to join them for lunch.

"Yeah, I'll be right down. Save me a seat."

Ethan and Charlene took their seats with an ocean view and ordered tea and coffee.

Noah soon joined them in the restaurant. "No word from anyone watching the house yet, I take it?"

"No. I figure if there's going to be any movement, it will be later tonight," Ethan said.

"If Renault is the mole, he'll know you're staying at the house, but he won't realize you have friends who are there protecting it now. He might believe, because of last night's botched attempt to break in, that you might not be staying there though."

"The guys will keep the chatter low so if he or anyone else comes to the house, they won't be able to make out their conversation or learn that there are five guys there. They'll have lights on when it gets dark out, play the TV, turn the lights out when it's a decent bedtime, and wait in the dark for something to happen."

"What do we do now?" Noah asked. "I really want to do something instead of just sitting around waiting for nightfall."

Just then Adam called Ethan. "Hey, we've got some action headed your way."

"Oh? What's up?" Ethan said to Noah and Charlene, "It's Adam."

"One of our police officers, Baker, took personal leave for the rest of the week," Adam said.

"Okay?" Ethan knew Baker was up to something or Adam wouldn't have called him about the officer taking leave.

"We figure he's trying to get in touch with Kroner or Oakley. Baker is headed your way."

"How do you know this?" Ethan figured if Baker was involved with this Kroner business, he wouldn't have told Covington, his boss at the bureau, or fellow officers where he was going.

"Tori and I are on his tail."

Ethan smiled. "More reinforcements."

"One way or another, we're going to nail these bastards. Wait, what do you mean there would be *more* reinforcements?"

Ethan explained how Leidolf sent five of their pack members to house-sit.

Adam laughed. "That sounds like Leidolf. But watch Kroner or his men not return to the house this time."

"Yeah, I know. At least we have reinforcements there if we need them close by. Are you and Tori driving together or separately?" Ethan asked.

"Separately. We'll swap out on following Baker but we're staying far enough behind him so that he doesn't catch on, keeping a vehicle or two in between us."

"Good. Did he say 'officially' where he was going?"

"Yep. He said he was going east to see his parents. His mother is supposed to be ill. But he's headed west toward the coast so we figured he was taking a trip to see Kroner or one of his buddies. We had already told our boss it looked like Baker was connected to the murder we were investigating. So he told us to tail him."

"What about Davis? What's up with him?" Ethan asked.

"He's still on the job for now. He might have done some illegal stuff with Baker, but maybe he has stopped, or Baker has just gotten himself deeper into criminal pursuits. Tori said she's staying with Charlene whenever you aren't with her, unless of course the other guys from the pack are watching over her. But she wants to make sure that she's always protected."

"Tell her thanks for me. When will you be in Oyster Bay?" Ethan asked.

"It will take us another two and a half hours."

"Okay, let us know where Baker goes, and we can help you with surveillance. Maybe we can take over tailing him with a different car so he doesn't get suspicious once you're closer," Ethan said.

"That sounds great."

Then they ended the call and Ethan let Charlene and Noah know what was going on.

"So wait, do you think that the two guys Renault identified as possibly being the moles in the DEA was just to take the heat off him? And the guys really didn't have anything to do with it?" Noah asked.

"That's possible. I hate to think that he could be throwing the agents under the bus to save his ass," Ethan said. "Still, after what Charlene had seen regarding Agent Cohen at the convenience store, I still suspect he could be involved."

"I agree. Hmm," Charlene said, "maybe I should talk to Renault and tell him that you and I broke up and I feel so bad about it. Maybe we could talk, and he'll finally slip up and tell me what he's up to."

"No," Ethan said.

Noah agreed with Ethan.

Charlene drank some of her water. "You guys are no fun."

They both smiled.

Then the server took their sandwich orders and left the table to turn them in.

"We just don't want you to get hurt, and if Renault is in league with Kroner, he's not a good guy. He's not the man you or Noah knew," Ethan said. "He's the enemy."

Charlene and Noah agreed.

After lunch, Noah opted to walk along the beach while Charlene and Ethan returned to their room to watch a movie, take another nap, and make love again. They showered before they headed out.

Ethan put Charlene in a taxi and he and Noah followed it to her house. Once she went inside the house and the taxi drove off, she called Ethan to let him know she was safe, and the other guys were there from the pack.

"We're off to do our work and then I'll see you when we return. I'll stay with you at the house after Noah drops me off in the woods so no one makes the connection between him and your house as long as no one has done so before this. I'll just make my way to the back door. I'll let everyone know when I'm on my way," Ethan said.

"Okay, thanks. I'll see you. Love you," Charlene said. "You and Noah be safe."

"You too. Love you, sweetheart."

"So Tori and I are going to have a girl's night in whenever you're away," Charlene said, sounding amused.

Ethan smiled. "Only when I'm away." He didn't want to have to lose his delightful mate during the evenings whenever he had the chance to be with her.

She laughed.

Ethan was glad Charlene wasn't upset that she wasn't involved in all the action. He could focus better on the mission if he felt Charlene was safe.

Then they ended the call and Ethan hoped they would catch these guys so he could just continue to enjoy his time with his mate.

Noah shook his head as he drove them to Shelby Bay. "Hell, you know all the right words to say to her."

"She's all that is important to me. When you find someone who makes you feel that way, then you'll have it made."

"That's for sure. I'm glad for you."

Ethan even more so. Charlene was a veritable treasure.

When they arrived at Oakley's house, they saw no activity again. Noah let out his breath. "I think they're spooked. Maybe they know we've come here watching the house before."

"I didn't tell Renault we were watching the house in Shelby Bay or the one in Oyster Bay. I really don't believe he thinks you are with me, in any event," Ethan said.

"Yeah, I agree. I got a text from him while I was walking the beach, asking me how things were going with selling my house in Destin. I told him I was enjoying the beach and so it fit with that scenario. I'm sure he believes I'm in Florida like I said I would be."

"What if he looks into it? What if he suspects you're here working undercover with me?"

Noah didn't say anything for several minutes. "My house is still up for sale, so if he looked to see if it sold, he would find it hasn't."

"Okay, good. But you have purchased a place in Portland already, correct?"

"Yes. But I haven't moved in yet. I'm still waiting on the closing. That's why this worked out so perfectly for me. I can stay in the DEA house, work on this case, and then when this is wrapped up, my new home should be ready to move into. I'll sign the contract via emails when my home in Destin sells, so I really don't need to return there. I have all my stuff in storage in Portland for now."

"That's good to know. I was worried Renault might have

had some indication you were out here working with me and then check to see if you were really back in Destin."

"I believe we're covered. The only way Renault would know the truth is if Kroner or one of his men saw me with you, took pictures, and shared them with him to check if I was an undercover agent."

"Right." Ethan sure as hell hoped not. Then Ethan got a call from Renault. Talk about eerie timing. "Speaking of the devil. It's Renault." Ethan had to alert Noah so he would remain quiet while he was talking to Renault. "Hey, Renault, any news of anyone seeing any sign of Kroner or Oakley?"

"I might have a lead. Do you want to go with me? I could drop by your house and pick you up."

Shit! That sure put Ethan and Noah in a bind. "Where are you now?"

"Staying at the Oyster Bay Inn. I can be there in about fifteen minutes."

"I thought that Grainger didn't approve of what you're doing." Ethan couldn't believe the latest turn of events.

"I think he changed his mind when we caught Thor."

"Right." But Ethan didn't trust that Renault had gotten Grainger's approval. If he had, Grainger would have informed Ethan. "Make it thirty minutes. I'll get ready for you." Ethan felt he didn't have any choice. "See you in half an hour." Did Renault believe Ethan might be conducting surveillance already? Ethan told Noah, "Go to Charlene's house pronto."

"What now?"

"A hiccup in our plans." Ethan explained what was going on.

"At least Renault's not staying at the Seabreeze Hotel, but this is problematic for us."

"I know. And Grainger hasn't approved it, or he would have told me."

Noah shook his head. "It could be a setup and they're planning on ambushing you while you're with Renault."

"Which is why you'll be watching us."

Noah smiled. "Talk about cat and mouse."

"Yeah, but I've got to get to Charlene's house before Renault heads over there."

"I'm on it."

"Just don't get caught speeding again."

"Just have your badge handy."

Halfway there, they saw flashing lights following behind Noah's vehicle.

"Damn," Ethan said. "We can't get a break."

"There must be a speed trap in here." Noah pulled over onto the shoulder and parked.

The patrolmen waited in his car, probably calling in the plate number.

"Hell, this is going to take forever," Noah said.

"The cost of being in a hurry."

The patrolman walked up to their car and said, "Hey, it's you two again. Do you need our help?"

It was the same officer—Jenkins.

"We're still undercover but we've got a situation. We need to return to the homeowner's house immediately," Ethan said.

"Did you call up reinforcements?" the patrolman asked.

"Yes, bodyguards, so she's safe, but we have a problem. Hey, how about you give me a lift to the house?" Ethan asked, thinking that might be the way to resolve the conundrum.

"Oh, that's a great idea," Noah said. "Then he won't chance seeing me. I'll be on the lookout for you while you head out with him and follow you without him seeing me."

"Is that all right with you?" Ethan asked the patrolman.

Jenkins appeared to be eager to do that, since it was more interesting than stopping speeders and ticketing them. "Yes, sir."

"Thanks so much," Ethan said.

"Good luck," Noah said to Ethan.

"Keep me safe," Ethan said to him in return. To Jenkins, Ethan said, "No word to anyone about this. We don't want the wrong people to learn of it or we'll all be dead."

"No, sir." The patrolman hurried back to his car and Ethan went with him.

Ethan called Charlene once he was in the car. "Tell everyone I'm on my way back to the house. We have a change of plans. An urgent one. Renault is coming to the house to pick me up so I can go with him on a stakeout."

"No. What if it's an ambush?" Charlene asked, sounding worried.

"Noah's backing me up."

"He'd better keep you safe or else."

"I know. I'll have the patrolman, Jenkins, drop me off at the woods before I reach the house. I'll slip in through the back door, just in case Renault shows up before I do. We"—Ethan smiled at the patrolman—"got stopped for speeding again. Maybe I can get something out of Renault to learn what's really going on."

"Okay, I'm telling everyone now," Charlene said.

Charlene was already dressed and hurried out of the bedroom to speak with the men guarding the house. "Ethan's coming through the woods. Don't show yourselves. Renault is coming to get him to conduct surveillance with him."

"Hell, no. What if Renault's working for Kroner?" Josh asked.

"Noah's supposed to be watching his back."

"I'm going too. I'll call Noah to have him pick me up." Josh called Noah then. "Hey, this is Josh Wilding. I'm going with you." He glanced at the others in the house. "All right. I'll meet you in the woods." Then he took off through the back door.

Maverick, his brother, said, "Josh will keep Ethan safe. They used to work together on cases when they had wolf situations to take care of and also when the police had to supplement the DEA missions."

"I'm glad Ethan has someone else to watch over him," Charlene said.

Then Charlene got a call from Ethan. "I'm nearly to the house," he said.

"Josh is going with Noah," Charlene told him.

"Okay, I see him in the woods coming toward me," Ethan said to her. "Hey, Josh, thanks a million."

"You bet," Josh said.

Then she heard a car pull up in the drive. "Renault is here now, Ethan."

"Tell the guys there that Renault can't see anyone in the house. Delay Renault if you have to," Ethan said.

"I will." God, what a mess. She couldn't believe how topsy-turvy everything was. She ended the call and went to the door while the other men slipped off to one of the rooms, but they kept the door open to listen in case she was in trouble and they would come to her aid.

Just as she was about to open the door to Renault's knock, Ethan came in through the back door. "I'll get it. You return to bed like you had been sleeping."

"No way." She gave Ethan a quick hug and kiss. "I'll get you a thermos of coffee like I love you and got up with you before you went off to war." Charlene headed into the kitchen and started to make some coffee.

Ethan smiled. "I love you." Then he answered the door. "I'll be out in a moment, Renault."

"Okay, I'll wait for you in the car." Renault returned to his car and Ethan shut the door.

Ethan embraced Charlene and kissed her much longer and deeper this time.

"If he tries to hurt you or is in league with the ones who want you dead, I will end him myself," Charlene promised.

"You won't need to. I'll take care of him. Love you, honey. I'll be back soon, hopefully with some good news."

"Take care, Ethan. Love you back."

"I will. You do the same."

She poured fresh coffee into a thermos for him while he took a bathroom break, then came back for another hug and kiss and the coffee. "I'll see you."

"Soon, hopefully."

Ethan hurried out of the house and Charlene locked the door. She knew Noah and Josh would try to take down Renault and Kroner and Oakley if they could while protecting Ethan. But she called Noah just to reassure herself. "Don't lose sight of Ethan."

CHAPTER 23

So far, so good, Ethan thought as he rode with Renault back to Shelby Bay, but Renault didn't drive to Oakley's house. Instead, he took a route to a more deserted area where a few businesses had closed down, including a couple of warehouses, a movie theater, a hardware store, and a couple of other nondescript shops at the edge of a wooded area.

"Where are we going?" Ethan tried not to sound like he was getting a little worried and ready to take Renault into custody before Ethan was ambushed.

"I told you. I have a new location where Kroner could be staying."

"How did you learn of it?" Ethan was wary of this whole situation.

"Ferret. He trusted me to take your place as his handler and gave me the new intel. Of course, we don't know if it will be any good, given that he gave Charlene's house address the last time with regard to Kroner, but what if it's right? It's worth taking the chance to check it out."

"What about Grainger? You know he can fire you if he learns you're going out on a limb like this without his approval. Especially since he already said no to you doing this on your own."

"Exactly. That's why I need you to be with me. You

legitimize the action since you're already doing the surveillance under Grainger's orders. I can just happen to be with you when we catch up to Kroner."

Hell. Ethan had known Renault hadn't gotten approval from Grainger. He just hoped they had been wrong about Renault and he could be trusted. He also hoped that Noah was following them to serve as his backup if this all went sideways and Renault hadn't lost him.

Renault parked near one of the warehouses that looked abandoned. Paint was peeling off the outer walls, but a side door looked secure, and so did a rolling, commercial steel garage door. Both doors looked out of place with the condition of the rest of the building. Which made it appear promising that the warehouse could hold some secrets related to a criminal enterprise. About a hundred yards to the west of the warehouse was an auto body repair shop that looked rather shabby on the outside but also had a new steel garage door and heavy-duty front door. To the south were woods and to the east of the warehouse, a couple of abandoned shops, the signs long gone. The windows were boarded up and the properties were listed for sale. Across the street was an old movie theater, also boarded up. It was a shame that someone couldn't come in and revitalize the area.

"Look," Renault said, pointing to a pickup truck near the smaller door.

"Hell, is that…" Ethan started to say.

"Lawrence Baker's truck? The police officer with the Portland Police Bureau? Yeah. What's he doing here if he isn't involved with Kroner?" Renault asked.

"It looks like Lawrence Baker is one of the moles."

"Yeah. Look, there's Agent Manx Ryerson," Renault said, motioning to the car that just pulled up. "One of our DEA guys."

It looked like Ethan and his friends had it right. Officer Baker and Agent Ryerson were involved if Kroner was here.

Two more cars pulled up and Ethan barely breathed while four men climbed out of one car and three out of another.

"Oakley," Renault said.

"Kroner. We need to call this in. We can't take all these men in on our own," Ethan said.

"Come on. We can take them," Renault said. "The element of surprise."

Ethan looked at Renault like he was crazy. No way could they take that many men down on their own. No telling how many others were in the warehouse.

Ethan texted Grainger with their location and names of all who were at the meeting at the warehouse, then told him that Renault was there with him, and Ferret had given Renault the information.

Grainger texted him back, despite the early morning hour. I'm sending the local police force your way, but you're in charge. Where's Noah?

Ethan texted: He's in another car. I ended up with Renault.

Have you cleared him of wrongdoing?

Ethan glanced at Renault. He was texting someone. No, sir.

Keep an eye on him. Take him down if you suspect he's in collusion with Kroner.

Yes, sir. Before Ethan could text Noah, he texted him instead.

Noah texted: We're right here.

Tori called Ethan on his cell, and he told her, "We've found everyone." He gave Tori the location of the warehouse. "Renault and I are watching the building now. Noah and Josh just arrived. We're waiting for local police backup."

"We followed Baker here. We're just pulling up now. My boss got word from your boss, but we also found the connection between police officer Elias Davis and Kroner," Tori said. "You didn't think Adam and I would let you take all the credit for taking these guys down, did you?"

Ethan smiled. "Good show." He wanted to ask her if her financial guy had learned anything about Renault's finances.

Then the police cars began pulling up, shining their headlights and spotlights on the warehouse.

Ethan had the officers surround the warehouse to make sure no one left it. He noticed then that the building had several security cameras. Probably so that Kroner would know if the police or any thugs who wanted to rip them off showed up.

Tori and Adam joined him. Ethan figured she would be glad when this case was over as far as him doing stakeouts and calling her all night long. Unless Noah started calling her on missions once Ethan was fully retired.

Then Noah and Josh Wilding joined them, and Renault's jaw dropped. "When did you get back to Oregon? Did Grainger send you, Noah?" Renault asked.

"I've been working with Noah undercover," Ethan said.

"We weren't supposed to tell anyone, but we all need to work together to take these men down."

"Well, hell." Renault gave Noah a hug. "Glad you're here for good now."

"Yeah, me too. Sorry. Our boss swore me to secrecy," Noah said. "I'm just glad Ethan was able to help you take down Thor. I wanted to help, of course, but I was watching over Charlene."

"Oh, of course. Ethan had worried that I might have led the stalker to Charlene's house," Renault said.

"Right," Noah said.

"I just hope Kroner and his men don't have some other way to exit the building that we are unaware of." Ethan spoke with Ty Richardson, the officer in charge of the support officers there. "I need the blueprints for the warehouse if you can get them quickly."

"On it."

"Okay, good. We need to keep the warehouse surrounded. These men are considered armed and dangerous, and we witnessed them going inside."

At least the building didn't have any windows so no one could shoot out of the building that way.

"An IT hotshot we called has disabled their security cameras," Adam said.

"That's good to hear," Ethan said. "I figured Kroner and his men were watching us, counting our numbers, sweating it out."

"Yeah, for a little bit until their screens went dark. The power's being cut too." Tori smiled. "I got hold of the electric company. I'm sure Kroner and his men are a bit rattled."

"That's where we want them to be." Ethan hoped Kroner was losing control of his men and everything was chaotic inside. At least wolves could see in the dark. These guys couldn't see a thing when the warehouse didn't have any windows even to let in a little illumination from the police lights set up. He was glad he could count on his wolf friends to work with him to tackle the problem.

Ty got on a horn and called for the men to come out and surrender. "We've got the place surrounded."

There was no response.

Ethan could envision them having a standoff for hours, days maybe if the guys inside had planned for a siege and had enough water to drink and food to eat.

Adam got a call on his phone. "It's Chief Covington." Then he said to his boss, "Putting the call on speaker so that Ethan and Renault from the DEA can listen in if it's all right with you, sir."

"Yeah, I'm keeping in touch with Grainger. Kroner called me and said that he has gotten Baker and one of Grainger's men, Agent Ryerson, as hostages," Covington said.

"No way," Ethan said. "Renault and I both watched them walk into the warehouse on their own, no coercion whatsoever. Unless their families are being threatened."

"Anticipating that, we've already picked up their families, just in case, but they said they haven't had any trouble," Covington said. "We believe it's just Kroner's ploy so that we don't approach them while they've got the so-called hostages. Though knowing Kroner and his murderous tactics, he might end up killing one of the officers to show he's serious. The corrupt DEA agents and the police officers should have known how ruthless Kroner can be and that all his men are expendable. He can get replacements for all of them with a snap of his fingers, promises of riches, and his innate charm, though I sure as hell don't see how people can fall for it."

"Yeah, me either," Ethan said.

"The water department cut off their water supply, so unless they have stockpiles of food and drink, we hope this won't last long. I've got to go. Let's keep each other informed," Covington said.

"Will do, sir," Tori said.

Trucks arrived to tow off Kroner and his men's vehicles.

Once the vehicles were gone, barriers were set up for everyone to stay behind. At least the warehouse was far from any other businesses that were still in operation, though it was quiet out here, dead even, so civilians shouldn't be in trouble.

The side door opened and a man who Ethan didn't recognize had Officer Lawrence Baker in front of him, his hands tied in front. Baker was sporting a black eye, and Ethan wondered if Kroner had his men rough Baker up a bit to make it look like he was really a hostage, or he did it because he thought Baker had led the police to him. If Kroner only knew Ferret was the one who had told them, he would want him dead.

"Ferret's going into the Witness Protection Program, isn't he?" Ethan asked Renault.

"Yeah, the minute he told us where Kroner was going to be and once you and I learned Kroner and his men were actually here, they whisked Ferret and his immediate family—mother, sister and her baby—away for their own protection," Renault said.

"I wonder how Ferret learned about Kroner being here." Ethan always asked Ferret when he gave him some good intel or bad.

"Oh yeah, I asked. He said he always liked you and you treated him like a person. He said Kroner was coming after you, making it his priority. Ferret has been going to all the places that he knows Kroner or his men hang out. About half an hour before all of this went down, one of Kroner's men was talking to another, and he said Kroner and a bunch of the guys were going to the warehouse. That he felt it was a death trap, and that Kroner was making it harder for the rest of them to keep from getting caught because of his vendetta against you."

Smiling, Tori shook her head. "I can't fathom an informant would be worried about Ethan's health when he had to believe that Ethan was retired and unable to help him out any longer while on the force."

Ethan had never told anyone, but he'd gone out of his way to see that Ferret's mother was getting some medical care and his sister was provided for when her baby came due. It wasn't just about the job. The guy had just needed a break and it never came until Ethan began to get tips from him and could help Ferret and his family out in some small way. Moving him and his family into the Witness Protection

Program, getting him into treatment, getting a job, all of that would hopefully set him on the right path.

"Yeah," Adam said. "You think Ethan's this tough DEA agent who eats drug dealers for lunch, but he has got a heart. At least Sierra always says he does."

"Me too," Tori said, winking at Adam.

Ethan felt his cheeks heat with embarrassment.

Noah was smiling. "That's pretty great that the people you work with feel that way about you, truthfully."

Ethan had thought Noah would believe he had been too soft on the job. Ethan also knew his friends were giving him a hard time because they figured this would be the last job he did.

Ty brought them the blueprints on the warehouse. Ethan and the others looked them over. There were six rooms, and the rest was an open space, no second story, no basement.

Ethan knew that all his wolf friends had their tactical backpack harnesses if they had to turn wolf. They were tucked away in their gear so that humans wouldn't ask what that was for. He didn't believe they would need them, but if they did, they would be prepared to run as wolves.

But for now, they were stuck playing the game as humans, armed to the teeth with guns.

CHAPTER 24

When Ethan texted Charlene that they had found the men that they were looking for, she was both thrilled and apprehensive. She hoped they got all the bad guys, and no one was injured in the process.

She wasn't sleeping in any event until this was all over. Then she heard someone walking on the deck. The four men staying with her immediately rose from the couches as soon as they heard the deck creak. Then they heard some rustling in the shrubs near the master bedroom window.

How many were there? This wasn't good. Maybe Josh Wilding should have stayed with them instead of going with Noah!

Maverick stripped off his clothes and shifted into his wolf, then rushed through the wolf door and around the house to see what he could see. Charlene wanted to go with him. She didn't like being locked up in the house where she couldn't observe what was going on.

She said to Brad, "I'm going with Maverick." She stripped off her clothes and turned into her wolf and raced out the door. She smelled Maverick's scent going around the back way. She figured it was better to stay together as part of a team and hurried to join him. When he heard her come up quietly behind him, he looked back and inclined his head, telling her he was glad to see her. He probably would rather that she was with him instead of going it alone and having no one watching out for her.

In the meantime, Brad had his gun readied, and he slipped out through the front door to make his way around to the deck where they'd heard someone walking.

But then the shooting began out front, and Maverick and Charlene ran around the front of the house to help Brad. When they came around the side of the house, they saw a tall, muscular man hiding behind the shrubs next to it. Maverick jumped at the man, startling her. He leapt onto the gunman's back, knocking him over. But she recognized the man's scent right away. He was Agent Pete Cohen! The agent who had bullied her at the convenience store.

Agent Cohen cried out in terror as Quincy and Pierre ran out of the house and grabbed his gun. Both Maverick and Charlene growled at the man, telling him in no uncertain terms to not even think of trying to get away.

As soon as Quincy tied Agent Cohen's wrists, Quincy and Pierce ran off to check for any more intruders. Charlene woofed at Maverick to go with them. She had Agent Cohen under her paw. She couldn't bite him, but she would keep him pinned down.

Then she heard movement in the woods. It sounded like someone was trying to flee. A shot was fired, and then she heard a thud. Agent Cohen tried to roll over onto his back, but she put her mouth on his neck, warning him that she would bite him and end his life if he so much as thought about trying to get up and run. Yet she couldn't really bite him, not without dire consequences. She could end up turning him, and he would be a danger to their kind. She smelled him pee his pants and knew he was terrified of her and rightly so. Thankfully, he stayed put after that.

After a few minutes, Quincy and Pierre were hauling two men up to the house through the woods, both of their hands zip-tied behind their backs. Luckily, no one had been injured during the shootout. Charlene figured the shooters couldn't see what they were shooting at all that well in the dark woods. She still couldn't believe one of Ethan's own coworkers would come here to kill him, or her. Then again, money meant more than anything to some people. And anyone who got in their way would be dead.

Maverick and Charlene went in through the wolf door while Brad got on his phone and called Ethan. "Hey, we got one of your DEA buddies, Pete Cohen." He glanced at Charlene still wearing her fur coat and he smiled. "Yeah, she's safe. We also have two other men, no ID, both armed, both firing shots at us. They'll go down big time."

She noted Brad didn't tell Ethan she'd been outside in her fur coat, helping to take down one of the men. Which she appreciated. She would tell Ethan all about it herself later.

Charlene went outside and listened for a few minutes. Then she went around the house and didn't smell any other men in the vicinity that would indicate someone else had been there and gotten away. With her homicide detective training, she wondered how the men had gotten there. They had to have a vehicle out here somewhere nearby. She wanted to disable it before anyone could come for it and take it away.

She started tracking their scents to learn where they'd come from, and a half mile away, she saw a black car sitting on the shoulder of the road next to the woods. Like a wolf on the prowl, she slipped behind the car and saw a blond-haired man sitting in the driver's seat. It had to be the getaway vehicle! They had to take this guy down too. She just hoped she wasn't making a mistake, and he was just some innocent driver, taking a break from driving, lost, or something.

First, she bit the right two passenger side tires and then she went around to the rear passenger tire and bit it. She did it so quickly that the driver didn't have time to see what was going on or react. She dashed into the dark woods and howled to let the others know they needed to grab this guy too.

The car door opened, and the guy got out, looked the car over, and cursed up a storm. He got on his phone and tried to call someone, but no one was picking up the call. And then he tried again, or maybe he called someone else. The guys who were zip-tied up in the house maybe?

She heard someone coming through the woods, headed straight for her. It was Maverick and he was coming to take this guy down. "Drop your gun and put your hands up," Maverick shouted, pointing his gun at the driver.

The guy couldn't see Maverick for the dark woods, but Maverick could see him perfectly well. Maverick immediately moved from the spot he'd called out from. When the guy raised his gun to shoot Maverick or at least in the direction his voice had been, Maverick shot the gun right out of his hand. The driver screamed out in shock.

"The next one goes through your head. It'll be self-defense. I have other men here with me who will testify to it," Maverick said.

She knew Maverick was trying to make out like there were more men with him to scare the driver into giving up peaceably. The others were watching the men incarcerated at the house. She would definitely be his witness—minus her fur coat—in a court of law if it came to that.

"Put your hands on the roof of your car," Maverick said.

The guy reluctantly did so, and then Maverick approached him with his gun pointed at him just in case the driver tried something.

Charlene came running around the other side of the car and growled at the driver, a man of about thirty, wearing a scraggly beard, his eyes heavily hooded, his hair black as coal. He glowered at her, and she knew if he'd still had his gun, he would have shot her.

She was so mad that these men would come to take Ethan and her down that she really wanted to bite him for it. But she was there in case the guy ran. She'd knock him down before he could get very far and act as a deterrent in case he attacked Maverick or did anything else that was rash.

Maverick got hold of one of the driver's wrists, but as soon as he did, the driver tried to get to Maverick's gun. Not hesitating to protect Maverick, Charlene leapt at the driver and, with her full wolf's force, knocked the man onto the ground on his back. She immediately went for his throat. *Don't bite him, don't draw blood*, she told herself.

Maverick said, "You brought this on yourself. If I gave her

the order, she would rip out your throat and I would give her a big hug and she would wag her tail for the praise."

She wanted to laugh at Maverick.

"Okay, you can release him now," Maverick said to Charlene. "As soon as the wolf releases you, you will flip over onto your stomach and put your hands behind your back, nice and cooperative-like. If not, we can go right back to doing this."

The man was sweating like crazy, and he looked like he was scared to death. It was dark out here and all he could probably make out was a big animal with glowing eyes, and the menacing growl she was making as she slobbered on his exposed throat.

"Okay," the driver said, sounding like he was trying to be tough, but he croaked out the words, his heart pounding furiously.

So was Charlene's. She had taken down several criminals over the years, but never in her wolf coat. She hadn't exactly been trained for this, though she supposed no wolf shifter would be. She didn't want to accidentally cut him with her teeth and mix her saliva with his blood. She would have to kill him, or they would have to take him into the pack. They wouldn't want a criminal in their ranks. Maybe he would turn out okay, with the right guidance. But what if he was a bad wolf too? Then they would have to terminate him, and it would be all her fault. Not to mention he could have a family and that would be double the trouble.

"You can let go of him now," Maverick said in a way that sounded like he appreciated her help, not that he was ordering her about like a master to a dog. She was surprised Maverick had called her a wolf and not a police dog or wolf dog even. Maybe to put the fear into the guy, but she could smell how scared he was.

Then she growled again, held on, not letting go immediately. She wanted the driver to know that she was a little… wild at heart and that she had to decide this for herself. Then she released him. Before the driver could roll over on his stomach like Maverick had told him to do, Maverick was flipping him over and getting the ties on his wrists. Then he pulled him off the ground and headed for the house.

"Good job," Maverick said to Charlene.

She howled for good measure, letting the driver know she was a wolf, or part wolf, if he was inclined to believe it. Then she saw the blue flashing lights of police cars coming to put these guys in jail. She stayed behind the driver, stepping on his heels a couple of times so he knew she was right there, making sure he didn't try to run off.

As soon as they got closer to the house, she melted into the woods. Maverick handed the driver over to the police and gave them the driver's gun, explained who he was, and joined the others in the house.

"You run the reindeer ranch with your brother," one of the officers said, smiling. "My kids love how you have them displayed at Christmastime at different locations. We would never have gotten to see them where your ranch is located. They loved the red wolves you brought too. Sweetest wolves ever."

The driver looked at Maverick with a scowl on his face.

If he hadn't believed Charlene was a wolf, he did now. "That wolf threatened to rip my throat out."

"What wolf?" the officer asked.

"That one!" The getaway driver motioned with his head to behind him, but Charlene was well hidden in the woods, listening to the conversation, amused.

"Yeah, tell another story. You'll go to prison with the rest of the men who are involved in this."

"The rest of the men?" the driver asked, sounding surprised.

What did he think? That his boss would get him out on bail?

"Your boss? The rest of his henchmen? They're all going down as we speak," Maverick said.

At least they hoped they were, Charlene thought, but she was glad they caught this guy and the others too at least.

CHAPTER 25

Ethan called Grainger and said, "We're just at a standstill here at the warehouse." Then he got a call notification from Charlene. "Got to go. Charlene's calling me."

"Hope everything is okay at her place. Out, here," Grainger said.

Worried that something bad had happened at Charlene's home and she was in danger, Ethan answered the call right away.

"Hang up on me if you're in a volatile situation and can't talk," Charlene said, always concerned for his safety.

"We're at a standoff with Kroner and his cronies inside a windowless warehouse, hunkered down and we've got them surrounded. What's going on at your place?" He suspected everything was all right when she didn't tell him right away that anything was wrong.

She explained everything that had happened, and he swore. He hadn't wanted her outside running around as a wolf, trying to take these men down.

"All of us are good. All the bad guys are in custody. I just wanted you to know there are a few bad men who will no longer be causing any trouble," she said.

"They were using police officer Baker as a hostage, not sure if he truly is at this point, since he walked inside the warehouse looking like he didn't have a care in the world.

Three law enforcement guys used as hostages will deter us from rushing the place, Kroner figures."

"Even though we're sure they're involved."

"Yeah. I doubt that anyone will take another chance of overrunning your house, but the guys are still there with you, right?" Ethan figured they would be until he returned home and they'd taken care of the men in the warehouse, even if it took a couple of days.

"Yes. Quincy and Brad are lying down while Maverick, Pierce, and I are keeping guard. After a few hours, we'll switch off."

"That sounds good. I love you. You stay safe."

"You too. Let me know what's going on when you can."

"Call me before you lie down so I don't wake you."

"If you end this siege, you call me, whether I'm sleeping or not. I probably won't be, worried about you until it's done."

"Okay. I love you."

"Love you too."

Then he pocketed his phone and Tori, Adam, Josh, and Renault were smiling at him.

"I never thought I would see the day that you would be head over heels for a woman." Then Renault frowned. "Charlene's okay, isn't she?"

"Yeah. Agent Pete Cohen and some of Kroner's men went after Charlene, but we had some other men in place to watch over her, so Kroner's men are in custody now," Ethan said.

"Cohen?" Renault said. "Other men were there? Good thing. I could kill Cohen myself for going after Charlene."

Josh shook his head. "I was so intent on being there with

Noah for Ethan that I didn't think I would be needed back at the house."

"It's all good. They've caught them," Ethan said, though he was furious that Kroner had sent the men and that one of his own fellow agents was involved in trying to break into the house. He knew they would have planned to kill both him and Charlene, had they been at the house without protection.

Renault frowned. "So who was staying with Charlene?"

"Friends." Ethan looked at the distance between the warehouse and the auto body repair shop. He wondered… "Do you think there could be a tunnel that leads from the warehouse to maybe that body shop? Or to the woods out back?"

"Yeah, that's a good bet," Adam said.

Ethan asked Josh, Adam, Tori, and Noah, "How about you accompany me to see if we can hear anything below-ground, in the event there are escape tunnels connected to the warehouse." He wouldn't put it past Kroner to have built something like that, figuring he would have a fast way out if law enforcement officials discovered he was dealing out of this warehouse. Most likely no blueprints would be available for any additions that were being used for an illegal purpose.

"Yeah, let's do it," Noah said.

"You need ground-penetrating, tunnel-detective sonar to locate tunnels," Renault said.

"Which they don't have here, so we need to improvise." Ethan knew the longer they waited, the more likely they wouldn't catch the guys if they did escape through a tunnel into the body shop or somewhere else.

Josh and Tori said, "I'm with you."

"Me too," Noah said.

Renault said, "I can't see that will do any good though. I'm going to go straight to the body shop over there."

Ethan spoke to Ty Richardson then. "Some of my people are doing a search for tunnels leading to the auto body repair shop. Can you send some men with Renault as his backup? He's going to the body shop. Can you get me some blueprints for that shop? And also learn who owns it?"

"Sure will. Do you want any of my men to help you?"

Ethan knew they wouldn't be able to hear anything like the wolves could, but if Kroner and his men were headed for the body shop, they would need some backup to search that shop. "Yeah. I want to search the area for any signs that a tunnel or tunnels might extend from the warehouse to the building closest to this one."

Adam quickly said, "I'll go with Renault to back him up."

Ethan had another six of the officers spread out around the second building to aid Adam and Renault. They needed some indication that there was a tunnel between the two buildings. Renault was on his phone texting someone as he and Adam ran toward the building. The auto body repair shop did have windows, but they were grimy and covered in cardboard. Ethan just hoped that if Kroner and his men were in the building, they didn't start shooting out the windows. It was impossible to see if anyone was inside.

Ethan and his wolf friends began to move away from the

warehouse, headed for the auto body repair shop about ten feet parallel to one another, listening for sounds of anyone moving and talking in a tunnel belowground.

Then suddenly Tori motioned to Ethan that she'd heard something where she was walking and he, Josh, and Noah hurried over. They could hear talking and then yelling. They couldn't make out the words, just heard the voices. Then three shots were fired in rapid succession underground.

Ethan called Renault on his phone. "Someone just fired three shots in a tunnel below us." Ethan was trying to give Renault the benefit of the doubt, though he was still keeping a close eye on him.

"Hell."

"We're still following their sounds, but you can see the direction we're headed," Ethan said. "It looks like they'll come out of the tunnel into the auto body repair shop. If they do and we try to stop them, they'll be ready to shoot it out. We don't know if anyone's been left behind in the warehouse either."

Then Ethan received a text with the blueprints for the auto body repair shop, and the name of the owner from Ty. But Ty also texted: Shop is under investigation for being a chop shop.

Was the owner in collusion with Kroner? Ethan wouldn't be surprised to learn that he was. He texted back: Thanks.

Ethan relayed the information to his wolf friends and Renault. They reached the building, and the wolves could hear movement and talking inside. Again, they couldn't make out the conversations, but something was going on.

Then they heard the roar of the engines of a couple of cars inside the auto body repair shop.

Ethan called out to the officers, "They're inside the building, getting ready to take off in a couple of vehicles."

Some officers scrambled to get to their police cars so they could pursue the vehicles as soon as they left the body shop. Then the garage door rolled up with a rumble. A black Chevrolet full-sized pickup shot out of the building. One man was driving the truck. It looked like no one else was in it, but they could be ducking down, hiding. Ethan suspected the truck was a decoy to draw the police away from Kroner.

Three police cars took chase after the first truck. Within seconds, a dark-blue GMC full-sized pickup truck roared out of the garage headed in the opposite direction and more police took off after it. Again, only the driver was visible.

Ethan, his wolf friends, Renault, and some of the officers went into the auto body repair shop, searching for anyone who might have been left behind. They had to find the tunnel and learn if anyone had been shot.

"Here's the hatch to the tunnel," Tori shouted out to the team. "Behind these barrels."

Adam joined her, but Renault and Josh continued to search every nook and cranny with Ethan, just to make sure that no one was hiding in the shop. Ethan wondered if the six vehicles still in there were stolen. None of the vehicles had any license plates.

A group of officers were still watching the warehouse to make sure no one escaped while others were in pursuit of the escaped vehicles. Ethan figured once the police called in the descriptions of the two vehicles, they would learn if the cars had been stolen.

They found no one in the chop shop so they went down into the tunnel, Ethan leading the way, hoping he didn't get shot at. But the tunnel was dark, so he felt like a wolf in shadows. Unless Kroner and his men had night-vision goggles, they couldn't see to shoot at Ethan and the rest, but they could just randomly shoot at anything in the tunnel coming to get them. They were quiet though, trying not to betray their presence.

Then Ethan smelled blood. Before he reached the body, he realized it was Officer Baker and he was still alive. Ethan hated to do it, but he turned on his phone light, hoping he wouldn't get shot at, but they needed the light for the other officers with them. "We need to get help for him, pronto. He might still live. He's a Portland Police Bureau police officer. Lawrence Baker."

Tori brought out her first aid kit and began to bind Baker's wounds. Two of the officers carried the wounded man back through the tunnel toward the auto body repair shop.

"Getting an ambulance." Adam was texting for one as they continued their way through the tunnel.

The money Officer Baker had received for working with criminals wasn't enough to make it worth nearly losing his life over. He still might not survive the ordeal.

Ethan smelled Kroner and Oakley's worried, frantic scents in the tunnel. They were recent. They also smelled the other men's scents, including Agent Ryerson's and Officer Davis's.

They continued on their way until they reached a ladder going up into the warehouse, Ethan assumed. He was afraid that as soon as he popped his head out of the hatch, he would get it shot off.

He opened the hatch and rushed up into the warehouse. Josh swore behind him, and Ethan knew he didn't like that Ethan was putting himself in danger. But someone had to do it. He didn't hear any sign of anyone. He was sure no one was in the warehouse any longer. The other wolves and officers joined them, and they spread out, looking for hiding places where any of the wanted men could be concealing themselves. Josh motioned to the others, pointing to another hatch.

"Unlock the door to the warehouse so the other officers waiting and watching the building can come in, search the premises further, and make sure we didn't miss anything," Ethan said. Though he smelled heroin hidden in the building.

"Right on it." One of the officers ran to the warehouse door and unlocked it.

If Kroner and the others went down into another tunnel, and this wasn't just a storage room, the men were probably long gone. Ethan pulled open the hatch and listened. He didn't hear any sounds, but he went down the ladder and smelled several men's scents, including Kroner's and Oakley's. They were recent too. The other men and Tori followed Ethan underground.

Ethan texted Ty to tell him about this tunnel and where he thought it might lead to, though it could angle off in another direction. When he reached the next ladder, he was disappointed that they hadn't found anyone in the tunnel. The men had escaped.

As soon as he opened the hatch, he breathed in the chilly

night air and the men's scents. He climbed out and the others soon joined him. There was nothing out there but vacant land, trash that people had illegally dumped, and wooded acreage. The men had scattered to the wind.

Ty and the other officers joined Ethan. "What now? The cars that left the auto body shop were stolen. They've been stopped, and the men arrested. Only the drivers were in the cars and the wounded officer is on his way to the hospital. He's in critical condition."

"I hope he pulls through." If for nothing more than to charge him for criminal misconduct and put him in prison for his crimes. Ethan didn't want him to die for his greed and stupidity. Baker might testify against Kroner and the others after one of them had attempted to kill him, which should help the DEA's case. "Keep searching the area. I'm going to head this way."

The police officers were using flashlights to look for the culprits. The wolves weren't.

Ethan and his friends searched in the direction that they smelled Elias Davis, the bad cop, Max Ryerson, the bad DEA agent, Oakley, and Kroner's scents. The four men had separated from each other to avoid being captured together.

Josh and Noah had gone after Oakley's scent. Adam and Tori went after the bad cop, Davis. They had to rely on the other officers to capture Agent Ryerson and the rest of the men who had been involved in Kroner's business.

As if Renault knew Ethan was hot on the trail of one of the men, he stayed close to him. Ethan finally realized Kroner was headed to the coast.

CHAPTER 26

For the first time since Charlene had left the police department as a homicide detective, she wished she was still working at the job, only in Oregon so she could be with the guys and Tori out there to help bring down the rest of the men. Kroner was bad news for everyone decent. Charlene hated not knowing what was going on with Ethan and the others.

"They'll get them," Maverick told her as she went back to the kitchen to get everyone some more coffee. "You rocked when you went after the driver of the getaway vehicle while the rest of us were here with the guys we had captured. Not to mention that you guarded the one guy until we could get him wrist-tied and ready for transport."

"Yeah, but I wish we could be out there helping Ethan and the others," she said.

Brad shook his head. "If you hadn't gotten that driver, we might never have ever caught up with him. By being here, we got more of Kroner's men."

"I agree with the other guys. You were amazing. We only just learned you had been a homicide detective in Destin. You didn't even give any of us bachelor males a chance to get to know you." Quincy winked at her.

Pierce smiled and agreed with his brother.

She was glad that she had helped the men take down a couple of the bad guys.

"So Ethan wouldn't tell us how he met you exactly," Pierce said.

"He raided her house," Brad said. "Ethan was just lucky as hell that she forgave him for that."

Pierce and Quincy laughed. "If we had done that, she probably would have given us a piece of her mind and never had another thing to do with us," Pierce said.

"And Leidolf would have been all over our cases," Quincy said.

Ethan texted Charlene: In pursuit of Kroner. Love you.

Charlene texted back: Love you back. Stay safe.

She wanted to tell him not to take any unnecessary risks, but she knew him, and truthfully, he was a lot like her. To get the job done, they did whatever it took. She relayed the information to the men staying with her. She was sure Maverick was worried about his brother just as much as she was worried about Ethan.

After a short while, Ethan heard gunfire off in the distance behind them. It sounded like the other officers had found someone to pursue. Ethan just hoped none of the officers would be injured during their search for the criminals. Ethan and Renault couldn't disengage from their pursuit of Kroner to join the firefight. He knew the rest of his friends would also continue to trail the men they were after.

Renault looked like he wanted to go to the other officers'

aid though. "Should we help the other men? Maybe the ones we're after went that way."

"I smell Kroner's cologne wafting this way," Ethan said.

"All right. You always steer us in the right direction, though I don't know how you do it," Renault said.

They got quiet again. Ethan was certain Kroner and the others would keep moving. They might not have a car anywhere close to the woods, but if they could reach any place that had one, they would steal it for sure. He and his team just had to stop them before that happened. Ethan was afraid if they didn't, Kroner would finally leave the state or the country. Though Ethan wondered if the reason he hadn't left already was he was trying to make this one last score at the warehouse before he could ship out.

In the direction they were headed, Ethan smelled the scent of the ocean and heard the waves splashing at the bottom of the cliffs. To the north, Kroner would find beach homes along the coast, and Ethan worried Kroner would try to break into a home and take hostages. He'd done it before. Ethan had to stop him before that could happen.

He knew he needed to run as a wolf, despite that his injured arm hurt every time he did. But they had to get these men at all costs.

Ethan stopped Renault, wishing now that he'd had one of his wolf friends with him. They would have made a much better team. He kept his voice low so only Renault would hear him. "Stay here and I'll see if I can track him down. He might be hiding around here, so if he moves, you take him down. But if I find him moving away from here, I'll let you know."

"Are you sure that you want us to separate?"

"Yeah. If he's hiding here, one of us needs to stay and apprehend him."

"All right." Renault sounded glad to be staying behind.

Ethan ran off in the direction he smelled Kroner's scared and angry scent. Ethan was still pursuing Kroner's scent when he saw a cabin to the north, its porch lights on and a van parked in the driveway—perfect for a getaway.

Ethan didn't see any sign of Kroner though. He hoped he hadn't lost him. Ethan removed his clothes, tucked his gun, phone, zip ties, and his clothes into the tactical wolf backpack and tied his boots onto it. The backpack was designed similarly to the ones offered for sale for dogs but were more advantageous for wolves who needed to take their clothes with them on a mission. The wolf who came up with the idea was a genius.

Ethan pulled the straps over his arms and around his chest, cinched it, shifted into his wolf, and pulled the cord to tighten the gear around his wolf body. But Ethan realized he'd lost Kroner's scent once he was on the move. Instead, he picked up Officer Davis's scent. What the hell had happened to Kroner? But Ethan was glad that he had caught up with Officer Davis's scent at least.

Ethan hoped he could take down Davis before Kroner linked up with him, if he planned to. Davis would never expect a wolf to be following him, and Ethan had the advantage of running much lower to the ground. Davis wouldn't see him until it was too late. After searching for the bad cop's scent again, Ethan saw movement—a silhouette of a man standing up behind thick underbrush. *Davis*. Davis started to move toward the beach house, but he got tangled up in a blackberry bush bramble. He was swearing up a storm as he was trying to free his pants stuck in the thorns.

Hoping Kroner wouldn't come to his aid, Ethan dashed forward, needing to end this chase now before Davis could get away. Davis was still struggling, continuing to curse when Ethan leapt twelve feet in his direction and took him down in the middle of the thorny bush.

Davis fell hard, not sure what had struck him, his phone dropping in the brambles. The phone light flipped toward the ground, the dark engulfing him and Ethan. While Davis was still stunned and caught even worse now in the brambles, Ethan leapt away. In the darkness of the woods, Ethan quickly loosened the cord on his backpack, shifted, dressed, and grabbed the wrist ties from the pack. The brambles were on a slope and Davis's head was facing down the slope, so he couldn't get up at all. Ethan leaned over and tied Davis's wrists together, the thorns scratching Ethan's hands. Ethan's injured arm was killing him, but then he located Davis's guns—Davis had three on him that Ethan could find—and bagged and secured them.

"Who... What the hell," Davis said.

Ethan texted Renault: Go toward the cliffs and then directly north. You'll see a cabin with porch lights on and a van sitting in the driveway. I've got Officer Davis caught up in a blackberry bush just south of there in the woods.

Renault texted: On my way.

Ethan read Davis his rights. "This time you're not going

to get away with all the criminal activities you've been involved in."

"Agent Masterson?" Davis said, still sounding like he wasn't quite with it and, in the dark, he couldn't make Ethan out.

"One and the same." Ethan could smell Baker's blood on Davis's clothes, but he didn't have gunshot residue on his hands. None of the guns Davis had on him had been fired recently. Davis hadn't shot Baker.

"But a wild animal jumped on me and knocked me down. I'm sure of it. Something huge and furry with glowing eyes." Davis's eyes were wild with fright, his heart beating hard, like he was afraid the wolf would return.

"I chased the wolf away. You're lucky I came to your aid so he didn't end you." Like Ethan had *wanted* to do. He texted Grainger: Got Officer Davis.

Grainger texted back: He's not getting away from facing charges and you're due a retirement.

But they hadn't gotten all the guys. Like Kroner and Oakley, as far as Ethan knew, and Agent Manx Ryerson. Ethan felt it was his obligation to finish this fully.

"Damn it, get me out of here. These thorns are cutting me to shreds," Davis said. "They're stabbing me in the back."

"Just hold still. My partner's coming and we'll get you out of there. So who shot your partner, Baker?"

"Kroner. We all thought we were next."

Ethan finally heard movement in the woods and saw Renault. Ethan turned on his flashlight to guide Renault the rest of the way to where Davis was still stuck in the brambles.

Renault finally reached them and shined his flashlight down at Davis. "It looks like he's stuck there for good."

"Get me the hell out of here," Davis said.

"Getting him out of there with him being practically upside down and as big as he is will be a job," Ethan said.

He and Renault just studied him.

"What the hell are you waiting for?" Davis growled.

Ethan texted Ty: Renault and I have Officer Davis. We're by the cliffs at the coast. There's a cottage just north of us with a van out front and porchlights on. If you can have a patrol car sent there, you can pick him up.

Ethan gave him the coordinates to their location.

Ty texted back: We've caught four of Kroner's men. We'll have a car sent your way.

Ethan texted: Thanks. We have to cut him out of some brambles, but we'll be there shortly.

In truth, Ethan wanted to leave Davis in his thorny bed until the police car arrived. As big as Davis was, it would be better to have more officers to help. Though Ethan had pulled three guns off him, he might have a knife or another gun on him that he hadn't been able to reach because they were concealed on his back.

Renault glanced at Ethan, waiting for him to give him the go-ahead to get Davis out of the mess he was in.

"Ty's sending a police car to pick him up. We'll wait until the car is at the beach house. Davis is so heavy and because of the odd angle he's at, it will probably take four of us to get him out of there." Whether or not that was true didn't matter. Ethan just didn't want to take any chances with the guy.

Renault nodded. "Sounds good to me."

While Ethan and Renault waited for the police backup, Ethan got text updates from the other wolves. Oakley and Ryerson were still at large with Noah, Josh, Tori, and Adam in pursuit.

Ethan heard a car coming along the road and he saw it was a police car. Relieved, he waved his flashlight at them. They couldn't reach their location by vehicle and parked, then two officers got out of the car and headed toward them through the woods.

Ethan had a flash of apprehension crawl across his skin as he worried that these men might be on Kroner's payroll like the two DEA agents and the two Portland Police Bureau officers.

"Hey, thanks for helping out," Ethan called out to the two men.

"Yeah, we're glad you got this one. Others are still out searching for some of his men," the one officer said.

Ethan, Renault, and the two officers worked on cutting Davis out of the blackberry bush. Once they freed him, they took him to the police car and the officers drove off with him. Ethan noticed a white-haired woman, a bystander, glance out the beach house window, a light behind her showing her highlighted between the curtains. He didn't blame her. With the police car's lights flashing, she had to worry that something bad had happened.

Ethan said to Renault, "Oakley, Kroner, and Agent Ryerson are still on the run. Are you ready to hunt them down? Ty said they've caught four of Kroner's henchmen."

"It's going to be getting light out soon and that will help us to find them," Renault said.

Unfortunately, Ethan couldn't run as a wolf when it grew lighter out.

CHAPTER 27

Ethan and his team headed back in the direction they had come, hoping on the way back to come across Oakley, Kroner, or Agent Ryerson's scent trail before the men had split up and the wolves had taken different paths to search for them. The sun was beginning to rise, and Ethan smelled Renault's own scent change from being more anxious to relieved. Ethan was glad he had such great night vision. He couldn't imagine how hard it would be to fumble around in the dark otherwise.

He heard someone coming and motioned for Renault to get down. Both of them crouched behind some shrubs as they watched and listened. He was certain Renault hadn't heard anyone coming yet.

Then Ethan saw movement off in the distance. He frowned. It was Noah and Josh. They were still some distance from him and Renault, scouring the area. Ethan motioned to Renault that it was their guys out there. Ethan and Renault remained hidden in case Noah and Josh chased one of the guys they were after in their direction and they could ambush him.

That's when Ethan heard someone moving low in the brush closer to them. Whoever it was had been hiding, but he must have heard Noah and Josh coming up on him, so he had to move. Hell, good news. It was Agent Ryerson.

Ethan indicated to Renault that their prey was headed straight for them, to keep down low until it was too late for Ryerson to change course. Noah and Josh would also be closer and the four of them could take the agent down.

Agent Ryerson was practically right in front of them when Ethan jumped out of the brush with his gun at the ready, Renault following his lead. Ethan shouted, "Down on the ground now. You're under arrest."

"What? You're making a mistake. I was searching for Kroner to arrest him. I was sure he went this way." Agent Ryerson was sweating profusely, despite the chilly morning air, and he smelled anxious.

"Sorry, not buying it," Ethan said, disarming him. "Grainger put me in charge of the operation, and he would have told me you were joining us."

Renault shook his head. "Not to mention we watched you go inside the warehouse with Kroner. Care to tell another story?"

Not that Ethan or Renault would believe anything he was going to tell them.

Josh and Noah ran to join them, now that they didn't have to worry about the agent ambushing them.

"He's playing the innocent, that he's just one of us trying to catch Kroner," Ethan told them while Renault zip-tied the agent's wrists and read him his rights.

Ethan texted Ty: We've got DEA Agent Ryerson in custody. We'll take him to the same place where your other officers picked up Officer Davis and you can transport him out of here.

Ty texted: Good show. Sending a car to pick him up.

Then Ethan texted Adam: We got Agent Ryerson. As soon as he's hauled out of here to face charges, we'll be joining you. Josh and Noah are here with us too.

Adam texted: Good. We found Oakley's scent again. He's headed to the coastline.

Ethan thought it was way too much of a coincidence that Kroner, Oakley, Officer Davis, and Agent Ryerson had headed to the coastline. To steal a car from one of the oceanside homes? Or was one of the homes another of their safe houses?

Ethan texted: Kroner, Officer Davis, and Agent Ryerson were headed that way also. What are the odds that they have a place along here where they planned to hole up?

Adam texted: Good thinking.

Ethan texted Ty: Oakley was also headed to the coast. Can you learn who owns the houses cliffside near where we found Davis?

Ty texted: I'll check into it.

To hopefully speed things up, Ethan asked Agent Ryerson, "Which house were you going to along the coast?"

"I don't know what you mean."

Really? Ryerson was going to play dumb now?

Ethan folded his arms. "Listen, you know you're in a lot of hot water. If you cooperate, the DA might give you a break."

"He'll kill me."

"Kroner?"

"Yeah."

"You think he's going to let you live anyway? If he has

contacts on the outside, you know you're a dead man. He could very well believe you had everything to do with us learning he would be at the warehouse." Ethan raised his brows, waiting for that bit of news to sink in. "Who tried to kill Officer Baker?"

"Kroner."

Ethan was glad they had confirmation from both Davis and Ryerson as to who had shot Baker. "So see? If he believes you're going to spill the beans on him, disagree with him in any way, the next thing you know, you're dead."

"Is Baker going to pull through?" Ryerson asked.

"The odds are in his favor. That means he'll talk and put Kroner away for life, and you'll be stuck with the rest of the gang in prison for nice long-term sentences. So where's the hideout you were headed for?" Ethan asked.

Agent Ryerson let out his breath. He didn't have anything further to lose so he finally said, "I'll show you the way."

"Who all knew about this?" Ethan asked as they walked with him to where the house would be. He was hoping Oakley and Kroner would be on their way there and they could give them a nice welcoming party.

"Kroner and Oakley. Me, Baker, Davis, and Agent Pete Cohen. But none of the other men working for Kroner knew about it. Kroner figured if too many people knew the location, someone might talk. He trusted us because he needed us on the law enforcement side of the house to keep him out of trouble."

"So much for that working out," Ethan said wryly. "Why did Kroner shoot Baker?"

"Baker said Kroner had put them all in danger when he'd called the meeting at the warehouse and had them all arrive at the same time. I think we all agreed with Baker, but we kept our mouths shut because we knew how volatile Kroner could be. Baker had been paranoid about getting caught for his participation in all these drug deals for some months now. He told me on more than one occasion he thought the detectives who conduct internal criminal investigations were looking into him."

"Did he tell Kroner that?" Ethan asked.

Agent Ryerson shook his head. "He told me, Agent Cohen, and Officer Davis that he was sure Kroner would kill any of us if he thought we could be up on charges and then be flipped to testify against him. And Baker couldn't quit. You can't just say to the boss you're not going to do this anymore and live to tell of it. But he was getting more vocal, maybe hoping the rest of us would agree with him and convince Kroner it wasn't a good idea. Kroner was getting a big payment for a shipment of heroin and Kroner wanted everyone there to make sure he had the muscle to ensure the guys delivering it didn't stiff him.

"So Baker was the one saying he didn't want to be there, that he felt something would go wrong. Kroner assumed he had talked to the DEA about it. In the tunnel, Kroner accused Baker of setting him up and shot Baker, then left him for dead. All of us were shocked and we thought any one of us could be next on the chopping block. But then Kroner said men would drive two stolen vehicles out of the auto body repair shop garage to lead the police on a chase. If it worked, they could get out of there and not get caught. Still, whoever took the job knew they were serving as the decoys, and nobody wanted the job.

"Kroner said either he got a couple of volunteers, or all of us would end up like Baker. Finally, two of the men said when they were younger, they used to race cars down the city streets in the middle of the night. They thought they could get away with it, so they finally volunteered. It didn't matter to Kroner who did it. He just wanted to make sure *he* could get out another way and not get caught."

"So he and the rest of you backtracked through the tunnel into the warehouse and took another tunnel out of there," Ethan said, "bypassing a wounded Baker."

"Yeah. He looked like he was dead. Maybe he had been playing possum. Smart of him, really. None of us had known about the tunnels. I figured the only reason Kroner told us about them then was so that there would be a bunch of us out running in the dark like chickens with our heads cut off. Then those of us who knew where to go—Kroner, Oakley, me, and Officer Davis would go to the safe house. Believe me, I was afraid that when I got there, Kroner would have me killed as a loose end. But I had the notion he and Oakley might not make it, and I could slip into the house and be safe until I could figure out what to do next."

Ethan noted that not once had the agent mentioned the hurt his family or the other families could be in if Kroner went after them. "So what does your wife think of all this?"

Agent Ryerson's face lost all its color. The guy had two little girls, ages five and seven. Ethan couldn't understand how these men who had good jobs—had an income, although maybe not like the criminals had—found it so easy to risk it all for just some extra money. Risked losing their families. Or was there more to it than that? The thrill of being the bad guy for once? Ethan couldn't understand it.

"She doesn't know about any of it," Ryerson finally said.

When they reached the beach house, Ty arrived with a search warrant and handed it to Ethan. "The owner is Clara Snyder."

Hell. The grandmotherly, retired teacher hadn't been a sweet, old lady who had been bamboozled into buying cars for these guys. She appeared to be in the middle of all this business.

Ethan pounded on the door and when Clara answered it, her eyes widened. But she was fully dressed, looking tired with dark bags under her eyes like she'd been up all night. "Yes?" she asked, sounding perfectly innocent, but it appeared she was up to her eyeballs in working with Kroner.

"We have a search warrant." Ethan handed it to her. "If you're hiding anyone who is wanted by the police, you'll be charged with aiding and abetting and obstruction."

Clara pursed her thin lips but didn't say anything. Then she finally motioned for them to enter the house. "I'm calling my lawyer."

"You're free to do so." Ethan headed into the house with his wolf friends and Renault, smelling for Oakley's scent. He followed that scent down the hall toward the bedrooms.

Some of the investigators were looking for evidence that the men used this as a safe house and found plenty of it in the other rooms, as Ethan heard one of the men say they found a stash of drugs, guns, and money.

Ethan heard the shower running and moved quickly toward the bathroom. Josh was right behind him, and Adam and Tori went into the bedrooms on either side of the bathroom. The shower was running in the bathroom, the window open, water all over the floor and below the windowsill, but Oakley couldn't have climbed out the small bathroom window.

"Someone's headed out the back way," Adam called out from one of the bedrooms. "He went out this window."

"That's Oakley," Ethan confirmed for them. They all ended up climbing out the window, the fastest way to catch up to the bastard.

Other officers stayed back at the house to gather evidence.

As soon as Ethan and his team were outside, he immediately smelled Oakley's scent headed toward the cliffs.

Ethan, his wolf friends, and Renault were in the lead, headed straight for Oakley while the other officers had spread out, searching for him. But Ethan and the other wolves were hot on Oakley's scent trail, Renault keeping up with the rest of them.

When they reached the cliff, Ethan peered over it and saw Oakley hanging on precariously. Idiot. Ethan couldn't believe Oakley would attempt to escape that way. The waves were crashing down below, the tide fully in so he couldn't even go anywhere if he made it down to the beach.

"Give it up," Ethan called down to him. "You have nowhere to go."

Oakley just glowered at Ethan. "Who told you we were at the warehouse?"

"Wouldn't you like to know? Climb back up here before you end up killing yourself. Think of how your great-aunt will feel if you commit suicide."

Oakley's eyes widened.

"Clara's being taken into custody. Was your great-aunt involved also?" Ethan didn't believe so, but who knew? Maybe she *was* just as involved. He was surprised Clara might be a lot more invested in all this business too.

Oakley wasn't making a move to climb up the cliff. Ethan figured he just really didn't want to give himself up to the police, as if he had much of a choice.

"Come on," Ethan said. "You're going only one way if you don't come up and join us, and that's to your death at the bottom of the cliff."

Reluctantly, Oakley finally started to climb up to the top of the cliff. As soon as he was within reaching distance of pulling himself up over the edge, Ethan, Adam, and Noah grabbed his arms and hoisted him up. Then Renault handcuffed him.

"So where's your buddy, Kroner?" Ethan asked.

"He hasn't been caught yet?" Oakley shook his head. "Figures. I swear he can get away with everything and anything."

"Who shot Officer Baker?" Ethan asked.

Oakley's eyes widened. "Hell, he was shot? I have no idea."

Ethan hadn't expected that Oakley would spill his guts.

Then Ethan contacted Ty. "We have Oakley in custody.

We just need him picked up." They would transport Kroner's men to Portland once he'd questioned them. He just wished they had caught Kroner too.

"We found the heroin they had stashed in the warehouse," Ty said. "It has been confiscated."

"Good. Kroner won't have the money from the sale of the heroin then," Ethan said.

"Clara Snyder is being taken in for questioning too."

"Okay, I'll be by to also speak with her."

"What about Kroner?" Ty asked.

"I need to interview the men we caught and then go from there. Maybe someone will have an idea where he is or might have gone," Ethan said.

Once Oakley was taken off to jail, Ethan said to Noah and Renault, "Let's go talk to these guys."

"And the rest of us?" Josh asked. "I'm all for going back to Charlene's place and watching over her."

"Yeah," Tori said. "I'm all for doing that too."

Adam agreed with them.

Ethan was glad about it, and then they all headed to the house so Ethan could see Charlene before he went to speak with the men they had caught. Ethan called Charlene on the way back with Renault and said, "We caught Oakley. Everyone except Kroner is accounted for."

Charlene said, "Wonderful! Not about Kroner, but about the rest of them. The other bad agent? The bad cops?"

"Yeah, all of them. We're dropping by the house. Tori, Adam, and Josh are staying with you. Noah, Renault, and I are going to interview everyone who was arrested."

"Okay, so I'll see you soon?"

"Yeah, we're on our way back from Shelby Bay now. Love you, honey."

"I love you. Can't wait to see you."

Though Charlene was really hoping that Ethan and the others had taken down Kroner, she was glad they had captured all the rest. She couldn't wait to see Ethan and hold him tight, to know that he hadn't been shot again.

She told Brad and the others what was going on. Maverick said, "Yeah, I just got a text from Josh."

"That's not good that Kroner wasn't caught," Brad said.

"I had an idea though. If Kroner still wants to take down Ethan, maybe we can go to the pack leaders' ranch and have our mating celebration party. If Kroner follows us there, the whole pack can welcome him with wolf jaws wide open," Charlene said.

"That's not a bad idea," Brad said.

"Let me check with Ethan and see if he agrees to it." Charlene called Ethan back. "Hey, how about having our celebration at the pack leaders' ranch and see if we can lure Kroner there?"

"Yeah, that works for me," Ethan said.

"Okay, then that's the plan. As soon as you join us back here after your interviews, we'll go to the ranch," Charlene said.

"I'll tell Leidolf and Cassie what we plan to do. They'll get everything set up for a party and more," Brad said.

They heard cars pull into the driveway, and Charlene peeked out and saw that it was Ethan and the others. She hurried outside and welcomed him like a loving mate would her returning wolf hero. He kissed her like crazy. She was kissing him just as much, loving him for who he was.

He walked her into the house, and everyone was smiling to see the two of them reunited in such a passionate way. She figured every one of the mated males there felt the same way about their mates after a difficult mission.

Then they all sat down and shared their experiences again, comparing stories, trying to figure out what might have happened to Kroner. Charlene and Maverick had fixed everyone breakfast before Ethan, Renault, and Noah went to interrogate the people they took into custody.

"I don't know how Renault and I could have been following Kroner and then ended up catching Officer Davis and losing Kroner," Ethan said, sounding perturbed with himself.

"What if he went down the cliff like Oakley had done, but he was able to get low enough that you couldn't...um, smell his cologne?" Charlene asked.

"Yeah, not at the same place Oakley had gone, but farther away from Clara's house," Ethan said. "The ocean breeze could have carried it away."

"I would sure like to know what her story is," Charlene said.

"Yeah, we all would," Renault said.

After breakfast, Ethan gave Charlene a hug and a kiss and then left with Renault and Noah to get these interviews over with.

Charlene packed a bag for both Ethan and her for the trip to the pack leaders' ranch. She knew they would stay overnight or maybe a couple of nights at the ranch, with Kroner still on the loose. She sure hoped they could catch him once and for all.

CHAPTER 28

ETHAN WANTED TO INTERVIEW OFFICER BAKER FIRST since he was the one who had been shot, and he might be willing to talk if he was out of surgery and able to communicate.

He, Renault, and Noah went into Baker's hospital room where he was handcuffed to the bed. A police officer was sitting beside the bed, another outside of the room. Ethan read Baker his rights. "I'm DEA Special Agent Ethan Matheson who has been working the case that you have been involved in." He'd worked with Baker before so the man knew just who Ethan was.

Baker looked awful, his skin pale. Ethan figured he had lost a lot of blood before they had found him lying in the tunnel nearly dead. He wasn't sure Baker was fully aware of his circumstances.

"Yeah," Baker said weakly. "I know who you are. I've worked with you before. You were after Kroner, and he wanted your head."

"You killed one of his competition," Ethan said.

Baker glanced at Renault, then Noah.

Ethan introduced them both to him, even though Baker would know Renault from joint missions, but not Noah. "Who shot you?"

"Kroner. Bastard, and yeah, I'll testify against him."

Great! Ethan hadn't even had to tell him they would ask

if the DA would give him a lighter sentence if he flipped on Kroner. Hopefully, Baker wouldn't change his mind.

"I–I didn't think it would go this far," Baker said, wiping away tears that streaked down his face. "Once I started to take money from him, he owned me, threatened me that he would reveal I was taking illegal bribes, that he would tell my family."

"And the drug dealer that Kroner had you get rid of?"

Baker let out his breath. "He was a drug dealer, guilty of several murders. And Kroner threatened me. I told you. My job, my life, exposing my extracurricular activities to my family, and knowing Kroner, if he'd had to take it that far, he would have gone after my family to get me to comply."

"What about you pulling Charlene Cheswick over? You hassled her after she was harassed by Agent Pete Cohen when she witnessed him taking drugs off a man at a convenience store and keeping them."

Baker's lips parted and then he clamped them shut.

"That was one of the reasons we knew you and Agent Cohen were in collusion."

Baker wouldn't comment.

Ethan suspected Baker hadn't realized he knew about that business too—that he and Cohen were taking illegal drugs from dealers and not reporting them, but keeping the confiscated drugs for themselves for whatever sordid purpose. "What about your partner? Davis?"

"Davis"—Baker cleared his throat—"wanted a part of the action. I just wanted to have him at my back if Kroner gave me trouble, but I know now that was a stupid idea."

"Davis didn't back you up that time, eh?" Ethan said.

"No. He knew Kroner would shoot him too. He didn't, did he? Later, I mean?"

"No. We arrested Davis and the agents who had been in collusion. They were lucky Kroner hadn't turned on them, but truthfully, Kroner probably hoped we would catch the others so he would have a better chance to get away."

"Did Kroner get away?"

Ethan hated to have to tell him he had. "He did, but we've got a couple of guards on your room."

"He hates you with a passion. He wants you dead."

"That's why he sent Agent Cohen and others to take me out at the home I had been staying at?" Ethan said.

"Yeah."

"But not you. And Cohen had no problem taking on the job." Ethan just couldn't believe a fellow DEA agent wouldn't have any trouble killing him.

"He volunteered for the job. Maybe he planned to save you. I don't know. Or maybe he thought the rest of us being with Kroner and Oakley was riskier, and he took the easy way out. Even Davis, Agent Ryerson, and I wanted on that detail."

"To kill me."

Baker sighed. "I hadn't planned to kill anyone. Not you or the woman. I'm not a gun for hire. I just knew the lot of us would be captured and go to prison. I didn't expect Kroner to shoot me and leave me for dead, or that my good friend Davis wouldn't try to come to my aid. I have to thank you for that. If you hadn't sent me to the hospital, I would have died."

The doctor came in and said that Baker had to rest from his injuries.

Ethan said to Baker, "We'll talk more later."

Baker nodded.

Then Ethan and the others left and headed over to the jailhouse before the other men were transferred to Portland. Ty met them there and showed Ethan and Renault into the interview room where they spoke with Agent Cohen first. Noah and Ty watched the interviews through the two-way mirror.

"So exactly why did you, and more of Kroner's stoolies, trespass on my property, showing up at my house carrying guns and knives, sneaking around in the dark?" Technically, the house was in Charlene's name, but she called it their house, and Ethan thought it would have more impact on Cohen if he was told it was Ethan's, which meant Agent Cohen had been after Ethan, or both him and Charlene.

"I don't have anything to say to you," Cohen said.

"We'll see you at trial." Ethan just hoped they would get some of the others to testify against Cohen and anyone else who wouldn't give them the truth. He guessed Cohen hadn't volunteered to go to the house to *save* Ethan and Charlene.

After that, Ethan interviewed Agent Ryerson. "Your buddy, Cohen, and you were working with Kroner and his men on drug deals. You were afraid you were going to get caught and so you wanted to go with Cohen to kill Charlene and me at our house."

"Who told you that bullshit?" Ryerson asked.

"We've got witnesses' statements. They outline your and

Cohen's involvement and also Officers Davis and Baker's part in all this." They didn't. Not yet. But they would get them by playing them against each other.

"Hell, I would never have gotten involved in any of this until Cohen convinced me it was easy money, and no one was suspicious of anything he was involved in. He said it was foolproof," Ryerson said.

"Committing criminal acts is never foolproof."

"Yeah, well, I know that now. I'll...I'll come forward. What about my family?"

Finally, he asks about his family? "They were taken to a safe house in case Kroner went after them."

"Thank God."

"No thanks to you," Ethan said, angry with Ryerson for not even considering his family when he became involved in all this.

"I'll testify against Kroner and Oakley."

"What about Cohen?"

Ryerson ran his hand over his head. "Yeah, because he talked me into all this shit."

And, Ethan thought, Ryerson would want to do it before Cohen threw him under the bus instead.

Afterward, Ethan talked to Officer Davis. "So whose idea was it to start taking graft money? Yours or Baker's?"

Davis held his stomach, was pale, and looked like he was feeling sick. He finally released his breath and said, "Baker. He said he talked to Agent Cohen, and he was convinced this was going to be a moneymaker and we would never get caught. Baker was really adamant at the last that we were going to get caught and that's when Kroner shot him. I nearly died. Baker and I went on fishing and hunting trips. We had been best of friends for years. Our kids are about the same ages. They played together all the time." He shook his head. "I can't believe I agreed to do this with him. Is he okay?"

"Yeah, he's coming out of it and he's testifying against Kroner and the others."

Davis nodded. "I will too."

Once Ethan talked to several of the other men who worked for Kroner, he had enough testimonies to put Kroner, Oakley, Thor, and Benny away for life. The rest of the men involved would get prison time too. Now Ethan and his team just had to catch Kroner.

Charlene was thrilled when Ethan arrived home. Brad, Josh and his brother, and Quincy and his brother said they would see them later and returned to Leidolf's ranch for the celebration. Ethan, Charlene, Tori, Adam, Renault, and Noah were seated in the living room in Charlene and Ethan's house. They had a lot of questions for Renault.

"Okay, we want to know exactly what the deal was with you going to Oakley's house and speaking with someone there," Ethan said to Renault. "Noah and I were watching the house for any sign of Kroner or Oakley to appear, and lo and behold, here you show up."

"You had his place under surveillance?" Renault sounded shocked and he was sweating a little now. "I told you I was trying to pretend I wanted a deal like fellow agents Pete Cohen and Manx Ryerson had. Of course that was if they had really been the moles but I suspected they were. Kroner's thugs weren't buying it, but they said either he or Oakley would determine if I was really willing to play the game. I suspected to allow me to join them, they would have had me kill somebody and then they would witness it. Just like Baker did when he killed Kroner's competition."

"Once we saw you go to Oakley's house, we knew Grainger hadn't sent you," Ethan said. "He would have told us he was having you help us with the investigation. And he would have told you about us already being on the case."

"You did a good job. I never saw you," Renault said.

"That was the whole point," Noah said.

"And you. Great work on being undercover with Ethan. I never had a clue that you were here with him. I thought you were really in Florida. The sound of the ocean in the background when we spoke had me convinced of it."

"I still think the business with the roses you sent me was suspicious," Charlene said.

Renault sighed. "I didn't know where Ethan was living, but I easily discovered where you were staying. The two of you were getting together, and then it was like I said. I had someone following me. I wasn't sure if Ethan would want to stick his neck out for me when he was retired, but I had to take the chance."

"Why did you make up the other story?" Charlene asked.

"I thought it sounded more reasonable, but in hindsight the truth was better," Renault said.

"You can't believe how annoyed I was that you thought someone was following you and could have led him to Charlene's house," Ethan said.

"I really believed I had kept him from tailing me to the house. I had made multiple switchbacks and driven to hell and back. I didn't see any sign of him when I made it to Charlene's place. I had to tell you I was in trouble. I figured that one of Kroner's men was going to kill me. I couldn't do it on my own. In no way did I believe I would have brought any harm to Charlene."

Charlene said, "It gave Ethan a good excuse to stay with me."

Renault smiled. "See? I did you a favor, Ethan. But I truly would never have come here if I had known anyone would follow me. At least you were prepared with all your additional muscle watching over Charlene when Cohen and Kroner's men arrived at the house."

"Yeah, I was lucky. I'm glad Ferret came through on the warehouse tip," Ethan said.

"I'm just glad we could be there to help out too," Adam said. "If we hadn't been tracking Baker, we wouldn't have been there in time."

Tori agreed.

"Yeah, thanks. Great work, everyone," Ethan said.

Then they said their goodbyes and Renault left to return to Portland. Adam was going to Portland to pick up his mate, Sierra, and head to the ranch. Noah and Tori drove their own vehicles out there.

Once everyone was gone, Ethan gathered Charlene in

his arms. "I can't believe the rogue agents put their families through all of this."

"They didn't think they would ever get caught." Charlene kissed his jaw. "Speaking of families…"

"We have the perfect place for children."

"Just my thought. And anytime is good for me."

Ethan smiled. "Just what I wanted to hear." He grabbed Charlene's and his bags, and they headed to the pack leaders' ranch.

It was time to have a celebration of becoming mated wolves and joining the wolf pack and to celebrate the capture of so many of the bad guys. Then work on having their own family in the most pleasurable way possible.

CHAPTER 29

THE CELEBRATION AT THE PACK LEADERS' RANCH TURNED out beautifully. A feast of trout, hot dogs, grilled burgers, fresh fruits, potato salad, and corn on the cob was laid out on tables. Music was playing in the background. The kids in the pack were playing ribbon tag, ring toss, and just plain chase.

Everyone was welcoming to Charlene and Noah to the pack, and congratulations were given in abundance for Ethan and Charlene's mating.

"Do you think Kroner will come here?" Charlene asked.

"None of us saw any sign of anyone following us to the ranch," Brad told Ethan and Charlene.

Janice squeezed Brad's hand. "My mate has to be at the heart of the excitement whenever he can be. He was thrilled to help you all out. That's his Navy SEAL training coming to play."

"We were glad he was there for me," Charlene said.

Maverick said, "We were all watching for any sign of anyone following us all the way to the ranch, but we figured if Kroner was watching the house, he would have waited until Ethan and Charlene were alone."

Maverick's mate, Gina, snuggled up to him. "I'm just glad you all were okay. When Maverick told me he was assisting you with this case, I was relieved he was helping to take care of Charlene."

Josh's mate, Brooke, said, "At least Maverick stayed with Charlene and didn't run off with Noah and Ethan to try and take down a bunch of the wanted men."

"Right, then Maverick was taking down one of Ethan's fellow agents," Gina said, shaking her head.

Sierra reached over the table and patted Charlene's arm. "I'm thankful you were safe. When Adam told me he and Tori were serving in protection mode, I was sweating it out. I know they're good at their jobs, but they were going after quite a lot of bad guys."

Tori said, "You know I always watch out for Adam."

Adam laughed. "Yeah, she does."

"I'm glad for it," Sierra said.

Leidolf and Cassie joined them at the table. "We have men watching the gate to the acreage and security videos out there. Usually, whoever is on guard duty won't let anyone on the property without checking them out and making sure they're wolves, but in this case, they'll let Kroner onto the property and warn us he's on his way. That way we have him for trespassing and you can arrest him for all the myriad of crimes he has committed."

Charlene glanced at the children who were playing and hoped they didn't get into any trouble if Kroner came in shooting. Though she couldn't imagine him doing that in front of tons of witnesses. Trying to follow them home would probably be a better bet, but they were staying here overnight with Leidolf and Cassie.

Unless, of course, Kroner waited for them at their home. But her security cameras were working, and she and Ethan were both monitoring them from time to time to make sure no one entered the house.

"What if Kroner did come onto the property and we were removing our clothes and shifting into wolves to go running?" Charlene asked.

"We'll change at Leidolf and Cassie's ranch house," Ethan said.

"Yes, exactly," Cassie said. "We'll run out the wolf door and head to the woods. We'll have fun."

Charlene couldn't wait. "Well, if everyone's done eating, I would love to run as a wolf."

"Yeah, I'm ready," Cassie said.

Charlene couldn't believe she would be running with not only her mate, but also a large wolf pack. After losing her family, she hadn't expected to have a mate and a whole pack of wolves who treated her like family. Coming here to reconnect with her fond memories of her vacations here with her grandfather had opened up a whole new world for her.

She realized Noah hadn't sat with them at their table while they were eating. She smiled when she saw he was busy talking to three different she-wolves.

Ethan followed her gaze and smiled. "Looks like Noah's glad to be part of the pack."

"Yeah, and he's getting a nice welcome."

Then Ethan took her hand and everyone who wanted to run headed into the homes on the ranch to remove their clothes and shift, then raced out wolf doors and began running, spreading out, barking, while a few stopped to howl.

Charlene had to stop and howl then, to let everyone

in the pack know her by her howl. Ethan howled, showing he was with her, and she licked and kissed him, loving him. Then Noah howled, and she wanted to laugh. He was running with the three she-wolves, each of them stopping to howl. Charlene wondered about Noah's interest in Tori. Maybe she was a little too hot for him to handle.

They crossed a creek, splashing water everywhere, snapping at it, seeing the fish swimming there, which made her want to fish. One leapt out of the water in front of her and she jumped at it, catching it midair, but released it before she injured it. Tonight was all about the run, not about fishing. This was so much more fun than running in Florida. Not that the park there hadn't been beautiful to explore, but running with a whole pack of wolves? And Ethan, of course. This was the life.

They had run for about a half hour, some with younger wolves, when they began to head back to the ranch. Ethan and Charlene nuzzled each other and slowly walked back, taking in the beautiful sun setting in the night sky. She was thinking how lovely it had been here and how much fun it would be to participate in other pack celebrations too.

The wolves began to howl, and Ethan and Charlene joined in on the chorus. When they finally reached the pack leaders' home, they enjoyed strawberry daiquiris with Cassie and Leidolf, and then Charlene and Ethan retired to the guest room on the other side of the ranch house where they would have privacy. Charlene couldn't wait to make love to her mate.

Ethan and Charlene took a shower together and then joined each other in bed, kissing and ready to make love after all that had gone on, when Ethan got a call from Grainger. He sighed and put the call on speakerphone. "Yes, sir?"

"Clara Snyder was released on bail. She has never done anything wrong that we could learn of, though the IRS is looking into the gifts she has received and not reported them or paid taxes on them. We're still trying to learn if she is who she says she is, and if not, who she is. So it's going to take a bit of digging. But everyone else has been moved from the jail near the coast and brought here to Portland," Grainger said.

"Good. Though if Clara is this mixed up in their financial business, I wish we could have kept her in jail. Otherwise, she could be a flight risk."

"She's wearing an ankle monitor, just in case."

"Oh, good."

"Are you ready to retire after catching the majority of the ones involved in the gang?" Grainger asked.

"Only after Kroner is caught. Unless it takes years. Then he's all yours."

Grainger laughed. "Hopefully, he is still hanging around. Just so you know, both Renault and Noah are your backup. Renault is moving into the safe house in Oyster Bay in the morning."

Ethan frowned. "Okay."

"All right. Talk to you later."

"Thanks, sir. Good night."

"I felt bad that Renault couldn't have been here with us tonight to celebrate," she said.

"Yeah, he deserved to be here, except for the not-being-a-wolf part. But..." Ethan shook his head.

"What?"

"Grainger is having Renault stay with Noah at the safe house, and he's going to work with me to catch Kroner. I–I don't know."

"You still wonder if he's telling the truth."

"Yeah. Though no one we caught acted like they knew Renault was working for Kroner. Which seems strange if Renault is one of Kroner's henchmen."

"We'll figure it out."

"We will." Ethan was ready to make love to his mate, with no more thoughts about Renault or anyone else on the case.

He began to slide his hands up Charlene's shirt, cupping her breasts, squeezing, feeling her aroused nipples push back against the palms of his hands. Scrumptious.

Likewise, she jerked his shirt tails out of his pants and slid her hands up his chest. Charlene traced her finger around Ethan's nipples and kissed them. Her touches pumped up his libido instantly and a raging ache in his loins ensued. She licked his nipples, making them pebble and crave her erotic caresses. His needs raged to the forefront when they kissed and touched each other.

Ethan's body was so attuned to Charlene's touch, her smell, her pheromones bumping up their interest in each other. He kissed her luscious mouth that was begging him to take his fill. She kissed him with the same enthusiasm, breathing him in like he was breathing her in, fanning the flames of need.

He deepened his kiss, their tongues dancing until she sucked on his tongue, nearly sending him over the edge. He moved against her soft body, tantalizing, his hands covering her luscious curves, his body molding against hers.

Their hearts were racing as he enjoyed her sculpted, feminine beauty. She was running her hands over his body, feeling his muscles, appearing to enjoy the planes of his body just as much.

"You are mouthwatering," she said.

He smiled and rubbed his body against hers before he separated enough from her so that he could run his hand over her flat tummy and then he was moving lower, stroking her between her legs, feeling her tense with pleasure.

"Oh, so good," Charlene whispered and kissed Ethan's lips again.

He pleasured her mouth with just as much enthusiasm and she loved the way he always treated her like she was a treasure to him, just like he was her treasure—the best thing that had ever happened in her life. But now, he was stroking her, then inserting a finger between the folds and practically sending her to the moon. She surrendered to him completely, seduced by the wolf.

She slipped her hand over his hip and buttocks, and he groaned a little. She smiled. She loved it when she could make him feel so good while she was touching him. He made her feel on top of the world as he continued to stroke her into a state of ecstasy. She sank into the mattress, overwhelmed by the orgasm, and he entered her, then began to thrust.

He was so masculine, so alpha, just the perfect mate for her as he turned her world inside out in the best way possible. She wanted him closer, inside and outside, connected in every way. Her heart thundered through her veins, and she could hear his heart beating just as hard.

"You're just perfect," he whispered against her ear, kissing her cheek and then her mouth, pumping his throbbing manhood deeper between her thighs.

He was just perfect for her, and she felt she was coming again under his beautiful ministrations. "Ohmigod," she said, feeling as though she was breaking apart into millions of happy pieces as he came.

"Oh God, Charlene, you are the best."

"You are too."

They cuddled together and kissed further. "I love you," she said, being so happy she had met and mated him.

"I love you too," Ethan said, and he was glad they were at the ranch, surrounded by protective wolves and just enjoying each other.

Before they left for home the next morning, Charlene and Ethan had breakfast with Leidolf and Cassie.

"Since the agents are still looking for Kroner, that means

you'll be left all alone," Cassie said. "We would like it if you stayed here with us for protection, Charlene."

"Kroner might have left the country. Even if he hasn't, it could take years to catch up to him." Charlene took another sip of her coffee. "You know how it goes with criminals and locating them. I do have a gun. Living alone on the coast, I figured one might come in handy if anyone thought to break in."

"We could send someone to stay with you," Cassie said.

"Thanks, but I'll be fine. I appreciate the offer."

"We'll take turns watching for Kroner—Renault, Noah, and me," Ethan said. "So someone will always be with Charlene."

"All right," Leidolf said, as if that would work for him.

Charlene was so not used to having pack leaders. But she loved them for taking their pack members' welfare to heart.

After breakfast, they thanked Leidolf and Cassie and finally left for home. Noah had chosen to have breakfast with the three single she-wolves that morning and was still at the ranch as far as they knew.

"So what do you think about Noah and the three she-wolves? I don't know any of them, but you do," Charlene said.

"He's interested in Tori." Ethan smiled at Charlene as they drove home.

"Why would he eat with the other women then? And run with them as wolves?"

"He's probably playing the field a bit to show Tori that he could and to make sure he isn't making a mistake of falling for the first single she-wolf he'd met while here. But their work will mean they'll cross paths in Portland, and I'll bet you anything that they'll work up a friendship," Ethan said.

"Maybe he can work on his relationship skills then."

Ethan laughed. "The other she-wolves will make sure of it."

Charlene smiled. "I'm glad he's moving on with his life. So what are you and the guys going to do next? As far as going after Kroner?" Charlene asked.

"I want to question Oakley's great-aunt. I want to know if she has any clues to where Kroner has gone."

"She might be afraid Kroner would come for her if she talks."

"Right. Which means we need to make sure she's safe too."

"Yeah, I agree."

"We'll have lunch and then decide who goes first to question Oakley's great-aunt," Ethan said.

"Should we have lunch with the guys and then you can decide on who goes?"

"Yeah, let's see what everyone wants to eat," he said. "I can grill burgers."

"That sounds great to me."

Ethan called Noah and said, "How do grilled burgers sound for lunch to you and Renault?" He smiled at Charlene. "Okay, see you at eleven." He ended the call and half an hour later, they arrived home.

A few minutes later, Renault and Noah showed up at the house. Ethan finished grilling the burgers while Charlene brought out the french fries. They ate their burgers on the deck to enjoy the beautiful summer day while the ocean breeze whipped around them.

"So who is staying here and who is going?" Charlene asked.

"I'll go with Ethan," Renault said before anyone else could say anything.

"That works for me," Noah said, "if Ethan and Charlene are good with it." Then Noah got a text, and he checked it out.

Was the text from one of the three she-wolves Noah had been talking to?

"Sure." Charlene suspected Renault wanted to be in on the action.

"We need to have a celebration when we catch Kroner," Renault said.

"That's for sure," Charlene said, thinking it would be a great idea for the four of them so that this time Renault could enjoy the camaraderie.

Noah was quiet, contemplative, and Charlene wondered what was going on with him. She wondered if he was a little put out that he would be left behind watching her and not there to help take Kroner down if he was at Oakley's great-aunt's house.

After they finished eating, Ethan kissed and hugged Charlene before he left with Renault.

She sighed as she shut the door on their departure. She figured they would be gone a couple of hours, but what surprised her was when Noah said, "Grab your gun. We're going to be Ethan's tail."

She was all for it, though she was surprised that Noah had wanted to do it without talking to Ethan about it first. Then again, maybe he suspected they would find Kroner at the great-aunt's house, and he wanted to be there to help arrest him. Knowing Noah, that was the reason.

She grabbed her purse and her gun. "So why are we following them? Do you really feel like Kroner will be at the great-aunt's house?" She climbed into Noah's car.

"I want to be there just in case Kroner is. Ethan and Renault will need more of a backup, but I want you to stay in the car in case this goes down when we get there."

"Sure. That sounds good." Still, she was surprised Noah hadn't just asked Ethan about doing it this way. She figured he didn't want Ethan to say no, worried about Charlene being in the area if they had a fight to capture Kroner. "I take it you didn't want to ask Ethan about doing this."

Noah let out his breath. "I don't know. I–I just want to make sure Renault is on the up and up."

"Wait a minute. You still think he might be involved with Kroner?" Now that changed the situation entirely.

"I just want to make sure that everything is all right."

She knew Noah better than that. "You have to have some reason to suspect Renault."

"It's just everything. The roses he ordered for you and sent anonymously. Renault taking Ethan to the warehouse without notifying the police or Grainger of what he thought they might find there. So then I tried to get ahold of Ferret to see if he told Renault that Kroner was at the warehouse. I learned Ferret was already in Witness

Protection which means no one could have asked him where Kroner was—as far as the warehouse location went. So how did Renault know? He had to have lied to Ethan about how he knew of it."

"Ohmigod, when did you learn this?"

"Just after we ate lunch. That was the text I got. I didn't want to bring it up in front of Renault."

"So you think he's turning Ethan over to Kroner," she said, getting her phone out at once.

"Possibly. There might be another explanation, but I want to be there if Ethan's in trouble."

She texted Ethan: Noah wanted to question Ferret about the warehouse tip, but he was in Witness Protection and Renault couldn't have talked to him. Noah and I are following you to the great-aunt's house in case he's leading you into a trap.

Ethan texted back: Hell, if he is, he's going to regret it. I'll update you if anything suspicious happens.

She texted: All right. Don't go inside the house to speak with the great-aunt until we're there.

Ethan texted: That works for me. And you stay in the car.

She smiled and texted: I've heard that one before. I have my gun with me. And yes, I'll stay in the car.

CHAPTER 30

Man, was Ethan shocked. Ethan texted Grainger, hoping he could get to the truth of the matter. Maybe Renault had talked to Ferret before he was put into Witness Protection.

Grainger got back to Ethan: I just checked with the U.S. Marshal's office, and one of them spoke to Ferret. Ferret said that he saw the breaking news on the arrests you made at the warehouse, but he had no idea that's where Kroner had been. He said the only agent he ever gave information to was you, Ethan.

Ethan glanced at Renault.

"Anything wrong?" Renault asked him.

"No." Ethan texted Charlene: Confirmed Ferret didn't give the location of the warehouse to Renault.

Charlene texted him: We see Renault's car parking at the great-aunt's house. We're close by, keeping out of his sight.

"Is that Charlene?" Renault asked.

"Yeah. She's talking about wedding plans," Ethan told Renault.

Renault laughed. "I wouldn't mind having a girlfriend, but the idea of marrying anyone is too scary to think about. Are you ready to speak with Mrs. Osburn?"

"Yeah, just a minute." Ethan texted Ty Richardson with the local police department: Can you send backup to Mrs. Osburn's home?

WHAT A WOLF WANTS 353

Ethan gave him the address.

Ty texted: I've got a couple of people near there. I'll send them now.

Ethan was glad that he didn't have to explain the situation.

"What are we waiting for?" Renault asked, sounding anxious, smelling worried. He was starting to perspire. "Can't texting Charlene about the wedding wait?"

"Yeah, just texting her that I love her one last time. You never know when you might not have that chance again." Ethan texted Charlene: Ty's sending a couple of men as backup.

She texted: Good. Love you.

Ethan smiled for Renault's benefit and texted: Love you right back.

Then Ethan opened the car door and said, "Okay, Renault, let's do this."

Renault looked relieved and hurried to leave the car.

"Since I'm retiring, I'm going to let you go first and talk to Mrs. Osburn," Ethan said.

"But this is your case," Renault said, looking a little panicked.

Which was true, but since Renault wanted Ethan to be the lead on this, he figured he just might have a dark reason for it. "Right, but you know what? You could be the one in charge of it if I retire. I'm certainly not going to spend years trying to track Kroner down."

Renault finally knocked on the door and Mrs. Osburn answered it. She smiled at Renault. "You're here. We thought you weren't coming. Come in. Come in."

We. Ethan had his gun out but concealed. He heard someone coming up behind him and he suspected it was Kroner, but when he looked over his shoulder, he was relieved to see it was Noah, hurrying to join him before he went into the house.

Then their favorite patrolman, Jenkins, and another officer pulled up and hurried to join them.

Renault was so intent on getting through the door that he didn't see the reinforcements Ethan had called on. Ethan quickly grabbed Mrs. Osburn's arm and pulled her out of the house to get her out of harm's way.

One of the officers took Mrs. Osburn back to his patrol car for her safety.

Ethan was using Renault as a shield, figuring if he was involved with Kroner, he could take the risk of getting shot first. All hell broke out then as Kroner started shooting, and despite figuring Renault was in cahoots with him, Ethan dove for him, slamming him to the floor behind a sofa to protect him.

Noah was shooting back at Kroner and so was Officer Jenkins.

Sirens alerted them that Ty had sent more patrol units to help them with their case. Ethan was grateful to him.

Kroner cried out and Ethan was certain he had gotten shot. Ethan motioned for Noah to stay with Renault, who looked surprised that he wasn't allowed to help out further. "I've got this," Renault said.

"You just stay here with me," Noah said.

Then Ethan and the patrolman moved to take Kroner

into custody. He was gasping for air, and it appeared he'd taken a bullet in a lung. Ethan called for an ambulance while the patrolman secured Kroner's weapons.

"Renault is just as dirty as the rest of your friends," Kroner said to Ethan, his voice coming out in gasps. He was so angry that his face was chili-pepper red.

"Hell, that's not so," Renault shouted from where he was standing with Noah.

As soon as Ethan read Kroner his rights, the EMTs arrived, and the patrolman and his partner provided security as they took him to the hospital.

What they were unprepared for was to hear someone in a back room, and Ethan hurried back there to learn who was in the room. What surprised him was to find Clara Snyder hiding in a bedroom closet.

"You can come out now," Ethan said. She hadn't been tied up or beaten. She looked like she was there of her own free will. He suspected she was just as guilty as everyone else they had arrested. "We're taking you in for questioning."

They were also taking Mrs. Osburn. But when he hauled Clara outside, he found a tearful Mrs. Osburn. And his beautiful mate, Charlene, was speaking with her. Since Charlene had been a homicide detective, she knew how to interview a person.

"She was Kroner's hostage," Charlene said to Ethan.

"But you knew Renault," Ethan said to Mrs. Osburn.

"Yes. He has seen Kroner any number of times. I know my grandnephew was involved in some shady business dealings, but he was always good to me. Oakley took me to church sometimes and he would take me out to have a nice lunch afterward. Kroner was a bad influence on Oakley. He always has been. I tried to get Oakley to make new friends, but Kroner is…just persuasive in an evil way." Mrs. Osburn wiped away tears. She saw Clara coming out of the house and Mrs. Osburn pointed to her. "She's the one in charge. She'll pretend like she's a sweet old lady, but she's the mastermind behind it all."

"How do you know this?" Ethan asked, surprised.

"I've got recordings of lots of their meetings."

Ethan couldn't believe it. Here he'd thought Mrs. Osburn was either a sweet old lady or involved in a cover-up with her grandnephew. But in retrospect, she had been gathering intel for them just when they needed it.

"It shows Kroner threatening me if Oakley didn't do what he said, so it's all yours now that you've caught the bastard. Just don't let him go again. And that woman?" Mrs. Osburn said, pointing at Clara Snyder. "She pulled all the strings. Look at her now, pretending to be so innocent. She was never a schoolteacher. She has been involved in all this for years. Her husband used to run things, and when he was shot, she took over the business. Renault was the sneaky one though. The other bad cops and DEA agents never knew he was working for Kroner. When I was participating in sewing circles or bingo nights with my friends, Oakley would have his meetings with Kroner, Renault, and Clara. That's when I began recording them to see what they were up to."

Ty ended up at the scene and Ethan said to him, "Agent Renault Green and Clara Snyder are under arrest. Kroner is on his way to the hospital. Mrs. Osburn has some information to help us with the investigation."

But Ty was glancing at Renault like he couldn't believe it.

"Yeah, apparently Renault wanted a piece of the criminal action like Agents Ryerson and Cohen," Ethan said.

With all the bad guys and the woman in charge in custody, Ethan needed to interrogate everyone at the police station. He said to Ty, "Can you have a couple of guys watch Charlene and her place until I can return after interrogating everyone?"

"Yeah, I sure will."

"Thanks." Ethan called his boss then and filled him in on the details.

"Hell, finally. Renault was dirty. Damn."

"Yeah, I know. I'll let you know more once I've done the interrogations."

"I'll be waiting to hear the news."

Then Grainger and Ethan ended the call and Ethan hugged and kissed Charlene while Mrs. Osburn went inside her house with Noah to get all the information for them.

When they came back out, Noah said, "Renault's car needs to be towed and investigated."

"Yeah, I need you to drive us home and drop Charlene off. Then you and I can go in and question everyone," Ethan said.

"What about me?" Mrs. Osburn asked.

"You'll come with us. You can fill us in on anything we've missed," Ethan said.

When Ethan spoke to Renault, he still couldn't believe his partner, though he hadn't been one for all that long, had worked with notorious drug dealers. "Did you work with Agents Ryerson and Cohen with Kroner and Clara Snyder?"

"Hell, they were on the take. Not me. I can't believe you still think I'm involved," Renault said.

"Why would you be? Money? That's all? You wanted me to follow you to protect you from Thor. You knew I would offer, but you figured Thor would take me out. You thought I was retired and probably didn't have a gun or badge on me. I know it was a shock to you when you learned I was still on the force and Thor was taken into custody."

Renault didn't say anything.

"The only reason you sent roses to Charlene was to learn where I was. It was the only way you could set me up so that Thor could take me down. You would have been in the clear but would have done what Kroner wanted you to do. You knew Kroner would be at the warehouse, and I suspect you thought that was going to go down a lot differently than it did. Thanks to Noah, he learned you had lied about Ferret telling you that Kroner was at the warehouse."

"As if you can believe everything a snitch says," Renault said.

"You had no access to him. You didn't realize he was in protective custody. You've wanted to be with me every step of the way to put me in Kroner's or one of his henchmen's line of sight. Except for the one time when Agent Cohen came for me at the house. But you couldn't kill me yourself because you were afraid you would be found out."

"All speculation on your part," Renault said.

Then Ethan played some of the security tapes that Mrs. Osburn had taken. They were damn good and perfect to use in convicting every one of the guys and the head honcho they had in custody.

Renault was frowning at the laptop showing him talking to Kroner about setting up Ethan so he could be taken down.

Tori called Ethan then and said, "You wanted me to check into Renault's finances, and my preliminary investigation of his accounts showed nothing out of the ordinary. But then I found where he had paid off his home, moved his kids to a private school, and bought a new Porsche, though he has it hidden in his garage."

"Money, greed. Thanks, Tori." Ethan looked at Renault. "So now we know it was all for money."

"You were supposed to be retired."

Ethan smiled. "So you thought if I had been retired, I wouldn't have seen you coming? We've got enough on you to put you away for a good long time."

Ethan told the officer to lock Renault up. Both Clara and Kroner wouldn't talk until their lawyers were present, though Kroner was going to be in the hospital for a while longer.

When they were done, Ethan told Mrs. Osburn, "How would you like to come to our house for dinner and have a nice grilled steak?"

She smiled. "I would love that."

"You, Noah?"

"Yeah, sure."

Ethan called Charlene. "Hey, honey, we're coming home and I'm grilling steaks for us. Mrs. Osburn is our guest of honor, and Noah is coming so we can celebrate." Forget celebrating with Renault.

"I'll be ready."

Twenty minutes later, they arrived, and Ethan started the steaks while Charlene asked if everyone wanted a margarita.

"Oh, my, yes, dear. As long as I'm not driving home." Mrs. Osburn took a seat in the living room while Noah worked on making mashed potatoes and Charlene served up the drinks. "So what do you do?"

"Manage house rentals on the coast, but I was a former homicide detective," Charlene said.

"Oh, me too. Not the house rentals, but I was a former homicide detective in Sacramento, California," Mrs. Osburn said.

"I'll be damned," Ethan said.

Mrs. Osburn smiled. "Everyone thinks I'm just a little old lady who goes to church on Sundays, knits, sews, and plays bingo, but I was a great detective in my time. Just like your sweetheart, I imagine."

"So what made Oakley take a different path in life?" Ethan asked.

"He liked the thrill of criminal pursuits. He always did. No matter how many times I tried to steer him onto the right path, I just didn't have any sway like Kroner did," Mrs. Osburn said.

"And Clara Snyder?"

"Oh, yes. She was a black widow. Some believe another

drug lord took out her husband, but I was certain she had him eliminated so she could take over the operation herself. My, this drink is really good."

"Thanks," Charlene said.

Ethan was so glad things were wrapping up and after dinner, he and Charlene would have their time together. And now he wasn't going to worry about Kroner or Clara or Renault any longer. His parents' killers would finally face justice. For that he was grateful, especially since his mate, who he loved with all his heart, had been at his side.

Charlene still was shocked to learn not only that Renault was involved like they thought he might have been, but also that Clara Snyder had been the real boss. She was glad to know Mrs. Osburn was a nice lady, one of the good guys, and had provided enough videotaped evidence to prove who had ordered what done and what they had received in payment.

"Didn't your grandnephew know what your job used to be?" Charlene asked Mrs. Osburn.

"You know kids. They never think us old, retired folks know anything." Mrs. Osburn smiled. "But old habits die hard and when Oakley began to have meetings with Kroner, Renault, and Clara at the house, I recorded them while I was with my friends."

"Here we had a secret weapon at the house, and we didn't even know it," Ethan said, bringing out the steaks while

Charlene made up some salads and Noah served up the mashed potatoes and butter.

"I was going to turn them over to the police once Kroner was caught," Mrs. Osburn said. "I knew he would kill me if he learned I had turned them over and he was still on the loose. Though I had left a note in my will as to where to find them if I died before that happened."

Charlene was glad Mrs. Osburn had lived to see all her hard work pay off.

When they were done—everyone talking about old cases they had worked on and then thanking Mrs. Osburn for being so instrumental in the case—Noah and Mrs. Osburn said good night and he drove her home.

"Wow, here we thought she might have even been involved in all this," Charlene said.

"While we kept waffling about Renault." Ethan finished cleaning the grill while Charlene put the dishes away.

"Now you can retire."

Ethan smiled, took her hand, and headed to bed. "I sure can. But now my boss is going to have to hire three new DEA agents."

She gave Ethan a look to say he better not even think of staying on the force any longer.

He laughed and swept her up into his arms and carried her to bed. "This is my new job—maintenance manager of beach houses, and your lover at your beck and call."

She chuckled and kissed him. "That's just what I want to hear, because that's what I want to be for you too."

EPILOGUE

Charlene loved Ethan so much and was so glad he was perfectly healed up now. She couldn't believe that the DEA raiding her rental home in Portland would have led to her finding a wolf she adored and ending up mating. Returning to the Oregon coast where she had loved spending time with her grandfather had given her and Ethan the perfect place to start their own family and their own pack. Though they would think of it as a pack within a pack because they cherished being part of the red wolf pack out of Portland. And their own little family was going to be expanding soon, which she couldn't have been more thrilled about.

She and he had even managed to move into the new home, rent out the other, add wolf doors to all the rentals and their main home, and decorate them with the photos she and he had taken on the special trips they'd made—during walks on the beaches, while on the whale excursion, viewing the sunsets off the ocean, visiting the iconic shipwreck of the *Peter Iredale*, and while at the parks in the area.

Their home was truly their home with a combination of his and her tastes and they loved it, but mostly they loved each other.

Ethan adored Charlene. He couldn't be happier for the way everything had turned out after what had started as a disastrous first meeting—her naked in her shower, him with a weapon at the ready, and her shifting and biting him.

They loved their house that together they'd turned into a real home, and he loved being retired and helping to manage the rental houses. He would never have thought that he would end up retiring on the coast, but with Charlene, it was just the most perfect place to live as wolves on the wild side.

Even the wolves of the pack thought so and the rentals were always booked. Wolves had really taken over the rentals, and they loved that the homes all had wolf doors and safe places to run in their fur coats. Word was spreading to other packs too. They'd had some billionaire wolves from California rent them, and wolves from even as far away as Silver Town, Colorado. And Arctic wolves from Ely, Minnesota, had rented a couple of them at one time for their whole pack.

Ethan and Charlene settled on one of the couches on the back porch to watch the sunset as they drank some hot cocoa. "Oh, I didn't tell you," Charlene said. "We have some jaguars coming from Texas who are staying in one of the rental homes."

"Jaguars."

"Yep. I can't wait to see them in their jaguar coats."

"That would be cool. We'll have to have them over for burgers."

That was the thing about their shifter guests. They weren't just renters. They were like an extended family.

Charlene and Ethan always offered their guests grilled hamburgers for lunch or dinner on one of the days during their stay, and everyone was always thrilled to participate.

Did Ethan miss the excitement of being a DEA agent? Not with Charlene in his life. They had testified against all the men and the woman they'd taken into custody, and all the criminals were now serving long prison sentences.

And Mrs. Osburn? She had been a brilliant witness in court, even though it pained her to use tough love on her grandnephew. But she'd gained friends in Charlene and Ethan and at least once a week, they would visit with her at her place where she would make them chocolate chip cookies, or they would take her for walks on the beach or on hunts for berries and make jams with her at their place. And once every couple of weeks, Ethan would drive her to the prison to see Oakley. She didn't regret turning over the evidence she'd had on all the players one bit and was delighted to have Charlene and Ethan in her life now.

"Well?" Ethan asked, pulling Charlene onto his lap to cuddle her on the back deck. He'd found her pregnancy test kit in the bathroom, and he was dying to know if they were going to have little ones soon.

She smiled and kissed him. "Yes! The baby or babies are due the first week in May."

He couldn't have been more thrilled. "That means we need to get to decorating a nursery."

She hugged him tight. "When we know how many babies we're having and what their sex is."

"I so love you and our little ones." He rubbed her tummy.

"I love you." She kissed him and shivered. "Are you ready to run as a wolf and then…"

"Take you to bed? Hell, yeah. I guess we can't tell the pack yet about the babies."

Charlene smiled. "After we know what we're going to have."

"And Mrs. Osburn?"

Charlene laughed. "Yes. She will be thrilled."

Mrs. Osburn had been asking them weekly when they were going to have babies. They would be sure to share the news with her soon.

"I still think she would make a great wolf," Ethan said.

"I know, but at her age, it might be a little hard to take all the changes in her life. She would need to stay at Leidolf and Cassie's ranch for her own safety."

"Maybe if someone around her age could help her along the way…"

Charlene laughed. "I never knew you were into wolf matchmaking."

They headed inside the house with their empty cocoa mugs and set them on the dining room table. They began pulling off their clothes and then they shifted, nuzzled each other in a loving wolf way, and then he chased her out the wolf door.

Life with each other couldn't get any better than this. And one of these days, they would have little ones and show them the ropes too. The pack had stretched its boundaries all the way from Portland to the Oregon coast and everyone had been thrilled about that, especially Charlene and Ethan, two red wolves in love.

Read on for an excerpt of another Red Wolf series favorite, *The Best of Both Wolves*

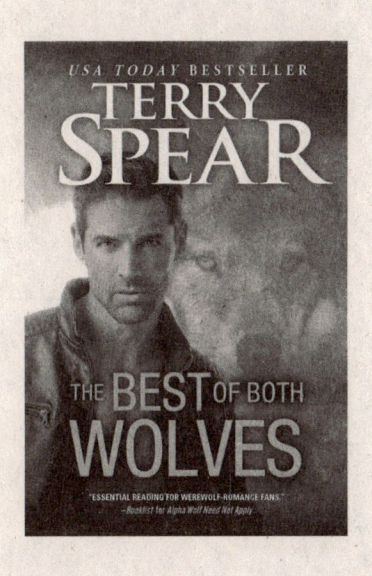

CHAPTER 2

Seven months later

ADAM WAS GLAD SIERRA HAD COME TO WORK FOR THE Portland Police Bureau seven months ago as their part-time sketch artist and still had time to teach art lessons to the kids a couple of days a week and adults in the pack at night, mainly because she was so good at her job and she seemed to love doing both. He'd had a ball when he had gone to her first adult art class where she'd showed them how to create photoshopped artwork and was teaching them about perspective, lighting, and shadows. Most of her class had been made up of bachelor males vying to win her attention, even though she was still seeing an out-of-state wolf who used to work with her in the army.

Adam had been trying to learn about art from her, but he was truly smitten with her—the way she smiled at her students and the way she tirelessly showed them over and over again how to create a simple picture using clip art and different layering techniques, laughing at some of their sillier comments and questions. She appeared to enjoy teaching them as much as they enjoyed getting to know her better.

But now it was back to the grind for him. Since he had to investigate the case of a stolen rental car from the airport and Sierra had to catch a flight, he was on his way to her house to give her a lift, which worked out well for both of them. Though the reason she was flying out of Portland bothered him. She was still seeing her boyfriend in Texas, and he sure wished he could convince her that she didn't want to leave the pack. To be honest, Adam didn't want the boyfriend to join them here either.

On the way over to her place, Adam got a call on Bluetooth from Sierra's brother, Brad. He suspected Brad hoped Adam could convince Sierra she didn't want to leave for Texas today or any other day. Not that Adam had told Brad he was taking her to the airport. "What's up, Brad?"

"You should tell Sierra you're taking the boat out the weekend she gets back. We'll go with you. Ask Josh and Brooke and my sister-in-law, Dorinda, to come too, and maybe Sierra won't think it's anything more than a family and friends get-together."

Adam chuckled. "I've asked her before, and she said no."

"Yeah, but right after she has seen her boyfriend, she's more willing to go out. I think she feels everyone understands she's 'with' him so none of the bachelors make a move on her."

"I'll ask." Adam was certain she would decline the invitation again.

"Okay, I'll keep working on her at this end."

Adam laughed.

"It's hard for Sierra to deal with change all at once. Retiring from the army, then moving here, she's having a hard time letting go of the last tie she has there. But he's not good for her."

Adam didn't know if that was really true or if Brad just wanted his sister to live close by.

"Okay, I'll ask."

"All right, good. And be sure and take another art class of hers. The more we can convince her that everyone needs her to stay here, the better."

Adam smiled. "I am. She put them on hold to take a trip back to Texas, but I'm on the list for her next one coming up." He didn't think he'd ever really be able to do anything art-related that was newsworthy, but he was having fun taking the classes because she was teaching them. "Talk to you later."

Adam dropped by the coffee shop and picked up a chocolate-caramel-hazelnut coffee for Sierra—her favorite. He'd gotten into the habit of getting it for her at work once she'd teased him about drinking boring coffee and he had learned that was her favorite. Of course his former partner, Josh Wilding, had told him it was obvious Adam was making a play for her.

After Sierra had drawn the police sketch of the man who had tried to rob from her hotel room, the police had also rounded up three staff members at three other hotels who had given the robbers access to the rooms. Sierra identified Dover Manning in a police lineup, though the robber denied he'd ever seen her before. Because he'd been armed with a gun and threatened her with it, even though she was a wolf at the time, he was charged with first-degree robbery. During the trial and his testimony, he had stated that he'd been protecting himself from a vicious guard dog. Of course no one—hotel staff, cleaning crew, or police officers—had seen any sign of a "guard dog" so Dover Manning was looking at twenty years in prison.

Adam arrived at Sierra's one-story brick home with flowers filling its flower beds and planters. He hadn't realized she was quite the little gardener, never having been to her place before. While he was getting out of the Hummer, she came out of the house carrying two bags and he loaded them in the back of the vehicle.

"Thanks, Adam." Sierra pushed a loose red curl behind her ear—the rest of her curly hair held in a chignon, a few wisps of tendrils framing her face—and climbed into the passenger seat.

He sure wished he could change her mind about going back to Texas so *he* could date her. He couldn't imagine successfully being in a long-distance relationship like that. And the fact that she'd left the boyfriend behind had to say something about their relationship.

"No problem. I had to be at the airport anyway," he said. Her eyes were a clear blue like her brother's and were spellbinding. She was petite but when she tussled with her brother as wolves, she was more than aggressive, and Adam would love to play with her like that. "Did you get everything you needed?"

She checked her purse. "Yeah, I've got my ID. We're good. Last year, I was behind a woman at the check-in counter at the airport who had forgotten her ID. She said she would never get back to the airport on time if she went home to get it. She was in tears when she left. I always remember that whenever I have a flight scheduled and check to make sure I have my ID on me."

"I don't blame you. I bet the woman was upset."

Sierra took a deep breath of the aroma of the coffee and eyed the cup sitting in the console for her. "Ohmigod, I can't believe you got my favorite coffee before I go on my trip." Sierra smiled at him. "You are my hero." She sipped some of the coffee and sighed. "You sure know how to help me unstress in a big way."

He smiled at her and drove in the direction of the airport. In a subtle way, he kept hoping he could convince her she didn't need to return to Texas to see the boyfriend ever again.

He was glad he had convinced Sierra to work with them at the police bureau. He loved watching her work on witness sketches. She always had such good rapport with everyone at the bureau and with witnesses she worked with. And with the pack members too. She was fun to be around at pack functions, but she avoided going out with any male wolf alone that could signal she was dating someone other than the out-of-state-wolf.

He didn't think she would say yes to a boat outing, but since Brad had spoken to him about it, he had to ask. Again. "Hey, I was going to take the boat out the weekend after you return from your vacation and—"

She gave him a look that said he was pushing his luck.

He smiled. "It would be with your brother, his mate, and his sister-in-law. And Josh and Brooke will come too."

"I'll see how I feel when I get back."

He figured that was a no.

Ever since she'd moved in with the pack, Adam had been interested in her but disappointed she was still seeing another wolf. He'd hoped once she began working for the bureau as a sketch artist and teaching art to the kids in the pack, who adored her, she would realize her home was truly here with the pack, her brother, and his mate. Even though Adam was an alpha wolf and would love to try to change her mind about dating the other guy, he just didn't feel right about it. He considered himself one of the good guys.

Stealing another wolf's potential mate wasn't something he was interested in doing. He supposed it had to do with that happening to him when he was a younger wolf in love with a she-wolf. A wolf passing through had convinced her to leave the pack and go away with him. Adam figured the woman he'd been dating wasn't as interested in him as he'd been in her, but he wouldn't do that to another wolf.

"I'll see if my brother can pick me up at the airport when I return." Sierra was wringing her hands and appeared to be uncomfortable about something. Flying? Seeing the boyfriend?

He hoped she was having second thoughts about returning to see the guy.

"Sure." Adam didn't offer to pick her up. He could be in the middle of an important criminal case when she returned for all he knew and wouldn't be able to spare the time. He didn't want to dig deeper into the feelings he had about her. The fact that she was seeing someone as a possible mate—that she wasn't free for him to pursue. If he had been seeing her, he would have damn well made sure he could pick her up from the airport. Criminal case or no.

He wasn't the only one who didn't want her flying out to see the boyfriend in Texas. Even her brother had told her several times she needed to give the guy up. Adam suspected Brad knew who he was, but he wouldn't tell anyone his name. Neither would she.

If she was *that* interested in him, wouldn't she have mentioned him by name at some time or another and let on how much she cared for him? Maybe she wouldn't share her feelings with the guys, but why not with the she-wolves in the pack?

He got a call from his dad and answered on Bluetooth.

"Hey, are we still on for fishing this weekend?" his dad asked.

Adam and his dad were close, and whenever he had a chance, Adam tried to run down to fish with him at the pack leaders' ranch or they would go out on the boat. Since his dad was a retired police officer, he was working security for the pack leaders' ranch now. So was Adam's mother, who had met Adam's father on the police force. His mother would undoubtedly be going on a shopping trip in town with some of her lady friends when he and his dad went fishing.

"I sure am, Dad."

"Hey, about Sierra…"

"I'm taking her to the airport." Adam had to warn his dad she was in the Hummer before his dad said something that would get Adam into trouble. "She's off to see her boyfriend." Why did she always have to go to see the boyfriend? Adam wanted to tell the boyfriend it was *his* turn to make the effort and come see her. He should have checked out the pack to see that Sierra was fine living here with them. Did he at least pay for her airfare?

"Oh, hey, Sierra, have a great time. I've got to run," his dad said.

"Thanks." Sierra frowned at Adam.

"See you and Mom Saturday, Dad." Then Adam ended the call. *Hell.* He shouldn't have mentioned on their last fishing date how he wished Sierra would call it quits with the boyfriend. His dad had instantly believed Adam had the hots for her and had started in on how Adam should change Sierra's mind about leaving town to see the guy. No matter how many times Adam told him there wasn't a lick of truth to it—because he didn't want his dad slipping up like this in front of Sierra—his dad knew him too well and didn't believe him.

In reality, a bunch of hungry bachelor male wolves would jump at the chance to date her if she wasn't still seeing the guy.

She looked over at Adam. "What about me? What was your dad going to say before you cut him off?"

Great. He would have to tell his dad not to mention anything more about this. "I have no idea, but I wanted him to know you were with me."

ACKNOWLEDGMENTS

Thanks so much to Donna Fournier and Darla Taylor for beta reading for me to catch my initial bloopers, which I swear won't be there, but they find them anyway. And to Deb Werksman who loved my first book where wolves rode in SUVs—you know, to carry all the wolves—that led to over a decade of shifter books for readers. Thanks to the cover artists who give us outstanding visuals of what the book is about before readers even open that first page.

ABOUT THE AUTHOR

Bestselling and award-winning author Terry Spear has written over a hundred paranormal romance novels and a dozen medieval Highland historical romances. Her first werewolf romance, *Heart of the Wolf*, was named a 2008 *Publishers Weekly* Best Book of the Year, and her subsequent titles have garnered high praise and hit the *USA Today* bestseller list. A retired officer of the U.S. Army Reserves, Terry lives in Spring, Texas, where she is working on her next wolf, jaguar, cougar, and bear shifter romances, continuing with her Highland medieval romances, and having fun with her young adult novels. When she's not writing, she's photographing everything that catches her eye, making teddy bears, and playing with her Havanese puppies and grandchildren.

Website: terryspear.com
Facebook: terry.spear
Wordpress: terryspear.wordpress.com